The Experts Praise

THE GOOD SPY
By Jeffrey Layton

"The excitement never stops in *The Good Spy* by Jeffrey Layton. Richly detailed and bristling with fascinating political intrigue, the story sweeps between the United States and Moscow as the danger intensifies. This is high adventure at its very best."
—**Gayle Lynds,** *New York Times* bestselling author of *The Assassins*

"An explosive high-stakes thriller that keeps you guessing."
—**Leo J. Maloney,** author of the Dan Morgan thrillers

"Layton spins an international thriller while never taking his eye off the people at the center of the tale. A page-turner with as much heart as brains."
—**Dana Haynes,** author of *Crashers, Breaking Point, Ice Cold Kill,* and *Gun Metal Heart*

"Breathless entertainment—a spy story with heart."
—**Tim Tigner,** bestselling author of *Coercion, Betrayal,* and *Flash*

"A fast-paced adventure that will challenge readers' expectations and take them on a thrilling journey—even to the bottom of the sea. Written with authority, *The Good Spy* is a visceral yet thoughtful read about an unusual pair of adversaries who join forces in an impossible mission."
—**Diana Chambers,** author of *Stinger*

A spy without a country . . .

Yuri Kirov is a wanted man. A former intelligence officer for the Russian Navy, he is living incognito in the United States. But the Russians are not through with him. He is recalled to duty and ordered to complete one last mission: infiltrate a Chinese naval base and install spy hardware on their newest nuclear submarine.

As a Navy veteran and expert in underwater technology, Yuri is the perfect man for the job. But with his family in danger in the U.S., he is also the perfect pawn. By the time Yuri discovers the true purpose of his mission, it is too late. A new Cold War is heating up. And it's about to go nuclear . . .

Visit us at www.kensingtonbooks.com

Books by Jeffrey Layton

The Forever Spy
The Good Spy
Vortex One
Warhead
Blowout
The Faithful Spy

*Published by Kensington Publishing Corporation

The Faithful Spy

A Yuri Kirov Thriller

Jeffrey Layton

LYRICAL PRESS
Kensington Publishing Corp.
www.kensingtonbooks.com

First Electronic Edition: October 2018
eISBN-13: 978-1-5161-0558-8
eISBN-10: 1-5161-0558-3

First Print Edition: October 2018
ISBN-13: 978-1-5161-0560-1
ISBN-10: 1-5161-0560-5

Printed in the United States of America

To my sisters, Pamela and Julie

Chapter 1

The interrogation cell reeked of stale vomit and rotting urine, leftovers from the previous occupant. A bullet to the back of the skull was the routine measure dispensed here for traitors.

Chilled to fifty-eight degrees Fahrenheit, the twelve-foot square unfinished basement room was buried deep under the Lubyanka Building in the Meshchansky District of Moscow. A single light bulb dangling from the ceiling illuminated the drab concrete walls and floor. Nastasia Vasileva sat on a metal chair, her left wrist handcuffed to the bracket bolted to a table. She wore a paper-thin oversized gray jumpsuit that concealed her curvy, sensuous frame. Sneakers sans socks and laces encased her feet. Other than plain cotton panties, no under clothing was allowed.

To complete the humiliation, they had sheared her mid-back length golden locks to a butch bob.

Nastasia shivered, an expected reaction to the frosty environment and her skimpy attire, but gut-churning dread amplified her body quakes. She struggled to maintain bladder control. She waited for nearly half an hour before he returned.

A stub of a man, Mikhail Kireyev was bald, rail-thin, and in his early forties. He worked for the Federal Security Service—*Federal'naya Sluzhba Bezopasnosti*. The FSB was the Russian Federation's FBI—and then some. Kireyev sat in the chair on the opposite side of the table. A major in the FSB, he was not in uniform today. Instead, he wore an off-the-rack dark wool suit with a starched white shirt and nondescript red tie. Kireyev placed the file folder he carried onto the tabletop and looked his captive in the eye. "I don't believe you," he said, his tone arctic. "We have not been able to verify your story. You are lying."

"No, that's not true. I was working to turn him, just what my directive required."

"We know you made at least three unauthorized visits to Seattle to collaborate with him."

"It was my mission. I had operational control. I did what was required."

Kireyev, an expert in counterintelligence interrogations, opened the file and removed a color photo. He held up the print of a mammoth yacht. "What was he doing with this boat?"

"He used it as his home base when he was in North America."

"How did he acquire the Mark Twelve?" He'd asked this particular question numerous times during previous interviews.

"I don't know anything about it. I never saw it and he never mentioned it." Nastasia reached up with her free hand and caressed her left shoulder. The post-operative ache remained. Her shattered clavicle, reassembled with metal pins and plates, refused to heal. Major Kireyev rubbed the stubble of his chin while staring at the woman he considered a turncoat. Nastasia looked away, knowing he'd already decided her fate.

Kireyev pushed his chair away from the table and stood. He collected the file and without another word exited the room. The steel door slammed shut with a shudder that signaled finality.

* * * *

The two men watched as Major Kireyev departed. A closed-circuit high-definition camera mounted in a basement ceiling corner provided live audio and color video of the interrogation of Russian operative Nastasia Vasileva—cover name Elena Krestyanova.

The directors of the brother intelligence agencies sat in posh chairs inside a well-appointed office half a dozen levels above the subterranean holding cell. They drank tea while staring at the 65-inch wall-mounted flat panel screen.

"I agree with Kireyev," FSB General Ivan Golitsin said. "She's obviously dirty." A month beyond sixty with thinning blond hair, Golitsin wore a black business suit that did nothing for his thick, stocky build.

"Maybe, maybe not," said Borya Smirnov. In his early fifties, he wore a Savile Row navy herringbone classic fit suit. The custom tailor-made ensemble complemented his lanky frame.

"Come on, Borya, I know she was one of your stars, but Kwan obviously turned her. Your own man in the field said as much."

"She was granted broad authority, like she said. He's a juicy target and her mandate was to bring him over, whatever it took." Smirnov was the director of the SVR and Nastasia's—Elena's—boss. The SVR—*Sluzhba Vneshney Razvedki*—was the successor to the former First Chief Directorate of the KGB. Responsible for foreign intelligence operations, the SVR functioned as Russia's CIA.

General Golitsin studied Elena's video image. The thirty-two-year-old woman remained seated at the table with her head slumped forward—defeated.

"Perhaps she got too close to Kwan. Could she be in love with him? That would explain much."

"No. She's not capable."

"Her training?"

"That plus all those years in the orphanages—she was abandoned at two years old."

"Orphanages—nasty business," Golitsin offered.

The men studied the video image of the prisoner. SVR chief Smirnov set his empty cup on a side table. He turned to face his counterpart. "I believe there may be a way to salvage this situation."

Golitsin leaned forward, his head angled to the side. "What do you have in mind, Borya Mikhailovich?"

Chapter 2

Day 1—Sunday

Laura Newman sat in a lounge chair on the expansive deck of her hillside home, overlooking the tranquil waters of Lake Sammamish.

It was half past six and the July sun arced low in the western sky. With temperatures still in the high eighties, it was the tenth day of the "heat wave" for the Puget Sound region—a rarity for the Pacific Northwest. Laura luxuriated in the warmth, wearing a bikini halter top and low-rise bottoms. Even with her chocolate complexion, she took precautions, applying sunscreen over every square inch of her exposed skin.

An exotic blend of Scandinavia and equatorial Africa, Laura had inherited her Swedish mother's high cheekbones, full ripe lips, azure eyes, and russet hair. Her father's tall willowy frame, broad nose, and cocoa skin, all linked to his distant Bantu ancestors, complemented her mother's genes.

Laura cherished the downtime. This was the first weekend in several months that she didn't bring her work home. She'd promised Yuri that she would avoid all email and switch her cell off. Still, she couldn't help but think about the coming week. The pressure cooker would ramp up tomorrow morning when she returned to the downtown Bellevue high-rise that served as the headquarters for Cognition Consultants. As one of the three owners of the two thousand-plus-employee IT firm, Laura was in high demand. Grateful for her company's phenomenal success—and the enormous financial rewards she benefitted from—Laura grew weary from the daily grind. Nevertheless, she would soldier on. Only thirty-three, she envisioned running full-throttle for another ten years and then maybe backing off. Yuri wanted her to put the brakes on now. She'd already accumulated more wealth than they would ever need—for several lifetimes.

Laura glanced at the color monitor on the deck table next to her chair. The image of her daughter asleep in the nursery filled the display. Two weeks shy of her first birthday, Madelyn Grace Newman had ash-blond hair, sapphire eyes, and when she smiled, the cutest dimples any mother could wish for. Laura's ex-husband was the child's biological father, but Yuri treated Madelyn as his own—a blessing Laura cherished.

Laura would limit herself to just one glass of wine. She was still nursing Maddy, but tonight she would use a warmed bottle of her own milk stored in the freezer. They had decided it was time for a nanny. Laura interviewed nearly a dozen candidates before making her choice. The references and background checks were now completed. A twenty-six-year-old from Bellingham would start work the following week. Laura hoped that Maddy and Amanda would connect, but not so much that Laura's own bond would suffer. Laura had promised herself—and Maddy—that she would not become a part-time mom, no matter what demands her business generated.

Thinking ahead to a critical meeting she would chair tomorrow afternoon at Cognition, Laura's thoughts clicked on pause when Yuri walked onto the deck from the living room. A strapping six-footer with slate-gray eyes, jet-black hair, and a trim beard that complemented his square-jawed face, Yuri Ivanovich Kirov was a couple years younger than Laura was. He wore a tank top and swim shorts that revealed his well-muscled, athletic build. He carried a platter of thick steaks, New York strips from Trader Joe's.

"Time to barbeque," Yuri said as he stepped to the built-in gas grill at the end of the deck. A trace of his Russian accent remained.

Laura sat up. "You need help?"

"I've got everything covered—just relax." Half an hour later, they sat together at the deck table enjoying Yuri's feast—sizzling beef, corn on the cob, Caesar salad, and grilled vegetables. Maddy continued to sleep.

"This is wonderful," Laura said. "Thank you for making dinner."

"My pleasure."

"Did you talk with Bill this afternoon?" Laura referred to Bill Winters, chief engineer for Northwest Subsea Dynamics. Laura owned the controlling interest in NSD. Yuri managed the company for her.

"Yes, we caught up."

"Does he still want you to go to Barrow?"

"He does, but I was able to put it off for a couple of weeks."

Laura shifted her legs. "How's the cleanup going?"

"It's still a mess. Pockets of oil are continuing to leach from the remaining ice as it melts. There's an armada of cleanup vessels but they're not enough."

NSD was under contract with the U.S. Coast Guard to monitor an enormous oil spill in the Chukchi Sea offshore of Barrow, Alaska. An oil well blowout in nearby Russian territorial waters during the previous winter had contaminated large swaths of the Arctic with crude oil. For the past several months NSD's autonomous underwater vehicles had kept track of the oil-laden ice that reached Alaskan waters.

"So, this could go on for some time," Laura said.

"I'm afraid so. The ice pack moves around so much that the remaining floes containing oil might freeze up in the fall. The whole mess could start over again next spring."

Laura arched her eyebrows, knowing the awful toll the renegade oil had already taken on the environment. Videos of oil-soaked birds, seals, whales, polar bears, and other wildlife frequented the nightly news.

Dinner was over. Laura and Yuri sat side by side in lounge chairs enjoying the retreating sun. Laura held Maddy as she nursed from a bottle. Yuri was enjoying an ice-cold bottle of Redhook ale.

Laura decided it was the right moment to revisit a subject that both had ignored for too long.

"Honey," she said, "I think it's time for us to make that trip to D.C."

"Hmmm," Yuri mumbled.

"The attorneys in Washington say it would be best for you to make a formal request for asylum directly with the State Department. They will set it up for you. Because of who you are, it will likely reach the secretary's level."

"But that will drag you into my mess. I don't want that."

Laura had prepared for Yuri's argument. "They assure me that I will be treated as an innocent party."

Yuri muttered something in Russian and then turned to face Laura. "My actions put you—and Maddy—in so much danger that it taints everything."

"You're ignoring what you did. The U.S. Navy will be grateful when we tell them what happened."

Yuri gazed lakeward. "One way or the other I will still have to deal with the FBI—and the CIA. That goes against everything I've stood for."

Laura knew how bull-headed her lover could be at times. "Yuri, we can't go on like this much longer. Sarah Compton's family deserves to know what happened. My Seattle attorneys can only keep the police at bay for a while longer. Eventually, we'll have to reveal what went down.

If we start at the top by talking with the State Department, it will be much easier to deal with the local issues."

Yuri turned to face Laura. "You're right. I need to get this over with. Please have the law firm set it up."

Laura beamed. "I will."

Chapter 3

Day 2—Monday

"You need any help?" Yuri asked. He stood by the garage door watching Laura as she secured Madelyn in the child car seat in the rear of the BMW sedan. It was 7:47 A.M.

"I'm good."

"What time do you think you'll be home tonight?"

Laura closed the door and turned to face Yuri. She wore a sleek silk blouse with a knee-length pleated skirt that displayed her shapely legs. "Probably around six."

"Great, I'll have dinner waiting. How's grilled salmon sound?"

"Wonderful."

Yuri stepped toward Laura and gave her their ritual morning kiss. "I love you, sweetie," he said with a glowing grin.

"I love you, too."

Yuri watched as Laura and Maddy drove up the private hillside road and disappeared from view behind a cedar tree-lined curve in the asphalt driveway.

Yuri returned to the living room of their residence. After picking up an electronic tracking device about the size of a paperback novel, he methodically walked around the perimeter of the space, eyeing the digital readout as it probed for bugs. He repeated the same procedure in the study, office, bedrooms, and bathrooms of the 5,000-square foot house. Yuri checked for listening devices at least once a week. The FBI was always a concern, but his principal worry was Russia's FSB. He had managed to evade his birth nation's security service for over a year but was now back on its radar screen. China's Ministry of State Security was an equivalent fear. Earlier in the year, Yuri had confronted MSS agents and military operatives of the People's Republic of China who plotted against both Russia and the United States. Yuri considered the United States his home; he had no desire to return to Russia.

Satisfied that the house remained free of spying ears and eyes, Yuri returned to the garage and climbed into his Toyota Highlander. His office was fifteen minutes away.

Laura was unaware of Yuri's weekly bug hunt; she already had too much strain in her life. Yuri didn't want Laura to fret over the possible electronic invasion of her sanctuary.

As Yuri headed to work, he couldn't help but recall the DVD he'd watched the previous evening with Laura. It was from one of the attorneys in Washington, D.C., preparing Yuri's case for requesting political asylum. The *60 Minutes* video segment featured a Cold War KGB-trained spy from East Germany who hid out in the United States for nearly twenty years, evading the FBI. After ten years of espionage operations, the KGB ordered the spy to return home but he managed to disappear from Russia's U.S. spy operations using a clever ruse. He subsequently raised a family, embraced suburban life, and ascended to upper management of a major American company before a fluke incident revealed his presence to the FBI. In the end, he was allowed to stay in the United States.

The story had buoyed both Yuri and Laura's spirits. His "non-status" as an American would soon be over, allowing Yuri to enjoy a normal life with Laura and Maddy.

Still, a knot remained in Yuri's gut. Asylum was not a slam-dunk. He was a military spy who had engaged in espionage operations against the United States. Yuri's only hope was to prove his new allegiance to the USA by telling everything. That briefing would take weeks and in the end, it would entangle Laura. The consequences to his lover troubled Yuri far more than his own fate.

Chapter 4

Nicolai Orlov was the only occupant in the code room of the Consulate-General of Russia. Located on the thirteenth floor of a polished high-rise near downtown Houston, Texas, the windowless interior room was about twenty square feet. To defeat electronic snooping by the FBI and the National Security Agency, the room's perimeter walls, ceiling, and floor were lined with special copper wiring.

Tall and trim with stylish dark hair and a chiseled face, Nick was nearing forty. He had appealing looks that were received well by females and envied by males. The SVR had recruited him just after he completed his university studies in Moscow. He rarely spent time in Russia. His last duty assignment had been at the San Francisco Consulate until Washington forced its closure as part of an ongoing diplomatic dispute between the Russian Federation and the United States. He had recently relocated to Houston, where he was promoted to SVR *rezident* of the consulate. Single with no strong family ties to the homeland, Nick found that his itinerant lifestyle suited him.

Nick sat at a table in the center of the room. It was mid-morning. His eyes focused on the monitor positioned at the end of the conference table. His boss was eight time zones ahead on the opposite end of the encrypted satellite circuit. SVR chief Borya Smirnov was alone in his office at Russia's foreign intelligence headquarters, located in the Yasenevo District of Moscow. "So, the hard drive is useless," Nick said, responding to Smirnov's summary.

"Yes. Our tech people were not able to recover any meaningful data."

The computer storage device belonged to the People's Republic of China. Nick had appropriated the drive from an MSS operative. Multiple attempts by SVR techs to crack the mechanism's encryption code triggered a self-destruction feature that bit-bleached all digital evidence.

Nick reached for the cup of tea on the table. He took a swallow and said, "We still don't know everything they were up to."

"Not completely. We're certain they were behind the Sakhalin debacle and probably the oil spill in the Arctic. And from what you uncovered there's no doubt China was playing us off against the Americans."

"They tried to trick us into war," Nick said.

"They obviously wanted us to tear at each other's throats."

"Bastards."

Nick watched as the SVR director removed a color photograph from a file folder. He studied the image before turning the photograph of the attractive blonde toward the camera. "I assume you remained convinced that she was turned."

Nick shifted in his chair as he eyed the photograph of Nastasia Vasileva, aka Elena Krestyanova, his fellow spy and past lover. "In my opinion, her actions in Seattle and Vancouver went beyond her assignment. Kwan got to her somehow… It's the only thing that makes sense to me."

Smirnov remained silent.

"Did she confess?" Nick asked.

"No. She's consistently stated that she was working to turn Kwan and played along with his requests to build trust."

"Bullshit."

Smirnov tossed the photograph of Krestyanova aside and removed another print from the folder. He directed the file photograph of a Russian naval officer in uniform at the camera. "What's Kirov's current status?"

"He remains in the Seattle area."

"Are the Americans still in the dark about him?"

"We believe so. He continues to work at the same company." Nick hesitated. "I believe all he wants is to be left alone. He saved all of our collective butts from what the Chinese had planned."

"I understand, Orlov. But remember, he's still in the navy—our navy."

"Yes, sir."

"I need you to contact him."

"Sir?"

"He's needed back home. We have a new mission for him."

Chapter 5

After completing the security check at home, Yuri made his daily commute to Redmond, where he repeated the electronic sweep of his personal office at Northwest Subsea Dynamics. Finding no threats at the residence or his workspace, he was able to concentrate on business. Yuri sat behind his office desk. It was 9:15 A.M. Sitting across the desk was Bill Winters. Short and rotund with a shaggy graying-blond mop, Winters served as NSD's chief engineer.

"How long do you think it will take to finish?" Yuri asked.

"We need at least another week, possibly two, to work out the bugs, and then a month of sea trials."

Yuri clasped his hands. "I promised Aurora that we'd start the survey on time. It's going to be close."

"I know, but with *Deep Adventurer* out of the picture, we remain behind the eight-ball." At forty-eight, Winters was NSD's oldest employee and one of the original founders of the high-tech marine company. NSD designed and manufactured cutting-edge autonomous underwater vehicles—AUVs. It used those underwater robots to map the ocean depths, conduct geophysical surveys, monitor environmental conditions, and assist in the worldwide hunt for subsea oil and gas deposits.

Yuri fidgeted in his chair. Winters was charitable in his reference to the loss of the half million-dollar autonomous underwater vehicle. Several months earlier, Yuri lost *Deep Adventurer* during a test dive for a prospective customer—or so Yuri told Winters. The replacement AUV—*Deep Guardian*—was under construction in the warehouse section of the NSD building. Yuri looked up, meeting Winters's eyes. "Do the best you can but we'll still need to ship it up on time."

"Okay. But without a thorough set of sea trials we're taking a big risk."

"I know, and it's on me."

Winters owned 25% of the company. Laura Newman held the remaining shares. She purchased controlling interest of NSD for Yuri, who served as general manager. Bill reported to Yuri.

Yuri shifted gears. "What's the latest from Barrow?" He referred to NSD's offshore survey operation in Barrow, Alaska.

"*Deep Explorer* keeps chugging along. No problems, but she's way overdue for an overhaul." *Deep Explorer* was NSD's flagship machine. It was monitoring the massive oil spill in the Chukchi Sea offshore of the northwest coast of Alaska.

"If we get in a bind, any chance we can pull her off the spill and move her north as backup for the *Guardian*?"

"It's such an awful mess up there. With the breakup and trapped oil still seeping out of the ice just about everywhere, the Coast Guard is overwhelmed. They bitch when we pull the *Explorer* off surveillance for routine maintenance and battery charging. If I even hinted about re-tasking her, they'd go ape shit for sure."

"I get it, Bill. I was just hoping that with all the equipment up there now, we'd get a break."

"That damn oil entombed itself in multiple layers within the ice. There are millions of chunks up there now, floating around and slowly melting, each one bleeding shit. Trying to keep track of the stuff and predicting where the next major spill is going to erupt is a frigging nightmare. The *Explorer* is the only unit that is up for the task."

Yuri smiled. "I know, Bill. You and your team are doing a magnificent job. Laura is extremely pleased with your work—and so am I."

"Thanks, boss. I appreciate the vote of confidence." He stood. "We'll do our best to get the *Guardian* ready in time."

"Thank you."

Yuri remained alone in his office. He was grateful that Laura had not wasted her funds on the purchase of the once-struggling NSD. The company was now well into the black. With the notoriety of its Arctic work, new customers were placing orders for surveys at an unprecedented rate.

Yuri glanced at the poster-size framed color photograph hanging on the wall opposite his desk. The image depicted the *Deep Explorer* mounted to its launching cradle aboard a workboat in Puget Sound. It was the inaugural voyage. Canary yellow, twenty feet long, and three feet in diameter with a bullet-shaped nose cone, stubby tailfins, and a ducted propeller, the autonomous underwater vehicle looked like an apparatus of war. RESEARCH stenciled in black paint on both sides of the fuselage identified its stated purpose.

Unknown to Bill Winters and the NSD staff, Yuri had converted the *Explorer*'s sister submersible, the *Deep Adventurer*, into a real war machine. Its last mission wreaked wholesale havoc on an adversary who had blackmailed Yuri and harmed his family. The peril had diminished but Yuri sensed it was not over.

Chapter 6

Only forty-three, Kwan Chi often felt like eighty-three. But today the pain level had dropped a notch. For most of the afternoon, he was able to move about his apartment without the damn walker. However, he still needed a cane this evening. His right tibia continued to mend—pinned together with a network of screws and stainless-steel plates. Kwan was lucky to have kept his leg. The burns to his wrists and forearms remained a concern. His doctors warned that additional skin grafts might be needed. He dreaded the thought of having to endure that awful procedure again.

He shuffled to the living room of his Kowloon condominium. Perched on the fifty-third-floor of the glimmering tower, the penthouse unit had an awesome vista of Hong Kong's Victoria Harbour.

Tall for his race, Kwan eased his sinewy frame into his favorite chair by the window wall. He gazed seaward at the nightly lightshow. Scores of workboats, ferries, and yachts scurried about the harbor, marked by profuse cabin illumination and nav lights. Although the view was breathtaking, Kwan's thoughts focused on the events of several months earlier.

With his mission aborted by Beijing, Kwan retreated aboard his yacht the *Yangzi* accompanied by most of the assault team. The other team members followed in the workboat. The plan was to avoid U.S. waters, staying at least fifty miles offshore. Once Kwan reached Ensenada in Baja Mexico, he would return to China aboard his private jet.

But within just a day, as the superyacht cruised southward along the Washington State coast approaching Oregon, Kwan's escape plan collapsed into catastrophe.

While Kwan had napped in his palatial forward cabin high up on the fourth deck, a massive explosion near the stern rocked the 305-foot-long yacht. Tossed from the bed, he smashed into a cabinet, snapping his shin bone with a sickening crack. In shock, Kwan crawled through the cabin door onto a passageway and peered aft. Half of his ship was missing. Flames fueled by 10,000 gallons of diesel oil raced through the remaining superstructure, blocking his only escape route.

Kwan ended up in the sea. He clung to debris with seared arms, managing to keep his head above the water. He endured mind-numbing cold for twenty minutes. The workboat following the *Yangzi* plucked him and one other survivor—a female assistant steward—from the chilled waters.

Kwan closed his eyes while taking in a deep breath. He pictured his adversary, knowing the Russian had someway sabotaged the *Yangzi*, just as he'd upended Operation Sea Dragon. *Yuri Kirov—you son of a bitch!*

Chapter 7

"Welcome back. We've missed you," the Chief of Mission said.

"Thank you, sir. It is good to be back." Elena Krestyanova's flight landed at Vancouver International late Saturday evening.

"Please, sit down and share tea with me."

Elena took a chair facing Alexi Popov, who sat behind an antique Russian desk. The tall and thin fifty-two-year-old balding diplomat poured steaming tea from a pot into two Russian crystal hot-tea glasses with vintage Podstakannik metal holders. He passed one to Elena. They were alone in a corner office of the Russian trade mission. The office overlooked a park in downtown Vancouver, British Columbia.

Popov noticed the change the instant she walked through the door, escorted by his secretary. "You cut your hair. Very nice," he offered. He had learned of her pending return the previous week.

Elena hated the butch cut but had no choice in the matter. "Thanks—I was tired of the old look. Time to try something new."

Popov was attracted to Elena from day one. Her lovely face, blond tresses, and sumptuous curves were irresistible. Yet he knew his limits. Although he was the boss, she was out of bounds. The SVR controlled Elena, not the Ministry of Industry and Trade. He was tasked with assisting her as needed. "Tell me, Elena, how are 'things' back in Moscow." Popov knew little about Elena's four-month absence. Moscow had informed him that she was recalled for a special project but provided no details.

Elena said, "In a word—tense."

Popov tilted his head to the side. "Sanctions?"

"Yes. The Americans are ruthless."

The envoy's forehead wrinkled. "I thought so. They're causing problems here, too. Washington is pressuring Ottawa to cut trade ties with us. Very serious situation."

Russia's continued harassment of its neighbors, coupled with its refusal to participate in the oil spill cleanup in the Arctic, resulted in a new round of penalties imposed by the United States. Trade relations between Russia and the West were at an all-time low.

"I imagine our position on the oil spill is a sore point for the Canadians," Elena offered.

"Yes. Most of the oil is now offshore of Alaska and Canada. The president has made it clear that he holds the U.S. responsible for the sabotage of our well and will not contribute a ruble to the cleanup in their waters. I think he has a point."

Elena nodded her agreement but knew otherwise—the USA was innocent. Prior to embarking on her new assignment, the SVR director instructed Elena to perpetuate the hoax.

The trade envoy took another draw from his tea glass. "There is some good news on the trade front. Our Chinese friends have stepped up and are really helping out."

Elena smiled. "I know. That's what I've been working on."

"I thought so. What can you tell me?"

"Moscow has tasked me to work with China about a cooperative arrangement to develop our offshore Siberian oil reserves."

Popov's eyes widened. "That's impressive, Elena."

"It's a reflection on you and your office, sir. You've had much success in Canada."

"Well, thanks, but your prior work in China has put you in the driver's seat."

"You helped train me, Alexi."

Popov was hooked. "How can I help with your assignment?"

They talked for fifteen minutes and then Elena returned to her office. It remained just as she'd left it earlier in the year. As directed by Moscow, the trade mission continued the payments on her apartment and the lease of her Mercedes.

Elena settled into her chair and turned on her PC. She keyed in the password to gain access to the desktop. It still worked. She opened her documents file, displaying two dozen folders. *So far, so good.* She had feared the SVR had erased her working files after copying the contents.

Elena selected a file. After keying in another password, the encrypted document opened. She found the color photograph and stared at the image of Kwan Chi. "Hello, lover," she whispered.

* * * *

It was evening at the Newman residence. Dinner was over and Laura had just rocked Maddy to sleep. She slipped her daughter into the crib in the nursery and joined Yuri on the deck fronting the living room. Yuri sat in a lounge chair, taking in the view. It was twilight and a comfortable seventy-eight degrees Fahrenheit. A runabout raced across the lake surface, towing a water skier making one last run. The sun had dropped behind the Olympic Mountains five minutes earlier. As the boat sped away, Yuri took a deep draw from a bottle of Redhook.

Laura sat in a deck chair beside Yuri. She had changed into cargo shorts, T-shirt, and sandals after arriving home from work. She was drinking a chilled glass of lemonade.

Laura sensed that something was wrong at dinner but let it pass. She decided it was now time to probe.

"Honey, you seem to be a little down this evening. Is there a problem at NSD?"

Yuri turned to face Laura. "We're doing well... My only concern is that we're a bit behind with testing for the *Guardian.* We need it to get certified so we can ship it north."

Laura was privy to the delivery issue for the replacement AUV. "I'm sure Aurora will give you some additional time—you're a hero to them!"

"Maybe, but I don't want to ask unless it's absolutely necessary. I made a promise."

Laura crossed her ankles. They sat quietly, enjoying the solitude of the evening as the sun's afterglow receded. A few minutes into darkness, Yuri confessed. "Nick called me today."

"At the office?"

"Sent me a text first. I called him back on my burner."

"What's going on?"

"I have to meet with him at the consulate tomorrow afternoon."

"In Houston?"

"Yes."

"Oh no... you can't go."

"I have to. Orders from the Navy."

"What do they want?"

"An interview."

"About what?"

"Nick doesn't know—or has been ordered not to say. Anyway, I have no choice in the matter."

"Yes, you do. We can fly to D.C. instead. This morning I authorized the attorneys there to set up an asylum interview with the State Department."

"No. I don't want to do that. It'll just drag you further into my mess."

Laura was about to protest when Yuri stood up. "We both know this day has been coming for a long time. I need to deal with the situation directly."

Laura rose and stood beside Yuri. "You can't trust them. They could make you return to Russia."

"I don't know. Maybe."

"Then I'm coming with you. They wouldn't dare do anything knowing I'm around."

"Absolutely not. I have to do this on my terms. I don't want to be worrying about you and Maddy."

Yuri headed inside.

"Where are going?"

"To pack. My flight leaves at 5:35 in the morning."

Chapter 8

Day 3—Tuesday

The Boeing 737 touched down at Houston's George Bush Intercontinental Airport a few minutes before noon. Yuri made his way through the crowded terminal to the designated place. The United Airlines counter was stacked three deep with customers. He stood aside, waiting as instructed.

The woman made contact two minutes later. "Mr. Kirkwood?" she asked with a glowing smile, her eyes veiled by sunglasses. The cute brunette in the professional pantsuit was in her late twenties, five-foot-six, and slim.

"Yes," Yuri said, responding to his alias, John Kirkwood.

"I'm Marina, from the consulate. Nicolai sent me."

"You work for Nick?"

"I do." She smiled again. "Any luggage at baggage claim?"

"No, all I brought was my carry-on." Yuri gestured to the wheeled case resting at his side.

"Very good. We can head to the parking garage and I'll drive you back to the consulate."

She led the way.

* * * *

"Now who do you suppose that turkey is?"

"No idea. No hits on the database."

The two U.S. Customs and Border Protection agents in the Department of Homeland Security's operations center at Houston International stared at the wall-mounted video screen. Yuri Kirov's HD image filled the display.

A recently installed beta test version of a new facial recognition software system at the airport identified Yuri's escort when she entered the terminal from the parking garage. The software ignored the wig and Ray-Bans she wore. Marina Kazakova's Russian passport photo had been scanned into the system four weeks earlier when she arrived from Moscow. Classified as a clerk, she worked in the Houston consulate's visa section. The FBI speculated that she really worked for the SVR. Homeland Security had followed Marina's progress through the terminal with overlapping closed-circuit cameras. The CBP agents watched the pair as they walked back to the parking garage. Five minutes later, another camera captured the Ford Expedition as it pulled onto a southbound lane of John F. Kennedy Boulevard. The Russian consulate was thirty minutes away near downtown Houston via the Hardy Toll Road and I-610.

As directed by the consultant's security officer, Marina wore a disguise. She also rented the SUV rather than drive one of the pool cars with diplomatic plates—an automatic red flag to the Feds. Not known to Russia's intelligence services, however, was how well DHS's new facial software worked.

"Do you want me to notify the FBI field office?" the junior agent asked.

"Yeah, let 'em know there's a new player in town. Maybe they can figure out who he is."

"Will do."

* * * *

"I'm honored to meet you, Captain-Lieutenant Kirov."

Yuri reached forward and clasped the offered hand. "Thank you, Captain."

Yuri settled back into his chair as the forty-two-year-old Russian naval officer took a seat on the opposite side of the table next to Nick Orlov. They were inside a secure conference room in the consulate. It was 2:04 P.M. Prior to the scheduled interview, Yuri and Nick lunched privately in Nick's office. They used the forty minutes to prepare for the meeting.

Captain First Rank Vladislav Zhilkin was the naval attaché assigned to the Russian embassy in Washington. A bear of a man, he stood six-foot-four and weighed a muscular 220 pounds. His tailored dark suit hugged his athletic build. Zhilkin opened his briefcase and removed a file folder, placing it on the table. He extracted a ten-page document from the folder and glanced at Yuri. "I assume that you've had a chance to review Major Orlov's briefing report on the incident."

"Yes, sir. I read it during lunch."

Zhilkin removed another document, a color photograph of a bulky cylindrical object resting in a steel cradle. The image of the torpedo mine came from a classified Russian Navy weapons catalogue. Zhilkin passed the photo to Yuri. "You're certain that the unit deployed was a Mark Twelve?"

Yuri glanced at the photograph. "Yes, sir. No question about it. I trained with it while at Sevastopol."

The attaché shook his head, puzzled. "How the devil did they get hold of it?"

"No, idea, sir. We found a manual aboard the yacht but nothing to indicate how they acquired the weapon."

Zhilkin removed another color photo, a screenshot from a Seattle television station news broadcast. He passed it to Yuri. "This was your work?"

Yuri stiffened as he took in the image of the blazing yacht. "I don't know for certain but I expect that I may have been responsible."

"Serves the pricks right. Good job, Kirov."

Nick joined in. "They deserved it, that's for sure." Nick lost four of his men on the mission—the first casualties he'd ever suffered in his seventeen-year career with the SVR.

Zhilkin asked several follow-up questions regarding the sinking before moving on. "Tell me, Kirov, what do you think the Chinese were really up to?"

Yuri expected the question. He and Nick discussed it during lunch and he'd thought about it numerous times during the past several months.

"It's my opinion that the Chinese government deliberately tried to start a war between us and the Americans."

Zhilkin clasped his hands. "The Kremlin agrees with you—and so do I."

Nick responded. "Captain, if Yuri had not intervened when he did, that war might have gone hot. We were that close."

"I agree." Zhilkin again looked Yuri's way. "We are indebted to you for your quick thinking."

"Thank you," Yuri said, flattered—and at the same time perplexed about the praise. *Where is all of this headed?*

He soon had his answer.

"Well, Kirov," Zhilkin announced, "it's now time for payback—and we need your assistance."

Damn!

Chapter 9

The two FBI special agents just connected. The on-call duty agent who initiated the telephone call was in his office at the Houston Field Office. The recipient was in her office at headquarters in Washington, D.C. The call came in just before Ava Diesen planned to leave for the day.

"We don't have anything in our system about this guy," Diesen said. The forty-four-year-old mother of three leaned back in her chair. She caught a reflection of her sandy blond hair in a nearby window. She needed to make an appointment for a trim and coloring.

"He's obviously someone important," the caller said. "They sent a car for him."

Counterintelligence specialist Diesen took another look at her desktop computer screen. Yuri Kirov's image stared back. She had just run the image through the Bureau's catalogue of known Russian spies and come up with zilch.

"All I can suggest for now is running through the airport's surveillance system. Maybe you can ID the aircraft that he flew in on and backtrack from there. That assumes, of course, that was the reason he was at the airport."

"I was afraid of that. I just hoped we might get lucky."

"Sorry. I'll make a few more inquiries here. But working from your end looks like the best option at this time."

"Thanks for checking."

"You're welcome."

Supervisory Special Agent Diesen hung up the phone. Yuri's photo remained on the computer display. *You're handsome. Just who are you and what are you up to?*

All Russian outposts in the United States were under extraordinary scrutiny. Relations between the two nations were dismal. The two presidents remained distrustful of each other over spilled oil in the Arctic and the catastrophic damage to their respective nations' oil and gas infrastructures. Saber rattling seemed to escalate weekly.

Alerted by Homeland Security, the FBI's hidden cameras monitoring the Russian consulate picked up the Ford Expedition when it drove into the garage of the eighteen-story office building on West Loop Street. Agents from the Houston Field Office would continue to track the visitor until he was identified and the purpose of the visit determined.

Diesen decided to make a few inquiries tomorrow. Maybe her contacts at CIA or DIA could shed some light on the mystery man. She didn't expect much to come of the effort.

He's probably some kind of consultant or maybe a lobbyist—yeah, that's probably it!

Ava shut down her computer and stood. It was time to head home—ninety minutes earlier than usual. Her middle child had a must-attend event this evening. She'd promised ten-year-old Ella that she would not miss the last competition of her squad at the summer cheerleading camp.

* * * *

After meeting with Captain Zhilkin, Yuri and Nick relocated to Nick's office. It was 3:35 P.M. During their earlier face-to-face, there was little time to catch up. They now had half an hour. Yuri stretched out his arms as he sat in the chair that fronted the oak desk. Nick drank from a cup of tepid tea. The spacious office contained a desktop computer, a two-drawer metal file cabinet and a hanging plant next to the window. A painting of a three-mast square-rigged tall ship charging through a turbulent sea dominated the wall next to Yuri. There were no photographs of loved ones or family memorabilia on display in the office. The only personal item was a San Francisco 49ers gold mini speed helmet. About the size of an orange, it sat on the right-hand corner of the desk.

Yuri reached forward and picked up the helmet. "Nice," he said as he examined the faceguard and chinstrap.

"Gift from a friend."

"I bet this doesn't go over well in this town."

Nick laughed. "No one cares here. None of the consulate staff are into American football."

"So, it's just you and your beloved Forty-Niners." Nick remained an ardent fan of the Bay Area pro team.

"Yep."

"Do you think they'll have a better season this year?"

"I can only hope." The NFL preseason was a month away.

"You still have season tickets?"

"Yeah, I kept them." Forced to vacate the San Francisco consulate with the other staffers, Nick relocated to the Houston consulate. Assigned to watch over the closed outpost, Nick made periodic visits to San Francisco to conduct security checks of the seven story Pacific Heights building that remained in the ownership of the Russian government. Russia planned to reopen the consulate when the U.S. regained its senses.

Yuri returned the helmet. "How do you like Houston?"

"People are nice—real friendly. Weather sucks. Too humid for me."

"Miss San Francisco?"

"I do."

Yuri took a draw from a plastic water bottle. Grimacing, he changed subjects. "I thought for sure Zhilkin would grill me about the *Neva*. But he barely mentioned it."

"He's Navy. You remain a hero for saving the crew."

Yuri wrinkled his brow. "But I'm AWOL."

"I think that's all in the past. Taking care of the Mark Twelve cancelled that indiscretion."

Yuri was not convinced, but let it go. "The charter Zhilkin arranged, what kind of aircraft is it?"

"Gulfstream. Very nice."

"You should come along. I could use the help."

Nick laughed again. "Right, a landlubber like me with all of you Navy guys running around the North Pacific. No thanks. Plus, my boss would have a fit if I took off now."

Yuri tugged on his beard "I'm worried about Laura. Who knows how long I'll be gone? I don't like leaving her alone. There are too many loose ends."

"China?" Nick asked.

"Yes."

"Kwan's dead, and so is Wang. You took care of that problem with the little surprise you left aboard the *Yangzi*. And their whole op was blown. If anything, China's going to remain low-key. If the Americans ever find out..."

"They should be told. That was my original plan."

"I understand," Nick said. "But Moscow does not want to risk it now. Maybe when things cool off."

"The *Neva*'s mission?"

"Yes."

Over a year earlier, Yuri was aboard a Russian spy sub that penetrated deep into Puget Sound and the Strait of Georgia. He was tasked with spying on U.S. and Canadian naval installations. Yuri said, "The Americans need to know what China was up to—how close they came to pulling it off."

"I know, but not now."

Yuri raised another troubling item. "Zhilkin is over-optimistic about this new mission. What he laid out is going to be a nightmare to pull off. The chances of success are dismal."

Nick frowned, unsure of where Yuri was headed.

Yuri continued, "I have no choice but to participate, which I will do. The promise of allowing me to retire and return to the U.S. is the incentive. But if I don't survive it will devastate Laura."

"Don't talk like that. You've been through much worse."

"I was lucky. But luck always runs out." Nick was about to protest when Yuri continued, "If I don't make it, you'll have to tell Laura. No one else will be around to do it."

"Of course, but it's not going to be needed."

"One other request, Nick. If the worst happens, please watch over Laura and Maddy as best you can."

"I will."

"Thank you, my friend."

Chapter 10

"Hi, honey—just checking in." Yuri parked his cell phone next to an ear. He sat in a chair inside the plush lobby of a private airport west of Houston. It was late afternoon. Captain Zhilkin stood at the counter twenty feet away, checking on the status of their flight.

"How did it go?" Laura was in her Bellevue office.

"Okay—about what I expected."

Nick Orlov arranged for the clandestine delivery of Yuri and Zhilkin to the airport. Knowing the FBI monitored the consulate twenty-four-seven, Nick and his staff took precautions to evade the snooping Americans. An NOC—non-official cover—Russian operative whisked the naval officers out of the consulate's parking garage, hiding them in the back of a rental van disguised as a florist's delivery vehicle. At the same time, Marina Kazakova drove Yuri's double in the Ford Expedition to a home in nearby Piney Point Village. The three million dollar residence served as guest quarters for visiting Russian diplomats and bureaucrats. The SVR officer masquerading as Yuri wore a wig and a false beard; he easily passed as Yuri from a distance.

"Are you coming home tonight?" There was hope in Laura's voice.

"No, I'm sorry—I've been recalled."

"Damn!" Laura rarely swore. "I knew this was going to happen."

"It's going to be okay. I need to help out for a couple of weeks and then I'll be back for good."

Laura's voice quavered. "Just where are you going?"

"I can't say."

"When do you leave?"

"I fly out tonight."

"Two weeks—are you sure about that time?"

"It's just an estimate."

"Will Nick be with you?"

"No."

Laura's moan vibrated over the speaker. "Can you call me to let me know how you're doing?"

"That won't be possible."

"How about email or text?"

"Unlikely." Yuri hesitated. "I know this is troubling, but it's a chance for me to take care of the outstanding issues—for good."

"You can't trust them... you said so yourself."

Yuri sensed Laura was losing it. "It's going to be okay. Please trust me."

Yuri asked Laura to relay instructions to Bill Winters regarding NSD operations during his absence. They talked for five more minutes, both continuing to use care with their words for fear of electronic eavesdropping. Captain Zhilkin turned away from the counter and made eye contact with Yuri.

Yuri raised a hand in acknowledgment.

"Sweetie, it's time for me to go."

"Promise me you'll be careful."

"I promise."

"Remember, I'm expecting you home in two weeks."

"I want to be home by then, too."

"I love you."

"I love you."

Yuri returned the phone to his coat pocket and stood up. Zhilkin stepped toward Yuri. "It's time to board."

"Okay." Yuri reached down beside the chair and grabbed his carry-on bag. Yuri and the Russian Navy captain walked through the private gate with just a nod from the attendant. The gleaming Gulfstream 650 sat on the tarmac fifty feet away.

Chapter 11

Day 4—Wednesday

"Kirov, wake up. We'll be landing soon."

Yuri blinked open his eyes. Captain Zhilkin stood in the aisle beside Yuri's chair. "How long?"

"We touch down in ten minutes."

"Thanks."

Zhilkin returned to his seat on the opposite side of the aisle.

Yuri rarely slept on aircraft. But the ride that carried him and Zhilkin across the Pacific was a posh flying carpet. The seats in the G650 were incredibly comfortable, allowing him to catch six solid hours of sleep. They had the luxurious twelve-seater to themselves.

Ownership of the charter jet was officially listed as a holding company based in Belgium. But that was just the beginning of the chain of title, which extended to eight successive entities. At the end was a Russian billionaire. To remain in favor with Kremlin, he made the jet available at very favorable rates without any questions. Before departure, the pilots filed the flight plan as a non-stop trip to Seattle. The total time in Seattle was fifty minutes. After filing a new flight plan and topping off the fuel tanks, the G650 commenced the transpacific flight.

The jet was capable of flying direct from Houston to Vladivostok but the first stop was orchestrated to throw off the FBI. If the Houston Field Office checked with the private airport, the flight to Seattle would not raise alarms.

Yuri stretched out his arms and faced the adjacent oval window. The Gulfstream was descending as it flew westward over the Bosfor Vostochnyy

Bridge, approaching Vladivostok. Although it was 8:50 P.M., the summer twilight conditions provided plenty of light to view the port city. The ocean-fronting bridge spanning the Eastern Bosporus Strait, coupled with the sheltered inner harbor areas and the hilly terrain, had earned the city a catchy moniker: Vladivostok—Russia's San Francisco.

As the G650 sped by, Yuri spotted the naval base tucked away in Uliss Bay, just inside the Bosfor Vostochnyy Bridge. He knew the base well from past deployments; it served as the principal moorage for Russian nuclear submarines.

After passing over the city, the twin-engine jet turned right and headed north up Amur Bay. Their destination was a couple of minutes away. Yuri leaned across the aisle. "Are we landing at Uglovoye?"

"No. Orlov recommended against that. It would be a problem for the pilots. We'll be using the civilian airport."

"Okay."

In the past, Yuri had always landed at and departed from Uglovoye. It was easier that way—no issues with customs or border entry. The Russian Air Force base was home to several squadrons of top of the line fighters. Vladivostok International Airport was four miles away.

Yuri reached into his coat pocket and removed his credentials. Nick had provided Yuri with new updated papers identifying him as an active Russian naval officer. The written orders directed him to report to Pacific Fleet Command for a new assignment. Yuri also carried a thousand U.S. dollars in cash, two credit cards, and his fake IDs—a Washington State driver's license in the name of John Kirkwood and a Canadian passport in the cover name of Peter Kirkinski from an earlier op. Yuri made eye contact with Zhilkin. "Where are we staying tonight?"

"I have a driver waiting for us. We'll drop the pilots off at a hotel in the city and then take you to the Headquarters BOQ. There will be a room for you."

"Okay." Yuri knew from experience the bachelor officers' quarters near the Pacific Fleet Headquarters building would be spartan. He expected that Zhilkin had a lavish hotel room reserved for his personal use. The next day, the charter pilots would make a deadhead run to Singapore for a new charter.

As the Gulfstream passed over the north end of Amur Bay, Yuri peered through the window. He could see the runway ahead, lit up with a string of strobe lights. Although he had slept during half the flight, fatigue again settled in. The time zone issue was part of it, but not knowing what lay ahead sapped his mental well-being. Russia was out for blood, and he was at the tip of the Kremlin's spear, about to be hurled at the enemy's heart.

* * * *

"Is he still there?" asked the FBI supervisor. She called from her office in the Houston Field Office.

"Yes, ma'am," replied the special agent. "We followed him from the consulate to the residence yesterday afternoon. We've had eyes on the house all night and through the morning. He has not come out yet."

"Anyone else staying there?"

"Not that we're aware of."

"Maybe they're coming to see him. Keep on it. Call me the minute he shows his face or if he has any visitors."

"Will do, ma'am."

It was half past noon. The FBI team surveilling the Russian consulate's guest quarters occupied a nearby residence in the high-end neighborhood west of downtown Houston. Several days would pass before the FBI discovered the ruse.

* * * *

Laura Newman sat on a sofa in the living room working with a laptop when her cell phone chimed. She checked the caller ID. "Hi, Bill," she said.

"Good evening, Laura," Bill Winters replied. "Please excuse my late call. I've been out of the office and just got your voicemail about John."

"Don't worry about it. You can call me anytime." Laura glanced at her daughter. Maddy cavorted on the carpet near Laura. "John had to leave suddenly for a family emergency. His sister in Denmark is gravely ill."

"Sorry to hear about that… Any idea when he'll be returning?"

"It's up in the air but at least a week."

"Will he be available to talk by phone?"

"It's pretty stressful for him right now. I'd like to let him deal with the situation there without having to worry about company matters—at least for a while."

"Got it. So, do you have a few minutes to talk about our contract with Aurora?"

"Absolutely."

The conversation ended ten minutes later. Laura provided Winters with the direction he needed regarding an ongoing project in Alaska for Aurora Offshore Systems.

Laura relocated to the nursery. She changed a diaper and dressed Maddy in her pajamas. Her conversation with Winters lingered. Laura admired Bill, as did Yuri. She didn't like perpetuating the myths about Yuri's identity and his sudden departure. Laura carried Maddy into the master bedroom and sat in a chair by the bed. As she nursed Madelyn, she prayed.

Dear Lord, please watch over Yuri. Keep him safe, and please bring him back home to me.

* * * *

Elena Krestyanova stepped out of the shower onto the tile floor. After toweling off, she used the cloth to wipe condensation from the bathroom mirror. She stared at her naked form. The scar across her left shoulder was still inflamed. While showering, she'd directed the nozzle's steamy flow onto the wounded tissue. Fifteen minutes of pulsed hydro-heat helped mitigate the ache.

After spending a full day at the mission, she arrived at her high-rise apartment in downtown Vancouver in the early evening. She should have gone home earlier—the pain in her shoulder kicked in full force in mid-afternoon. The over-the-counter meds she relied on failed her today. Elena reached up with her right hand and traced a finger over the revolting four-inch-long blemish. She'd suffered through two surgeries at the same location. The first repaired the clavicle, shattered by a nine-millimeter slug four months earlier while on a mission in North America. The follow-up operation occurred just two weeks ago at an FSB medical facility in Moscow. One of the stainless-steel plates used to stitch bone fragments together had malfunctioned. Its replacement would help heal the festering wound and relieve the chronic pain—or so she was told. That's when they installed the tracking device.

A radio frequency identification device embedded within the replacement plate kept track of Elena's location twenty-four-seven. When energized by a unique RF signal emitted from a remote transceiver, the RFID tag under the skin broadcast a confirming signal. Technicians from the SVR's Science and Technology Directorate installed the micro transceiver in the cell phone issued to Elena upon her departure from Moscow. The iPhone emailed Elena's location to an SVR-monitored anonymous address every hour.

The constant tracking of Elena's whereabouts was an annoyance, but there was more. Attached to the replacement plate was a plastic capsule filled with a neurotoxin synthesized from an amalgam of venomous marine creatures. Should an attempt be made to remove the capsule or to disable the RFID tag, or should twenty-four hours of consecutive failure to communicate between Elena's cell phone and SVR headquarters occur, another microprocessor connected to the capsule would release the poison. Once absorbed into the surrounding tissue, the toxin would short-circuit the nervous system, blocking transmission of electrical signals from the brain to the body. The result would be paralysis of the diaphragm and cessation of breathing—an especially awful way to die. SVR director Smirnov made it clear to Elena that should she make a run for it or fail to complete her mission, death was guaranteed.

Elena put on a terrycloth bathrobe and relocated to the living room. The elevated view of the city was breathtaking. Elena picked up her cell phone from the charger on the desk, verifying it was fully charged. She carried two extra batteries, one in her briefcase and the other in her purse. As long as she remained within fifty feet of the iPhone, she was safe.

Elena sank into a sofa by the gas fireplace. She used an app on the cell to check the time in Hong Kong and saw it was mid-morning.

She dialed a number from memory, knowing the recipient would be awake by now. It rang three times before he answered. The dialect was not her native language, but she recognized his voice.

"Hello, Chi," she said using English, a common tongue to both. "It's me—Elena."

Chapter 12

"Take a seat, Kirov."

"Yes, sir." Yuri sat in a chair fronting the elegant desk. On the other side of the Italian handcrafted oak writing table sat Admiral Oleg Belofsky. His predecessor accepted the lavish desk and matching chair from the commander of a squadron of Italian warships visiting Vladivostok during a goodwill tour of East Asia.

Pushing sixty, Belofsky was bald and heavyset. His leathery, wrinkled face telegraphed heavy smoking. He wore wire-rimmed eyeglasses. There were three gold stars on the epaulettes of his uniform jacket.

Yuri was in uniform, too. When Captain Zhilkin had dropped him off at the BOQ, he was dumbfounded to find his uniform, freshly cleaned and pressed, hanging in the closet. Somehow, it had survived the transpacific crossing aboard the crippled *Neva* and was rescued before the submarine was scrapped. Yuri had also shaved off his beard this morning, knowing the Russian Navy frowned on facial hair.

The admiral poured tea from a sturdy pot into two mugs. He passed one to Yuri. They were the only occupants in the office. It was late morning.

"Thank you, sir," Yuri said.

Belofsky sipped his steaming beverage. Yuri followed his lead and gazed out the windows. As head of Russia's Pacific Fleet, Belofsky occupied a corner office on the top floor of the Fleet headquarters building. The view overlooked Vladivostok's Golden Horn Bay, a natural inlet that extended about four miles inland from the open bay waters. Yuri spotted the sculpted support towers of the Golden Horn Bridge to the east. The majestic cable-stayed structure spanned the waterway, providing a shortcut to the southern half of the city. Warships lined the quays fronting the headquarters building. Commercial craft were moored alongside the wharves and piers on adjacent shorelines.

Belofsky met Yuri's eyes. "I served under your grandfather's command early in my career. Admiral Fedorov truly was a legend, a terrific leader and an inspiration to all of the junior officers."

"Thanks, sir. He encouraged me to join the Navy."

"Indeed."

Belofsky took another draw from his mug and then picked up one of the several file folders stacked on his desk. He retrieved a document and thumbed through a twenty-five-page report prepared by the Fleet Intelligence Directorate. He glanced back at Yuri. "I've read this briefing on the mission half a dozen times—just incredible work." He returned the report to its file folder. "I wanted to take this opportunity to personally thank you for your work with the *Neva*."

"Thank you, Admiral."

Belofsky picked up another report and scanned the executive summary. "You received treatments in Seattle for your injuries. Tell me about that." Belofsky referred to Yuri's bouts with decompression sickness.

"I had multiple hyperbaric treatments and several months of physical therapy."

"Your leg is now healed?"

"The paralysis is gone."

"Good." Yuri kept waiting for the bomb to be dropped. "Tell me, Kirov, how did you like living in America?"

"They're good people, sir. Not unlike us."

"I had a chance to visit the United States as a young officer. I too was impressed with the Americans and their wealth."

Yuri did not comment, unsure of Belofsky's track.

The admiral continued, "The American woman who helped you—is she the reason you remained there so long?"

"It is, sir. I'm in love with her."

Belofsky removed a color photograph of Laura Newman, downloaded from Cognition Consultants' website. "She's quite beautiful—and from what I've read, a brilliant businesswoman."

Yuri decided it was time to launch his defense. "She is, sir, and if she hadn't assisted me the *Neva* and its crew would never have survived. She risked everything to—"

Belofsky cut Yuri off. "Relax, Kirov. I know what she did and I can't fault you for wanting to remain with her." He adjusted his glasses.

Yuri waited for the inevitable "but" that would come.

Belofsky said, "She certainly was your ally and as you say she risked everything. But can she still be trusted?"

"All she wants is to be left alone."

"And you would like to remain with her, correct?"

"Yes, sir."

"I don't blame you." Belofsky returned Laura's photo to the file.

Yuri perked up.

"Kirov, you're still a commissioned officer in the Russian Navy with remaining obligations, the least of which is your unauthorized leave, regardless of your injuries."

"Yes, sir," Yuri said, now expecting reprimand.

"Before we discuss those issues, I have questions about your recent actions." The admiral picked up another file and removed a color photograph. He passed it to Yuri. "Can you confirm this is the man you know as Kwan Chi?"

"Affirmative, sir."

Belofsky extracted a second photo and handed it over. "Please identify this individual."

Yuri scanned the image. "David Wang—at least that was his cover name."

"Were you aware he was a PLAN officer with the grade of lieutenant-commander?" Belofsky referred to the China's People's Liberation Army-Navy.

"Yes, he so identified himself." Yuri returned the photos to the desk.

The admiral retrieved Wang's photo. "Are you certain the weapon Wang used was a Mark Twelve and not a knockoff?"

"No question about it, sir. The Viper used was legitimate."

"How did they get their hands on it?"

"I don't know."

"Well, thanks to your intervention, this prick was deep-sixed." He tossed Wang's photo aside and picked up another collection of photos from the file folder. "Unfortunately, Kirov, your surprise package was only partially successful." He handed over the color prints.

The surveillance photos were grainy, shot from long distance with aid of a telephoto lens. The images focused on a man in a wheelchair on the ground floor of a high-rise building. "*Govnó!*"—shit—muttered Yuri as he stared at the image of Kwan Chi. Stunned, Yuri looked back at Belofsky. "The news report said there were no survivors."

"That's what we thought, too. But one of our agents in Hong Kong discovered otherwise. Apparently, Kwan was severely injured and spent a couple of months in a hospital. He returned to his apartment only recently. He was photographed in the lobby."

A cascade of fears engulfed Yuri. He'd assumed that with both Kwan and Wang dead, he was safe. But with Kwan alive, everything changed. Somehow, Yuri needed to warn Laura.

"Kwan was behind everything," Yuri said. "He's exceedingly dangerous and powerful. I'm sure that he's tied directly into the Politburo Standing Committee."

"He is."

Yuri fidgeted in his seat.

"We will deal with him in due time. Right now, more pressing matters require your assistance."

Oh no—here it comes.

Chapter 13

After meeting with Admiral Belofsky and a quick lunch with Captain Zhilkin in the commissary, Yuri relocated to the Fleet Briefing Room two floors below the admiral's office. Yuri was the lowest ranking officer of the six men present, and the youngest. Captain Zhilkin was in charge. A map of the People's Republic of China filled the screen at the head of the darkened room.

Zhilkin used a laser pointer to highlight map features. "As you all know, China has three fleets: North Sea, East Sea, and South Sea. The North Sea Fleet is based at Qingdao. East Sea Fleet headquarters are at Ningbo and the South Sea Fleet operates out of Zhanjiang and Hainan Island. We'll start first with Zhanjiang."

Zhilkin advanced to a new sequence of slides, all high-resolution Russian spy satellite images. "Zhanjiang is a natural harbor along China's southern coast. It's one of their busiest ports." He used a laser pointer to mark the slide. "Donghai Island protects the harbor from storm waves from the South China Sea. The principal shipping channel runs north-south in this estuary. The main fleet mooring area is along the east bank in this area. As you will note…"

Yuri half-listened to Zhilkin's drone-like briefing on the navigational approach to the People's Liberation Army-Navy's largest installation. The warships moored along the wharves and piers of the estuary were for the most part modern and lethal. China's program to update its navy was well underway.

Zhilkin continued, "Compared to the other PLAN bases, the Zhanjiang moorage is far from the ocean, which complicates our mission."

"What's the water depth in the channel leading to the fleet moorage?" asked a captain first rank. Yuri did not know the submarine officer or any of the others in attendance.

"The main navigation channel is around six to seven meters deep but there are shoals."

"We cannot run a submerged boat up that far—too damn shallow."

"That's correct. The approach will need to be conducted remotely. That's why we have brought in an expert on AUVs." Zhilkin turned to face Yuri. "Captain-Lieutenant Yuri Kirov will be in charge of installing the recorders remotely."

Yuri stiffened as others around the table turned his way.

"Operating from the deeper bay water north of Donghai, Kirov will use a state-of-the-art autonomous underwater vehicle to make the penetration and then—"

"What about those damn underwater sensors?" interrupted the same sub commander. "I'm sure the place is loaded with them. You know how the PLAN is—they're paranoid about base security. And because their latest antics turned to shit, Beijing's going to expect some kind of response."

"Very true, Captain. Kirov has experience in those matters." Zhilkin turned to Yuri. "Kirov, provide us with your approach to defeating the sensors."

Yuri stood and walked to the head of the conference table. Zhilkin handed off the laser pointer and slide control.

Yuri advanced to a new slide titled "Evading Subsurface Sensors." He turned to face his audience. "As you would expect, the key component to underwater security systems is acoustic." He clicked to the next slide, which displayed a diagram of a hypothetical harbor protected by underwater devices. "The various sensors operate in either passive or active modes, just like ASW systems. The difference is…"

Yuri wrapped up his presentation fifteen minutes later. After covering similar intelligence operations against China's North and East Sea Fleet homeports, Captain Zhilkin concluded the meeting. Yuri was about to leave when one of the officers approached him. "Excellent presentation, Kirov. I'm Petrovich." He extended a hand.

Yuri accepted the offered hand. "Thank you, sir."

Captain First Rank Leonid Petrovich had asked most of the questions during the ninety-minute briefing. He stood five-foot-ten with a solid, muscular build and close-cut graying auburn hair. The decorations on his uniform jacket included a submarine icon.

"Were you the Kirov assigned to the *Neva* under Captain Anatolii Tomich?"

"Captain Tomich was my CO."

"I recognized your name," Petrovich said. "Thank you for what you did—saving the crew and the boat. Absolutely amazing."

"Thanks, Captain."

"I heard about what happened to Tomich. We were classmates at Peter." Petrovich referred to the Higher Naval Submarine School located on the St. Petersburg Naval Base. The school was similar to the U.S. Naval Academy at Annapolis but with a five-year curriculum directed toward training future submarine officers. Yuri also attended Peter after graduating from the Nakhimov secondary school in St. Petersburg.

Petrovich continued, "Anatolii was a great friend and an outstanding officer. Damn shame what happened to him—and to the rest of the crew."

"Captain Tomich was a pleasure to serve under."

"What have you been doing after you left the *Neva*?"

Yuri shifted his stance, not certain how much Petrovich knew about his recent past. "Working primarily with AUVs."

"Good, we're going to need your expertise to carry out this mission. I look forward to working with you." Yuri was about to ask for clarification when Petrovich continued, "I have command of the *Novosibirsk*."

The *Novosibirsk* was based on Russia's newest class of nuclear attack submarine—*Severodvinsk*-class. Designed to challenge the U.S. Navy's best subs, it contained a deadly arsenal of torpedoes and cruise missiles. A recent modification to the *Novosibirsk* also allowed the submarine to support underwater espionage operations. "Excellent, sir. I look forward to serving with you."

"Captain Zhilkin and I are dining together tonight at the Sword & Shield. Please join us at nineteen hundred." The restaurant that catered to senior navy staff was just a block away.

"Thank you, Captain. I look forward to it."

"Excellent."

Petrovich left. Yuri was now alone. He walked back to where he had been sitting and collected the briefing papers and other documents provided by Zhilkin. The last thing Yuri wanted this evening was to dine with two senior officers. Jetlagged and overwhelmed by his shockwave reentry to military life, he dreaded the shoptalk that would undoubtedly end up with resurrecting the *Neva*'s mission. Questions about how he worked behind enemy lines would likely be asked by Petrovich. Zhilkin knew most of the details, including Laura's involvement. Yuri decided he would not mention Laura; he hoped Captain Zhilkin would do the same.

All Yuri had going for him was the hope that his recent actions on behalf of Russia—and the USA—had earned him respect from Russia's president. If not, he would never see Laura again.

Chapter 14

Fourteen-time zones behind Vladivostok, FBI Supervisory Special Agent Ava Diesen sat at her desk on the sixth floor of the J. Edgar Hoover Building in Washington, D.C. This morning she wore a white oxford blouse with a knee-length bell-shaped skirt and a pair of pumps.

She arrived at a quarter to eight. The commute from Fairfax took forty minutes longer than usual—another fender-bender on I-66 gummed up the eastbound lanes. Her husband, Arthur, ensured that their three children made it to their respective schools on time. His commute consisted of walking from the kitchen to his office in the basement. As an IT software consultant, he could work from just about anywhere. His flexible schedule complemented Ava's career as a federal agent.

A fifteen-year veteran of the FBI, Ava had moved with her family four times since she graduated from the FBI Academy in Quantico, Virginia: Anaheim to Anchorage to Dallas to New York City to FBI Headquarters. She was on the fast-track in the Bureau for upper management, currently serving in the Counterintelligence Division. After receiving her law degree from Pepperdine University, Ava spent five years with the Orange County District Attorney's Office in southern California, where she prosecuted drug and gang related cases. For as long as Ava could recall, her ultimate career goal was to work for the FBI. This morning, Ava scanned through overnight email traffic while enjoying her first cup of coffee. The sixteenth message caught her eye. It was from her counterpart at the Defense Intelligence Agency responding to the John Doe inquiry from the Houston Field Office.

"I'll be darned," she said as she scanned the message. The DIA had a possible ID on the John Doe. Ava opened the attachment included with the DIA email. The image of a young Russian naval officer in uniform filled the right screen on her desk. She next retrieved the John Doe photo taken at the George Bush Airport and opened it on her second monitor. Ava switched between the two images. The John Doe was older and had a trim beard. Nevertheless, she could see the similarities.

This is the guy!

Ava reread the email text. She transcribed the key facts on the yellow legal-size notepad she kept on her desktop—a habit from her days as a prosecutor:

- 93% probability John Doe in photo is Yuri Ivanovich Kirov
- Captain-lieutenant in the Russian Navy
- Trained as a submarine officer–St. Petersburg
- Specialty: underwater intel—dive training at Sevastopol—Black Sea
- Assigned to Pacific Fleet Intelligence—likely GRU
- Last known duty station—Rybachiy Submarine Base at Petropavlovsk-Kamchatsky
- 31 years old
- Single
- Father: Ivan Kirov—retired Army colonel. Lives in Moscow
- Mother: Irina Kirov (deceased)
- Grandson of Vice Admiral Semyon Nikolayevich Fedorov (deceased)

Ava ran a hand through her hair as she mulled over the DIA info. *There's been no sign of him for over year. So, just what has he been doing and where has he been? And why did he all of a sudden show up at the Russian consulate in Houston?*

Ava checked her watch: 8:17 A.M. D.C. time, 7:17 A.M. in Texas. She decided to call her contact at the Houston Field Office in an hour.

Ava gazed again at the side by side photos. *What's this guy up to?*

She decided to keep mining. *His maternal grandfather was a hot-shot in the Navy. Let's start there.*

Chapter 15

Kwan Chi refused to use his cane, knowing his superior would view it as a weakness. He walked into the office and took a seat as offered. "You look better than I expected," said the balding fifty-two-year-old man sitting behind the elegant table desk—a replica from mid-Qing Dynasty. Guo Wing served as the deputy minister of operations for the Ministry of State Security. The MSS was responsible for foreign intelligence, counterintelligence, and political security. Guo wore a Hong Kong summer suit over his squat, thick frame.

"The recovery is going well." Kwan changed position in the chair, attempting to relieve the pain in his right leg.

Guo said, "You certainly captured our interest with your Russian contact. We all thought she would have been terminated by now."

"I also thought I'd never hear from her again." Kwan remained bewildered by Elena Krestyanova's call from the grave.

"So, what's your take on the situation?" Guo asked.

Kwan had duly reported the contact by the Russian agent and was subsequently ordered to report to Beijing for a meeting with Guo.

"I don't have an opinion yet. She provided no details when she called, just that she had returned to the trade mission in Vancouver and was hoping to get together soon."

"You're certain it was her?"

Kwan clasped his hands. "I believe so. Her voice was as I remembered and I found nothing out of the ordinary in our conversation. She was careful not to mention any operational matters."

Guo opened a file folder and slid a stack of enlarged photographs across the desk. "Is that her?"

Kwan picked up the photos and took his time thumbing through the half dozen color images. He tilted his head. "Her hair is much shorter but yes, this does appear to be Elena Krestyanova."

"Our people in Vancouver recorded these yesterday. She drives the same vehicle, resides in the same apartment, and spent the day inside the Russian trade mission."

Kwan looked across the desk. "It really must be her."

"It does appear so."

Kwan rubbed his forehead. The headache that had plagued him all morning intensified. "Sir, have you been able to do any back checking?"

"All we know so far is that she took a commercial flight from Moscow to Vancouver. She arrived last weekend."

"She didn't wait long to contact me."

"Yes, why do you suppose she did that?"

"I don't know… maybe she's trying to reestablish our business arrangement. She earned around five million U.S. from our prior arrangement."

"But she was forcibly returned to Russia by the SVR—you said so in your mission debrief. How could she have been cleared from what happened?"

"She was never privy to the operation. We only used her on the perimeter. Plus, she was wounded."

Guo scowled. "What are you getting at?"

"Her original assignment was to recruit me. Perhaps she managed to keep that charade going." Kwan wavered as a new thought developed. "She could argue that she was continuing to work me as a potential asset when our operation soured."

Guo was not convinced. "What about the computer hard drive the SVR took from the *Yangzi?*"

"If the security measures worked, perhaps the Russians were not able to access it."

"That's a big assumption."

"It is, sir. But if that's what happened, Moscow would have no concrete proof regarding Sea Dragon." Kwan met Guo's eyes. "Has there been any hint that Moscow knows?"

Guo rubbed his chin "None. It's been four months and nothing has changed. Actually, our relations continue to improve."

Kwan cheered up. "If the drive self-destructed and she stuck to her original assignment to recruit me, she might still be in play. As far as the Russians would know, the operation was directed only against the Americans." He pursed his lips. "Sir, Elena Krestyanova is cunning and clearly motivated by money."

"So, you think she wants to work for us again?"

"It's a distinct possibility."

"But she could also now be playing us as triple," Guo said.

"True."

Guo swiveled in his chair, glancing out the window wall. It was over ninety degrees Fahrenheit with no wind. Beijing remained shrouded in an awful veil of smog. He turned back to face Kwan.

"We need to know what Krestyanova is really up to. You are authorized to reestablish your arrangement with her."

"Yes, sir."

* * * *

Yuri Kirov occupied a chair in a small conference room in the Naval Headquarters Building. Across the table from where he sat this morning was an officer equal to his own rank but three years his senior. Captain-Lieutenant Stephan Maranovich kept his ash-blond hair cut short. At six feet two and a solid 220 pounds, Maranovich's physique telegraphed athlete.

"What's the endurance?" asked Yuri

"The batteries are good for twelve hours at five knots."

"That's all?"

"Yes, but it should be sufficient for our needs."

Yuri slipped a hand behind his lower back and massaged his spine. The BOQ mattress he'd slept on was too soft for his liking. He glanced back at the wall-mounted screen. The PowerPoint slide of a Russian-manufactured autonomous underwater vehicle filled the display. Code named *Starfish*, the AUV was cylindrical, about two feet in diameter and sixteen feet long. A propeller and rudder assembly with fins were located at the stern. The bow cap consisted of a rounded nose cone. The entire steel casing was painted navy gray.

"Obviously, it fits through the tubes," Yuri said.

"Correct. Once the tube is flooded, it will swim out on its own and the fins will unfold."

"How about retrieval?"

"Manual."

This did not surprise Yuri. Divers would be needed to maneuver the AUV for reinsertion into an open tube. "I assume it has sidescan sonar survey capability as well as ranging sonar."

"It does." Maranovich advanced to a new slide filled with bullet points. "This provides a summary of the surveying and navigation equipment incorporated into the *Starfish*."

Yuri scanned the specs. He was not impressed but did not let on. The Russian Navy's top-of-the-line AUV was a dinosaur compared to the technology developed by Northwest Subsea Dynamics.

Yuri looked back at Maranovich. "It would be helpful if you could provide me with details of missions where you have deployed the *Starfish* and how it functioned. I'm interested in any problems that developed with the unit itself."

Maranovich narrowed his eyebrows.

Yuri caught the glare. "It's been my experience that we learn much from our mistakes, and please believe me, I have had way more than my share of screw ups with AUVs." He smiled. "If it can go wrong, it will and it has for me."

Maranovich's frown rolled into a grin. "I understand. We've had trouble with the *Starfish*. When we received the first unit, the battery pack failed on the first mission."

"Manufacturing problem?"

"Yes. We ended up scrapping the batteries and purchased replacements from Sweden."

Yuri was not surprised. Russian manufacturing practices were not yet close to the quality of the West's. "What about electronics?"

Maranovich sighed. "The GPS module worked fine as well as the ranging sonar, but the original sidescan was crap. We replaced it with an American-made unit." He named the unit and summarized its design specifications.

"How did you get that though the sanctions?" Yuri asked. The United States imposed a long list of penalties against Russia for harassing its neighbors and interfering with American elections. Near the top of the list of restricted commerce items were specialty electronics that could be adapted for military uses.

"We used a third party."

Yuri smirked. Maranovich used code. The GRU obtained the blacklisted gear by either outright bribery or blackmail.

Yuri asked several follow-up questions regarding the *Starfish* before moving on to question Maranovich about his background.

"How much diving experience do you have?"

"Basic dive training at Sevastopol—SCUBA and hardhat."

Yuri grabbed a plastic water bottle from a tabletop tray. He removed the cap and took a swig. "What's your deepest dive?"

"Just forty meters—basic certification." Maranovich also helped himself to a water bottle.

After another swallow Yuri asked, "Any experience with rebreathers?"

"A couple of shallow-water training dives. How about you?"

"Extensive training and experience—numerous hundred meter-plus operational dives."

"My God," muttered Maranovich. "What were you doing?"

"Installation and retrieval of surveillance equipment."

Maranovich glowered. "Well, I hope you're not expecting me to participate in those activities." He hesitated. "No way that I can go deep like that."

Yuri clasped his hands. "From what I've seen so far about the mission, I don't see the need for diving deeper than twenty meters or so."

"Good," Maranovich said, relaxed.

Yuri looked back at the screen image of the *Starfish.* "I need to observe the unit in the water. Is there someplace around here where we can test it without drawing attention?"

"I already checked. No testing allowed."

Yuri was about to protest when Maranovich said, "We're too close to China. They have electronic eyes on us constantly—like the damn Americans. Plus, who knows how many agents they have planted in the city."

Yuri frowned. "I've got to become intimate with the unit if we're going to have any hope of pulling off what the Kremlin wants."

"I understand. I'll talk with Captain Petrovich. I think it's time that we head to Rybachiy. We can check everything there in private."

"Good."

Maranovich excused himself to confer with Captain Petrovich. Yuri remained behind, thumbing through the slides. His worry quotient ratcheted up a notch. He was less than impressed with the *Starfish.* Its range was seriously deficient, regardless of Maranovich's opinion. But his principal concern was the AUV's lack of stealth. He again scanned the slide displaying the electric motor's performance characteristics. *I bet she's a noisy bitch. She'll never get past the sensors.*

How the hell do I fix that?

Yuri stood and stepped to a map pinned to a wall on the right side of the conference room. The map depicted Russian military installations in Russia's Far Eastern Province. Prominently identified on the lower left side was the naval base at Vladivostok. To the far upper right of the map was another naval installation near the southerly tip of the Kamchatka Peninsula. Located nine miles across Avacha Bay from Petropavlovsk-Kamchatsky—the region's capital—the naval base was homeport to several squadrons of attack boats and Russia's newest ballistic missile submarines. The Rybachiy Submarine Base was also Yuri's last duty station.

Over twenty months earlier, Yuri departed from Rybachiy aboard the nuclear-powered attack submarine *Neva*. After crossing the North Pacific and taking extreme care to avoid detection by the U.S. Navy's Integrated Undersea Surveillance System, the sub entered the Strait of Juan de Fuca. The twelve-to-eighteen-mile-wide waterway separated Washington State from British Columbia. Hugging the bottom, the *Neva* sailed far into enemy waters where Yuri commenced his mission—planting subsea recording devices and spying on U.S. and Canadian naval installations.

The mission was nearly complete when an accident sent the *Neva* to bottom, over 700 feet below the surface. Using high-tech diving equipment from his espionage operations, Yuri escaped the underwater tomb—barely. Suffering from decompression sickness, alone, and a hundred miles inside enemy lines, Yuri had to rescue the *Neva*'s remaining three dozen survivors before the U.S. Navy discovered the marooned spy sub.

Yuri thought of his diving partner and friend, Senior Warrant Officer Viktor Skirski. Viktor perished along with fifty-three others. He made the first dive after the accident to inspect hull damage but never returned. Yuri wondered if Viktor's widow, Alma, and her son still lived in Petropavlovsk-Kamchatsky. *If I have time, I'll try to look her up!*

Yuri returned to his chair and took a swig from the water bottle. He reminisced about other survivors, reliving the nightmares and triumphs they had all endured. None of them should have survived the initial accident—it was simply luck that the entire casing didn't flood. And then Yuri somehow survived the escape ascent despite suffering from the bends and hypothermia. Was that luck or something more?

Yuri shivered as his body recalled the freezing water and the untold hours he spent immersed in it after escaping from the hulk. *Nick— thank God for Nick!*

Moscow dispatched Nicolai Orlov to investigate Yuri's sudden and unauthorized appearance behind enemy lines with the express task of returning him to Russia. But Nick became an ally, sympathetic to the plight of the stranded crew. *Elena—what a cold-hearted bitch.*

Elena Krestyanova accompanied Nick Orlov. She helped but the *Neva*'s survivors meant nothing to her. Later, Elena caused Yuri untold apprehension and heartache.

Prison—that's where she belongs. Lock her up and toss the key away.

Yuri could never forgive Elena for her recent treachery that nearly cost Laura and Maddy their lives.

Laura—sweet Laura—you are the light of my life. I could never have done it without you.

Yuri closed his eyes. He pictured Laura, her sunny smile, her sweet voice. *Lord, please watch over Laura—and Maddy. Keep them safe.*

Yuri's mother sparked his early belief, but her guidance ceased after she succumbed to cancer a week after his twelfth birthday. With a nonbeliever father, Yuri's faith languished. But surviving the trauma of the *Neva*'s sinking had rekindled his conviction. *Lord, please help me through the mission, and let me return home.*

Chapter 16

"Sir, I believe we have another FBI surveillance operation underway at the guest quarters."

Nick Orlov looked up from his desk. The consulate's security officer, a young man in his late twenties, stood in the open doorway of the office. It was 2:35 P.M. at the Russian consulate in Houston.

"What's going on?"

"One of our cameras detected movement in the home across the street."

Nick signaled for the visitor to take a seat. Oleg Babin wore civilian clothes but was on loan from Russia's military intelligence service, the *Glavnoye Razvedovatel'noye Upravlenie*, aka the GRU. Medium height with a trim build, Army Captain Babin's most distinct feature was a two-inch scar above his right eye. Shrapnel from an IED in Syria had clipped his forehead, resulting in a concussion and a permanent tattoo that reminded Babin everyday how lucky he was. Two other GRU officers in the vehicle lost limbs. Babin placed four photographs on Nick's desktop. The color blowups showed the partial image of a male peering through the narrow gap of a set of window blinds, backlit by lights from inside the home. Time stamps on the photos revealed the photos were recorded the previous evening.

Nick picked up a photo. "Have you IDed this guy?"

"Yes, sir. He's an agent assigned to the FBI's Houston Field Office." Babin recited the name.

"How long have they been in the unit?"

"At least the last twenty-four hours." A clerk assigned to the security office reviewed the video images every morning, accessing the cloud-stored data file from the consulate. "They could have been watching us longer."

Nick waved the photo. "This guy was sloppy. Others might take more care."

"Yes, sir. I see your point."

"I want you to go back for at least a week and examine every photo and video we have on the building. Look for other anomalies. Lights on. Background movement behind the blinds, pedestrian traffic in front of the home, vehicles coming and going, anything out of the ordinary."

"I'll get right on it, sir."

The officer stood and started to collect the photographs.

"Leave them," Nick ordered.

"Yes, sir."

After Babin departed, Nick picked up another photo. *What are they up to now?* The residence in question was almost directly across the street from the main entrance to the consulate's guest quarters. If it had been Nick's op, he too would have chosen the house.

The SVR had long suspected the FBI had human as well as electronic eyes on the guest residence. About a year earlier, they finally had the proof. A search of public records revealed the home was purchased by a company registered in Montgomery County, Maryland. Further mining by SVR staff in the Washington embassy ascertained that the FBI controlled the shell company.

Nick considered the development, again perusing the photo. *So, Mr. FBI man, just what are you doing?*

It had been several months since federal agents occupied the home on an around-the-clock basis. The last campaign occurred when the Russian Foreign Minister paid a visit to the consulate during an international conference held in Houston.

Nick tossed the photo onto the desk and stared out the window. His office had a view of Interstate 610. He reflected on the events of the past few days. Worried that Yuri might have been tagged at Houston International, Nick was thankful he'd taken extra precautions to ensure Yuri's surreptitious return to Russia.

They must have followed Yuri's double! After spending a night at the guest residence, the SVR officer masquerading as Yuri departed the next morning on foot using the backyard and a connecting greenbelt to access a residential street. He then used Uber to return to the consulate.

They must think he's still there.

Although pleased that the evasion tactics worked, Nick's worry quotient ratcheted up a notch.

If Yuri was spotted, then he might really be on FBI's radar!

Chapter 17

Day 7—Saturday

Elena Krestyanova settled into the business-class seat of the Canada Air 777. The Boeing was third in line for departure from Vancouver International. She glanced out her window; it was raining this late morning. A summer front had moved in overnight, casting a gray pall over British Columbia's lower mainland. While in the terminal waiting to board, Elena had checked the weather of her destination. For the next week, the forecast for Hong Kong called for scorching daytime highs, windless clear skies, and dripping humidity. Never a fan of sticky climes, Elena would avoid the outdoors wherever possible.

As far as the Vancouver trade mission knew, Elena was on a follow-up assignment to a trade delegation team she'd led from Vladivostok earlier in the year. She would renew contact with Chinese government trade officials. But it was cover only.

Elena's real assignment, dictated by SVR chief Borya Smirnov, was to reestablish her personal relationship with Kwan Chi.

After checking into her hotel, Elena would text Chi. If he responded, her new op would commence. If ignored, she'd complete the trade mission charade and then fly to Vladivostok, where she would report her failure to Smirnov by encrypted email. Under no conditions was Elena to attempt any communications with the SVR while operating in Hong Kong. The PRC's Ministry of State Security would have digital eyes and ears on her the instant she stepped off the wide-body jet at Hong Kong International.

China's One Nation, Two Systems policy toward Hong Kong provided a modicum of independence for the former British colony. When the UK's lease for Hong Kong expired in 1997, China allowed Hong Kong to police itself, along with a pledge not to import mainland security forces to the enclave. That promise, along with others, didn't last long. The MSS now operated freely in the city of seven million.

Another scenario vexed Elena. While in Hong Kong, the MSS could collect Elena at will. Rushed to the mainland by any manner of transport, she might end up in a holding cell in Beijing. Foreign spies caught operating in the People's Republic of China sometimes earned a rifle shot to the back of skull without even the pretext of a trial. As the triple seven throttled up for a sprint down the runway, Elena's body tensed. She was now committed—no turning back.

Elena reached up with a hand to massage her wounded shoulder. The ache persisted but, thankfully, a little less each day. Fifteen minutes later, as the jet climbed above Vancouver Island to cruising altitude, a flight attendant announced over the cabin intercom that portable electronic devices could now be turned on. Elena removed her cell from the handbag at her feet and checked just one app, which bypassed airplane mode.

The iPhone and the RFID tag embedded in Elena's shoulder continued the hourly check-ins. Although Elena's cell could not email her GPS coordinates to the anonymous address until the 777 landed, the non-stop flight time to Beijing was well under the twenty-four-hour death limit.

Elena would limit the cell's use to local calls and texts while in China. Nevertheless, she would keep the phone nearby at all times—her own private reminder of Moscow's ultimate control. Elena carried a pack of spare batteries and a backup phone with the same app already installed—just in case.

Although plagued by the burden of carrying her own demise twenty-four-seven, there was one positive element to her predicament. If arrested, the MSS would undoubtedly confiscate her phones. By the time technicians dissected the iPhones and discovered the RFID query device, it would be too late.

No more torture, no more pain—just the end.

Chapter 18

The North Pacific offshore of the Kamchatka Peninsula remained docile this afternoon. Low and slow swells tracked from the northeast, rolling under the workboat as it strained to maintain station. The 130-foot-long vessel hovered in place, employing its main diesel engine in combination with bow and stern thrusters.

Yuri Kirov and Captain-Lieutenant Stephan Maranovich stood near the stern of the *WB-112*. The Russian Navy support vessel was several miles east of Petropavlovsk-Kamchatsky. Yuri and Maranovich had arrived at the Rybachiy Nuclear Submarine Base the previous day. They'd hitched a ride aboard the military transport that ferried the *Starfish* and its support gear.

"How's it checking out?" Yuri asked. Maranovich held a tablet. He squinted at the screen, fighting glare from the overhead sun. "Everything is in the green."

"Let's turn it loose."

"Okay." Maranovich tapped the screen with his right index finger. The wireless transmitter broadcast a coded signal. The two-foot wire antenna atop the *Starfish's* twenty-two-inch-diameter cylindrical hull intercepted the radio single, transmitting the start command to the autonomous underwater vehicle's central processing unit. Thirty feet to the west of the *WB-112*, the *Starfish's* propeller bit into the water. Ballast water tanks near the bow and stern of the sixteen-foot-long robot flooded. Within ten seconds, the AUV disappeared.

Yuri turned to face Maranovich. "What's the expected time to the first obstacle?"

Maranovich consulted his tablet. "Thirty-two minutes."

"Let's head back in and wait for her to show up."

"Okay. I'll let the captain know."

Yuri had designed the exercise. After departing Avacha Bay, the *WB-112* stopped just beyond the harbor entrance where Yuri deployed an acoustic sensor. Sitting on the sandy bottom seventy feet below the surface, the hydrophone listened for mechanical sounds, propellers in particular. A reinforced fiber optic cable connected the bottom sensor to a radio-equipped buoy that bobbed on the surface.

The sole purpose of the test sensor was to determine if the *Starfish* could penetrate Avacha Bay without detection. Yuri had his doubts.

Yuri felt a shudder in his feet as the *WB-112*'s engine throttled up. Two minutes later the workboat headed west at twelve knots—triple the AUV's velocity.

Yuri glanced northwestward. Mount Koryasky loomed ahead. Rising over 11,000 feet from the seashore to its snowcapped peak, the volcano was one of scores that stretched along the seventy-eight-mile-long Kamchatka Peninsula. Eruptions and earthquakes were as common to the peninsula as traffic jams were to Seattle.

Other than Petropavlovsk-Kamchatsky and a handful of lesser communities, Kamchatka was pristine wild. Bristling with salmon, deer, and grizzles, the peninsula was one of the few natural preserves left largely untouched in the northern hemisphere.

Half an hour passed. The *WB-112* drifted, its engine set to idle. The buoy marking the hydrophone sensor on the seabed bobbed seventy feet to the west. As swells rolled by, the buoy's antenna unhurriedly arced back and forth. Kirov and Maranovich stood in the wheelhouse next to the chart table. The *WB-112*'s captain, a chief petty officer, manned the helm.

A radio receiver occupied one corner of the chart table. Linked to the buoy's antenna by a wireless circuit, the receiver waited for a response from the hydrophone.

"Anything?" Yuri asked.

"Looks good," Maranovich said. "I think the *Starfish* defeated the sensor."

Yuri checked his watch again. "Let's wait another five minutes. The tide is still ebbing. That might have slowed it up."

"All right, but I think we're good."

Ninety-five seconds later, the radio receiver came to life: *Warning Warning Warning. Unidentified Submerged Vessel Detected. Warning Warning Warning. Unidentified...*

"Shit," muttered Maranovich.

Not surprised, Yuri concealed his thoughts regarding the *Starfish. Piece of junk. It will never work as Fleet planned.*

* * * *

The USS *Colorado* lurked ten miles east of the *WB-112*. The *Virginia*-class attack submarine hovered at observation depth; a narrow steel tube projected several feet above the sea surface. The antenna sniffed the air waves for radio traffic, scanning hundreds of frequencies per second. It locked onto and recorded the open-air broadcast. A digital voice analyzer translated the Russian signal into English, transmitting the converted message to a speaker in the *Colorado*'s control room. "They must be running a test," Commander Tom Bowman said. He stood near the center of the command compartment. Although a month away from turning thirty-nine, he retained the same youthful looks he'd had when he'd graduated from Naval Academy seventeen years earlier—close-cropped black hair without a speck of gray, square-jawed face, and a muscular five-foot-nine frame.

"That AUV is a noisy machine," Commander Jenae Mauk said. "Not surprised that we picked it up." A petite brunette, the thirty-six-year-old mother of two served as *Colorado*'s second in command. Like the captain and the rest of crew, she wore a standard navy-blue jumpsuit. Jenae had been aboard the *Colorado* for over a year. Also a product of Annapolis, she'd graduated near the top of her class. When the Navy opened up subs to women, she transferred from the surface warfare program to the submarine service. After completing nuclear power school, she served on a boomer for three years before transferring to the *Colorado*. It was her dream job.

Captain Bowman turned to a nearby console and addressed the lead sonar technician. "What's the status of that AUV?"

"It's gone quiet, Captain." Twenty-nine-year-old Petty Officer (Second Class) Richard "Richey" Anderson was short and plump. A whiz with digital systems, Anderson was *Colorado*'s senior sonar technician.

Unlike other U.S. submarines, the *Virginia*-class boats do not have separate sonar compartments. "What about Sierra Eight-Four?" asked Bowman.

"Throttled back to idle and drifting."

"Keep monitoring. Let me know of any changes."

"Aye, sir."

Bowman turned back to Mauk. "Sounds like they're retrieving the AUV."

"I agree. Their sentry system appears to work well, so they probably had a successful test."

"Maybe."

Colorado's executive officer—XO—cast a questioning look at her boss.

Bowman responded, "If it was the AUV they were testing and not their harbor defense system, then it failed—miserably."

"It certainly did."

Bowman and XO Mauk stepped to the nearby plotting table, a freestanding platform with a four-foot-square LCD screen. Superimposed over a digital nautical chart, the video screen displayed all known surface and submerged contacts in the ocean within a radius of fifty miles. A red icon marked as Sierra 84 identified the *WB-112* on the plotting board. The Sierra designation represented a sonar contact.

"Captain, perhaps we should break off and head back out to deeper water. The Russians may have other monitoring devices in the area. No sense pushing our luck."

"Not yet. Let's hang around here for a while longer and see what develops. I'm curious as to what they're up to. Something doesn't smell right to me."

"Very good, sir."

Earlier, the *Colorado*'s sonar team had tracked the *WB-112* after it passed through the entrance to Avacha Bay and entered the ocean. The workboat, or one of its sister vessels, typically preceded the deployment of ballistic missile submarines homeported at Rybachiy. Using a potent hull-mounted multi-beam sonar system, the workboat would sweep the bottom for hazards several miles beyond the harbor—hunting for seabed mines in particular. But today, the *WB-112*'s sonar suite was silent.

The *Colorado*'s mission was to follow and track Russian ballistic missile submarines deployed from Petropavlovsk-Kamchatsky. It had been on station for nearly a week, waiting in vain. Satellite reconnaissance of the Rybachiy base noted a spike in activity on the pier that moored the *Borei*-class boomers, which suggested that a sub was preparing for a new patrol. *Colorado*'s commanding officer was a patient man. He would wait, always vigilant. When Russia's newest and deadliest missile boat departed Avacha Bay, he would order the *Colorado* to follow. And, if directed by the President of the United States, Captain Bowman would issue the kill command without hesitation.

* * * *

Yuri Kirov and Stephan Maranovich stood on the aft deck of the *WB-112* as it powered into Avacha Bay. The sun remained overhead but the wind had kicked up to twenty-five knots from the northwest, generating an annoying quartering sea chop. The *Starfish* was at their feet, secured in its custom cradle. The harbor sentry unit, also retrieved from the bottom, rested on the steel deck plates near the AUV's bow.

"Stephan, I need to be direct here. The *Starfish* is not up to what the mission requires."

"We can make adjustments—fine tune the propulsion unit."

Yuri ran a hand across his chin, still not used to the smooth skin. "I'm not going to recommend its use to Fleet."

Maranovich squatted down next to the *Starfish*, eyeing the propeller and rudder assembly. "This is the best unit we have."

"I know, and it's not a reflection on you." Yuri knelt next to Maranovich. "The *Starfish* is obsolete. The propulsion unit probably can be improved, which would help, but the real problem is the AI software. It's rudimentary, and that problem cannot be remedied overnight."

Maranovich glared at Yuri. "What do you mean by rudimentary?"

"The code is at best third-generation. The United States has units in the water running on fifth generation software, soon to be six."

"How do you know this?"

"Because I've been using it, working as a civilian contractor."

Maranovich stood; Yuri followed. "You have been working in the United States?"

"For over a year. The Americans have AUVs that might be able do what Fleet wants, but we don't. The probability of failure with the *Starfish* will be unacceptable to command."

"Are you saying the mission is technically not doable?"

"Not as currently planned."

Maranovich puckered his brow. "We can't tell Fleet that. You know what will happen."

"I do but there's another way."

"What way?"

Yuri told him.

* * * *

"Captain, just picked up a hit on the wide aperture array. We have a new visitor."

Commander Bowman took a couple steps to the *Colorado*'s sonar section located on the port side of the control room. "Russky boat returning home?"

"Negative. It's not Russian. It's a Chinese boat—one of their new ones, Type Zero Ninety-Five class." Sonar tech Anderson pointed to the console's video screen, his finger tapping the left side of the LCD screen.

Bowman stared at the sonar display, nicknamed "the waterfall" for the way the broad spectrum of undersea noise was graphically displayed on the monitor—a continuous flow of data moving from the top to the bottom of the display. "Isolate and play it back for me."

"I've got it ready for you, sir." Anderson handed Bowman a set of headphones. He keyed in a new command on the keyboard. A soft hiss broadcast through the Bose speakers.

Bowman smiled. "Nice work, Richey. How far out is it?"

"About sixty miles. Maintaining a heading straight for Petro at fourteen knots. Depth 600 feet and change."

"Let's designate it Master One." The Master designation stood for an upgraded sonar contact, possibly hostile.

"Master One, affirmative."

"Keep on him."

"Aye, aye, captain."

As Bowman walked back to his station, he considered the change in the tactical situation. *The Chinese must be just as curious about the* Borei *as we are. The next couple of days should be interesting.*

Chapter 19

Two men met in a private dining room for a Sunday luncheon. Both were members of the exclusive club—perks of their positions. Situated on the bank of the *Moskva* near the Kremlin, the establishment catered to the wealthy and powerful. The middle-aged males were government employees drawing respectable salaries, but their positions demanded respect from the millionaires and occasional billionaires who also frequented the place. General Ivan Golitsin commanded the FSB's military counterintelligence directorate. SVR chief Borya Smirnov directed Russia's foreign intelligence operations. The intelligence chiefs' personal aides stood outside the room door, ignoring each other. Undercover security forces occupied the lobby and patrolled the grounds. Technicians had already swept the room for listening devices. Lunch was over; it was time for business.

"So, she's on her way," General Golitsin said.

"Yes, she's in Hong Kong. I should know soon if she's able to reestablish contact."

"Kwan will be suspicious."

"Of course. But she's skilled—and motivated."

The FSB general chuckled. "I must admit, Borya, implanting that device was brilliant. I've never heard of such a thing. Where did you find it?"

SVR chief Smirnov replied, "The Stasi came up with the original idea in the eighties but never implemented it. My technical group ran with it, using current technology."

"Well, let's hope she's successful."

"I have confidence that she will complete her mission." Smirnov reached behind and massaged his lower back, his spine disliking the softness of the chair. "Where are you with your mission?" he asked.

"It's moving along. The Navy is cooperating fully. Personnel and equipment are being assembled. Deployment is probably around two weeks away."

"Good." Smirnov drained his cup. "What's the status on Kirov?"

"He's now at the Rybachiy Naval Base helping plan the mission."

"He seems to have reintegrated well."

"Yes, he too is motivated." General Golitsin reached for the nearby teapot and refilled both cups. After taking a drink, he said, "What about your other work in Washington—how's that going?"

"Underway. The information should be passed on soon."

"Your State Department operative?"

"She is quite skilled. The rumor will be subtle. Her MSS handler will listen and he'll report it back home."

"Excellent. That should spook 'em."

"Yes, and if Krestyanova also succeeds, those *zhópas* in Beijing will truly go berserk."

Both men laughed at that proposition.

Chapter 20

Elena walked from the bathroom, her naked body swaddled from neck to ankle by an Egyptian cotton robe. She stepped through the master bedroom into the living room, which was adorned with priceless artifacts from the Ming dynasty. She passed through an open door onto the terrace. The apartment occupied the entire top floor of the high-rise building. It was early evening, the sun in full descent to the west. Victoria Harbour remained alive as watercraft dashed about. Although the temperature was still in the low nineties, the humidity was tolerable.

A sunken spa occupied a corner of the spacious deck area. Kwan Chi was already inside the eight-person tub, relaxing as multiple Jacuzzi jet nozzles massaged his broken and weary body. A silver platter with a chilled bottle of California Riesling and two crystal glasses sat on the shelf next to the spa's control panel.

Kwan eyed Elena as she approached the spa. She gracefully slipped out of the robe and draped it over a nearby deck chair. Kwan stood, revealing his trim athletic torso. A handsome man, he offered Elena a hand as she stepped into the turbulent steaming basin.

"You look fabulous as always," he said, his voice raised to counter the hiss of the water jets.

"Thank you."

Elena slid into the swirling liquid. It was just the right temperature—he always remembered. She closed her eyes, relishing the mini vortexes that raced over and across her body, kissing and caressing every square inch of her tingling skin. For the next few minutes, they remained immersed in the pleasing cocoon, choosing not to chat.

When the automatic timer shut down the jets, the rush of white noise ceased. "Would you like me to run the jets longer?" Kwan asked.

"Maybe later." She glanced at the bottle. "What I'd really like is a glass of wine."

"Of course!"

Kwan filled both glasses and offered one to Elena.

"Thank you."

They clinked their flutes, the crystal ring echoing in the now still night air.

"I'm so happy to see you again," Kwan said, his remark authentic.

"And so am I." Elena flashed a counterfeit smile. "I was sorry to learn that you were injured so badly."

"I'm recovering." He held up his left forearm; the skin grafts covering the scorched flesh remained beet red.

"Must be painful."

"A little less each day." He scooted across the submerged bench seat next to Elena. "Your wound—does it still bother you?" He scooted closer to examine the blemish marking her left shoulder.

"Yes—aches off and on." She set her wine glass on the top edge of the spa. "The doctors tell me it should improve over time."

Kwan lowered his lips to kiss the scar. He looked up, grinning. "There, that should make it better."

Elena chuckled, her response true. "Thank you, Chi—all better now."

They finished the bottle, making small talk as they caught up. Neither mentioned business, both on guard and both anticipating what was to come.

Elena wondered if Kwan's injuries had sapped his desire. During previous encounters, Kwan's prowess rose to supercharged grade when they made love in spas, either in the apartment or aboard his yacht.

When Kwan kissed Elena, she opened her mouth to receive his tongue. She slid her hand down his muscled abdomen, probing his groin.

Kwan was more than ready.

Chapter 21

Yuri Kirov and Stephan Maranovich stared at the widescreen LCD display inside a video conference room at the Rybachiy Submarine Base. Captain First Rank Leonid Petrovich's digital image filled the screen, transmitted over an encrypted satellite link. He occupied a similar facility at Fleet headquarters in Vladivostok.

"Captain, the *Starfish* is not adequate for our mission."

"What's the problem, Kirov?"

"There are several issues, sir. First, its stealth is piss-poor. It was detected by the test unit we planted on the bottom and the sensors on that particular unit are over five years old. That's a lifetime for underwater tech. The electronics available now will detect the *Starfish* before it ever penetrates restricted waters." Yuri rubbed an ear. "Its endurance is also marginal at best. If there's the slightest delay, it could become stranded. And finally, the AI software is rudimentary. That severely limits its capability for anything beyond simple bottom mapping."

Captain Petrovich mulled over Yuri's conclusions. "I can't say that I'm surprised at your findings. The sanctions by NATO and the Americans have hindered our ability to update our software and electronic packages for numerous weapon systems."

Punishing its adventurism in Ukraine, Georgia, Syria, and elsewhere, the West had cut off Russia's access to cutting-edge technology. Nearly anything that could be adapted for military use was prohibited. Russia had countered by attempting to surreptitiously acquire electronics through shady intermediaries. And where they could, SVR and GRU spies outright stole the technology. But it was slim pickings for Russia. For once, the West remained united in its effort to thwart the bullies in the Kremlin.

Petrovich said, "We might be able to replace the batteries with new ones from another source. That should increase the *Starfish*'s endurance."

"From Israel?" asked Maranovich.

"Yes—you know about that?"

"I heard about it from our propulsion engineers."

"They're supposed to have twenty-five percent more capacity."

Maranovich and Petrovich discussed the battery situation for a couple of minutes before moving on to software issues. Petrovich addressed Yuri. "I agree with you about the code. We're far behind what the Americans are doing."

"Artificial intelligence is a rapidly evolving field."

"What about the company you were involved with in the States? Can you get access to the AI software?"

Yuri had anticipated the question. "The code is not directly applicable to the mission. The AI software I worked with in Seattle is based strictly on mapping for subsea oil and gas deposits. It might be adaptable but would require a complete overhaul."

"How long would it take?"

"Months at least, sir. It's far beyond my coding skills. We'd need a team of experts."

"We don't have that kind of time." Obviously peeved, Petrovich swiveled his chair, turning away from the monitor.

Yuri let him stew before commenting. "Captain, I have an alternative plan that I would like you to consider."

Petrovich turned back. "And what is that?"

"Rather than relying on an AUV, I propose a manned mission using a midget with divers. The midget would penetrate harbor defenses, allowing the divers to install the recorders."

"Hmmm," Petrovich muttered, surprised at Yuri's suggestion. "The mission planners specified that an autonomous vehicle is to be used. There's nothing autonomous about a midget and divers."

"I understand. But from what I reviewed at Fleet, it's reasonable to expect the Chinese already have a robust underwater warning system in place at their key bases. They're not worried about our capabilities."

"Americans?" Petrovich asked.

"Exactly. U.S. Navy subs with their AUVs are no doubt running ops deep inside Chinese waters, just like they do to our facilities."

Petrovich squirmed in his chair. "They certainly have newer equipment than we do."

"Yes, sir. And that's why the Chinese are paranoid about the security of their capital ships while dockside. American AUVs launched from their *Virginia or Seawolf*-class boats are capable of sinking everything PLAN has moored at Qingdao, Ningbo, and Zhanjiang."

"What's your experience with midgets?"

"About five years ago, I trained with an underwater comms intercept unit out of Kaliningrad."

"What about recently?"

"Nothing recent—but Stephan has." Yuri gestured for Captain-Lieutenant Maranovich to proceed.

"Yes, sir," Maranovich said. "I do have current experience. There's a minisub squadron here at Rybachiy that I've worked with in the past—training missions only." Maranovich keyed a laptop on the table next to where he sat. The video screen at both venues split into two viewing frames. The smaller frame continued to show the conference participants. The larger panel displayed a photograph of a black hulled minisub floating alongside a quay—a wharf. The steel teardrop hull was about a hundred feet long and twenty feet in diameter at its widest point. An eight-foot-high sail rose above the deck about a quarter hull length from the bow.

"This is the newest mini we have—Project Eight One Five," Maranovich said. "It has an air independent propulsion system with an electric motor powered by oxygen-hydrogen fuel cells. Uses an anaerobic diesel generator for hydrogen production and battery recharging. Based on the *Kronstadt*'s AIP system."

"What about the exhaust from the diesel generator?" Petrovich asked.

"No exhaust is discharged overboard—it's recycled. No snorkeling required." Maranovich advanced to a new slide. The design drawing illustrated the *P-815*'s interior. He used a cursor to point out key features. "Control station, galley, and mess room in this area. Accommodations for eight. Toilet here. Propulsion in the stern compartment with liquid oxygen and diesel tanks. Batteries are in the bilge." He moved the cursor to the bow. "There's also a bottom-opening lock-in lock-out chamber in the forward compartment for divers."

"Weapons?"

"It can carry a variety of external packages. Two exterior mounted dispensers carrying twenty bottom mines, 600 kilograms each. Or four Mark Twelve Vipers in canisters with anchors. Another option is two diver-operated mine delivery vehicles with a total of 10,000 kilograms of mines. It can also remotely carry two naval Spetsnaz delivery vehicles and has internal space for up to twelve operators." Spetsnaz was short for *Spetsial'noye naznacheniye*, which means special purpose.

Yuri joined in next. "Sir, the hull has an anechoic coating—just like our nukes. Sound suppression of the diesel generator is excellent. Minimal sound print. When running on fuel cells, she's virtually invisible sound wise."

"What about performance, endurance?"

Maranovich rejoined the conversation. "Eight knots transit speed—submerged. Burst speed submerged is eighteen knots and sustained speed is twelve knots. Submerged endurance is fourteen days."

"Impressive little bugger. What else can it do?"

Yuri said, "An ROV package can be mounted to the hull and controlled from the pilot's station."

Yuri waited for Captain Petrovich to respond.

"Okay, Kirov, sending in an autonomous vehicle is one thing, but how do you get a mini through the underwater monitoring systems? The *P-815* is at least a magnitude larger than the *Starfish*."

"With the right pilot and navigator, a midget like the *P-815* has a better chance of defeating an aggressive monitoring system than the best AUV. Under manned control, decisions can be made on how best to avoid or get around underwater sensors. For that type of environment, brains still beat the best AI software out there."

"Adaptability."

"Yes, sir—exactly."

"I get it, Kirov. We've got sub designers from Central telling us that they have plans for attack subs like the *Novosibirsk* that will be completely autonomous—no crew needed. That's just pure bullshit."

Yuri glanced at Maranovich and cracked a weak smile. He responded in kind.

Petrovich continued his rant. "There will always be a human captain in charge of a Russian warship—not some digital deviant."

"We couldn't agree more, sir. That's why we recommend you consider the *P-815* for the mission."

"I like the concept but its range is insufficient—fourteen days is not enough time for the distances involved."

"I understand that issue," Yuri said. "The only way it will work is for the mini to be transported to the operating area by another vessel."

"Hmmm. Sounds like you have the *Novosibirsk* in mind."

"I do, sir. It's ideal."

Captain Petrovich looked pleased. During a recent refit, the forward side-by-side twin vertical launch tubes for cruise missiles had been removed and replaced with a diver-support module. The purpose of the hull modification was to provide improved ingress and egress for special underwater operations teams.

"Access the mini from the diver-support unit?" Petrovich asked.

Maranovich answered. "That's correct, sir. A cradle for the mini can be welded onto the outer casing aft of the sail." He advanced a new slide of a sketch illustrating the concept. "The *P-815* is already equipped with a mating collar around the lockout hatch that will allow it to connect directly to the diver module's air lock. That will permit access between both vessels while underwater. This is particularly beneficial when…"

Maranovich completed his briefing two minutes later.

Captain Petrovich leaned back in his chair, contemplating. "Okay, gentlemen, I'm interested. Let's take this to the next level."

Petrovich spent several minutes issuing new orders before terminating the video conference. Yuri collected his notes from the table and stood. Maranovich followed his lead. "Nice work with Petrovich," he said. "I think he's on board."

"But it's your experience with the mini that won him over."

"All of my experience is training and simulations—no real covert missions."

"You'll be fine, Stephan. You know the *P-815* and its crew. That's why I recommended you for mission commander."

"Thanks for the vote of confidence, but I think you should be in charge."

Yuri met his colleague's eyes. "This is the kind of mission that will rocket your career. Most officers would give their left nut to have such an opportunity. Don't let it slip by."

"I'd like you to be my deputy."

"Thanks but you don't need me. Assign that task to one of the minisub officers. They'll be hungry to be involved."

"I'll think about it."

Maranovich left for another meeting. Yuri remained behind, sitting at the table and working on a fresh cup of tea. So far, Yuri's plan was headed in the direction he'd engineered. Yuri beamed. *Yes, this just could work!*

Chapter 22

Elena Krestyanova sat up in the bed and stretched out her arms. Sunlight flooded the enormous bedroom. She glanced at the vacant side of the king-size bed. Kwan Chi was already up. Elena checked the clock on the bedside table: 9:25 A.M. She'd slept soundly, almost eight hours straight. Jetlag contributed to her weariness but the sex had helped. Celibate for over four months, she had exhausted Kwan and vice versa.

Elena slipped her legs over the edge of the elevated platform bed and stepped onto the bamboo flooring. Nude, she walked into the bathroom. Twenty minutes later, Elena entered the living room. She wore a silk robe and a pair of slippers she found on a counter, both placed earlier by Kwan's housekeeper.

"Good morning," Kwan greeted, walking in from the kitchen. "I hope you slept well." He wore a plain white T-shirt and a pair of tan Bermuda shorts. Leather sandals covered his feet.

"I did, and I hope you did too."

"It was excellent. I haven't felt this good in a long time. Thank you!"

Elena flashed a friendly smile. "Is that coffee I smell?"

"It is. My housekeeper made a full pot plus a delicious breakfast. Please join me on the deck. It's wonderful outside this morning."

"Great, I'm famished."

Elena devoured the scrumptious omelet along with the smoked salmon. Kwan also cleaned his plate, which Elena noted was unusual. In the past, he rarely ate anything in the mornings.

Kwan poured a second cup of coffee for both and settled back into his chair.

"I'm so pleased that you're here."

"Thanks for inviting me."

Kwan decided it was time for business. "Have you heard anything new about Kirov?"

"Only that he's apparently still living with the woman and her child in the Seattle area."

Kwan took a swallow from his cup. "Although our arrangement regarding Kirov did not work out, we remain interested in continuing to retain your services."

"I'm very pleased to hear that. I too wish to continue."

"Good. Anything you can provide us regarding Pacific Fleet activities, submarines in particular, would be useful to us."

"I'll be visiting Vladivostok on my return trip. I'll see what I can find."

"Great."

Elena clasped her hands over the table. "When I was in Moscow, I heard something that might interest you—but it's not about the Russian Navy."

Kwan's eyebrows narrowed. "Please tell me."

"A few days before I left, I sat in on a classified SVR briefing regarding American operations in the western Pacific—Japan and China plus the Spratly Islands. Most of the discussion was related to the South China Sea and the waters disputed by—"

"They are not disputed waters," Kwan interrupted. "They belong to us."

"Yes, of course. I understand."

"Sorry for interrupting. Please continue."

"Near the end of the briefing, the officer reported that the Americans appear to be strengthening ties with Taiwan."

Kwan sat up rigid in his chair. "What kind of ties?"

"Military, as near as the GRU can determine at this time. Possibly related to stationing of U.S. forces on the island."

Cleary agitated, Kwan said, "How much confidence do you have in that report?"

"It was mentioned in passing during the briefing. Apparently, one of our operatives learned about Washington's overture to Taiwan from an agent in the U.S. State Department. That's all I know."

"Thank you. This is most helpful. What is your fee for this information? I'll make arrangements for immediate payment."

Elena shook her head. "No, don't worry about it. You've been so generous in the past."

Kwan smiled. "Very well, but anything else that you might uncover regarding this situation would be most appreciated. And we will compensate you handsomely for that effort."

"I'll try, Chi."

"Thank you."

* * * *

Two SVR officers sat at a table on the balcony of a luxury hotel suite that bordered Victoria Harbour. The building was over a mile southwest of Kwan Chi's penthouse. They had a partial line of sight of Kwan's unit from the hotel room, but relied on another surveillance device for up-front and personal views of the targets.

"She's hot." The older of the two Russian intelligence officers said. Although in his mid-forties, he retained a trim, athletic build.

"Yeah, she's not bad looking, but I don't care for the butch cut. She used to let her hair hang below her shoulders." The younger one commented.

"How do you know that?"

"There was a photo of her in the case file, taken a year or so earlier. She's much sexier with the longer locks."

A drone hovered over the bay about a thousand feet directly offshore of Kwan's apartment. Operating at the same level of the apartment, the zoom lens on the drone's HD camera captured vivid images of Elena and Kwan as they chatted on the exterior deck. The drone transmitted the encrypted images to the laptop parked on the balcony tabletop.

"I wonder how many times they screwed last night?" mused the older one.

"With her good looks, you've got to believe he wore himself out."

"Especially in that hot tub, he really worked her over."

"That's for sure—lucky guy!"

The surveillance team followed Elena from Moscow. The high-tech drone was already in place when they arrived, arranged by another Russian NOC stationed in Hong Kong. The specially modified unit's four propellers issued a whisper instead of the typical shrill high-pitched tone. It also came with an infrared camera for nighttime conditions.

"What do you think she's up to with that guy?" asked the junior officer. He was thirty-four. Slim for his nearly six-foot-tall frame, he was handsome with his soft blond hair and tan complexion.

"I have no idea. Moscow provided nothing about her mission, only that we're supposed to observe and report what we see."

"With a palace like that place, I bet she decides to hang out with him right there. He's certainly rich."

"There are lots of rich guys in this city—they're everywhere."

The two SVR officers entered Hong Kong with tourist visas, masquerading as an affluent gay couple on vacation from Germany. Besides their native Russian tongue, both men were fluent in German, having served in the Berlin embassy as security officers. Both remained single but were straight.

"Oh, looks like we've got a low battery," the junior officer said, reacting to a flashing low battery icon on the drone's handheld control device. The agent in charge studied the laptop screen; the camera remained focused on the couple. Both were holding coffee cups. "They're not going anywhere yet. Let's bring it back in for a charge."

"Okay. I'll issue the recall signal."

Although the drone had about fifteen minutes of flying time left, neither operative was about to take any unnecessary risk with the $50,000 mini-aircraft. Their Moscow supervisor informed them that if they lost the drone to carelessness, their salaries would be docked until the debt was paid off.

Six minutes later, the muted drone landed on the balcony table without operator assistance.

* * * *

SVR director Borya Smirnov relaxed in a comfortable leather chair in the library of his sprawling Moscow home. He gazed out the windows, taking in the late afternoon view of the garden. The serene vista was calming but it was the two shots of chilled Russian Standard burning in his belly that mellowed his outlook.

Before he had departed SVR headquarters for his chauffeured ride home, a hardcopy of the latest secure email report from his operatives in Hong Kong arrived. Decrypted and marked with a cover sheet containing the SVR's equivalent of a CIA "EYES ONLY" designation, the 22-page account detailed Elena Krestyanova's encounters with her target. He read the report during the twenty-minute commute.

The report's salacious details remained fresh. *Screwing in a hot tube on an exposed deck of a high-rise apartment! What an arrogant fool.*

Nonetheless, Smirnov smiled at the thought, almost envious of his Asian rival. *She must really be good—but Kwan is an idiot.*

Smirnov stood and walked a few steps to his bar. He opened the freezer compartment of the built-in German refrigerator and removed the bottle. He poured a third serving of chilled vodka into a glass. He returned to his chair and slugged down the shot.

Elena's doing her part—we'll just have to wait to see if they take the bait!

Elena Krestyanova was part of the deception. Smirnov also ran another operation in Washington, D.C.

One of the SVR's legacy plants working inside the U.S. State Department delivered another tantalizing morsel of intel data that would shake Beijing to its core. The MSS operative who thought she'd recruited an American spy by offering a pile of cash was clueless that her agent at Foggy Bottom was really a Russian operative. Smirnov smiled at the irony of the op.

They're going to pay us to get screwed!

Chapter 23

Yuri Kirov and Stephan Maranovich were aboard the *P-815*. The minisub was moored to a quay at the Rybachiy submarine base with the top of the hull ballasted down to within a foot of the water surface. It had rained this morning. The sky was a dull gray in all directions. "You'll be fine," Yuri said. "The lockout chamber is a piece of cake to operate."

"A what to operate?" asked Maranovich.

"Sorry, slang from my stay in America. The chamber is similar to escape hatches on submarines."

"All right but it looks tight in there."

"It'll be okay."

Maranovich wore a wetsuit with a scuba tank strapped to his back. A standby diver, already suited up, waited on the exterior deck next to *P-815*'s sail. A chief warrant officer sat atop the sail, his legs dangling over the forward edge of the fin. He wore a telephone headset. Yuri had a similar headset, plugged into the mini's com system.

Yuri said, "Stand by, Chief. We're going to start the test now."

"Ready here, sir."

"Very well." Yuri made one last check of Maranovich's equipment. "You're all set, Stephan."

"Okay."

Maranovich crouched down and crab walked into the lockin-lockout compartment. It was a tight fit with his lanky frame. His fin-tipped feet added to the awkward gait.

"I'm going to seal the door now," Yuri said.

Maranovich raised a hand.

Yuri closed the steel access door to the chamber, turning the handwheel that engaged the rack-and-pinion locking mechanism. He picked up a small hammer from a bulkhead receptacle and rapped the hemispherical hatch cover with three sharp bangs. Stephan signaled back with two clangs. Yuri made a mental note to come up with an improved system to communicate with the lockout diver. Banging on steel was not the best stealth for the upcoming mission.

Yuri heard the rush of water flooding the chamber as Maranovich activated a pump. Instead of allowing seawater to flow into the compartment, water stored inside the *P-815*'s internal side tanks was pumped into the chamber. This procedure prevented a radical change to the minisub's overall trim.

The water ceased flowing. Yuri checked his wristwatch. It should take no more than a minute for Maranovich to egress the midget. First, he would equalize internal and external pressure by opening a valve. Maranovich would next open the bottom hatch, step into the opening and descend fins first. After clearing the lockout chamber, he would pop up to the surface.

A minute passed. Yuri checked the control panel for the lockin-lockout compartment. The indicator light for the outer door remained closed. *There must be a fault in the line.* Yuri made another mental note to investigate the anomaly after the dive.

Yuri spoke into his headset mic. "Chief, he should be out now. Let me know when he surfaces."

"Copy that."

Half a minute went by. "Do you see him?" Yuri asked.

"No, and there're no bubbles or any kind of disturbance around the hull."

Yuri glanced at the chamber's control panel. The indicator light for the lockout door still signaled "closed".

"Get the standby diver in the water now. Check the outer door."

"We're on it, sir."

Yuri grabbed the hammer and whacked the interior door of lockin-lockout compartment. No response. *Govnó.*

The topside watcher made his report. "The diver reports that the outer door has not been opened."

Dammit. "Stand by. I'm going to drain the chamber. Come down to help."

"On my way."

Yuri activated multiple switches on the control panel, triggering the dewatering process for the chamber. The warrant officer clambered down the sail's interior ladder and joined Yuri.

"What happened?" he asked.

"I don't know."

Water flowed into the side tanks. When the control panel indicated that the pressure inside the chamber matched ambient level, Yuri spun the wheel on the access door and pulled it open. Captain Lieutenant Maranovich's torso flopped into the hatchway. His face mask remained in place but the breathing regulator with its mouthpiece dangled at the side of the air tank. Yuri dropped to his knees. "Stephan, what's wrong?" he called out.

No response.

Yuri ripped off the face mask and checked for signs of life. No chest movements. No breath signs. Eyes wide open.

Yuri unstrapped the SCUBA tank's shoulder harness and removed the weight belt.

He turned to the warrant officer. "Help me pull him out."

Maranovich lay on the open deck of the minisub's control center. After checking for a pulse and finding none, Yuri initiated CPR. He ordered the warrant to call for help.

A medic team from base headquarters arrived twelve minutes later.

Exhausted, Yuri moved aside to let the professionals take over.

The first responders worked on Maranovich for nearly half an hour before giving up.

After zipping up the body bag, the medics struggled to remove Maranovich from the confines of the *P-815*.

Yuri sat alone in the control center, stunned at the events of the past hour.

What happened?

Chapter 24

The two men drank green tea. They sat in a private dining suite in a Shanghai restaurant. While breakfasting on the exquisite fare, they caught up on family and mutual friends. With their bellies filled and personal updates completed, it was time for work.

"We remain convinced that the Americans are still in the dark," said Guo Wing. The overweight, middle-aged deputy minister of operations for the Ministry of State Security rubbed his neck.

"I would not underestimate them," said Lieutenant General Sun Jin. "They could easily be holding back." Sun served as chief of the Second Department (aka *Er Bu*) of the PLA's General Staff Department. The Second Department was responsible for providing intelligence services to China's military. A year older and nearly half a foot taller than his balding MSS counterpart, Sun had retained his hair but kept it close cut. He was not in uniform this afternoon; his summer suit revealed his gaunt frame.

"You are correct, of course. The Americans can never be trusted. Still, all indications are that they do not suspect what happened."

General Sun took a sip from his cup. "My main concern is the Russians— the hard drive from the yacht."

Guo sat up straight. "We have strong reason to believe the hard drive is no longer an issue."

Sun flashed a questioning glare.

Spymaster Guo continued the rundown. "My operative, Kwan Chi, reestablished contact with the SVR agent who assisted us with the early phase of Sea Dragon."

"Who are you talking about?"

"A trade mission delegate—her cover. Works out of Vladivostok and Vancouver."

General Sun tilted his head to side. "The blonde?"

"Yes—Elena Krestyanova."

"I thought she was arrested and sent back to Moscow."

"She did return to Moscow, but for treatment of a gunshot wound—multiple surgeries." Guo paused, taking a taste of tea before dropping the bomb. "A couple of days ago, she showed up in Hong Kong and reestablished contact with Kwan."

The general frowned, confused.

Guo continued, "After recovering from her injury, Krestyanova was sent back to Vancouver to continue her work at the trade mission. If the Russians somehow managed to work around the self-destruct feature of the hard drive, she would certainly have been imprisoned but more likely executed. There was plenty of incriminating evidence in it to reveal her spying for us—as well as critical details on Sea Dragon."

"That's your evidence—that she was sent back into the field because the hard drive was useless? What about their own people on the *Yangzi*?"

Guo's posture stiffened. "What did they know? Only that we had an op underway against the Americans near Seattle. They had no evidence other than what was on the hard drive. The yacht sank and all of our people on the mission either returned home or were killed. None were taken off that boat by the Russians."

"What about the mine? Some of them might have seen it."

"So what—how would they know what it was? Besides, it's gone, blown to bits along with the *Yangzi*." Guo returned his teacup to the table. "And consider our current relations with the Kremlin. Nothing has changed. Not a hint of trouble. In fact, we're about to start work on the new oil pipeline to Siberia. That's going to be a huge cash generator for Russia once the oil starts flowing."

Sun glowered, not convinced. "Come on, Guo, you don't think the SVR or FSB believe she's a double? Well, I don't buy that. They're trying to set you up."

Guo held up a hand. "Of course I'm concerned. But if what she told Kwan is accurate, everything changes."

General Sun took the bait. "What changes?"

"Operation Sea Dragon! We just might be able to resurrect it."

"We blew it. Beijing will not proceed with Sea Dragon."

"That may have been the case a few days ago, but no longer. Not after what Krestyanova told Kwan."

"Where are you going with this?" demanded Sun.

"We now have two sources. Krestyanova and one of our agents in the U.S. State Department. Beijing is going crazy."

"What?" the general asked, annoyed at Guo's build up.

"The Americans are preparing to base military assets in Taiwan."

"Tā māde,"—shit—muttered General Sun.

Chapter 25

Supervisory Special Agent Ava Diesen walked into her boss' office at FBI Headquarters. It was late morning in Washington, D.C. She carried a file folder.

"Morning, John. Do you have a minute?"

"Of course. Have a seat." Assistant Director of Counterintelligence John Markley was in his early fifties. He was average height with a trim waistline. He retained most of his russet hair with the exception of a retreating hairline. A pair of reading glasses was parked on his nose.

Ava sat down and opened the file folder. "I have an interesting situation I'd like to brief you on." She removed a photo and placed it on the desk.

Markley picked it up. "Russian?" he asked, noting the naval uniform.

"Yep. Capitan-Lieutenant Yuri Ivanovich Kirov. GRU Fleet Intelligence. Underwater intel expert. Last assigned to a sub based out of Petropavlovsk."

"And how did this guy get on your radar?"

"Homeland Security tagged him at Houston International last week. Our field office tracked him to the Russian consulate. But that's the last we have on him." Ava knew the rest of the report would upset her boss. "The Russians used a decoy to throw us off. They sent a double to the consulate's guest quarters."

Markley removed his reading glasses and gave Ava an accusing look. "You mean we don't have eyes on this guy?"

"We don't."

"Dammit, that shouldn't have happened."

"I agree."

Markley's forehead wrinkled. He studied the photo again. "What the heck is a submarine officer doing here, anyway?"

"It gets weirder, sir." Agent Diesen removed another document and handed it over.

He slipped on his glasses and thumbed through the papers. It took about twenty seconds for Markley to make the connection. "This is the same guy."

"Ninety-three percent confirmation on facial recognition."

"Tell me more."

"DIA made the original ID off a surveillance photo at the airport. I then asked Homeland Security to back-check every camera in the entire airport for the morning in question." She removed another photo from her file folder and held it up to show Yuri in civilian clothes walking out of an arrival gate. "He arrived on a United flight from Seattle."

"What name was he using?"

"John Kirkwood. Matched both his Alaska Air ticket and the Washington State driver's license he provided TSA when checking in at Sea-Tac Airport."

Markley reexamined the papers he held. "It says here that he's the general manager of Northwest Subsea Dynamics—what kind of company is that?"

"Very high-tech. Builds state of the art autonomous underwater vehicles and conducts underwater investigations. The company he works for has a multimillion dollar contract with the Coast Guard. It's involved in the cleanup of the oil spill in the Arctic offshore of Alaska."

"The Russian oil spill?"

Ava nodded.

"Damn! A Russian naval intelligence officer—running an American company that's under contract to an agency of the U.S. government?"

"That's what it looks like."

"Where is he now?"

"Unknown. As best as we can determine, he has not returned to Seattle. There's no indication of how or when he left Houston."

"They smuggled him out. That's the only thing that makes sense."

"I agree."

"What was he doing here?"

"We have no idea."

Markley rolled his chair back a few inches from his desk. "What do you have in mind, Ava?"

"My guess is that he was recalled home for a meeting or new orders. Something that required him to leave the country covertly, which could be arranged through the consulate. It was just a fluke that Homeland picked him up at the airport—CBP was testing new facial recognition software." Ava crossed her legs. "John, there's a chance he might be coming back. I'd like to implement a full-scale surveillance operation of where he works and lives in the Seattle area."

"By all means. Start setting it up."

"I will."

Markley said, "I'd also like a summary memo on this situation by two o'clock this afternoon. I need to brief the boss ASAP to get his blessing for a FISA hearing."

"Will do."

* * * *

Laura Newman took one last look at her reflection in the master bedroom mirror—silk pleat neck blouse, pinstripe jacket with matching ankle pants, and three-inch heels. Satisfied with the outfit for the day, she walked into the kitchen. "I'm about ready to head to the office," she announced, addressing Maddy's live-in nanny. Amanda Graham had started work the previous day. She would care for Madelyn from eight in the morning to when Laura returned from work, Monday through Friday.

"Wow, you look terrific," Amanda said. "May I ask where you bought your outfit?"

"Sure, it was Ann Taylor."

"It's very nice."

"Thank you."

Amanda was a tad heavy for her five-foot-four frame. A brunette with her hair bundled into a ponytail, she wore a pair of faded blue jeans and a sweatshirt with her alma mater's team logo: University of Washington Huskies. She sat at the kitchen table spoon-feeding Madelyn apple sauce.

Laura stepped to Maddy's side. She traced a finger along Madelyn's cheek, initiating the dimpled grin that stirred Laura's heart every time. "How are you this morning, sweetie?"

Maddy babbled a chorus of giggles. "Was she hungry?"

"She took most of the bottle."

"Good." Laura was in the process of weaning Madelyn. "There should be plenty of milk in the freezer."

"No problem."

"I should be home around six tonight."

"Okay, see you then."

"I'm going to order out tonight. How does Thai sound?"

"Great!'

"Okay, I'll take care of it."

Amanda occupied the guest quarters located over the three-car garage. The one-bedroom apartment contained a compact kitchen with the usual modern conveniences. An enclosed hallway linked the apartment to the second floor of the main residence. Since Yuri was gone, Laura had invited Amanda to join her for dinner. Sharing the evening meal also allowed the two women to get to know each other.

Laura walked into the garage and punched a keypad. While the door rolled open, she climbed in the silver BMW Seven Series. She started the car and buckled her seatbelt. As the sedan warmed up, Laura reached into her purse and removed her cell phone. She scanned through the list of telephone messages, texts, and emails. She had not checked since last night. *Still nothing! Where is he?*

Laura had heard nothing from Yuri for a week. Each day with no word further increased her anxiety. More than ever, she wanted to hear Yuri's voice, know that he was safe. But it was as if he had dropped into a black hole. Her duties at Cognition Consultants were mounting, and the pressure didn't help, either.

Although she ran for forty minutes this morning, the exercise-induced endorphins failed to relieve her stress.

Laura closed her eyes, silently reciting a prayer for Yuri's safety.

As she backed out of the garage a new thought flashed. Laura beamed. Maddy's birthday was this coming Saturday.

My sweet daughter. One year old already! Thank you, Lord.

Laura drove along the tree-lined private driveway that led to the street. When she pulled on to the public roadway, her bliss dissolved into disenchantment.

Yuri won't be there to celebrate with us!

Chapter 26

Day 11—Wednesday

"What happened to him, Kirov?"

"Heart attack, sir."

Yuri was on an encrypted phone in the communications center of the Rybachiy submarine base. Captain Petrovich was on the opposite end of the satellite link in Vladivostok. Yuri briefed the submarine commander on the autopsy of Stephan Maranovich.

"He was only in his mid-thirties. How can that be?"

"The medical examiner said he had advanced heart disease—clogged arteries. He also had water in his lungs. The doctor thinks he might have had a heart attack during flooding of the wet chamber, which caused him to panic. Somehow in that chaos he lost his breathing regulator and ended up ingesting water. Drowning is what killed him."

"With a condition like that, Maranovich should never have been assigned to field work."

"The doctor said he reviewed Stephan's medical records. His blood work during his last exam, which was..." Yuri paused to check his notes. "Four years ago, his blood chemistry was normal."

"Why wasn't he tested annually?"

"Don't know, sir. That's all that was in the file."

Yuri stared out a nearby window at the water of Avacha Bay. It was mid-morning with tranquil skies and waters. Today a faint brownish haze shrouded Rybachiy and Petropavlovsk-Kamchatsky. A forest fire 120 miles to the north polluted the otherwise pristine atmosphere.

"Well, Kirov," Petrovich said, "without Maranovich, the mission is in trouble."

Yuri had anticipated the captain's reaction. "I understand, sir. And I have a suggestion regarding a new commander for the mission."

"Go on."

"Operational experience with the mini is critical. I took the liberty of reviewing the records for the midget squadron based here at Rybachiy. There are at least three excellent candidates for filling Stephan's position."

Yuri briefed Petrovich on the officers.

Captain Petrovich was thoughtful. "They all appear qualified. Of the three, who would you pick if this were your mission?"

Yuri did not hesitate. "Senior Lieutenant Tumanov, sir. He has more time in minis than any of the other candidates. Plus, he has considerable diving experience, even deep water."

"Sounds like you."

Yuri did not respond.

"Okay, Kirov. We'll go with Tumanov."

"Excellent, sir." Yuri cleared his throat. "If I may, sir, I would like to recommend Junior Lieutenant Vassi Nevsky as Tumanov's executive officer. He has experience that—"

Petrovich cut him off. "That won't be necessary. Tumanov will be the XO."

"I don't understand."

"Tumanov is going to be your deputy. You're going to lead the mission."

"But—"

"It's final, Kirov," Petrovich said. "The decision has been made. I talked with Admiral Belofsky after receiving the notification of Maranovich's death. He concurred with my recommendation."

"Yes, sir. Thank you for your confidence in my skills."

"I want you to continue preparing for the mission. Bring Tumanov on board and anyone else you think might be needed. The schedule remains the same. My XO is going to ferry *Novosibirsk* to Rybachiy. I'll fly up when it arrives. And then we go."

"Understood."

Captain Petrovich terminated the satellite link without further discussion.

Yuri stood and walked to the window. The tide was out, preventing him from viewing the *P-815* moored alongside the quay fronting the communications building.

Govnó!

His scheme to withdraw gracefully from the mission by promoting Stephan Maranovich and playing down his own capabilities was in ruins.

They're never going to let me go.

* * * *

Elena Krestyanova selected the burnt orange side ruffle dress—one of her favorites. With a surplice neckline, ruched side ruffle, three-quarter sleeves, and a knee-level hem, the dress displayed her superb curves. A pair of nude four-inch heels with gold trimmed ankle straps adorned her pedicured feet. Elena scanned her mirror image in the hotel room. Satisfied, she slipped a gold bracelet onto her left wrist. *Georgii will love this!* She would meet him in the lobby in half an hour. Six months had passed since their last rendezvous. Elena wondered where they would dine tonight. She hoped for Italian food but suspected he had seafood in mind. It was a logical choice—like San Francisco, Vladivostok's restaurants were known for fin and shellfish fare.

Elena tolerated Vladivostok. Her hotel accommodations were first class and the view of Golden Horn Bay from the room was exceptional, but the seaport city just didn't click for her. Although its economy was robust and the city had a decent summer tourist crowd, Vladivostok's subculture of stark Soviet Union realism, mixed with Imperial Russia's extravagance, left her cold. Vladivostok was also a navy town, overflowing with horny young sailors and officers on the prowl, both single and married. Elena had frequently endured catcalls and wolf whistles during prior stays when she jogged along the waterfront or hiked on the trails in the nearby hills. When she visited drinking and eating establishments for a solo night out, she rarely ever bought her own drinks or meals. Sailors were sailors. Whether it was St. Petersburg or Kaliningrad or Sevastopol or Vladivostok, gorgeous women like Elena were targets. Trained to employ her femininity for specific purposes, Elena had put up with the unwanted advances during her earlier tenure in Vladivostok, waiting for the right opportunity.

That opportunity came; the first payout netted Elena half a million USD. After an unscheduled transpacific crossing delivered Elena to Vladivostok, she hooked up with a submarine officer stationed at the port's naval base. The squadron commander was careless, and Elena exploited his lapses. Captain First Class Georgii Seriyev inadvertently left a classified report on a desk buried under a stack of magazines in his apartment. After rendering the senior naval officer into a near-comatose state from three couplings in his bed, Elena took her time searching the rest of his quarters. She used her cell to photograph the treasure. Kwan Chi and his confederates in Beijing were ecstatic with the report that detailed the Russian Navy's Pacific Fleet submarine operations. That had been the start of their mutually beneficial relationship.

As Elena touched up her makeup, she planned her next coup. After dinner, Georgii would certainly pick a bar to continue the evening's festivities. She hoped he would avoid the officers' club at the base; the drab establishment with its cigar stench and cadre of drunks lining the mahogany bar counter was not her first choice. But then again, if Georgii wanted to show off his catch to his colleagues, Elena would play along—something she accepted as part of her career with the SVR.

Once Georgii reached vodka bliss, she would take him home in a cab. After finishing him off with multiple rounds of the best sex he ever had, she would again commence a treasure hunt.

Back on the payroll with Kwan, she would pocket what she could. SVR director Borya Smirnov would never know.

When Elena had returned to Vancouver from her Moscow internment, the first item she purchased was a new cell phone. While on a walk along the shores of English Bay, she used the smartphone to check her Luxembourg bank account. She feared the SVR might have discovered and drained it. The $5 million and change she'd earned from the MSS remained untouched.

The nest egg was Elena's only hope. Maybe she could buy her way out of Smirnov's bondage.

Chapter 27

Day 12—Thursday

A crew-cut blond in his mid-thirties opened the car door. He slid into the passenger seat, holding a pair of paper cups filled with hot tea.

"How's it going?" he asked.

"They're up, having breakfast."

The occupant behind the steering wheel removed his headphones, parking them on his shoulders. He accepted a cup and inhaled the steam before taking a drink. A few years older than his companion, the driver had shaggy auburn hair that brushed his ears and hung over the shirt collar behind his neck.

"He must have had a great time."

"No doubt—the lucky bastard."

The two SVR officers stationed in Vladivostok traded barbs as they contemplated imagined sex with Elena Krestyanova. Their Toyota Land Cruiser was parked half a block away from Captain First Class Georgii Seriyev's apartment building. It was a few minutes before ten in the morning.

"What do you think is going on?" asked the arrival. "Why would someone like her be working a naval officer?"

"Maybe she's not. They could just be bed buddies."

Both officers were aware that Elena also worked for the SVR.

The driver set his tea in a console cup holder. He retrieved a compact notebook from the dash.

After turning to the fourth page he reported, "Says here they have a history together. She's spent time with him before. Their last rendezvous was in January."

"Interesting. Maybe it's a budding romance."

"That might explain it."

"Too bad. I would have liked to have had a shot at her."

"She'd eat you alive, man—and me too. Neither one of us is in her class."

They laughed in unison.

* * * *

Elena and Georgii sat at the kitchen table drinking coffee. They just finished breakfast—a thick cheese omelet garnished with onions and peppers. Elena cobbled it together. White cotton robes covered their nude bodies.

"That was fabulous, Elena. You're a terrific cook."

An inch under six feet tall, Captain First Rank Georgii Seriyev had a barrel chest, muscled arms and legs, and thick mat of auburn hair that conveyed the vigor of a man twenty years younger.

"Thanks. Eggs are easy."

"Better than I could ever do."

After a final romp, the pair had climbed out of the bed forty minutes earlier. They showered and relocated to the kitchen. Georgii was in fine form this morning. He'd managed to capture seven hours of uninterrupted sleep, unaware that Elena had slipped a sedative into his final vodka shot.

Elena, on the other hand, was exhausted. Once Georgii passed out, she slid from the bed and conducted a careful and methodical search of the apartment. She left the lights off, using the flashlight app on her cell for illumination when needed. But there was no joy. Other than non-classified technical naval journals stacked on the living room coffee table, she found no secret materials.

Frustrated, she returned to the bed before sunrise. She slept about three hours before Georgii rolled onto her side of the bed.

Georgii cleared the dishes from the table while Elena finished the last of her coffee.

"When are you heading back to Vancouver?" he asked.

"Tomorrow. I have a morning flight to Seoul and then on to Vancouver."

"That's a long flight."

"You should come visit me. Vancouver's a terrific city."

Georgii returned to the table, refilling their mugs from the Mr. Coffee pot. "I'd like that very much, maybe later in the year."

Elena was about to suggest a date when Georgii's landline phone announced its presence.

"Excuse me."

Georgii walked to the counter where he retrieved the handset. "Captain Seriyev."

Elena turned toward the nearby window. The apartment had a partial view of Golden Horn Bay, but she ignored it. Instead she listened to the one-sided call.

"That's correct, sir. Petrovich will be in command.... It's scheduled to arrive in Petro next week.... Kirov is already there, prepping the mini.... Yes, sir, I'll let them know."

Georgii returned the handset to its cradle and walked back to the table. He reclaimed his chair and toyed with his cup.

"Everything okay?" Elena asked.

"Fine. Just routine stuff."

Elena glanced at the wall clock: 10:19 A.M. "Am I keeping you from your work?"

"No problem. That was my boss. He's a worrier. The chief called him and then he called me. You know, shit runs downhill."

"Chief?" Elena said.

"Admiral Belofsky. He's in charge of the Pacific Fleet."

"Ah, the top dog!"

Georgii's brow wrinkled, not catching the idiom.

"Sorry. I've spent too much time in North America. Top dog—the number one."

"Ah, yes, the admiral is number one around here."

Elena was about to return to the bathroom when Georgii said, "Dinner with me tonight—please. I won't keep you up late. I know you need to leave early tomorrow."

Prior to the call, Elena would have declined. "I would like that."

"Officers' club okay?"

"Sure, that'll be fun."

Elena relocated to the bathroom. As she combed her hair, using a brush from the counter, one thought dominated. *Kirov—could it be him!*

Chapter 28

Yuri Kirov was aboard the *P-815* with another officer. The minisub remained moored to a floating pier at the Rybachiy submarine base. It was half past one in the afternoon.

"How will we install the recording devices if we can't penetrate all the way into the harbor?" asked the twenty-four-year-old Russian naval officer.

"I'll lockout and tow it in with the DPV," Yuri said.

Senior Lieutenant Yakov Tumanov was a couple of inches shorter than Yuri was but weighed a dozen pounds more. Prematurely balding, he shaved his dome daily to achieve cue-ball smoothness. Tumanov glanced down at the diver propulsion vehicle resting on the deck beside Yuri. The two men were standing in a compartment next to the *P-815*'s lockin-lockout chamber. The DPV consisted of an aluminum cylinder about a foot in diameter and nearly four feet long. A ducted propeller occupied one end of the cylinder. A metal bar with a handgrip projected just over a foot above the propeller housing.

"Won't the bottom sensors detect the DPV?" Tumanov asked.

"This unit has been modified. The electric motor is virtually silent. The propeller blades are designed to minimize cavitation."

Captain-Lieutenant Maranovich had ordered the special gear from the St. Petersburg naval base. It arrived the previous day aboard a scheduled military air cargo flight. "Okay. That should work," Tumanov said.

Lieutenant Tumanov pulled open the inner hatch to the lockout chamber. He squatted and peered inside the cavity. "Poor Stephan. It must have been awful for him."

"Did you know him long?" Yuri asked.

"Just a couple of months. Good man. We all liked him."

"I was just getting to know him. I liked him, too."

Yuri and Tumanov relocated to the control room. Tumanov sat at the pilot's console. Yuri stood at his side.

"The integrated sonar system is just outstanding, sir." Tumanov handed Yuri a headset with a visor and then slipped on his own unit. "I'm going to run a simulation so you can get a feel for the three-D virtual reality features of the system."

The mini video screen covering Yuri's eyes flashed on, revealing the image of a sandy silt bottom with blades of eelgrass waving in the current. "This is from the video camera mounted on the bow. The test was inside the bay here, running from the shallows to the deepest part of the harbor."

"That must be a high-def camera," Yuri commented, impressed with the clarity of the images.

"It is. It also has special optics for low light conditions."

Tumanov advanced to the next phase of the test. "This is in about twenty meters of water now." The bottom was still visible in Yuri's visor screen but was devoid of vegetation other than sporadic clusters of macroalgae. "Sir, this next segment shows how the sonar system views the same conditions."

Yuri's visor screen blinked from the video to a computer-generated image.

"Wow," Yuri muttered, stunned at the clarity of the artificial view of the harbor bottom. The digital image had an azure background with bottom features that included a textured tan bottom and green splotches of vegetation.

Lieutenant Tumanov continued with the demonstration. "This next segment shows how the sonar system found the target that was pre-positioned on the bottom."

"But you didn't know its position ahead of time?"

"Correct, only the general area. Our mission was to run a grid search in an attempt to find it."

"How long did it take?"

"Just under an hour. Here's the target."

The virtual image of the telecommunication cable filled Yuri's visor screen. The three-inch-diameter cable was half-buried in the bottom muck.

"Here's the confirming video of the target," Tumanov said.

The screen again changed. The black cable snaked along the bottom.

"Impressive," Yuri commented, handing the VR visor back to Tumanov. "My only concern is the acoustic output. Remember, the Chinese will have the best sensors they can find."

"I know, sir. When on stealth mode, the sonar operates at an ultralow power level and mimics indigenous biological activity of the target waters.

The software can cloak the signal with over a dozen species, ranging from whales to dolphins."

"The Germans are very clever."

"They sure are." Lieutenant Tumanov turned toward Yuri. "Sir, how did we get this equipment, you know, with all of the sanctions?"

"I have no idea. Did you ask Maranovich?"

"He didn't know either, only that Fleet had the equipment installed and we were ordered to test it."

"Well, that's not for us to be concerned with. What counts is that the new sonar works exceptionally well and it might be the key factor to the success of our mission."

"Understood, sir."

After meeting with Tumanov, Yuri disembarked the *P-815* and headed back to the main administration building. As he walked alone, he considered Lieutenant Tumanov's inquiry about how the Russian Navy managed to obtain the cutting-edge German sonar system. Two scenarios came to mind—bribery or theft. *The GRU or SVR paid off someone to get around the sanctions—that makes the most sense.*

He was right.

Chapter 29

"Subject exited from five twenty and is now southbound on East Lake Sammamish Parkway. ETA is seven minutes."

"Follow until she turns down the driveway. We'll take it from there."

"Roger that."

After returning the radio handset to its receptacle, the seasoned professional sitting at a compact table in the cargo compartment of the Chevy van keyed her laptop. The command activated the street camera feed. It was 4:23 P.M.

"She's coming home early today," announced FBI Special Agent Michaela Taylor. Nearing forty, Michaela retained her good looks with black hair that just brushed her shoulders, a pleasing smile, and generous curves that filled out her gray pantsuit. Divorced three years, she had custody of her two daughters.

"Something must be going on." Special Agent Todd Rossi sat opposite a console packed with electronic hardware. Built like a fireplug, he was a month shy of thirty and single.

Both agents turned to eye the widescreen flat panel LCD video display mounted to the side wall of the van. There was no vehicle traffic on the narrow tree-lined asphalt paved roadway, but a couple of preteens on bicycles pedaled by the telephone pole that housed the surveillance camera. Disguised to simulate telephone equipment, the hi-def camera produced vivid imagery.

Five minutes passed before the sedan appeared on the screen. "Here she comes," Taylor announced.

The silver BMW slowed and, with a signal flasher activated, turned onto the private driveway that led down the hillside.

"That's a nice ride she has," Rossi said.

"Indeed."

"She must be loaded."

"Yep, no doubt about that." Sitting on the table at Agent Taylor's side was a three-ring binder full of background data on the target. For the past several days, she had immersed herself in Laura Newman's life. To say she was impressed with Newman was an understatement. Michaela was in awe of Laura's accomplishments—*summa cum laude* computer engineering graduate of Caltech, chief operating officer of a world class IT company, board member of three philanthropic foundations, and mother of a one-year-old—all at the age of thirty-three.

There were blemishes in the binder's documents. Abused by her husband, Laura called it quits about a year earlier. The divorce decree indicated that Ken Newman never made any court appearances and his current whereabouts remained unknown. An attorney representing the family of a missing bodyguard assigned to protect Laura Newman had recently sent an inquiry to the Seattle Field Office. Sarah Compton had been missing for several months now. What was that about?

Most disturbing of all was the impetus that convinced the United States Foreign Intelligence Surveillance Court of Review in D.C. to issue a blanket FISA—Foreign Intelligence Surveillance Act—warrant regarding the Newman residence, Cognition Consultants and Northwest Subsea Dynamics. Under the guise of national security, the FBI was authorized to surveil and obtain evidence regarding a Russian naval intelligence officer who managed a high-tech marine company owned by Laura Newman—and who also shared her bed. That made her a likely security risk. Laura's name was added to the target list, along with the names of key personnel at Cognition and NSD picked up in the wire taps.

FBI headquarters also issued a nationwide BOLO—Be On (the) Look Out—for Yuri Kirov. The notice included his Washington State driver's license photo.

The integrated FBI investigation of Yuri Kirov and Laura Newman was code named Red Rover.

Agent Taylor again keyed her laptop. A new image appeared on the video screen. The BMW Seven Series drove into the center stall of the three-car garage and stopped.

When Laura opened the trunk and removed a shopping bag, Michaela entered another command and the magnified image snapped into focus.

"Looks like she went shopping."

"Yep," Rossi replied, eyeing the same image.

Michaela focused on the image of the bag Laura removed from the trunk. "Nordstrom. She must have visited Belle Square today." She referred to the upscale shopping mall in downtown Bellevue near Laura's office building.

Agent Rossi checked his computer. "You're right. She left the building at one thirty-seven on foot. Visited the mall for about thirty minutes and returned. Says here she purchased a pair of shoes. Sam Edelman three-inch Tia ankle strap pumps—whatever those are."

Nice, thought Michaela. She needed a new pair herself.

Michaela again worked the laptop keyboard. The monitor split into eight equal-size view screens, one for each camera installed inside the residence.

"The nanny and kid are still in the living room," Rossi reported.

Michaela watched as Laura walked through the kitchen, leaving her shopping bag on the counter. She entered the living room. Amanda sat on a sofa by the window wall. Madelyn played on the carpet beside the couch, cooing to a stuffed bear almost her size.

"Turn the sound on," Michaela ordered.

"Got it."

Michaela watched as Laura scooped up Maddy. "Hi, sweet pea!" Laura said. "I missed you!"

Special Agent Michaela Taylor shook her head, bewildered.

Just who are you?

Chapter 30

Captain-Lieutenant Yuri Kirov stood in the narrow observation well atop the sail of the *P-815* as it powered across Avacha Bay. Mount Koryasky towered in the background. The skies were clear today.

The minisub's operating crew was below. There was no need—or room—for the typical three to four watch standers to man the sail, scanning the surrounding waters with binoculars. Instead, the HD camera mounted on the mast that extended seven feet above Yuri's head provided the *P-815*'s pilot with a sweeping 270-degree view of the approaching waters. The real-time images filled the main monitor of the pilot's control panel. A second camera and monitor system viewed the aft deck of the submarine. Yuri wanted a breath of fresh air and ascended the fin's internal hatchway.

The *P-815* headed toward its home berth at the Rybachiy submarine base. The training exercise had gone well. After departing from the harbor, the midget cruised eastward for six miles and descended to a depth of three hundred feet. It took just over three hours to sneak back into Avacha Bay, defeating the two antisubmarine warfare patrol craft assigned to guard the harbor entrance and an acoustic sensor planted on the bottom. The submersible's stealth was excellent, but it was the decoy Yuri deployed that made the difference. Designed to mimic the acoustic sound print of a minisub, the decoy soon attracted the hunters' attention. They locked onto the decoy's scent and hounded it with sonar pings. The robot executed evasive measures, leading the ASW ships on the proverbial wild goose chase. All the while, the *P-815* slipped into the harbor entrance without notice by the patrol craft. It also avoided triggering an intruder alert from the seabed acoustic monitoring device. *So far so good.*

The decoy worked and the midget's crew demonstrated competency. *But is it enough?*

Defeating the patrol craft and sensors guarding the Chinese harbor facilities would require other measures. He'd been thinking about the problem since the briefing in Vladivostok. The brainstorm hit the previous evening, while he rested on the bed in his quarters. Before the test cruise, he made a couple of email inquiries to colleagues on the west coast of Russia.

Yuri checked his wristwatch. 16:35 hours. It was still early in the morning at the St. Petersburg naval base. After the *P-815* docked, he would check his secure email using the code room at the base. If there were no responses, he would start working the phone, using the scrambler unit in the code room. As the minisub turned and made its final approach to the Rybachiy base, Yuri sensed he was on the right track.

Remoras and Crawlerbots—they just might be the key!

Chapter 31

It was early afternoon at the Ministry of National Defense headquarters building in western Beijing. The Central Military Commission meeting had started ten minutes earlier. The CMC was responsible for the command and control of the People's Liberation Army. Twelve men and three women sat around the U-shaped table in the secure conference room. Just one participant occupied the center of the table. The others sat in flanking chairs. All but three attendees wore uniforms. An enormous flat panel screen occupied a wall opposite the open end of the table. A color map of China's coastline filled the video display. Admiral Soo Xiao stood next to the screen. He served as Vice-Chairman of the CMC as well as Chief of Staff of the People's Liberation Army-Navy. At fifty-eight, Soo was one of the oldest in the room. He maintained a trim build that reflected regular exercise, healthy eating habits, moderate drinking, and complete distain for cigarette smoke.

"Mr. President," Soo said, addressing the occupant of the center table, "as you directed we are now carefully and quietly pre-positioning our forces in preparation for the resumption of Operation Sea Dragon. The North Sea Fleet is replenishing at Qingdao after sea trials." He used a handheld laser pointer to illuminate Qingdao. Bordering the Yellow Sea, Qingdao was the largest city in Shandong Province. Admiral Soo moved the pointer to the center of the map, identifying Ningbo. "Our East Sea Fleet continues to prepare for the scheduled war game." Ningbo was on the coastline of northern Zhejiang Province. China's top military officer pointed to the bottom of the map, highlighting Zhanjiang City and adjacent Hainan Island. "And lastly, our South Sea Fleet is standing by in Zhanjiang and Yulin, waiting for the go-code." Zhanjiang served as the South Sea Fleet's headquarters. Yulin was China's newest naval base located at the southern tip of Hainan Island. The huge island bordered the South China Sea.

"Admiral, you know the Americans are watching everything we do." Chen Shen, the President of the People's Republic of China, general secretary of the Communist Party, Chairman of the Central Military Commission, and First-ranked member of the Politburo Standing Committee, was fifty-six. A dark suit draped his trim, tall frame. He gestured at the video screen from the center of the table, a lit cigarette dangling from his fingers. "How will they not pick up the threat?"

Soo rubbed an ear. "For certain, Mr. President, they are surveilling our military assets, surface vessels, and submarines, as well as land-based aircraft. That is to be expected." Soo keyed the pointer, advancing to a new PowerPoint slide. An aerial photograph of Shanghai filled the screen. "What they will not be expecting is the conversion process for the commercial vessels." He pointed the laser at the screen, identifying half a dozen hulls, each in excess of a thousand feet long. "The work is complete. Each vessel can accommodate 15,000 troops."

The president looked pleased with the deception. Two years earlier, China had announced to the shipbuilding world that it was embarking on a new policy to promote tourism for its citizenry. A dozen cruise ships, designed to meet the needs of China's burgeoning middle class, would be constructed. The plan was to promote tourism within its own waters with its own floating palaces instead of relying on established international cruise lines. The plan was true to a point. However, prior to turning over the first six completed ships to the government-controlled agency sponsoring the project, the builders were required to give first dibs to the PLA.

The admiral continued his presentation. "If authorized, Sea Dragon would commence at the conclusion of a pre-scheduled war game in the South China Sea, code named Stalking Tiger."

A new slide filled the screen featuring the 250-mile long by eighty-mile wide island of Taiwan—aka the Republic of China—and the coast of mainland China. Separating the rebellious enclave from its parent nation was the hundred-mile wide Taiwan Strait.

Soo aimed the laser pointer at the center of the Taiwan Strait opposite Taipei. Serving as the ROC's capital, Taipei was located at the northern end of Taiwan. "After completing Stalking Tiger, the North and East Sea Fleets will begin their return voyage to their homeports. Once the bulk of the ships arrive offshore of Taipei, Sea Dragon will commence with a lightning missile attack from our land bases in Nanjing and Guangzhou. Approximately 5,000 weapons will be released in the first hour."

The slide advanced to a gif video that depicted a barrage of missile arcs originating from mainland China and converging on targets from one end of Taiwan to the other. "After the missile strike, coordinated attacks by mainland-based aircraft and naval units from the North and East Sea Fleets will commence."

Calculated to obliterate airbases, surface-to-air defenses, and military command and control infrastructure, the initial sneak attack would be followed by targeted bombing of naval and army facilities. Coinciding with the bombing campaign, airborne forces, 20,000 strong, would parachute into key coastal areas to secure port and harbor facilities. Naval special operators inserted by submarine would support the paratroopers. Later the same day, the main force of 150,000, escorted by naval units from Stalking Tiger, would cross the strait aboard a flotilla of commercial vessels—container ships, break-bulk cargo carriers, and the commandeered troop-laden passenger liners. The South Sea Fleet would remain at sea in the South China Sea as a reserve force to support the invasion if needed. Its principal purpose, however, would be to intimidate the Americans should they rush to Taiwan's defense. The invasion planners estimated it would take the People's Liberation Army ten days to secure Taiwan, at last returning the rebel providence to the homeland. The CMC had reviewed the attack plan on numerous occasions before so there were few questions, all related to timing issues. President Chen thanked Soo and the admiral returned to his chair.

Chen moved on, addressing one of the PLA officers. "General Sun, please provide us with your report."

Lieutenant General Sun Jin stood and faced President Chen. His uniform jacket bristled with ribbons. "Sir, I would like to introduce Colonel Eng." The deputy chief of the GSD's Second Department—military intelligence—gestured to the female sitting at his side. "She is responsible for Taiwan and with your permission will provide the Second Department's report."

"Proceed," Chen said.

Sun returned to his seat and Colonel Eng Hu stood. Forty-six-years old, Eng was single—wedded lockstep to her career. She spoke five languages fluently. Her straight black hair just brushed the collar of her uniform jacket. At five-foot eleven with a rail frame, she was taller than most of the men in the room. The spectacles she wore hardly detracted from her lovely face.

"Comrade President," Eng said, meeting her leader's eyes, "our operatives in Taipei have not detected any changes in military preparedness. The Air Force continues to run routine sorties over the ocean but avoids the Taiwan

Strait. Patrol watercraft run surveillance operations near shore around the entire island."

"What about the Americans?"

"Nothing new from our last meeting. Routine visits from U.S. Navy ships, taking on fuel and supplies. Occasional aircraft landings, ferrying military personnel to and from the United States."

"Have your people observed any new equipment or troops on the island?"

"No, sir."

"Hmmm." President Chen directed his attention to the Deputy Director of Operations for the Ministry of State Security. "Guo, you are the one who sounded the alarm. What about Eng's report? She says nothing is going on."

The plump and balding spymaster sat to the left of the president, several chairs away. The tan summer suit he wore contrasted sharply with the green and brown uniforms of the PLA general officers sitting on his sides. Prepared for the inquiry, Guo Wing said, "I think that's good news, sir. They have not yet moved any weapons onto the island. That will make it simpler for us."

"We could be getting played here."

"It's possible, but we now have another confirming source. I received the report last night from our embassy in Washington."

The president's eyebrows furrowed at the news.

Guo continued, "Our operative in the State Department reported that the deputy secretary for Asian Affairs met secretly with those Taipei dogs in Honolulu."

"When?"

"Last week."

"What was the meeting's purpose?"

"Defense of Taiwan."

President Chen muttered a curse. "What about stationing of ships?"

"That is unclear at this point. However, the meeting was held at the Pacific Fleet headquarters in Pearl Harbor."

"The swine—they must be preparing to stage American ships at their port facilities."

"That is a real possibility, Comrade President."

Chen turned to face Admiral Soo. "What about nuclear weapons? Would they dare bring them in on their ships?"

"They could do that, especially aboard submarines and aircraft carriers."

Guo Wing rejoined the conversation, "Sir, we still don't know for sure if the Americans will make such a bold move. They know what our reaction will be."

"Guo, how solid are your sources about what the Americans are up to?"

"We have two independent agents reporting new contact between Washington and the scoundrels in Taipei. One is an SVR officer who is in our employ; the other is an American collaborator who has been working for the U.S. State Department for eighteen years. We rate both agents as highly creditable."

President Chen considered Guo's comments. He rolled his chair back a few inches from the table and lit another cigarette. After taking a puff, he said, "We now have two separate sources that confirm the Americans and those Taipei dogs are meeting secretly. The nuclear weapons issue could be a bluff, but I can't afford to take that chance."

Chen again addressed Admiral Soo. "Admiral, how soon can you implement Sea Dragon?"

Soo scanned a document on the table. "We will need three weeks once we receive the proceed order."

"Consider this your authorization to proceed."

Chapter 32

"Please summarize what you've found so far," said Supervisory Special Agent Ava Diesen. She spoke into the speakerphone on her desk while seated in her office at FBI headquarters in Washington, D.C. It was sizzling outside this afternoon—upper nineties with ninety percent humidity.

"Routine. She arrives at her office between eight thirty and nine and returns to her residence between six and seven." Special Agent Michaela Taylor was calling in from her Seattle office. It was late morning in her time zone. Rain pelted the window next to her cubicle as a summer front raced through the Puget Sound region.

"Has she had any contact with the subject Kirov?"

"None. No phone calls, cell or land lines. No emails, texts, or social media messages." Taylor coordinated the entire surveillance operation, even pulling occasional van duty at the Newman residence. Her own home was a short drive away in Issaquah.

"How about her business—what's it called?" asked Diesen.

"Cognition Consultants. Nothing from his alias John Kirkwood or anything remotely linked to him."

"What does Cognition Consultants do?"

Taylor checked her notes. "It's a software company that specializes in analyzing Big Data. Uses artificial intelligence as part of its work. Makes a ton of money working for oil and gas exploration companies and recently branched out to assist power companies—something to do with electrical grids. Company headquarters are in Bellevue, Washington—near Seattle with a couple of branch offices."

"What does Newman do?"

"She's Senior VP of Operations—runs the technical stuff. Owns thirty-five percent of the company. Makes a couple mill a year."

"Public company?"

"No, it's private, but that might be changing. We've uncovered some internal email correspondence that suggests the company might go public. Cognition also has had several suitors trying to acquire the company."

"Michaela, what the heck is she doing with this Russian?"

"I don't know. Just doesn't compute for me."

Diesen moved on. "What about the company Kirov works for...the underwater survey outfit? What's the latest there?"

"A number of incoming phone calls asking for Kirkwood but nothing from him. Also, a fair amount of incoming email traffic. All calls and emails are directed to someone named Bill Winters. He is NSD's chief engineer."

"When a caller asks for Kirkwood, what are they told?

"The receptionist's standard line is something like this: 'Mr. Kirkwood is out of the country on a family emergency and will be away several weeks. May I refer you to Bill Winters?'" Agent Taylor hesitated. "When a caller is directed to Winters, he repeats pretty much the same thing but when pressed admits that Kirkwood is in Denmark—his sister is ill."

"Well, that's certainly BS. He's not in Denmark, more like Moscow."

"Yes, ma'am."

Diesen mulled over Taylor's surveillance report on Laura Newman. "What about the house? Any interesting visitors?"

"The nanny leaves in the early evening—she has a boyfriend who works at Microsoft. He has an apartment in Redmond. She spends a lot of time with the guy but manages to make it back to the Newman residence before seven o'clock in the morning."

"You check 'em out?"

"Yep. They're both legit."

Ava picked up a document from her desk. "I reread your contact report with the locals about the missing bodyguard..." Ava turned a page. "... Sarah Compton. Anything new about her?"

"Nothing since I talked with the detective handling the case."

"Missing for four months now—she must be dead."

"I agree. Everything points to it."

"Why did Newman need a bodyguard?"

"As best we can determine, there was a threat and Kirov arranged for her protection."

Diesen was perplexed at the report. "Newman claims she and her daughter were kidnapped and that this Kirkwood guy, aka Russian intelligence officer Yuri Kirov, paid the ransom without involving the police."

"That about sums it up."

"That's preposterous."

"It's out there, all right."

"Okay, Taylor, thanks for the update. Keep monitoring. This case is high priority."

"Understood, ma'am, and will do."

* * * *

"Sir, do you have a moment?"

Nicolai Orlov looked up from his desk; he was in the middle of composing a report on his PC. Army Captain Oleg Babin stood in the doorway.

"Come on in," Nick said.

The consulate's security officer took a seat. It was late afternoon in Houston. Nick liked Babin. Confident but humble, the intelligence officer carried out his work with diligence and expedience.

"What's up?" Nick asked.

"Ah, sir, something's come up on the FBI issue." The GRU officer squirmed in his seat, not at ease with the news he was about to divulge. "Moscow reports that the FBI is running a covert operation codenamed Red Rover."

Nick's right eyebrow wrinkled but he remained silent.

"As you suspected, the target of the operation is Captain-Lieutenant Kirov."

"*Govnó*," Nick uttered.

Babin continued, "One of our people in Homeland Security made the report." Despite Washington's Herculean efforts to weed out spies and turncoats, the American intelligence agencies remained infected.

"What do they know?"

"There's a nationwide alert for him issued by the FBI."

"What about the mission Kirov is on now?"

"The General Staff analyst who sent me the notice today indicated that at this point there is no reason to believe the FBI or other U.S. intelligence organizations know that Kirov has returned to Russia. It appears they believe he's somewhere in the United States conducting a covert operation."

"Have they traced him here—to the consulate?"

"We don't know. The alert is all we have at this time." The skin above the scar on Babin's forehead involuntarily twitched. "The FBI might be monitoring to see if Kirov returns to the consulate. That assumes he was spotted here. Of course, we don't know if that happened or not."

"Just assume they've been watching us twenty-four-seven—and the guest house, too."

"Yes, sir."

Nick reflected. "Kirov might have been surveilled at the airport when he arrived here."

"That's possible."

Nick turned away, peering out the office windows. Traffic on Interstate 610 crawled as commuters headed home. Babin waited for orders.

Nick had kept Babin in the dark about Yuri's previous activities in the Pacific Northwest but decided it was time bring him aboard.

He turned back. "Captain, we need to find out just how far the FBI has managed to probe into Kirov's activities while he was here." Nick turned to his right to access the electronic file safe bolted to the floor behind his desk. After keying in the combination and pulling open the door, he retrieved a file folder and placed it on the desk.

Nick opened the file and removed a color photograph. He held it up to Babin. "Her name is Laura Newman, and she lives in a suburb east of Seattle. Check with Moscow to see if she's mentioned in Operation Red Rover. I need to know if she's also on the FBI's radar."

Babin studied the photo and was about to ask a question when Nick read his mind.

"She's Kirov's lover—and someone who has helped us in the past."

"*Obaldét*"—Wow.

Chapter 33

Elena Krestyanova was in the code room at the Vancouver trade mission. The compartment contained the latest communication equipment that provided secure comms with the homeland. The video image of her boss, SVR chief Borya Smirnov, filled the widescreen monitor mounted to a wall near the conference table. A high-definition camera adjacent to the screen transmitted Elena's image and voice to a similar setup at Smirnov's residence in Moscow.

Elena briefed the SVR director on her interaction with Kwan Chi. "He clearly suffered severe injuries. Burns on his arms and a fractured leg. The burns are healing but remain painful. He uses a cane when walking." Elena maintained digital eye contact with Smirnov. "He's taking narcotics—oxytocin in particular."

"How do you know that?"

"I found the bottle in his bathroom."

"Continue, please."

"He's back working at his real estate company. But I'm sure he's not full-time."

"What about Kirov—did Kwan mention him?"

"Only in passing, wondering if I'd heard anything." Elena clasped her hands. "As you instructed, sir, I told him I had no information on Kirov."

"What about Orlov, was he mentioned?"

"No, sir."

"And what about you? Have you had contact with Orlov since you left Moscow?"

"No. Is there a problem?"

Nick Orlov and Elena were past lovers; Nick turned in Elena to the SVR, accusing her of treason. Elena did not fault Nick for his actions, knowing he had no choice given the circumstances.

"We have reason to believe Kwan may seek revenge against both Kirov and Orlov."

Elena chose not to respond. The spymaster moved on. "How did Kwan respond to the American situation?"

"He was clearly agitated when I mentioned the meeting between the U.S. State Department and Taiwan. I believe it stunned him."

"Anything else?"

"When the Spratly Islands came up that really upset him."

"The Americans ordering a warship to sail close to one of China's artificial islands no doubt pissed 'em off again."

"I'm sure it did. There was a lot of media coverage about it when I was in Hong Kong. Mainland China considers Washington a meddler and wants the U.S. Navy out of East Asia."

"We are of the same opinion, but for different reasons."

"Of course, sir, I understand."

Smirnov quizzed Elena for several more minutes regarding her activities in Hong Kong before moving on to her stay in Vladivostok.

Elena said, "I spent a couple of days reestablishing contacts with the trade office. Routine work."

"Was that all?"

Elena's heart fast-tracked, her mind raced. *What's that mean?* And then she put it together. "I went out with a man I'd dated before."

"The naval officer?"

How does he know that? "Ah, yes, Captain Seriyev."

There was no follow up question regarding the submarine squadron commander. Instead, Smirnov switched direction. "How have you been received in Vancouver?"

Sensing risk, Elena ignored the question and backtracked. "Sir, there was one thing I overheard in Vladivostok that was surprising."

"Go on."

"I heard Captain Seriyev speaking on the phone in his apartment to someone I presume from his base. In the course of that conversation he mentioned the name Kirov."

"Captain-Lieutenant Yuri Kirov?"

"I don't know." Elena's response was truthful. During drinks with Seriyev at the officers' club, she had made a subtle inquiry about Kirov but learned nothing.

Elena remained fixated on the video screen. Smirnov stared back. Adrenaline surged into her bloodstream. She feared a trap.

Director Smirnov said, "Kirov has defected to the United States."

Taken aback, Elena retained her poker face as Smirnov continued. "He disappeared a couple of weeks ago. He's being interrogated by the FBI and CIA in Washington, D.C."

Elena unconsciously massaged her left shoulder as the bombshell reverberated. *Kirov will burn me—my cover will be destroyed.* "Sir, how much damage can he inflict on us?"

"We're assessing it now, but it's likely to be severe."

The video conference concluded a minute later. Elena remained seated at the table, still reeling. *Kirov defected—damn!*

She again kneaded the scar on her shoulder, thinking of the time bomb just under the skin. Stress fed the ache.

They're never going to let me go.

SVR chief Smirnov ordered Elena to resume her activities in Vancouver. He offered no praise or criticism for her work with Kwan Chi. With her options narrowing by the day, Elena sensed impending doom.

It's just a matter of time and then they'll get rid of me.

* * * *

After speaking with Elena, Borya Smirnov again reviewed the daily digital summaries of her whereabouts for the past week. Fear worked wonders. The tracking system duly reported Elena's GPS coordinates. The radio frequency identification chip embedded in her clavicle responded to hourly inquiries from the special cell phone she carried around the clock. Elena followed all protocols requiring advance notice of air travel or other excursions beyond her assigned areas of operation that might interfere with the hourly updates that kept her alive.

But it was bogus. There was no vial of poison attached to the stainless-steel plate pinning her collarbone together. The item Smirnov pointed to on her X-rays when perpetuating the hoax contained the RFID tag but nothing else.

So far, Elena Krestyanova had toed the line. And she passed the Kirov test.

The voice-activated "bug" in Captain Seriyev's apartment recorded Elena's post-sex breakfast talk with Seriyev in its entirety, including his one-way telephone conversation with the sub base commander when Kirov's name was mentioned.

Elena's verbal briefing matched the surveillance recording. Had she not voluntarily mentioned overhearing Kirov's name, Smirnov was prepared to address the issue directly. The SVR director typed a command on his desktop PC, opening a Windows folder. He clicked on a file name. A color image of the official Russian Navy photograph of Yuri Kirov filled his LCD monitor.

Smirnov stared at the image. *Soon*, he thought.

Kirov was part of his grand plan. The rumor was already in the works. An SVR plant assigned to the Indian embassy in Singapore started the ball rolling the previous day. During a diplomatic reception at the embassy, she casually mentioned to her PRC counterpart the buzz about a Russian defection to the USA. No names were mentioned, only that the party involved was a submarine officer.

Beijing must know by now.

A turncoat Russian naval officer was big news in the diplomatic world. The rumor that the officer in question was a submariner would jolt the intelligence community. Submarine espionage represented the pinnacle of naval intelligence operations.

They will contact Kwan soon.

As in his own country, the SVR chief expected the defection news would pass instantly from diplomatic channels to the senior military echelon. Seeking confirmation, the People's Liberation Army-Navy would utilize its intelligence assets to mount an investigation. Eventually, those efforts would involve the MSS and Kwan Chi.

He will put it together.

A Russian naval officer assigned to submarines who defected to the USA—there was only one possibility for Kwan.

Kirov will be the trigger.

SVR Director Smirnov speculated that Kwan loathed Yuri Kirov for thwarting the PRC's plan to generate a war between Russia and the United States. If the Americans believed defector Kirov's account, China's treachery would soon be on full display to the world. Without a shot fired, weapons of ridicule, disdain and revulsion would eviscerate China's prestige and prowess, rendering it an international pariah. It might take a decade of reconciliation and kowtowing to recover its once-robust economy and budding superpower status.

Smirnov knew it was a decade the Central Committee of the Communist Party of China could not afford to lose. A rollback of China's growth could trigger rebellion. With about half of its 1.4 billion living a marginal or subsistence lifestyle and the rising specter that a majority of those on the other side of poverty equation might roll back into that abyss, civil unrest on an untold scale was just around the corner. It was a scenario China's Communist Party could never survive. *Kwan will reach out to Elena.*

Elena Krestyanova had originally injected Yuri Kirov into Beijing's plan to spark a war between Russia and the United States. Director Smirnov now expected Kwan would contact Elena, seeking confirmation of Kirov's defection.

He will believe her.

Instead of Elena initiating the contact, Kwan's expected call would provide the confirmation of Kirov's defection.

Operation Fall Harvest—SVR director Smirnov's brainchild—was now nearing its culmination. *Soon they will pay!*

* * * *

Laura Newman sat at her home office desk, holding Madelyn in her lap. A chocolate cake with a single candle occupied a corner of the table. It was half past one in the afternoon.

Laura peered into the desktop monitor at the Skype image of her adoptive mother. "I wish you could be here too, Mom."

"When I heal up, I'll be able to travel again." Margaret—Maggie—Wilson was in her mid-sixties but didn't look it. She retained her honey blond hair and just a few folds marred the fair complexion of her striking face.

"Don't worry about it, Mom. Come up whenever you can."

A widow, Maggie lived in Santa Barbara, California. Recovery from hip replacement surgery was taking longer than expected. She had planned to attend Madelyn's first birthday. "Well, I sure miss seeing you and Maddy—she's such a cutie."

"She sure is!"

Mother and daughter chatted for another five minutes and then signed off.

Laura and Maddy relocated to the living room. Maddy was in her playpen, lining up her toy horses while chatting to herself.

Laura sat in her favorite chair by the windows. The lake sparkled in the background. Laura rattled the ice cubes in her iced tea, thinking of her mother.

I'm so blessed to have Mom.

Adopted as an infant, Laura was forever grateful to William and Maggie Wilson. They doted on Laura as if she were their biological daughter. Will, an MD, provided well for the family, allowing Laura to have a carefree childhood.

They rescued me!

The cards are often stacked against biracial children born into poverty. The Wilsons saved Laura from that uncertainty.

I should take Maddy to visit Mom. We could also see Tom.

Laura's brother—Maggie and Will's biological son—was ten years older. Tom also lived in Santa Barbara with his wife and three daughters. Following in his late father's footsteps, Tom was a physician specializing in neurosurgery.

Laura finished her drink. Her thoughts switched to Yuri, knowing he too wanted to be home for Maddy's first birthday.

Where are you, honey? And when will you come home?

Chapter 34

Day 16—Monday

It was late afternoon in Hong Kong. Kwan Chi sat in a high-backed leather chair beside a magnificent black marble desk. The office was just a few blocks from his residence. The fifty-eighth floor of the Kowloon Tower offered commanding views of Victoria Harbour and the connecting waterways to the distant South China Sea. Kwan held a telephone handset to his right ear; he reacted to the bombshell news. "That bastard—how long has he been gone?"

"About two weeks," Guo Wing said. "We know he flew to Houston but then disappeared." The MSS Deputy Minister of Operations was in his Beijing office. Smog obscured the view from his mid-rise building.

"Where is he now?"

"We suspect that the FBI and CIA have him sequestered in a safe house somewhere in the Washington, D.C. area."

Kwan cursed.

Guo Wing continued, "From your prior contact with him, what are the implications for us?"

Kwan flexed his injured leg, reacting to a twinge. "Nothing absolute, only his word about what happened."

"They will believe him—eventually."

"Yes," Kwan agreed. "Sir, how did we did get this information?"

"Our ambassador to Singapore heard a rumor at a reception. We followed up with one of our agents in Washington. The FBI has an ongoing investigation regarding Kirov. There's an active alert looking for him but we believe he's already in custody."

"You're certain he was turned by the Americans?"

"That's what was reported—and it makes perfect sense for him. He obviously wants to remain in the United States because of his lover. Working for the CIA is the price he has to pay."

"Then my cover's blown."

"Yes. That means you can't take the chance of entering U.S. territory."

"I wasn't planning on any trips there. I can manage the American real estate holdings from here. I'll send one of my staff if a face to face is required in the U.S."

"That's acceptable."

Kwan reached down with his free hand and rubbed the ache in his lower leg. "Sir, if all of this is true, we can expect severe repercussions from the Americans."

"I agree, as does the president. However, we haven't detected anything yet."

"It will come—you can count on it."

"We are and we will be prepared."

"What about Sea Dragon?"

"That's the other reason I called. Sea Dragon has been advanced."

Surprised, Kwan asked, "Because of Kirov?"

"No, another matter, which I can't reveal at this time. Nevertheless, the Kirov issue complicates the situation."

"How can I help?"

"The SVR officer who made contact with you recently, where is she now?"

"Probably back in Vancouver. She said she had a stop in Vladivostok first."

"I want you to contact her and ask her to quietly check to see if the SVR or FSB are aware that Kirov has defected."

"Okay." Kwan wavered as a new thought jelled. "What if the Russians don't know Kirov defected?"

"It's possible the Americans might be planning to use him as a double and return him to Russia to spy for them."

"The Russians must know."

"Probably, I just need confirmation."

Kwan switched gears. "What about Laura Newman? She knows just as much about what happened as Kirov."

"We've decided it's time to remove that contingent threat."

"When?"

"Soon. It's in progress."

"And Kirov?"

"When we find him."
"Excellent!"

* * * *

Nick Orlov stood at the water's edge, gazing at the two-acre pond. It was 6:32 P.M. He was in a city park near the apartment that the consulate rented for him. Located inland, Houston lacked the water amenities Nick had grown accustomed to in San Francisco.

Nick reached into his coat pocket and removed a pack of Winstons. He lit up. As he inhaled, he took the opportunity to eye the woman sitting on a park bench forty feet away. He first spotted the attractive thirty-something brunette when he entered the park. Attired in blue jeans and a short-sleeved blouse, she fit in with other park goers enjoying a warm summer evening. But Nick suspected otherwise. Another Feebie, he thought, using the slang term for an FBI special agent.

This was the third tail he'd spotted during the past month. As SVR *rezident* for the consulate, Nick was under increasing security by U.S. counterintelligence agencies. The escalating tension between Russia and the USA sparked the harassment. It was now becoming a nuisance.

Nick finished his smoke and walked west along the path for five minutes, finding a vacant bench. After sitting he retrieved his iPhone and called up the national news on SFGate—a digital version of the *San Francisco Chronicle.*

He glanced at the headline but ignored the article. Instead, out of the corner of his eye he watched the brunette meander along the walkway. She strolled past Nick. Just before she passed out of view, Nick watched as she removed a cell phone from a hip pocket.

Calling in your report on me—is that what you're up to, honey? Nick settled into the seat and began reading the sports section.

You're not going to record anything hot tonight Ms. FBI—just the latest on the 49ers.

After racing through the article on his favorite team, Nick returned his phone to a trouser pocket. He crossed his arms and closed eyes. He thought back to earlier in the afternoon when his aide, Captain Oleg Babin, provided an update on the Kirov situation.

Dammit—the FBI knows about Laura.

The SVR's mole in the FBI confirmed that Laura Newman was a target in Operation Red Rover.

She doesn't have a clue.

With Yuri incommunicado, Laura remained in the cold. *I've got to warn her. But how?*

* * * *

Elena Krestyanova relaxed in her Vancouver apartment, listening to Stravinsky's *Le Sacre du Printemps* while finishing a plate of Thai takeout. It was early evening. She was thinking of going for a run when her cell chimed.

She checked the phone's caller ID and smiled. "Hello, Chi," Elena said, her voice warm and welcoming.

"How was your trip home?" Kwan asked.

"Fine. It was long but no problems. And how are you feeling?"

"I manage, you know, a little stronger each day."

"Good."

"Elena, I need your help."

"Of course—what can I do?"

"I need you to check your schedule to see if you can attend another meeting here later this month. We are interested in exploring the possibility of investing in the real estate venture in Vladivostok you mentioned at our last conference—the hotel property."

"Oh, excellent. When is the meeting?"

Kwan provided the date and time.

Kwan and Elena used code; it was part of their previous arrangements to thwart surveillance by the Americans and Russians—and, because Elena had returned to Vancouver, the Canadians. Tonight's operative word was "hotel."

"I think I can make it. I'll need to check a few things at the office tomorrow and then I'll email you confirmation."

"Excellent, thank you."

Elena jogged after the call. She was halfway along her normal route when she diverted from the waterfront boardwalk to a cyber café. She ordered a decaf and sat down at a vacant rental computer. After logging in to the anonymous Outlook email account, she checked the drafts folder. There was a new entry with an attached file. She downloaded the encrypted document to a flash drive she carried in a pocket.

Elena arrived back at her apartment half an hour later. She showered, changed into pajamas, and relocated to the living room. She sat sofa cross-legged on a sofa cradling her laptop. Elena inserted the thumb drive into a USB port, clicked on to the encrypted Word document from Kwan, and keyed in the password.

The message followed SVR director Smirnov's prediction with frightening accuracy. Elena would wait 48 hours before posting a new draft email in the Outlook account she shared with Kwan, confirming Yuri Kirov's defection to the United Sates.

Elena would request $10,000 for the information.

Chapter 35

Day 17—Tuesday

Commander Tom Bowman was in the *Colorado*'s control room. He stood beside the sonar section, responding to a summons by the senior technician. "What've you got, Richey?"

"Captain, Master One is slowing. Down to eight knots now."

"She may be preparing to surface. Let me know if they start blowing tanks."

"Aye, Captain."

After radioing COMSUBPAC (Commander, Submarine Force, U.S. Pacific Fleet) regarding the chance encounter with the Chinese submarine, the rear admiral ordered *Colorado* to shadow the boat. The Type 095 nuclear powered attack submarine loitered offshore of Petropavlovsk-Kamchatsky for forty-eight hours before heading south. For the past six days, SSN 788 tailed Master One to its homeport on the Chinese mainland. Bowman stepped away from sonar, joining his executive officer at the plot table. "What's your take, XO?"

Commander Jenae Mauk looked up; she had listened to sonar's report. "Continue to shadow, Captain. Once Master One passes the twelve-mile limit, break off surveillance."

Bowman rubbed his chin. "If I were to decide to continue on, what would you recommend?"

"One moment, sir." Mauk studied the electronic chart and scanned an adjacent computer monitor. She looked back at Bowman. "We still have several hours before sunrise, and traffic in and out of the port is minimal.

We could make a quick probe into the main harbor area, take infrared photos and then head back out before sunup." She consulted the chart again. "But we'll have to be extra careful—the harbor is shallow, even for us."

"Good plan, Jenae. Let's implement it. You have the conn."

"Aye, aye, Captain."

With a quiet but resolute voice, Commander Mauk issued orders to the *Colorado*'s control room crew. Mauk was aware her current assignment was a test, and she welcomed it.

Two hours and ten minutes passed. *Colorado* penetrated deep into harbor, its keel just twenty feet above the bottom. Bowman and Mauk eyed the control room's main video display. Unlike older U.S. submarines, the *Virginia* class boats were not equipped with an optical periscope. Instead, photonic sensors were used. The camera mounted on *Colorado*'s photonics mast transmitted high-definition video images of the harbor. A southerly breeze propelled three-foot-high waves past the mast.

"Captain," Mauk said, "I think we've pushed our luck far enough. I recommend that we head back out. Sunrise will be on us within an hour."

Bowman peered at the image of the distant, blurry shoreline. "I'd sure like to take a look inside that sub base. We've never had anyone in there."

"Send a probe—from here?"

"Yeah, what do you think?"

"I don't recommend that. We don't have time."

"I think we do." He smiled. "Nice job bringing her in. I'll take it from here."

"Thank you, sir." Mauk keyed the bridge intercom mic, "Captain has the conn."

Colorado loitered for nearly half an hour, preparing an AUV for launch from a torpedo tube. Concerned about the delay, Captain Bowman called the torpedo room and connected with the senior AUV technician. "How much longer, Chief?" he asked, using a hand microphone.

"Another five minutes, Captain."

"What's taking so long?"

"We had a system error. Ran a diagnostic and found the problem. It's been corrected but I had to reboot the program, which is ongoing."

"Very well."

Captain Bowman turned to face his XO. "Damn electronics—just can't trust 'em."

Commander Mauk checked her watch. "Skipper, the sun's coming up now. I recommend that we depart and try later. The water's so shallow in here the hull could be seen by aircraft."

"Duly noted." Bowman turned to the officer of deck. "Raise the mast."

The OOD repeated the order.

Bowman turned back to Mauk. "I want to peek topside and then decide."

The main display flashed on as the photonics mast rose above the water surface. The eastern horizon glowed orange as the sun rose.

"Sun's coming up, Captain," Mauk reported. Bowman was about to respond when the chief sonar tech's voice broadcast over the control room intercom. "Conn, sonar. I have high-speed propeller cavitation approaching from the west. Estimate speed forty plus knots."

Bowman stepped to the sonar console, with Mauk in his wake. "Where exactly is it headed?"

"Straight for us."

"Shit!" muttered Captain Bowman.

Chapter 36

It was 8:25 A. M. at the Kremlin. The two men sat in baroque chairs facing each other across a table extension that projected from a colossal mahogany desk. The president of the Russian Federation preferred the seating arrangement for one-on-one visits to his office. It allowed Pyotr Lebedev to make intimate eye contact with those seeking an audience.

Today SVR director Borya Smirnov occupied the hot seat.

"Where are you with your special project?" asked the Russian leader. Lebedev had a husky build for his five-foot-eight height. Although he was in his mid-fifties, his brown hair remained full with just a trace of gray.

"The first phase of Operation Fall Harvest is nearly complete. The Chinese have swallowed the bait and we've set the hook."

President Lebedev smirked. An avid fisherman, he embraced Smirnov's metaphor. The SVR chief continued the briefing. "We've already detected an increase in military activities—subtle movement of army units to pre-positioned staging areas, a spike in training drills at key missile bases, and increased air sorties with practice bombing and air-to-air combat missions."

"What about naval units?"

"Minimal changes to date, as we expected. Both aircraft carriers remain in port as well as most surface combatants. That will change, of course, when their scheduled war gaming exercise commences."

"When?"

"About three weeks. They confirmed the exercise two days ago by issuing an international notice to mariners that its naval and air forces will be conducting training operations in the South China Sea. The notice did not specify the actual operating area."

The president cupped his hands with his elbows planted on the desk extension. "How are the Americans reacting?"

"Washington remains silent on the war game but asserts that its Navy will continue to operate in the South China Sea regardless of what China does."

"And Taiwan?"

"Taipei is nervous, which is consistent with China's past naval war games. As you probably know, the GRU detected an increase in communication chatter between various defense units on the island. In reality, however, all they can do is watch, knowing they'll be squashed if the mainland decides to put an end to their independence experiment."

"But Beijing may think otherwise now," the president said with a sneer.

"Yes, sir. I believe they are now spooked."

"Excellent news," President Lebedev said, pleased with the SVR's disinformation campaign. Both the Chinese and the Americans remained in the dark regarding Operation Fall Harvest. The operation had commenced a month earlier. While Russia continued to embrace mainland China as its new economic and military partner, the SVR in cooperation with the GRU utilized Russia's vast network of operatives in Beijing and Washington to sow the seeds of doubt and mistrust. Experts at manipulating foreign governments for decades, Russian intelligence agencies salted truth with fabrication, expecting that the recipients would connect the dots on their own.

Key to the manipulation was China's absolute rejection of a nuclear-armed Taiwan. China remained convinced that the United States would soon base nuclear-capable cruise and medium range ballistic missiles on the island—a complete fantasy but one that SVR chief Smirnov calculated would send Beijing into a frenzy. The United States unwittingly assisted the deception by increasing it resistance to China's adventurism in the South China Sea.

Relaxed, President Lebedev said, "Your plan to implicate the Americans. How is that proceeding?"

"On schedule, sir. The navy continues to prepare for the mission."

"What about the special unit?"

"They will arrive in Petropavlovsk-Kamchatsky later this week."

"Very good. And the scapegoat—how is that progressing?"

"The rumor about a defection was passed on to the PRC in Singapore as planned. Details of the defection were also conveyed to the MSS by our mole in the U.S. State Department. The news should have reached Beijing by now." Smirnov massaged his scalp. "We have a backup operation with another senior MSS officer in the works, too."

"Will they believe it?"

"We have good reason to think they will—it fits what will be logical to them. To avoid prison for espionage and to protect his American lover, Kirov will offer up everything he knows to the Americans about what China did."

The president rubbed his hands together. "I agree. That will make perfect sense to those backstabbers." Lebedev continued to smart from China's attempt to incite a war between Russia and the USA.

"That's what we are counting on, sir."

"Once Beijing believes the Americans know the truth, they'll be expecting a response."

"And we will provide that response."

The Russian leader broadcast an approving smile. "Yes, we will. Excellent work."

"Thank you, sir."

President Lebedev stood; Smirnov followed his lead.

The two men shook hands.

As the president escorted his visitor to the door he said, "Payback will be sweet, Borya."

"Yes, sir. Very sweet indeed."

* * * *

Four thousand miles east of Moscow, the two men walked along the shoreline at the North Sea Fleet submarine base in Qingdao. It was a warm muggy afternoon with a slight haze over the still harbor waters. They had the waterside walkway to themselves. Both wore matching white trousers and short sleeve shirts and head covers with gold braid—summer uniforms for the People's Liberation Army-Navy.

"We had a visitor last night after we docked," the younger of the pair said. Lieutenant Commander Zheng Qin was thirty-one years old, slim, of medium height with jet-black hair cut to regulation length.

"I heard," said Commander Yang Yu. Of similar statue to his subordinate, Yang had graying hair that marked his eight years of seniority.

"Scuttlebutt says it's the Americans again."

"No doubt."

Yang and Zheng walked in silence until they reached their destination. A dozen paces away from the gangway that led down to the floating pier, they stopped and peered seaward.

Moored to the float, the *Heilong*'s sleek rounded bow was in full view. The sail rose nearly twenty feet above the deck. Over 360 feet in length, the Type 095 nuclear-powered fast-attack submarine extended well beyond the floating pier it was moored to. Several other submarines occupied duplicate nearby piers. Those boats were shorter and diesel powered.

Named after the Amur River in the northeast sector of mainland China, the *Heilong* represented China's newest and most technologically advanced underwater warfare weapons system. The English translation of the warship's name was *Black Dragon*. The 1,700-mile-long Amur-Heilong River forms the boundary between Russia's Siberia and China's Heilongjiang province, which is part of Manchuria. The river basin is the tenth largest in the world.

The captain of the *Heilong* leaned against the guardrail that capped the steel bulkhead. Yang Yu peered seaward at his charge. The submarine sat low in the water, its black hull coated with sound-absorbing rubberized tiles. The forward escape hatch was open. An armed sentry stood on the hull between the hatch and a gangplank that provided access to the adjacent floating pier.

The *Heilong*'s second in command stepped next to Yang. Lieutenant Commander Zheng reached into a pocket and removed a pack of cigarettes. He extracted a Furongwang and lit up, not bothering to offer his boss one, knowing Yang was a non-smoker. "Captain, do you think that intruder was following us?"

Yang rested his elbows on the guardrail. "I've been thinking about it all day. Yes, I believe it followed us in."

The junior officer voiced a curse in Mandarin.

Yang said, "Apparently, our sonar is not as good as we were led to believe."

The state-run defense contractor guaranteed to the PLAN that its passive sonar hardware and software could detect any subsurface threat the American Navy might pose.

Zheng took in a long drag and exhaled. "They must have been waiting for us when we surfaced last night ."

"Let's hope that's what happened."

Zheng's eyebrows arched.

Yang continued, "We could have been followed long before reaching Qingdao."

"But we didn't detect anything on approach. It must have been loitering offshore. That's got to be it."

"Maybe—but why didn't the base's offshore bottom sensors pick it up?"

Dozens of passive sonar hydrophones littered the seabed offshore of Qingdao. Linked together by a network of buried fiber optic cables, the underwater listening posts transmitted acoustic energy detected by the seabed sensors to a mainframe supercomputer at the base headquarters building. The Chinese-developed system filtered the firehose stream of underwater racket, searching for unique acoustic sound prints of alien submerged craft.

"That is troubling, sir," Zheng said. "Fleet ordered us to dock at Qingdao instead of Jianggezhuang because of improved harbor security. Nothing should have penetrated those sensors." Located about ten miles east of Qingdao, Jianggezhuang was China's oldest submarine base and in need of an upgrade. Its direct exposure to the ocean provided easy access for interlopers.

"You're right," Commander Kang said. "The trespasser never should have reached the inner bay."

"But part of the system worked," Zheng offered. "One of the sentries picked up something—that's how we found out."

Zheng took one last drag and flipped the butt seaward. He turned to his left and peered back at another floating pier near where they had started their walk. A dozen small boats moored along the sides of the float. The cabin-less runabouts were each 33-feet long. Equipped with a bow-mounted machine gun turret, torpedo and depth bomb launchers, and a 14-foot-high mast populated with video cameras, dual radar domes, GPS unit, and multiple secure radio comms, the autonomous surface vessels—ASVs—mimicked similar robotic systems deployed by the U.S. Navy.

Commander Yang followed Zheng's gaze. "The system eventually worked, Qin, but it was too late."

Zheng frowned, unsure of his CO's direction.

"I checked with base security. The robot picked up a radar contact, not a sonar hit. It appears to have been a periscope or some type of mast."

"A sub—not an AUV?" Zheng had assumed the underwater contact was from an autonomous underwater vehicle, launched from an American submarine lurking offshore.

"Yes."

"Inside the bay?"

"Yes, about four kilometers south of the base."

Zheng peered at the nearby harbor opening and muttered another curse. He turned back to address his commanding officer. "Did the robot have any video evidence?"

The ASVs contained a full complement of optic sensors including high-definition infrared video with live streaming capability. The Qingdao Naval Base deployed its new fleet of ASVs at night and during inclement weather conditions. Manned patrol boats guarded the base during daylight hours.

"No. The contact disappeared before the robot arrived on scene. Its sonar didn't pick up anything either."

"Bastards—sneaking into our waters like that—must be the Americans again."

"I think their captain is what they call a 'cowboy'."

Zheng squinted.

Yang said, "Kind of reckless, a showoff. Testing us to see what they can get away with."

"Yes, cowboy, that does seem to fit," Zheng replied as another troubling thought jelled. "Captain, if this cowboy followed us before we arrived offshore of the base, where did he pick us up? During our entire mission, we did not make any submarine sonar contacts."

"If I had to guess, right now I'd say he was north, monitoring Rybachiy."

"And he tracked us the whole way back?"

"Yes."

"*Gāi sǐ*"—Dammit.

Chapter 37

Day 18—Wednesday

The *Novosibirsk*'s wardroom was spacious compared to the last nuke Yuri Kirov spent time onboard. The oak table with brass trim easily accommodated a dozen. This morning, just two others sat at the table besides Yuri—Senior Lieutenant Tumanov and Captain First Rank Leonid Petrovich. Petrovich summoned the two junior officers for the 9 A.M. briefing. He arrived the previous afternoon at the Rybachiy submarine base aboard a military air transport from Vladivostok. The *Novosibirsk* sailed into Avacha Bay that morning.

"Moscow has issued new orders," Petrovich said while cupping a mug of tea. "We need to be underway by early Friday morning."

"But sir, we're not ready," Yuri said, dazed by the news.

"I know it's sooner than we planned, but there have been new developments. The Chinese are making waves again."

"About the Americans?" asked Tumanov. Both he and Yuri watched a Russian government television news broadcast the previous evening at the officers' club. During a speech at the United Nations, the Chinese ambassador condemned the United States' decision to send a carrier strike group into the South China Sea. A day earlier, the USS *Ronald Reagan* and its armada of escorts departed from a port call in Sydney, Australia.

"Yes," Petrovich replied. "It appears the U.S. Navy is going to test Beijing once again. Fleet expects multiple territorial encroachments on Chinese bases in the South China Sea."

"That'll really piss 'em off," Tumanov said while running a hand over his shaved dome.

"No doubt."

In an attempt to establish control of the South China Sea, the PRC embarked on an aggressive program of creating dry land outposts from reefs and rock outcrops in the Spratly Islands, an archipelago located between Vietnam and the Philippines. By dredging bottom sediments and using the material as fill, China created seven artificial islands. Beijing claimed national jurisdiction over the islands and the waters and airspace within twelve miles of each island's shoreline. China also invoked economic control zones, reserving all natural resources within 200 miles of each island. The United States, China's South China Sea neighbors, and the International Court in the Hague did not recognize China's claims. To protect its investment, Beijing armed the islands with missile batteries, squadrons of fighter aircraft, and an armada of combat naval patrol vessels.

Captain Petrovich continued the briefing. "Fleet expects Beijing will deploy a significant number of its naval assets to intimidate the Americans as part of the PLAN's scheduled war games. That means they'll be massing ships soon. Moscow wants us to have our equipment in place before that occurs to monitor their preparations."

Yuri was uncomfortable with the change in plans. "Sir, they'll likely increase harbor defenses as they prepare."

"I know, but that doesn't matter. We have our orders. Understood?"

"Yes, sir."

"Now that you know the schedule, tell me your plan for implementation."

As the designated mission commander, Yuri responded. "First and foremost, we need to mate the *P-815* to *Novosibirsk*'s casing."

"Here, at the quay?" asked Petrovich.

"We could, using the dockside mobile cranes to lift and then lower the mini onto *Novosibirsk*. But since we have so little time to prepare, I think it would be best to try it in the bay with *Novosibirsk* submerged. It'll be harder that way, but it will provide Tumanov and his team real-world experience."

Petrovich considered Yuri's request, draining his mug. "That makes sense from an operational point of view." He looked toward Tumanov. "Have you ever operated your mini on a boat before?"

"Ah, yes, sir. We trained with the *Barrakuda*."

"Using a cradle?"

"Yes, welded to hard points on the hull. Worked well."

"I assume you can oversee installation of the cradle onto my boat?"

"Certainly, sir. It's already quayside, ready to go."

"Good. How about provisions?"

Yuri signaled for Tumanov to continue. "I'll need to top off the fuel and oxygen tanks for the power plant. Our breathing gas supplies are at one hundred percent. Other than that, we're ready to…" Tumanov's voiced tailed off as an errant thought materialized. He turned to face Yuri. "Ah, sir, what about the special equipment you ordered?"

Petrovich tilted his head. "What special gear?"

Yuri said, "I contacted a couple of former colleagues at the St. Petersburg base. They've been working on new diver-deployed autonomous underwater probes. They're supposed to send two prototypes out. I thought we'd take them along and if the opportunity presents itself, we'll deploy them rather than the normal recorders."

"What's so special about them?"

Yuri described the capabilities of the spy gear.

"When are they supposed to arrive?" Petrovich asked.

Yuri checked the notepad he carried. "The flight is supposed to touch down here tomorrow evening. But you never know."

All three officers were well aware that the Pacific Fleet and especially Petropavlovsk-Kamchatsky were at the opposite end of the country. Scheduled air service by military transport was less than reliable. Mechanical breakdowns, crew unavailability, and harsh weather all contributed to delays.

"Interesting. Maybe the gear will be on the same flight?"

"Sir?" Yuri said.

"You're going to have two additional passengers—specialists, also from the St. Petersburg base."

"What kind of specialists?"

"Naval Spetsnaz. They are bringing some of their special equipment, too."

Yuri took a deep breath. "Sir, is there more to this mission than just installing recording devices?"

"I don't know. Moscow has not provided me any details on the Spetsnaz mission. We'll be briefed when they arrive."

* * * *

"What the devil?" muttered Nick Orlov.

Nick was in his office at the Russian consulate in Houston. It was mid-afternoon. He was halfway through a routine monthly personnel activity report from the Vancouver Trade Mission's security officer. It was part of

Nick's duties as SVR *rezident*. Besides Houston, the consulate monitored Russian outposts on the west coast of North America—Mexico City and Vancouver. Nick's office kept track of the whereabouts of all Russian nationals under its jurisdiction.

Nick read the entry again:

Trade delegate Elena Krestyanova resumed her duties at the Mission after completing a special assignment in Moscow. She continues to coordinate her activities in Western Canada and Northeast Asia. She completed a three-day trip to Hong Kong with a stopover in Vladivostok before returning to Vancouver.

Stunned, Nick set the report aside. *It can't be. Something's wrong!*

Nick attacked his keyboard, calling up an encrypted file of all personnel in the Vancouver Trade Mission.

Shit! Nick turned away from the PC monitor, still in shock.

How could they bring her back?

Nick's report to SVR director Smirnov four months earlier had been damning. Convinced that Elena was traitor, he laid out all of the facts. He was certain that she would be locked up for years—or worse.

She was working for Kwan and she screwed over Yuri! Why isn't she in prison?

How come no one told me?

Nick was about to call Moscow demanding answers when doubt set in. Elena clearly schemed against Yuri and orchestrated the abduction of Laura and Madelyn at the bidding of the MSS—this Nick knew from personal observation. *But could that have been part of her cover?*

Throughout the ordeal—just months earlier—Elena consistently maintained that she operated under SVR directives to infiltrate the MSS with goal of turning Kwan Chi into an intelligence asset for Russia.

But Nick still couldn't buy it. The damage she inflicted ran deep. *They must be running her as a triple.*

While she had originally been assigned by the SVR to turn Kwan Chi into a Russian agent, Nick was certain that Elena succumbed to his charms and the Ministry of State Security's fat wallet. But when Moscow discovered her treachery, Elena returned to her roots to save herself.

That's got to be what's going on!

The bombshell news conflicted Nick. *Working for the MSS against Russia and then returned to the fold without penalty?* And then there was their affair. Nick still cared for Elena—deeply.

I had no choice but to turn her in—but was I wrong?

Nick spent the next few minutes mulling over the revelation, planning multiple moves ahead. Hazards littered the chessboard he played. Yuri remained unapproachable, still on his secret mission aimed at China. He needed to know about Elena's change in status, but Nick was powerless to sound the alarm.

Laura Newman was under investigation by the FBI, but Nick could not warn her. He too was hounded by federal agents along with others in the consulate. He had picked up on another tail this morning during his commute. And use of his cell or even a burner was risky. The Americans were capable of intercepting any electronic communications directed to Laura Newman.

Nick had no choice but to back off and wait for the heat to abate. In the interim, Laura would have to fend for herself.

* * * *

"Hello, Amanda," Laura said as she walked from the kitchen into the living room. It was 5:50 P.M.

"Hi, Laura."

Amanda and Madelyn were on the rug next to the coffee table. As toddler Maddy propped herself against the table, she inspected the stable of toy horses she just finished lining up on the tabletop.

Laura knelt next to her daughter. "Hello, sweet pea," she said beaming. Maddy's face brightened into her trademark dimpled smile. Laura caressed Madelyn's angel-soft ash-blond hair. "Are you having fun with your horseys?" Maddy cooed a response as Laura kissed her forehead.

"We had lots of fun today," Amanda said as she moved from the rug to a nearby sofa. She launched into her review, something she did every day when Laura returned from work. "We went to the park this afternoon. The weather was perfect. Maddy had fun on the swing and then…"

Laura listened, asking for an occasional detail or clarification. So far, she was pleased with Amanda, who was always unpretentious and dutiful concerning Maddy when around Laura. The anxious mom hoped Amanda acted the same when she was at work. Laura had yet to install the nanny-cam she had purchased earlier in the week. She remained ambivalent as to whether she should spy on Amanda. It would have been so much easier if Yuri were around. He would know what to do.

Laura relocated to the kitchen carrying Madelyn on her right hip. "What would you like for dinner tonight?" she asked as she opened the refrigerator door. She removed a Tupperware container filled with organic vegetables she'd pureed the previous evening—carrots, sweet potatoes, and green peas.

After placing Maddy in her highchair, Laura warmed the blended vegetables in the microwave and took a test bite to make sure they weren't too hot.

"Here you go, Munchkin," Laura said as she held the baby spoon to Maddy's lips.

Madelyn turned her head to the side with sealed lips.

"Come on, honey. This is good for you."

Amanda walked into the kitchen and observed the standoff. "I fed her a bottle about half an hour before you arrived."

"Well, then, maybe we'll try this a little later." Noticing the windbreaker Amanda wore and the handbag she carried, Laura asked, "Taking off?"

"I'm meeting Tom at the Red Robin and then we're going to a movie."

"Great. Have fun."

"We will."

Laura relocated to the deck. She traded in her Armani pantsuit for a sleeveless blouse and a pair of Chaser lounge shorts. Maddy sat inside her playpen next to Laura's deckchair, busy with her horses.

As Laura watched the sun sink in the western sky, her thoughts turned to Yuri. Over two weeks had passed and not one word from Yuri. *Where are you?*

* * * *

"How much longer do you think we're going to have to babysit her?"

"I have no idea. Taylor doesn't share anything about this case."

The two male FBI agents sat inside the surveillance van three blocks from the Newman residence. It was dark outside; the sun had set half an hour earlier. The nondescript van moved to a new location every couple of hours. The video monitor displayed the feed from the camera in the living room. Laura Newman sat cross-legged in a sofa typing on her laptop.

"She goes to work. Comes home. Watches the kid for an hour or so before putting her to bed. She then works for another hour and goes bed. Boring. Boring. Boring."

"Hey man, this babe is one smart cookie. You see how nice this place is?"

"Yeah, I know she's loaded. I read the background report, just like you."

"So, what's your problem?"

"She's rich. She should be out there—enjoying herself. Like the other fat cats do."

"She's not like that."

"No kidding."

Chapter 38

Yuri knocked on the door. He was on the fourth floor of an apartment building in Petropavlovsk-Kamchatsky, a dozen blocks away from the north shore of Avacha Bay. It was late afternoon. Hearing footsteps on hardwood flooring, he braced for what was to come. The door opened.

"Hello, Alma," Yuri said with a glowing smile.

The twenty-six-year-old redhead remained frozen in place for a couple of seconds before a hand raced to her mouth. "Yuri!" she said, plainly stunned.

"Do you have a little time to talk?"

"Of course, please come in."

They sat at the kitchen table. The one-bedroom overlooked a forested area. Alma had just brewed a fresh pot of tea.

"Thank you," Yuri said after she filled his mug.

Alma topped off her mug and set the pot on the table. Recovered from the shock of the unannounced visit, she said, "How long have you been at Rybachiy?"

"About two weeks."

Yuri did not volunteer anything further, and Alma chose not to probe. As the widow of a submariner who'd assisted Yuri in highly classified underwater intelligence gathering operations, Alma accepted the secret world her husband had embraced.

Yuri took a quick look around the neat and clean modestly furnished apartment. In a corner of the adjoining living room on the top of a small table was a color photograph of Senior Warrant Officer Viktor Skirski.

Mounted on the wall near the official Russian Navy portrait was a simple cross. Viktor's determined expression, encouraged by the photographer, did little to diminish his boyish good looks. Yuri's heart fluttered as he recalled the last time he spoke with his friend and submate.

Yuri looked back at Alma. "Where's your son?"

"Napping."

"How old is he now?"

"Alek will be two next month."

The revelation hit Yuri with the impact of a Mack truck. *Maddy—her birthday was last week!*

Yuri recovered. "He must keep you busy."

Alma smiled. "He's a delight, a real chatterbox. "

Yuri listened as Alma went on about her son. He asked questions that eventually led to Alma's job.

"I'm a clerk at the base," she volunteered. "I guess the base commander took pity on me. Anyway, I help with keeping track of supplies and deliveries for the commissary." She ran a hand through her hair. "What really helps is I can leave Alek at the base daycare center while I'm working."

Alma's parents remained in Moscow. Viktor's mother, a widow, resided in St. Petersburg.

"Did the Navy provide you with any benefits from…" Yuri couldn't finish the question.

Alma heaved a sigh. "No death benefit but I do receive a modest pension based on Viktor's service. With that and my job, we're doing okay."

"I'm pleased to hear that." Yuri had worried that Alma and Alek might end up on the breadline. She'd married Viktor at eighteen and because of his frequent changes in duty stations, Alma never had the opportunity to attend college. She was exceptionally sharp with mathematics and during secondary school expressed interest in becoming an engineer.

Yuri continued, "I don't know what the Navy told you happened but—"

Alma cut him off. "They told us nothing—only that there was an accident and over half the crew was lost." Tears rolled down her cheeks. "Most of the wives were able to bury their husbands. But not me. All I have is a letter—a stinking letter from an admiral in Vladivostok saying Viktor died in the service of Russia. Died for what?"

"I'm sorry, Alma. Sometimes our government is coldhearted." Yuri rubbed his chin. "I wanted you to know that Viktor gave his life trying to save the survivors of the accident. He was incredibly brave."

"He was?"

"Yes—truly."

"Can you tell me what happened?"

"It was a rescue dive, very deep and extremely dangerous. There was an equipment failure—with his breathing gear."

"Oh, dear God."

"He went peacefully."

"You're sure he didn't suffer?" Her eyes teared again.

"It was like falling asleep."

"You were with him?"

"He went first—braver than anyone else. I followed and found him."

"His body—what happened to it?"

"We had a service at sea to honor his remains."

"Where?"

Yuri wanted to tell the truth but could not reveal mission details. "All I can say is that it was in the North Pacific Ocean."

Alma asked a silent prayer before meeting Yuri's eyes. "Thank you for telling me, Yuri." She wiped a droplet from her cheek. "You have helped me find a little more closure. I'm grateful."

* * * *

Yuri returned to the Rybachiy base. It was 8:55 P.M. Alma insisted he stay for dinner, which allowed him to meet Alek.

Yuri sat in a well-used chair beside the window of his room. He held his iPhone. The BOQ building was equipped with Wi-Fi. Ready to tap the screen and launch the transpacific call, he hesitated. A moment later, he switched off the cell. "Too risky," he muttered.

It was his last opportunity to call home yet it would have been a grave security breach. The GRU monitored all communications at the base. Yuri's orders prohibited any personal international calls, texts, or emails.

She's asleep anyway. It was nearly two o'clock in the morning in the Seattle region.

Yuri set the cell on a side table and peered out the window. The frugal quarter's one distinguishing feature was its third-floor view of Avacha Bay. As the sun retreated, he could still see the *Novosibirsk* moored at its berth several hundred yards away. Attached to the casing behind the sail was the minisub *P-185*.

The mating process had proceeded in textbook fashion during the morning. While Yuri observed from *P-815*'s control center, Lieutenant Tumanov and his crew maneuvered the midget over *Novosibirsk*'s partially submerged aft deck. They centered the mini's mating collar over the submarine's diver module hatch while simultaneously lining up key hull points with the steel cradle welded to *Novosibirsk's* deck. Divers checked the automatic locking clamps, verifying the mini was secured to the attack sub's casing.

After coupling with the midget sub was completed, Captain Petrovich ordered the *Novosibirsk* to the deepest section of Avacha Bay where the *P-815* and its host submerged. Like a baby humpback whale huddling with its mother, they dove into the deep.

The *Novosibirsk* conducted two test dives in the bay and then left the harbor. It conducted half a dozen deep water dives in the Pacific offshore of Petropavlovsk-Kamchatsky. Satisfied with the mating arrangement, Petrovich guided the *Novosibirsk* back to its berth.

When Yuri returned to the base after visiting Alma, he learned that the transport jet carrying the equipment he had requested from Peter was late. It was due to land just before midnight. The two special operators Captain Petrovich mentioned were also aboard the air freighter. The *Novosibirsk* would still depart at 2 A.M. Yuri had already packed his gear and planned to board at one o'clock.

The presence of the new players worried Yuri. *Naval Spetsnaz—why are they here?* Yuri questioned Tumanov on the subject but learned little. The *P-185's* crew had trained with special operators in the past but never participated in any real missions.

Yuri's thoughts shifted again to Alma and her son. He could see Viktor's likeness emerging in Alek, broad forehead, angular jaw, and brunette hair. It reminded Yuri how Maddy favored her mother. *She'll be just as beautiful.*

Yuri pictured Laura's dazzling face, heard her cheery laughter. *I miss you so much!*

Still reclining in the chair, Yuri watched as the last vestiges of sunlight faded. Base lighting already illuminated the quays and floating docks of the sub base. A new thought reemerged, one he'd purposely suppressed.

I had no choice—I had to do it.

Four months earlier while aboard Kwan's superyacht the *Yangzi*, Yuri fired twice, both rounds striking the target. It was a split-second decision—kill or be killed.

Yuri's foe fired first but missed him; instead, the errant round plowed into Elena's Krestyanova's shoulder.

The awful truth that Yuri took another human being's life weighed profoundly on him.

Yuri stood. The officers' club remained open until eleven o'clock.

He needed a nightcap, maybe two.

Chapter 39

Underway for seven hours, the *Novosibirsk* with the *P-815* riding piggyback was 660 feet below the surface heading south at twenty knots. The hydraulically efficient teardrop geometry of the minisub's hull resulted in minimal drag, allowing the combination to slip silently through the abyss. The towed sonar array stretched 1,000 feet behind the rudder, its sensors tuned to identify telltale sounds of other submerged submarines. The acoustic sensors in the bow-mounted spherical dome and running along each side of the hull also listened. The *Novosibirsk*'s chief sonar technician reported to Captain Petrovich that they were alone in this stretch of the North Pacific Ocean.

While the executive officer commanded the *Novosibirsk* from the attack center, Petrovich held a mission meeting in the officers' wardroom. It was 9:05 A.M.. Attending were Yuri, Lieutenant Tumanov, and the two new arrivals. Tea was served. The men sat around the mess table. The special operators from St. Petersburg were in their late twenties, confident and all business.

"Captain Petrovich, how close to the target area can you ferry the mini?" asked Lieutenant Mikhail Shtyrov. He was in charge of the two-man Spetsnaz detail. Average height with a barrel chest, muscled arms, and thick neck, his physique telegraphed wrestler.

"It depends on the defensive posture of the Chinese. If the approach is lightly patrolled, we'll probably drop the mini off ten to twelve kilometers away." Petrovich wore a one-piece cobalt-blue jumpsuit that stretched from neck to ankle and a pair of sneakers—the standard issue uniform while aboard the *Novosibirsk*. Yuri and the others in the meeting wore the same apparel.

Petrovich continued, "If the approach is hot, we'll have to turn you loose further out, maybe even beyond the territorial limits."

Shtyrov turned to face Tumanov. "If we encounter submarine nets, how will you counter them?"

"Sonar should detect their presence. We'll then use our video system to swim over or around any nets or other obstructions."

"But let's say your sensors don't pick up the netting and you run into it, what then?"

"Send out a diver and cut our way through. We carry cable cutters and other gear."

Chief Petty Officer Vladimir Dobrynin spoke next. "Lieutenant, does your vehicle have the ability to hover close to the bottom, say two meters above it?" With a slim build, Dobrynin was a few inches taller than Shtyrov. His close-cut russet hair accented his handsome facial features—strong jaw, Roman nose, and trimmed eyebrows.

"Yes, of course. It's not a problem. Why do you ask?"

"It'll be easier for us to move our equipment if we can let it drop to the bottom and then assemble the parts."

Yuri decided to join in. "Your gear, I'd like to know more about it. What kind of recording equipment is it?" Prior to departing Rybachiy, he watched as the naval Spetsnaz operators loaded their gear aboard the minisub. They did the work themselves, declining assistance from *P-815*'s crew.

"Routine acoustic monitoring gear, sir," responded Shtyrov. "But new improved models. Built into the casing is a mini buoy antenna system. On a preset schedule, every week or longer, the buoy is released—during the night. It pops to the surface and broadcasts an encrypted signal to an overhead satellite, providing a summary of what it picked up during the monitoring period. After the transmission, the buoy is reeled back into the pod to repeat the process."

"How long will your pod remain operational—using the buoy system?"

"Easily a year, assuming weekly transmissions. Maybe a little longer." Shtyrov said. "If the transmission schedule could be increased to every ten days or so, we might get another six months. The buoy retrieval system uses a lot of power."

Yuri was aware that the system described was under development prior to his last official mission.

Petrovich weighed in. "That should work well for our needs, Lieutenant." He next addressed Yuri. "What about the gear you're going to install?"

"I'll lock out and use the DPV to get in position to release the package."

"How far?"

"Each site is different and depends on harbor defenses. On average, I'm planning on a ten- to twelve-kilometer round trip."

"That's quite a way underwater."

"I know. But in order to have best chance for success, the closer I can get to the quays, the better it will be."

"These devices—how do they work?" the captain asked.

"They burrow into the bottom and—"

"How deep into the bottom?' interrupted Petrovich.

"Depending on the substrate—silt, sand or clay—anywhere from a quarter to half a meter deep." Anticipating a follow up question, Yuri continued. "The purpose of burying the units is to hide them from divers or AUVs that might check the bottom."

"How big are these things?" asked Lieutenant Shtyrov.

"I thought you might all be interested in that." Yuri reached under the table. "I brought a couple." He retrieved a canvas bag at his feet and placed it on the table. "This is one of the units," he said with just a trace of a grin as he removed the device and set it on the conference table. About a foot and a half in diameter with a six-inch-high domed profile, the high-tech spy gadget was similar in shape to a sea turtle's shell. Constructed of rugged epoxy plastic, it weighed about fifteen pounds.

Yuri's audience gawked at the creature-like object.

"Officially, it's called Project X One Five One," Yuri said. "Unofficially, we refer to it as the Remora."

"How does it work?" asked Captain Petrovich.

Yuri reached into a pocket of his jumpsuit and removed a key fob. He pressed one of the buttons.

The Remora sprang to life as ten aluminum mini leg-like struts protruded from its underside, five on each side. "Looks like a giant crab," muttered Petrovich.

CPO Dobrynin peered at the underside of the gadget, its base now elevated about three inches by the legs. "Are those suckers?" he asked, pointing to several cup-like rubber knobs protruding from the bottom.

"That's right, Chief. They're designed to grab hold and hang on, just like the remora fish you see on sharks."

"Grab what?" asked Lieutenant Tumanov as he examined the underside.

Yuri picked up the Remora, flipping it upside down. He triggered the fob and the legs retracted into the main body. He stepped to a nearby bulletin board fastened to a bulkhead. A duty roster, maintenance schedules, and other non-digital paraphernalia covered the board. Yuri picked a clear spot and placed the Remora on the board, holding it in place with his right hand. With his free hand, he pressed another button on the fob.

The suckers worked in unison, responding to a vacuum pump inside the robot. Yuri removed his hand. The robot remained in place, its underside flush with the board.

Yuri gestured to Dobrynin. "See if you can remove it, Chief."

Dobrynin stepped to Yuri's side. "Just grab it?"

"Yes, try to pry it free."

Dobrynin grabbed the Remora with both hands and pulled.

No movement.

He tried twisting.

Again, no movement. He braced himself and yanked hard, grunting in the process. "It won't move," he said, defeated.

"Nice try, Chief. Once it becomes attached to a host, it's damn near impossible to remove without the release command. Hang on to it again and I'll let it go."

Yuri pressed the fob. The robot dropped into Dobrynin's hands. He returned it to the table next to Tumanov.

"Just what is this thing supposed to attach itself to?" Captain Petrovich asked.

"The hull of a submarine—like the *Novosibirsk*."

Petrovich glared at Yuri. "Please elaborate."

"The Remora has been under development for several years at a robotics lab on the St. Petersburg base. It's designed to function just like you thought—a crab. In particular, it was modeled after the common rock crab, but much larger."

Petrovich gestured for Tumanov to pass the Remora his way.

While Petrovich examined the gadget, Yuri continued, "Once it's released, it will crawl along the bottom to a designated location and bury itself. It will then wait for the target to depart its mooring and—"

"But how will it know that?" interrupted special operator Shtyrov.

"It has a mini hydrophone that deploys as it buries itself in the muck. Looks like a twig." Yuri extended an arm, pointing at the dome side of the Remora. "It releases from this compartment with a tiny cable."

Yuri returned to his chair. "It sits there quietly listening, waiting for a reactor to start up. That process is relatively noisy for a sub that's been on shore power. The Remora's computer compares the sounds it detects to startup recordings for dozens of different types of submarine reactors. If it detects a similar pattern, that signal will be enough to activate it."

"But the Chinese boats may not have the same startup procedures," Petrovich said.

"Correct. The same applies to the American, British, and French subs. The Remora uses artificial intelligence software to assess whether what it hears is a probable reactor startup or not. It's already been field tested on several subs plus one of our surface nukes."

"What happens after it detects a reactor start?"

"It waits. The Chinese, just like the Americans, use divers to inspect all submerged hull surfaces before departing on a mission."

"Of course, we do the same," Petrovich said. "Looking for limpets or other types of mines or trackers."

"Yes, sir. After confirming reactor activation, the Remora waits until the boat moves away from the pier on its own power—divers would be out of the water at that time." Yuri said. "It has a bladder inside, similar to a ballast tank. After confirming departure, it backs itself out of the mud and inflates the bladder using gas from an internal high-pressure cylinder."

Yuri picked up the Remora and turned its underside up for all to view. "Now neutrally buoyant, it swims to the hull, homing in on the reactor area." Before the obvious question was asked, he once again activated the fob. Two openings about an inch in diameter appeared at either end of the device. "There's a hydraulic jet pump inside. Propels the Remora like an octopus—quite agile. Fast and silent."

Yuri continued the briefing. "It swims to the underside of the hull and flips over. It then attaches itself to the bottom. The suckers work well on steel surfaces and all known coatings and tiles." He referred to the rubber-like anechoic tiles used on modern submarines to absorb sound energy from active sonar and to attenuate internal noise generated by the sub.

"What about biofouling?" asked Lieutenant Shtyrov.

"Not a problem. The suckers work on algae-coated surfaces, even with barnacles."

Petrovich grinned. "The sub is just a giant shark. This thing gets a free ride."

"Exactly, Captain. But in our case the Remora is just getting to work."

"Please enlighten us, Kirov."

"The Remora is loaded with sensors. Besides internal hull acoustics, it records water depth and temperature and provides a record of where the sub operates."

"How does it do that?" asked Tumanov. "GPS doesn't work underwater."

"Correct. It has a micro inertial navigation module that continuously keeps track of heading and distance. Combined with the depth recording, a complete profile of the sub's mission can be resurrected when the data is recovered."

"And just how is that accomplished?" Petrovich said.

"Two options are available. First, it can wait until the ship returns to its original departure point or wherever it docks next and switches to shore power. It will recognize the reactor shutdown. The Remora detaches, sinks to the bottom and then crawls away from the target vessel. Later, during darkness it surfaces and broadcasts its data to one of our satellites. It sinks back to the bottom, digs itself in and self-destructs."

Lieutenant Shtyrov rejoined the discussion. "What's the other option?"

Yuri took a swallow of tea. "The second opportunity allows for quasi real-time tracking of the host."

That grabbed Captain Petrovich's attention. "That sounds interesting."

"It is, sir. Very clever."

Yuri spent the next five minutes describing the Remora's alternative tracking system.

"Incredible, Kirov," Petrovich said. "I've never heard anything like that before."

Yuri drained his mug. "Captain, amazing as the Remora is for tracking subs, the boys at Peter developed another modification that is truly unique." Yuri reached under the table and retrieved a similar but smaller version of the Remora already sitting on the table.

"This one is called the Crawlerbot," Yuri announced. "It's not designed to attach itself to a sub. Instead, its purpose is to secretly explore and record naval installations."

Yuri opened the device's cargo compartment. He extracted one of the objects stored inside the compartment, a tiny mechanical device that looked like an insect. Yuri held it in the palm of his hand. "Gentlemen, meet the Firefly."

"What is it?" asked Captain Petrovich.

"It's a miniature aerial drone that has mind-blowing capabilities."

Petrovich smirked. "Tell me more."

Yuri did.

Chapter 40

The two men sat inside a Toyota Highlander on State Route 520 heading into Redmond. Both men were in their early thirties. Each was dressed casually—designer jeans, short sleeve shirts, and track shoes. They had arrived in Seattle the previous evening on a non-stop flight from Shanghai, traveling with tourist visas.

It was 6:35 P.M. and the freeway remained sardine-packed. The Friday afternoon eastbound lineup stacked up for over a mile back to the Microsoft campus. The driver tapped his hands on the steering wheel. "This damn traffic is almost as bad as Shanghai."

"It's awful all right," the passenger concurred. "But at least the weather is better here."

"Warm but no humidity—that is nice."

The MSS agents spoke in Mandarin. The passenger checked the navigation display on his cell phone. "After she exits, it should clear up. When it does, don't get too close—she might spot us."

"I won't."

Laura Newman was five vehicles ahead in her BMW, inching forward.

The agents picked up Laura when she drove out of the parking garage of Cognition Consultants in downtown Bellevue.

* * * *

"Amanda, I'm running a little late. Five-twenty stinks again." Laura continued to crawl forward on the freeway off ramp as she phoned the nanny.

"That's okay. Don't worry about it."

"I probably have another fifteen minutes before I make it home."

"No problem."

"How's Maddy?"

"Fine. She's napping."

"Okay, see you soon. Good-bye."

"Bye."

Laura settled back into the leather seat. She had used the dashboard hands-free phone system to make the call. See issued a new verbal command: "Call Bill Winters's cell."

The phone rang twice. "Hello."

"Hi Bill, Laura here."

"Oh, hi."

"I'm heading home now and thought I'd just check in to see how you and NSD are doing."

"I'm well and so is the company, especially after you sweet-talked Aurora. That extra time really helped."

"I'm happy to hear that."

Several days earlier, Laura had called the CEO of Aurora Offshore Systems. She requested a two-week extension for the commencement of NSD's survey of a new Alaska offshore lease tract for the oil exploration company. When the oilman learned that Yuri's significant other was calling on behalf of NSD, he took the call. After Laura explained she was pinch-hitting for Yuri while he tended to an ailing sibling, the CEO agreed to the extra time without hesitation. Earlier in the year, Yuri and the NSD crew helped Aurora climb out of a very deep pit. The chief executive remained grateful.

Winters said, "We're all set to head up to Barrow next week and start the work. We have a workboat lined up, and the weather's looking good."

"How's the oil spill cleanup going?"

"Still a mess."

"Will that impact your survey work?"

"It'll be a nuisance but we'll work around it. Most of the time *Deep Guardian* will be submerged under pack ice, out of the spill zone. "

"Good."

Winters changed subjects. "How's John?" he asked, using Yuri's alias.

"Okay. I haven't heard much other than he seems to be coping."

"Any idea when he'll be returning?"

"Not yet. Everything's still up in the air."

"How's his sister doing?"

"Not well."

"I'm sorry to hear that. That's got to be tough on John—and you."

"It is." Laura invented the affliction—lung cancer—for Yuri's phantom sibling.

"Please tell him I said 'hi' next time you talk to him. Everyone here misses him."

"I'll let him know."

Laura pulled onto East Lake Sammamish Parkway NE and headed south along the lakeshore.

* * * *

"Here she comes," announced FBI Special Agent Todd Rossi.

His boss swiveled in her chair to view the wall-mounted flat panel screen. A silver BMW four-door turned off the public street and drove onto a hillside driveway. "She's a little late today," Special Agent Michaela Taylor said.

Rossi and Taylor occupied a private home near the Newman residence.

"I wonder if she'll order out again tonight."

"What's wrong with that?" Taylor glared at her charge.

"She doesn't seem to cook much."

"She's tired, Todd—works all day and then comes home to care for her daughter. Give her a break!"

"She must be up to something."

"I'm not so sure. She's just a single mom working her butt off."

"But she's loaded. Where'd all that money come from?"

Michaela retrieved an inch-thick file folder from the tabletop and tossed it onto the desk where her assistant sat. "Read her history then you'll see how she earned her way."

Rossi picked up the document and thumbed through it. "I know. I've seen this before." He set the report back on the desk. "It just seems to me that she must have had help to get where she is—all that money and still so young." Rossi's voice grew animated as a new thought flashed. "Maybe the Russian government set her up—like in *The Americans*."

"The TV show?"

"Yeah. Maybe she's an illegal and this Kirov fellow is her handler. He might be back in Moscow right now getting new instructions."

Taylor rolled her eyes. "Newman is not a plant. We know she was born here."

"But then why is she living with the guy?"

"My guess is that he's been using her as cover. Somehow, he won her heart and she takes care of him, not knowing he's really manipulating her."

Rossi rubbed his eyes. "I suppose that's possible." He checked his wristwatch: 6:55 P.M. "We've got a long night ahead. I think I'll brew a pot."

"Good, we'll need it."

Taylor and Rossi would be relieved at six in the morning. Michaela would never have been able to remain with the Bureau without her widowed mother's help. Her mom cared for the girls while Michaela pulled all-nighters and worked late at the office.

The FBI continued to monitor the Newman residence, but the around-the-clock team of agents no longer needed to use the van. Instead, they occupied a 4,400-square-foot contemporary four houses away. Technical staff had completed installing the equipment the previous afternoon.

The main floor of the home had a terrific western view of Lake Sammamish, but Agents Taylor and Rossi occupied a windowless utility room in the basement. Multiple widescreen displays mounted to a wall provided real-time surveillance of the interior and exterior of the target residence.

The FBI rented the home, using one of its surrogate businesses to execute the transaction. The bogus company signed a one-year lease, ostensibly as quarters for a visiting executive. If needed, the FBI would have purchased the home.

The investigation of Russian operative Yuri Kirov and his presumed American accomplice Laura Newman was now the number one case in the Bureau's Counterintelligence Division. FBI Headquarters ran the entire investigation from D.C.

Chapter 41

The MSS agents sat inside the parked Toyota SUV on the shoulder of the public street. The asphalt driveway that led to Laura Newman's home was adjacent to the right front fender of the Highlander. At a few minutes past three o'clock in the morning, there was no traffic on the road.

"Her house is down this drive."

"I don't see it. Trees are in the way."

"Here, look at this." The passenger peered at the Google Earth image displayed on the driver's smartphone. "This is where we are," the driver continued, pointing a finger at the edge of the road. "The driveway winds down the hill to the house."

"It's secluded. Is this only access point?"

"We could try coming in from the sides, but the vegetation is too thick. The driveway is our best bet on foot."

"When do we go?"

The driver checked his wristwatch. "I want to get this over with. Let's get going now."

"Where do you want to park?"

The driver again pointed to the Samsung's screen. "This side street up ahead should work."

"Good, let's do it."

* * * *

"What are they doing?" asked Michaela Taylor. She eyed the video monitor that displayed the feed from the high-def camera mounted to a telephone pole.

"Just sitting there." Todd Rossi sat at his desk, staring at the same video image. Set to infrared mode, the camera broadcast black and white images.

"Same vehicle?"

"Yep, plates match." Rossi checked a notepad beside his PC. "This makes the fourth drive-by. These turkeys are definitely up to something."

"I don't like this. Something's up, all right. Can you get any closer? I'd like to get a look at 'em."

"I'll give it a shot."

Rossi worked the PC's keyboard. The video image blinked, displaying a magnified view of the front end of the SUV. The heads and shoulders of the two front-seat occupants were visible but remained grainy.

"That's the best I can get," Rossi said.

"They could be anybody."

"Maybe they're Russians, trying to make contact."

"Maybe...but then again, these guys might be crooks, casing the place."

"Yeah, all of the homes around here are worth at least—" Rossi stopped as the Toyota pulled back onto the road. "They're leaving."

"Try to get better visual as they drive by the camera."

"On it."

A minute passed. Agent Rossi enhanced an infrared flash screen shot of the Highlander as it neared the HD surveillance camera.

Michaela stood behind Rossi, eyeing the PC screen. She squinted. "Asians."

"Yeah—not what I was expecting."

"They're definitely up to something."

"What do you want to do?"

"We need backup. I'm going to call Seattle and ask for help."

* * * *

Twenty minutes passed. Agent Rossi continued to monitor the video feeds on the main control panel. All fourteen cameras were live. The cameras inside the residence broadcast color images. The exterior feeds remained in night vision mode.

Michaela Taylor walked back into the surveillance room after visiting the kitchen to refill her coffee mug.

"Anything?" she asked while reclaiming her chair next to Rossi.

"Quiet—nothing new."

"Maybe I jumped the gun."

"Backup should be here soon. How do you want to—shit! Look at that!" Rossi pointed to the street monitor.

Two individuals crept along the edge of the roadway. They were about fifty feet from the Newman driveway. Although dressed in black, their body heat registered as gray tones on the video display.

They stopped at the edge of the light cone from a decorative pole fixture that illuminated the entrance to the Newman driveway.

"Home in on 'em," Michaela ordered. The screen blinked as the camera zoomed in on the pair. "Damn—they're armed," Rossi said.

Both men carried pistols in their hands. One of the men aimed at the light. The street light blinked off. Unaffected by the action, the video feed from the FBI's street cam remained unchanged.

Stunned, Rossi said, "They're using suppressors. What should we do?"

Michaela Taylor reached for her cell. She hit a speed dial. "Taylor here, what's your ETA? Dammit, step on it. Armed intruders are approaching the house as we speak."

"How long?" asked Rossi

"They're fifteen minutes out."

"This could be over by then."

"I know."

"What do you want to do?"

"Let me think."

* * * *

Laura woke when the telephone on the bedside table blared. It was a landline, rarely used.

She reached for the handset, noting the time on the adjacent clock: 3:33 A.M.

"Hello," she said, her tone showing annoyance.

"This is your security company. There are potential intruders on the grounds. Please activate the perimeter lighting and take protective shelter immediately. The police are on the way."

"What?"

"Please, there isn't much time. Activate the perimeter lighting and take protective shelter."

Laura tossed the phone aside and launched herself out of bed. She sprinted into Maddy's room, picked up her daughter, and wrapped a blanket around her sleeping form. Laura raced down the long hallway, passing through a door that opened to another hall that led to the guest quarters over the garage. Laura used her free hand to bang the door.

"Amanda, wake up!" she yelled.

Madelyn's nanny opened the door, clad in a T-shirt and panties. "What's going on?"

"Alarm company called. Someone's trying to break in. We need to get into the saferoom."

"The what?"

"Please, just follow me."

The trio returned to the master bedroom. Laura stepped into Yuri's walk-in closet. She pushed aside a rack of his shirts and removed a wood trim panel on the back wall. Inside was a key code reader. She punched in the code. The hidden door rotated inward.

Handing Maddy to Amanda, she said, "Quick, get inside."

Amanda complied while Laura pulled the shirts back in place and replaced the wood trim over the key pad. She stepped inside the safe room, flipped a light switch on, and closed the door.

The room was just eight feet square with two folding lawn chairs and a foot locker next to the far wall. A security alarm panel was mounted to the wall next to the door. Laura triggered the exterior lighting system. She opened the locker and removed the weapon.

Amanda's eyes widened as Laura racked the Mossberg 12-gauge 500 Tactical Adjustable Stock shotgun.

* * * *

"Where are they now?" asked FBI Special Agent Michaela Taylor.

"I'm not sure. When the lights came on, they bolted into the brush." Rossi pointed to the edge of the video screen. The camera monitored the south side of the home.

Michaela spotted movement in one of the other monitors. "Locals are rolling in now."

A police cruiser raced down the driveway. Half a minute later, another cruiser pulled into the parking court. Both officers got out of their vehicles with pistols drawn.

Michaela picked up her cell and speed dialed. The phone was answered on the first ring. "Center."

"This is Taylor again. I need you to call Newman and let her know the local police have arrived."

"Yes, ma'am. Will do."

The FBI call center functioned twenty-four-seven, available for undercover and stakeout operations. When Michaela first called the center, she provided the basics to the on-call facilitator located in Washington, D.C. The female agent in the headquarters building called Laura Newman, issuing the warning. She next called the Sammamish Police, masquerading as Laura's security alarm monitoring service. The line was untraceable.

"Now what?" asked Rossi.

Michaela checked the master bedroom monitor. "They're still in the saferoom, so they're okay for now." She scanned the remaining monitors. "I don't think those guys are burglars."

"Not with suppressors." Rossi checked his wristwatch. "Our backup team should be arriving any minute."

"Tell 'em to come here for now. I don't want to have to explain to the Sammamish cops what we're doing—at least not yet."

"Roger that."

Michaela thought about calling her boss but decided to wait. The immediate crisis was over. Still, uncertainty plagued her. *What's going on here?*

Chapter 42

Forty-seven hundred miles west of Sammamish, Washington, the *Novosibirsk* continued its southbound track. Underway for over forty hours after departing Petropavlovsk-Kamchatsky, the submerged warship paralleled the Kuril Island chain. It would soon pass through Le Perouse Strait near the northern end of Japan's Hokkaido Island and enter the Sea of Japan.

The attack submarine was navigating 500 feet below the surface. Yuri was aboard the *P-815*. He had entered through the minisub's lockin-lockout chamber after passing through the *Novosibirsk*'s diver access module. He was alone in the compact galley and mess compartment. Lieutenant Tumanov and his crew, along with the two Spetsnaz operators, remained sleeping aboard the *Novosibirsk*.

The mother sub was massive—390 feet long and almost fifty feet in diameter. Yet, like most warships, it was packed with equipment, supplies and people. There was no privacy. For the next couple of hours, Yuri would have the mini to himself.

Sleep eluded him. Anxiety over the pending mission left him restless. He cherished the solitude as he sat at the four-person mess table. Laid out in front of Yuri were a navigation chart and a collection of aerial photos. Yuri had expected the mission to be directed at the Jianggezhuang submarine base, located east of Qingdao. Jianggezhuang was China's oldest nuclear-powered submarine base and the homeport of ballistic missile submarines. However, orders from Vladivostok sent over an encrypted satellite communication network called for the *P-815* to spy on a PLAN submarine berthed at the Qingdao Naval Base.

Qingdao served as the homeport for the North Sea Fleet's squadron of diesel-powered subs, but recent satellite imagery revealed that one of China's newest nuclear attack boats, a Type 095, also moored at the base. Fleet mission planners targeted the Type 095 for underwater reconnaissance. Russia considered it a direct threat to its own submarine force.

Captain Petrovich had expressed his reservation about the approach to Qingdao. Commercial vessel traffic into and out of the harbor would help mask the *Novosibirsk*'s minuscule sound print, but new intelligence updates from Vladivostok suggested the People's Liberation Army-Navy had increased harbor sonar sweeps. Onsite GRU assets noted a flurry of daytime activity by antisubmarine warfare craft within the inner harbor area and offshore waters. ASW corvettes and patrol boats constantly ran transects as if conducting a coordinated search. An uptick in unmanned patrol craft was also observed in the evenings and early mornings. At first, Yuri and Petrovich thought the Chinese were running an exercise. However, when radio reports from Vladivostok indicated the activity continued into the next day, doubt set in. *Something must have spooked them.*

But what?

Yuri tossed the photo aside. Standing, he walked aft into the accommodations compartment and climbed into one of the bunks.

Lying on his back, he settled into the mattress, arms clasped behind his head. The *P-815* was tomb quiet, its engine and generator shutdown. Electrical power from *Novosibirsk* powered the minisub.

Yuri could hear the faint rush of water next to the hull. He closed his eyes. His last conscious thoughts were of Laura.

* * * *

Laura Newman stood in the foyer of her home, talking with two King County deputy sheriffs. The City of Sammamish contracted with the county for police services. Sunrise was about an hour away.

"What have you found?" asked Laura.

"Some footprints around back, but nothing else."

The deputy was young—mid-twenties, over six feet with a rugged build. The name tag on the chest pocket of his shirt displayed *Halvorson*. His Latina partner was about the same age but diminutive, barely over five foot four and slim. Her name tag read *Fernandez*.

"Are they still out there?"

"Doubtful, ma'am. You certainly have an impressive perimeter lighting system. I suspect they bugged out as soon as it was triggered."

"Ms. Newman," Fernandez said, "do you have exterior sensors for the lights?"

"Yes, for lights around the house itself, but the lights along the edge of the woods are manually controlled." Laura brushed a hand through her hair, realizing she must appear disheveled in her robe and pajamas. "The deer and other wildlife were constantly triggering the system and one of the neighbors complained, so we disengaged the auto function."

"We?" asked Halvorson.

"My partner programmed the computer. He's out of town."

"So, it's just you and the young lady with your child?"

"Yes. Amanda Graham is Madelyn's nanny."

Amanda had returned to her apartment after placing the still asleep Madelyn in the spare crib in Laura's bedroom.

Fernandez jotted a couple lines on a notepad. "The intruders must have triggered some kind of alarm to have woken you."

"I guess so. The alarm company called and woke me up. Said there were intruders on the grounds and requested that we take shelter, which we did—in our saferoom."

"So, they must have called us, too?" Fernandez asked.

"They said the police were coming."

"Which security company is that, ma'am?" asked the male cop.

Laura recited the name and the officer recorded the information.

"If you don't mind me asking, where is your saferoom?" Halvorson asked.

"In our bedroom." Laura reluctantly decided it was time to reveal another factor, knowing it would eventually come up. "It was installed several months ago along with the enhanced outdoor lighting system... ah, after the home invasion."

That admission spiked the interest of both officers.

"Could you provide us with background on that?" Halvorson asked.

"My daughter and I were abducted. A ransom was paid and we were released unharmed. It was done without police involvement, as demanded by the kidnappers."

"Wow," Officer Fernandez commented. "We've heard nothing about that."

"We cherish our privacy. Anyway, we have cooperated with your department." Laura mentioned a detective's name.

"Okay, we'll check in with him."

Laura yawned. The adrenaline rush was over.

Fernandez smiled. "We'll be out of here soon, ma'am."

Laura waved a hand. "That's okay. I'm thankful you're here."

Fernandez glanced down at her notes. "Do you think what occurred tonight could be related to what happened before—the abduction?"

Laura retained her neutral face. "I don't think so. There have been burglaries in this area, as you know."

Fernandez smiled. "Yes, ma'am, we do."

Halvorson added, "We'll make another walk around before heading out."

"Thank you. I really appreciate it."

"No problem, ma'am."

The police officers drove out of the driveway five minutes later. Laura relocated to Yuri's home office. She replayed the security camera videos, stored on a dedicated hard drive. The outdoor cameras revealed nothing.

Laura switched off the monitor.

They were probably kids, looking for an easy way in to rip-off stuff to buy drugs.

Laura headed back to her bedroom, unaware the FBI had saved the lives of Maddy, Amanda, and herself.

Chapter 43

Day 23—Monday

FBI Supervisory Special Agent Ava Diesen walked into her boss' office. It was 8:35 A.M. in Washington, D.C.

"Excuse me, John," she said standing in the threshold of the open door. She held a file folder. "I need to run something past you."

Deputy Assistant Director for Intelligence John Markley looked up from the Dell monitor on his desk. "Sure, come on in." He pushed his keyboard to the side.

Ava took a seat facing Markley. "It's about the Seattle op."

"The missing GRU officer?"

"Yes, we're still looking for him but something troubling has happened." Ava reached into the file and removed a grainy black and white photograph enlarged to eight by ten. "The woman Kirov is living with, Laura Newman, had unwanted visitors early Saturday morning. They were armed with suppressed weapons."

Markley frowned as he reacted to the image. The blowup of the surveillance video frame revealed two individuals in all black apparel. Each carried a handgun with an extended barrel.

"Who are these guys?"

"We don't know, but they were casing Newman's residence. Our people running the surveillance became so concerned that they initiated imminent threat protocols."

"Was our op blown?"

"No. Our measures worked. The perps bugged out. Neither the local police nor Newman was aware that we intervened."

Ava slid another photograph across the desk. "One of our cameras picked up two men in an SUV driving by Newman's driveway earlier. We think they were surveilling the place."

Markley studied the photo. The blowup showed the front of the Highlander. Through the windshield, two males were visible.

"Asians?" he said, looking Ava's way.

"That's our assessment."

Markley again examined both photographs. "She's been targeted."

"I think so."

"Anything on the vehicle?"

"Rental—from the airport." Ava checked her file folder. "Someone named Chou from Shanghai. We checked with Homeland. He arrived at SeaTac Airport on a tourist visa a couple of days before the incident."

"No doubt a bogus name. What about the other one?" Markley placed the photos on the desk.

"We're still checking."

Markley scratched an ear. "What have you learned about Newman since your last briefing?"

"Squeaky clean. There've been only a couple of telephone conversations where John Kirkwood aka Yuri Kirov's name has come up. She's been consistent in her response that he's attending to family matters—an ailing sister."

"I assume there's been no contact from him."

"None that we've recorded." The federal warrant authorized monitoring of all of Laura's communications—residence landline, cell phone, business phones, Internet, and even her snail mail at the local Post Office.

Markley clasped his hands. "She may be an innocent party to whatever Kirov's been up to."

"It's possible but we just don't know yet. I'm still perplexed about her acquisition of the underwater tech company that Kirov has been running. What's that about?"

"Technology transfer?"

"Maybe," Ava said. "The file says he was assigned to submarines."

Markley again picked up the photos of the gunmen. "These guys might be coming back."

"I agree."

"Have you coordinated with the local PD yet?"

"No, they remain in the dark about our surveillance."

"Okay, let's run a BOLO on these turkeys, see if we can pick 'em up."

"Will do, John. I'd also like to beef up our security measures in case they come back."

"Go ahead."

Chapter 44

Day 24—Tuesday

"How much time do we have?" asked the president of the People's Republic of China.

"Maybe a week, perhaps two." The Chief of Staff of the People's Liberation Army-Navy faced his boss across an elegant teak desk.

"What can the Americans do?" asked President Chen Shen.

Admiral Soo Xiao squirmed in his seat. "They will likely condemn us in the United Nations and then impose economic sanctions."

"Military activity?"

"We just don't see that happening," Soo said. "They have no solid evidence that directly implicates us."

"Sinking the oil tanker and blowing up the pipeline—I'd say that's solid evidence."

"But our cover story remains intact. All they have or will have are allegations from the Russians."

President Chen was not sold. "The Americans will believe Kirov."

"I understand your concern, sir. But please consider that the weapon was obliterated when the *Yangzi* caught fire and blew up. In fact, we now think that it was the Mark Twelve that detonated, which resulted in the sinking."

"How could that have happened?" Chen tapped his left foot on the carpet. Over an hour had passed since his last cigarette.

"Kirov might have sabotaged the device."

"Didn't our people check it?"

"We don't know. Kwan Chi claims the *zhongdui* officer in charge of the operation checked the Mark Twelve after recapturing the ship and told him it was safe."

"Sounds like something might have been missed."

"Yes, it does."

Chen stood up. "I need a break."

"Of course, sir."

Admiral Soo followed China's president through a rear door in the office into a hallway that led to a stairwell. After ascending two flights, the two men stood under a covered roof awning located at the peak of the mid-rise tower. It was a miserable afternoon, sticky hot with no hint of a breeze. Beijing's world-class smog shrouded the spire, spoiling the view of the sprawling metropolis.

The president lit up, enjoying his fifth Marlboro of the day. Soo endured the stench without comment.

Screened with tinted, bullet-resistant glass panels to prevent snooping eyes from nearby buildings, the smoking palace provided the president with a convenient location to indulge his principal vice half a dozen times each day.

Chen was halfway through the smoke when he said, "Admiral, you may be right about the Americans' reaction, but what about the Russians?"

"We believe they remain in the dark about Kirov."

"But Moscow knows something happened. Besides Kirov, they had SVR agents aboard the yacht."

"Correct. But all they know is that the yacht was involved in an operation directed against the United States—not Russia."

Chen took a deep drag. "Washington will no doubt blackmail us with this information."

"That's possible."

"It's what I would do."

"Yes, sir."

"Is there any way that we can get to Kirov? Without him, the Americans will have nothing."

"Guo Wing and his people, along with the *Eu Bu,* are looking at that option. The FBI has him rat-holed somewhere. It's unlikely they will find him anytime soon."

"What about his woman?"

"Despite the initial setback, the operation is still underway."

The president was privy to the scheme engineered by Guo Wing and his MSS operatives. The money trail would lead to the SVR. The Americans would conclude that Moscow hired the gunmen to kill Laura Newman as revenge for Yuri Kirov's treason.

President Chen crushed the butt in an ashtray stand. "Let's hope all of this works, Xiao. We need to string them along to give us time to get ready."

"So, you have decided to continue with Sea Dragon."

"Yes."

* * * *

President Chen returned to his office. Admiral Soo had just departed. Chen poured himself a second cup of coffee, another of his vices. He had fifteen minutes before his next meeting and welcomed the downtime. Doubt consumed Chen as he settled into in his chair. Admiral Soo's steadfast bearing helped bolster Chen's apprehension over reauthorization of Operation Sea Dragon. Still, the dread remained. *We're sinking deeper into the abyss each day and I can't stop it!*

Two years earlier, the Standing Committee of the Central Political Bureau of the Communist Party of China, aka the Politburo Standing Committee, mandated that Chen address the American problem. He was the logical choice.

Groomed for high office in the Communist Party due to his father's influence as a government minister, princeling Chen Shen earned a BA from Cornell and an MBA from Stanford University. The six years he spent in the United States provided him the opportunity to study the enemy's strengths and weaknesses. Although he led a pampered life as a student and was constantly monitored by the MSS to ensure his protection as well as prevent him from straying, Chen admired America by the time he returned to his homeland. *They're good people—generous people.* Chen also respected the freedoms American citizens enjoyed, knowing such liberties were impossible in China under his party's rule.

Nevertheless, the quality of life in China was improving under authoritarian capitalism. With an expanding middle class powered by a colossal export machine and a burgeoning military, China was on the verge of earning superpower status. One obstacle remained.

Washington continually tries to box us in! They block us on every front—fearing our eventual dominance.

The United States government's policy toward China could be summarized in one word: containment. *They say we don't trade fair. We trade to win—whatever it takes. That's in our DNA!*

They chastise us on human rights, claiming we abuse our citizens. We are different from the West—our people need strong leadership at the top that extends downward to all levels. We are surrounded by enemies. Our military must be able to protect the homeland and secure our economy.

Several years earlier, the economic forecast authorized under secret decree by the Politburo Standing Committee had cast the first warning. China's export juggernaut had peaked. The model predicted a steep decline in annual growth with cascading consequences. Tens of thousands of state-run enterprises were identified as in jeopardy. Operated inefficiently for decades and ripe with corruption, the government-owned companies could not compete on a global level without continual renourishment from the central government. But with growth slashed, China's cashflow also tanked. Severe pushback from the United States on China's predatory trade practices further aggravated the state of affairs. The once endless gusher of yuan was drying up. President Chen's and the PSC's principal worry was jobs. *It's already started! Twenty thousand lost just this week!*

No longer able to prop up the SREs that could not compete, Beijing had no choice but to allow the slaughter. The economic model predicted stability if half of the SREs were shut down. But the price was astronomical.

Forty million jobs! How can we ever allow that to happen?

The middle class would take the brunt of retooling China's economy. With looming massive unemployment, the Communist Party's days would be numbered. China's next revolution was already in the making, and that realization struck fear in every member of the Politburo Standing Committee.

We must divert the workers' attention to provide time to make the transition.

Operation Sea Dragon was the designated diversion. The invasion of renegade Taiwan and its return to the homeland would galvanize the populace. Confiscating the island's assets would bolster China's wealth. Legions of unemployed mainlanders would take the jobs of the hapless Taiwanese.

The one obstacle to the PSC's grand scheme was the United States. *The original plan would have worked wonders. Let Russia and the USA beat each other's brains out and then we take Taiwan—a real cakewalk.* But not now. Chen and the PSC no longer wondered if the USA would help defend Taiwan. Recent intelligence reports revealed the Americans were about to base military assets on the island.

It can still work, but we must catch them by surprise.

Admiral Soo can do it!

Chapter 45

Yuri sat at the *Novosibirsk*'s wardroom table with Captain Petrovich and Lieutenant Tumanov. Petrovich had called the meeting.

"Well, gentlemen," Petrovich said, "we'll be arriving offshore of Qingdao in about ten hours. It will be dark then—twenty-two hundred hours local." He pointed to the paper navigation chart. "Depending on what we encounter, I plan to release the *P-815* in this area."

Yuri eyed the chart scale and made a quick estimate. "Sir, that's about twenty-five kilometers out. It was my understanding that we'd have a shorter run."

"I know, but the situation has changed. Vladivostok just provided an update. The *Liaoning* returned to its berth in Qingdao along with its escorts."

Tumanov groaned and Yuri's spine stiffened. The *Liaoning* was China's first aircraft carrier and the pride of the North Fleet. When a warship is at anchor or moored alongside a pier or wharf, it is essentially defenseless—vulnerable to a host of hazards that include aerial attack, underwater sabotage and assault from shore.

Petrovich continued, "With *Liaoning* and its strike group docked at Qingdao, I think you both know what that means."

"Harbor defenses will be at maximum," Tumanov offered.

"Correct. With almost the entire North Fleet beached, you can expect the PLAN will deploy all assets to provide maximum protection."

Yuri said, "Captain, do we have any idea how long the *Liaoning* battle group will remain at berth?"

"Fleet estimates a couple of days, and then it'll head south."

Yuri turned to face Tumanov. "We'll really have to watch out for their ASVs." Yuri referred to autonomous surface vessels—unmanned patrol craft controlled by artificial intelligence software.

"How capable are they?"

"Very. They can swarm and overwhelm a target with multiple units. Similar to what the U.S. Navy uses."

"Are these the ASW craft for which the Chinese got access to the software?"

'Yes," Petrovich said. "It was stolen from the American contractor that developed the AI system for the U.S. Navy."

"That means it works well."

"I'm afraid so."

Yuri picked up one of the aerial photos stacked on the table. He pointed to the image of Qingdao while facing Tumanov. "Lieutenant, perhaps we should make our approach by hugging the eastern shoreline and staying on the industrial side of the harbor. We could then head toward the center of the bay for deployment."

Petrovich glowered. "You'll still have a long swim to the sub base— maybe five to six kilometers."

"I know. That's about maximum range with a DPV, so we'll really have to watch power usage."

"That sounds marginal, Kirov. The entire mission will be blown if any of you end up stranded and captured by the PLAN."

"I understand, sir."

"Well, you and Tumanov rethink your plan." Petrovich stood, signaling the end of the meeting. "Remember that we've got to repeat the same process for the East and South Fleets. Our activities cannot be detected at any of the locations."

Yuri and Tumanov stood and Yuri spoke for both of them. "Understood, sir."

* * * *

One hundred fifty-two nautical miles northwest of the *Novosibirsk,* the two-hour briefing at the Qingdao Naval Base concluded. The commanding officers and executive officers for the twenty-two warships based at the People's Republic of China's naval base attended the top-secret meeting.

The *Heilong*'s CO and XO were dining together at the officers' mess in the naval station's headquarters building. Less than a year old, the sprawling four-story structure occupied a prime section of waterfront along Jiaozhou Bay. The two men sat at a table in a corner, away from the clamor of the main dining area. Both ordered noodles and steamed bass with green tea.

They continued to decompress from the briefing where they learned the *Heilong* would soon be heading to the South China Sea along with the majority of the North Sea Fleet to participate in China's largest maritime exercise.

"The Americans will be watching us during the entire operation," offered Lieutenant Commander Zheng Qin.

"I'm sure they will—just as we do to them," Commander Yang Yu said.

"I don't like it. They want war."

"I'm not sure about that. We might be pushing a little too hard."

Zheng looked up from his plate, his brow crumpled. "What do you mean, Captain?"

"Our South China Sea policy. The rest of the world does not see it our way."

"But they're wrong. The Nanshas are ours. We discovered the South Sea Islands 2,000 years ago!"

"I know the history, too, Qin. But remember, we lost the case with the Philippines."

"That tribunal in the Hague—what do those morons in Europe know about our waters?" Zheng boosted his voice. "What gives them the right to judge us?"

"Calm down. You're too emotional over this."

Heilong's executive officer exhaled. "Sorry, sir."

"Regardless of how you and I may feel about the situation, we have orders and we will carry them out."

"Yes, sir."

The *Heilong*'s first task was to escort the *Liaoning* battle group to Hainan Island, where the ships would join the rest of the taskforce assembling at the Yulin Naval Base. While the taskforce prepared, the *Heilong* would remain at sea, sanitizing the war game site near the Spratly Island group.

Commander Yang took a bite of bass before continuing. "As you correctly noted, the taskforce will be watched the entire time by the Americans. They will have at least one submarine shadowing everything we do."

"We should force them out. Those are our waters. They should not be allowed to spy on us."

Yang almost rebuked Zheng a second time but contained himself. His young second in command remained brainwashed by Communist doctrine, which limited his ability to see beyond lockstep protocols. To survive in subsea warfare, Yang knew from experience that the commanding officer of an attack submarine must remain flexible in his response to the ever-changing battle environment. Following rules without seeing beyond the "cube" was a pathway to a sinking.

"Consider our task as a blessing, Qin. We will be allowed to seek out and identify any unknown submerged contacts. We can run through the full fire control procedures on a real target. We can't actually fire but it will force the Americans into countermeasures."

Zheng smiled, the light turning on. "And we'll be listening at the same time. We'll learn much about their evasion maneuvers."

"Exactly."

With their meal finished, Yang and Zheng refreshed their mugs. Executive officer Zheng remained fixated on the U.S. Navy.

"Sir, what did you think of the Americans when you observed RIMPAC?"

"Courteous, competent, and very confident."

Commander Yang had served as an observer aboard a PLAN destroyer that participated in the previous year's Rim of the Pacific naval exercise. Twenty-two nations, forty-eight ships, six submarines, over 250 aircraft, and 27,000 personnel participated in the month-long exercise that took place around the Hawaiian Islands and off the California coast. China's contingent consisted of five ships but no submarines. Beijing declined to send a submarine for fear of spying by the West.

"What did you think of their ASW capabilities?"

"Lethal. Their systems are superior to ours." Commander Yang's principal task was to assess antisubmarine warfare tactics employed by the U.S. Navy and its allies. It was a true eye-opener.

Zheng slumped in his seat. "I've heard that before, too."

"The new Boeing platform is particularly concerning. They had several at RIMPAC." Yang pursed his lips. "Just one of those jets was able to orchestrate the hunt for the target sub in the main exercise—a nuclear powered boat from Great Britain. The Poseidon coordinated with four destroyers and half a dozen helicopters to track and then execute a kill—within just three hours."

The U.S. Navy's P-8A Poseidon Sub-Hunter was based on the Boeing 737 airframe.

"Hmmm," mumbled Zheng. "At least we won't have to worry about that during the exercise."

"Not for in-water monitoring. That would be too provocative. But you can be certain the Americans will have aircrafts watching from a distance—possibly a Poseidon."

Zheng was still agitated. "I suppose they'll also have one of their new hunter-killers shadowing us."

Commander Yang nodded. "You can count it. Might even be the same one that followed us into port."

Yang referred to the U.S. Navy's *Virginia*-class fast-attack submarine. Nearly 380 feet long with a beam of thirty-four feet, the $2.7 billion nuclear powered vessel was packed with cutting-edge electronics and weapon systems envied worldwide, especially by the PLAN. The *Virginia*-class boats could operate in shallow brown-water situations just as well as deep-blue conditions. The *Heilong* and its sister nukes lacked shallow water maneuvering capability.

Zheng reached into a shirt pocket and removed a pack of cigarettes. He was about to light up when Yang pointed to a nearby wall sign. PLAN bureaucrats recently decided to implement a new program to prohibit smoking in mess areas. Zheng frowned and returned the Furongwang to the pack.

"The damn Americans spread their crap everywhere. I can't even enjoy a smoke after a meal now."

Commander Yang smiled. "Sometimes they have good ideas."

"You watch. Before long they're going to take away the smoking compartment on the boat."

Yang laughed. "You're probably right."

* * * *

Commander Yang jogged along the park pathway. It was late afternoon. After lunch with Zheng, he had attended to a stack of digital paperwork aboard the *Heilong* before returning to his apartment in northeast Qingdao. He changed into running gear and set out on a ten-kilometer run. Situated on a hillside, the park provided scenic overviews of the sprawling city of nine million. He enjoyed his posting to Qingdao. The seaport city was a pleasing blend of modern building construction and traditional Chinese architecture. Tucked between the surrounding hills and broad reaches of Jiaozhou Bay, the coastal city lived up to its moniker as China's Sailing City. The smog enveloping portions of the city was not nearly as awful as in Beijing and other thriving regions throughout China. The ocean breezes helped flush away the after-products of the region's spectacular commercial growth.

Yang approached a lookout. He could see the peaks of elegant towers marking the navigable sections of the Jiaozhou Bay Bridge. With an overall aggregate length of nearly twenty-six miles, it ranked as the world's longest overwater bridge.

Yang jogged in place at the overlook, now facing southwest. In the distance he could see the naval base. The towering superstructure of the aircraft carrier *Liaoning* was visible along with dozens of other warships. But his command sat too low in the water.

Soon, the *Liaoning* taskforce would set sail with the *Heilong* clearing the path ahead. Yang looked forward to the challenge but remained apprehensive. The *Heilong* and its crew were ready—that was not the concern. Nor was it the Americans and their powerful naval forces. The discussion with his mother the previous evening lingered.

Yang's parents resided in his hometown of Langfang, located about thirty miles south of Beijing. He sensed trouble as soon as Ling called. Eventually, she confessed. Yang's sixty-two-year-old father, Jin, had lost his job. After graduating with a mechanical engineering degree, Jin worked for nearly forty years at the same company—a state-owned enterprise that manufactured knockoff replacement parts for American-manufactured automobiles and trucks. He worked his way up the political hierarchy of the business from junior plant engineer to senior operations engineer to shift supervisor and, finally, to general manger. After years of losses resulting from political graft and deliberate inefficiency to maintain scores of unnecessary jobs, Beijing tired of propping up the company. The central government stopped its annual infusion of capital that had ensured the business's solvency. The plant closed and all employees were let go, most without severance pay.

The folding of Jin Yang's employer was not an isolated event. Dozens of state-owned enterprises throughout China collapsed each week. The PRC's unholy fusion of capitalism and communism had run its course. Commander Yang's father was fortunate compared to most of the fired employees. He received a modest severance package—six months' salary. But it was not enough. Yang's parents were careful with their money. They consistently saved at least twenty percent of Jin's monthly pay, which was not unusual for China's evolving middle class. Although the Yangs had amassed a sizeable nest egg, the Chinese government limited the interest banks could pay savers, and it prevented most citizens from moving their savings abroad for higher returns. That left just two alternatives: the wildly fluctuating Chinese stock market and real estate.

The Yangs opted for real estate. They poured most of their life savings into an upscale condominium apartment building in Lanzhou, purchasing two units on the twenty-fifth floor. They shelled out $300,000 in cash to the developer. The promise was twofold: appreciating unit value and high rents from lessees. For several years, the units appreciated but remained unrented. The Yangs were patient, knowing renters would eventually come knocking on their door.

After six years, the units remained vacant, as did the entire building along with neighboring towers throughout the development. The Ponzi scheme was in freefall. To spur growth and create jobs, the Chinese government purposely maintained low interest rates to encourage real estate developers and builders to reinvent China. It worked far better than the central planners had expected. With cheap loans, the builders went to work creating spectacular housing developments throughout China, erecting new modern cities on a vast scale. And with limited investment opportunities, the middle class climbed aboard. The result was a frenzy of building and buying.

There was one problem, though. The new residential developments catered to the middle and upper-class Chinese and were priced accordingly. Unfortunately for the investors, many of the new cities were constructed in regions where the populace could not afford to purchase, let alone rent, the apartments. The multitudes living near the boom cities were barely above peasant status. They were lucky to have enough left over each year to buy a new bicycle.

Yang's mother cried when she revealed the awful truth. His parents' retirement plan was in shambles. They might be lucky to receive twenty cents on the dollar—if they could ever find a purchaser.

Although it had not come up in their conversation, Yang sensed what was coming. *They will want to come and live with me.*

It was not unexpected but just sooner than he had planned.

I need to care for them.

Yang had a spacious apartment with a water view, which he cherished. And he was often away at sea for months at a time. *Yes, it could work.*

But there was a downside. His mother would surely restart her campaign about offspring.

He would counter with his usual mantra—he had not found the right woman. And besides, there were so few of them. China's one child per family policy had decimated female birthrates for decades—parents always preferring a male to carry on the family name. Still, there was another hitch.

What about Tao?

Yang feared his parents would eventually discover the true reason for his aversion to marriage. He and Tao had a longstanding relationship. The married businessman who owned a thriving restaurant in the financial district of Qingdao hooked up regularly with Yang when he was in port.

As a senior military officer and the commander of one the People's Republic of China's most lethal weapons system, Yang was destined for flag rank. But his career would be in jeopardy if his sexual orientation were revealed.

Yang headed west along the pathway, picking up the pace. He would have to call Tao when he returned to the apartment.

Chapter 46

"Up periscope depth," ordered Captain Petrovich.

The watch officer echoed the command and ten seconds later the mast rose eight feet above the surface of the Yellow Sea.

Petrovich and the entire attack center team viewed the dark waters and even darker night sky. Four-foot-high swells rolled in from the northeast. Like the American *Virginia* class, the *Novosibirsk* employed photonics instead of optics. The high-definition video camera mounted to the periscope mast transmitted crisp images to an outsized flatscreen panel display mounted to a forward bulkhead.

"Switch to night vision, Captain?" asked the executive officer.

"Not yet." Petrovich used a joystick hand control connected to his pedestal-mounted captain's chair to rotate the camera lens to the port. After it traveled about thirty degrees of arc, smudges of light appeared in the video image. He next worked the focus control until the shore lights sparkled in crystal clarity. Petrovich swiveled in his chair to face the two observers who stood on the starboard side of his command station. "Well, gentlemen, there's your target."

"How far out are we now, sir?" Yuri asked as he took in the lights of Qingdao.

"Twenty-two kilometers."

"Any chance we can come in a little closer?" Tumanov asked.

"No. We've been lucky so far—no submerged contacts and just routine commercial traffic on the surface."

For the past six hours, Petrovich had followed an inbound container ship using the vessel's noisy propeller to further mask the *Novosibirsk*'s miniscule sound print as it transited the shallow sea.

"The entire fleet must be docked by now," Yuri said.

"That's consistent with what Vladivostok reported."

Yuri checked his wristwatch: 2157 hours. It was set to local time. "Sir, we should get underway now. We need all the dark we can get."

"Agreed. You men head aft and prepare for separation at 2230 hours."

Kirov and Tumanov left the attack center, heading aft with Tumanov in the lead.

When they entered a narrow passageway, Tumanov stopped and turned to face Yuri. "I sure wish he'd launch us closer in."

"He's being careful."

"I know, but if we have problems inside the bay, twenty-two kilometers is a long way to get back here."

"Yakov, just follow your training and you'll be fine."

"I understand, sir. But what really bothers me is our passengers."

"What do you mean?"

Tumanov made a quick check of their surroundings. They were in a corridor that bypassed the reactor compartment. It was vacant. Most personnel chose not to linger in that section of the ship. "Have you noticed how guarded they are about their equipment?"

"It's highly classified."

"I know. But just the same, I find them standoffish. I think they're hiding something."

Yuri frowned. "They're spooks—like me."

Tumanov looked confused.

Yuri realized he used the English word. "They're with the GRU. Spies, like me."

Lieutenant Tumanov altered his stance. "Well, sir, with all due respect, I still believe they aren't being upfront with either of us." He reached into a pocket of his jumpsuit and produced a plastic item about the size of a credit card. Yuri recognized the dosimeter. Everyone aboard was required to carry one. It recorded radiation exposure. Both Yuri and Tumanov had similar cards clipped to the chest pockets of their jumpsuits. Russian nukes—even new ones like the *Novosibirsk*—were notorious for accidental radiation releases.

"I know this isn't the best place to be showing this." Tumanov removed a small electronic reader from another pocket and inserted the card. He then handed the device to Yuri.

"It's been exposed," Yuri said after he scanned the electronic readout.

"Yes, it's low level but there shouldn't be anything other than background on it."

"What about your badge?"

"Clear."

Yuri unclipped his dosimeter and inserted it into the reader. *Thank God!* Yuri looked back at Tumanov. "Where did this exposed card come from?"

"The cargo compartment of the mini."

"Why check there?"

"There's one in every compartment on the mini. Standard operating procedure when we're mated to a nuke."

"Hmm, okay." Yuri went on, "What about the other compartments?"

"All clear."

"And the rest of your crew?"

"No exposure—just like our own cards."

Yuri searched his brain for an explanation. "You think the radiation source is coming from the gear Shtyrov and Dobrynin brought aboard?"

"Their recorders were stored inside that compartment with the dosimeter. The rest of our equipment is clean."

Yuri considered the facts until an explanation clicked. "I bet I know what's going on. The recording units have a low-level radiation source for some kind of power backup system. They're designed to sit on the bottom for months."

"Have you used units like that before?"

"No, but I've read about the concept."

"That must be it, sir." Tumanov lowered his eyes. "Sorry to bother you."

"Don't worry about it. Good job on letting me know." He held up the exposed dosimeter. "I'd like to keep this. I need to let Shtyrov know he's got some kind of leak."

"Very good, sir."

* * * *

Yuri and Tumanov relocated to the *P-815*. Tumanov manned the pilot's console while the rest of his crew occupied their duty stations. Yuri entered the minisub's storage compartment. Lieutenant Mikhail Shtyrov and Chief Petty Officer Vladimir Dobrynin were checking gear. They both knelt on the deck next to the recording device. The black cylinder was about eighteen inches in diameter and two feet long.

"Hello, sir," greeted Shtyrov.

"We're about to decouple from *Novosibirsk*. You guys set?"

"We are. Just running final diagnostics."

Yuri squatted for a better look. "How are these units powered?"

"Lithium ion batteries."

"How long are they good for?"

"At least a year."

"Do you have any kind of backup system in case the primary battery goes out?"

"No, sir. It's just battery operated." Lieutenant Shtyrov's brow furrowed. "Is there a problem?"

"The last recording unit I used also had lithium batteries but it failed—damn thing burned up after it was installed." Yuri invented the storyline. "I hope your gear doesn't have the same type of batteries."

Chief Dobrynin joined in. "Ah, sir, these are new batteries, purchased from Israel. They've been thoroughly checked out."

"Good to hear." Yuri stood. "We'll be getting underway soon."

"Very good, sir," Shtyrov said.

Yuri headed forward, uneasy with his conversation with the Spetsnaz operators. *I gave them plenty of opportunity but they didn't budge.*

Maybe their recorders are just powered by batteries.

He almost confronted the pair about the exposed dosimeter but elected to postpone. All three were about to depart on a dangerous high-risk dive. The last thing he wanted to do was cast doubt. *Something else must have exposed the dosimeter.* Yuri decided to deal with the mystery later. He also made a metal note to tell Tumanov to keep his finding to himself.

Chapter 47

The *P-815* crept into Jiaozhou Bay, hugging the bottom. It was half past midnight. Yuri stood behind Lieutenant Tumanov, who occupied the starboard pilot's console. The *P-815*'s co-pilot, Junior Lieutenant Vassily Nevsky, sat in at the port control station. Of average height and build, Nevsky had blond hair, sapphire eyes, and a handsome face that had earned him the moniker of "Hollywood" at the naval academy in St. Petersburg. He was the youngest aboard, just twenty-three.

Both Tumanov and Nevsky wore virtual reality visors. Yuri donned a spare unit. Fiberoptic cables connected the goggles to the minisub's supercomputer. Hull-mounted sensors fed a firehose stream of data to the CPU. The processer digested the chorus of underwater sounds that clamored throughout the bay. The racket ranged from propeller wash of 5,000-horsepower tractor tugs that assisted the docking of a three-football field-long container ship to the snap, crackle, and pop of mating shrimp. Acoustic reflections from low-powered pulses generated from the *P-815*'s navigation sonar were also processed. The frequency range and tonal pattern of the nav pulses simulated indigenous bottlenose dolphins. Software randomized the outbound sound waves to conceal the transmissions.

Short-range blue green laser scans of the approaching water column supplemented the acoustic data. The combined result produced three-dimensional images of the bottom terrain in the VR goggles.

"What's that at two o'clock?" Yuri noticed something projecting out of the bottom.

"I'll check." Tumanov maneuvered the minisub until it was ten feet from the contact. "Switching to visual," Tumanov said, parking the visor on his forehead.

Yuri tilted his visor up and stared at the video monitor mounted to the forward bulkhead. The screen flashed from background blue to a slightly gray-washed picture. The search light illuminated the bottom, providing enough light for the video camera to generate images. A cylinder half-buried in the silt was visible.

"Looks like debris," Tumanov reported.

"Is that a barrel?" Yuri asked.

"Yes, sir. I expect the harbor is loaded with crap like this."

"Good."

Tumanov made eye contact with Yuri. "How is that good, sir?"

"We want our gear to blend in to the bottom." Yuri turned to his left. "Right, Mikhail?"

"Absolutely, sir," replied Lieutenant Shtyrov. The Spetsnaz officer stood beside Yuri. Like Yuri, he wore his dry suit with the hood folded behind his neck. Shtyrov moved forward for a better view of the video monitor. "The more junk on the bottom, the easier it will be for our recorder to fit in without raising suspicion."

"Got it," Tumanov said.

"How deep are we here?" asked Shtyrov.

"Sixteen meters. We're still in the dredged channel."

"Are the floodlights visible from the surface?"

"Not at this depth. Lots of sediment and plankton in the water column tonight. But as we get shallower, no lights allowed."

"Let's proceed as planned, Lieutenant," Yuri said.

"Understood."

Tumanov switched off the exterior lights and slipped his visor down.

Yuri faced Shtyrov. "We're about ten minutes out. I'll help you launch."

"Very good, sir."

Fifteen minutes later, Yuri stood outside the lockin-lockout chamber. Shtyrov was inside the pressure vessel, along with the underwater recorder. It was a tight fit. Dobrynin waited on the bottom. The *P-815*'s keel hovered ten feet above his position.

Yuri triggered the intercom speaker. "Let me know when you're set and I'll flood the chamber."

Shtyrov extended the thumb of his right gloved hand. Yuri observed the signal from the newly installed observation porthole—a thick slab of acrylic that filled a four-inch-diameter hole in the side of the chamber. Yuri had insisted on the installation of the viewport and the intercom prior to starting the mission.

"Flooding," Yuri announced.

He flipped a switch, triggering a pump that transferred water from internal tanks into the chamber. Soon Shtyrov was completely submerged. He equalized pressure and opened the bottom hatch. Yuri watched as Shtyrov lowered the acoustic recording cylinder through the hatchway. He used a line lashed to the unit to prevent it from free-falling. The Spetsnaz operator then made his exit.

Yuri remotely sealed the bottom hatch and dewatered the chamber, pumping the water back into the internal side tanks.

He was next.

* * * *

Yuri stood inside the pressure chamber. The water level was waist high and rising. Clad head to toe in a black dry suit and equipped with a rebreather backpack and a buoyancy compensator, he appeared ready for a spacewalk. The flooding water reached his chest. He pulled up his right arm and checked the control panel lashed to the neoprene covering just above his wrist. The breathing gas and CO_2 scrubber were in the green. The water reached his neck. Yuri tried to breathe normally but remained apprehensive, waiting for complete immersion. His dive mask gripped his face and gas flowed through the mouthpiece, but leaks were always possible. The claustrophobic chamber didn't help either. There was barely enough room to turn around, let alone adjust his gear if needed.

No leaks, Yuri thought as the water surged past his head. *Thank you, Lord!*

With the chamber filled, Yuri's hooded head bounced against the overhead. *Too much air!*

He reached up with a gloved hand and pressed a valve on his buoyancy compensator, releasing a stream of bubbles. He descended, his fin-tipped feet landing on the bottom hatch.

Yuri and the Spetsnaz divers did not use traditional weight belts to counter the buoyancy of their dry suits and to provide a quick escape to the surface in an emergency. Instead, lead weights placed in pockets sewn inside their neoprene suits provided ballast. If they had an accident, the Russian Navy did not want the corpses of their underwater spies floating to the surface.

Yuri turned to the side and peered through the lens of his facemask at the chamber porthole. Tumanov was on the other side. Yuri signaled thumbs up with both hands. He dropped to his knees and turned a gate valve, hearing a slight hiss as the pressure inside the chamber equalized with the exterior water. Next, he triggered the release mechanism of the bottom hatch. It rotated away, revealing a black hole. Yuri removed the diver propulsion vehicle from its mounting on the side of the chamber. It was slightly negative. He flipped a switch on the control panel. The LED display lit up. He scanned the readings. All systems were normal. Turning to the cargo stowed on the deck next to the open hatch, he removed the Remora from its lashings and held the underside close to his facemask. The indicator light broadcast a faint green.

Good, everything's working. Yuri slipped the Remora into an open mesh container with a tether connected to the diver propulsion vehicle. He next clipped a second line attached to the DPV to a D-ring on his chest harness. He took one last look at the porthole and again signaled thumbs up to Tumanov. Yuri dropped the DPV and the Remora through the hatch. He followed, sinking fins first.

Yuri hovered just above the bottom as the beam from his handheld dive light pierced the gloom. His fins kicked up a silt cloud from muddy bottom sediments. He checked the depth gauge strapped to his left forearm. *Sixteen meters*—fifty-two feet.

He rotated three-sixty. Shtyrov and Dobrynin had already departed for the south side of the entrance channel to the Port of Qingdao. Yuri's mission would take him along the north side of the channel.

He pulled on the tether to his underwater ride, retrieving the four-foot-long by one-foot diameter aluminum cylinder from the bottom. He grabbed hold of the DPV's handgrip, a metal bar that extended about a foot above the ducted propeller housing. Yuri triggered a switch on the handgrip, energizing the diver propulsion vehicle's control panel. The screen mounted on top of the handgrip displayed compass heading, water depth, speed, and battery capacity. After verifying the DPV was operational he cinched in the Dacron line reducing the tether to about three feet in length. The second line securing the Remora stretched out behind Yuri.

He turned to the side and aimed his light at the *P-815*. The minisub loomed in the background. Knowing Tumanov and crew were watching with the underwater video system, he waved an arm. Yuri switched off the dive light, which produced instant gloom. He would rely on the DPV's LED compass display for navigation. He checked the heading and verified the course. Now ready, Yuri engaged the electric drive.

The DPV lunged ahead. With both hands gripping the handle bar, Yuri hung on. Propeller wash jetted under his elongated form as he sped northeastward at four knots. The Remora, also tethered to the DPV, trailed several feet behind his fins. Virtually silent, the DPV's battery powered electric motor towed Yuri and the Remora with ease. Designed to minimize cavitation, the propeller generated a minuscule sound print.

Despite the DPV's stealth, Yuri fretted. Acoustic sensors might detect the noise as he closed in on the sub base. He also worried about the *P-815*. Once he departed, the mini would ground out on the bottom and wait for the divers to return. A homing signal transmitted by the minisub's nav sonar mimicked the clicks of a short-finned pilot whale. Receivers attached to the rebreather backpacks that all three divers wore would guide them back to the rendezvous point.

On paper, it was a doable exercise. Each team would install their special equipment on the bottom and return to the *P-815*. The mini would then reconnect with the *Novosibirsk*.

But it could all turn to crap in a heartbeat. This Yuri knew from experience. Rebreathers could fail, forcing a diver to the surface. A DPV could peter out too soon, stranding a team. Underwater listening devices might detect extraneous noise from the electric drive of a DPV. Even respirations could give away the divers. And magnetic anomaly detectors might discover the *P-815*. Despite the demagnetization of its steel hull, a faint signature remained.

If a diver suffered a gear casualty or hostile surface forces began searching, their orders were unambiguous: Depart from operations area immediately. Rendezvous with the *P-815* and promptly leave Qingdao harbor.

Yuri relaxed his grip on the handle bar, transferring the hydraulic drag of his body from his arms to the chest harness line that connected with the DPV. The tether now took the burden of hanging onto the underwater tug as it towed Yuri east. He checked the DPV's heading display. He remained on course.

Yuri planned to continue for another ten minutes on the same compass course at four knots. He would then carefully ascend to the surface to verify his location. It was slack high tide, but residual currents still surged through the bay. He would take a GPS fix and adjust course as needed to home in on the entrance to the Qingdao Naval Base.

* * * *

Shtyrov and Dobrynin reached the head of the harbor inlet thirty-five minutes after locking out from the *P-815*. Their actual destination differed from what they had told Yuri and the others aboard the minisub. Instead of installing the recorder in the entrance channel to the Qingdao base, they diverted to a commercial waterway located to its south.

On their journey to the Port of Qingdao's Middle Harbor, they encountered a massive barge with a clamshell bucket dredge. Illuminated by racks of floodlights, the dredge worked around the clock deepening the navigation channel that served the commercial harbor. The Russian divers welcomed the racket from the operation, which masked their penetration.

While Dobrynin remained on the bottom next to the package, Shtyrov ascended. He eased his head out of the water. His wrist compass told him he was facing north. Through his facemask, he observed half a dozen fishing boats and workboats moored to floating docks about 150 feet away, their hulls silhouetted by pole-mounted lights on the adjacent jetty. He kicked his fins, rotating one-eighty. A collection of large vessels, a hundred to three hundred feet in length, lined the wharf along the southern edge of the waterway. Just beyond the wharf, Shtyrov spotted several high-rise towers, each blazing with hundreds of lighted windows.

Govnó! The presence of the twenty- to thirty-story residential apartments stunned Shtyrov. He had expected only port facilities.

Are we in the right location?

Shtyrov lifted his right arm out of the water, allowing the GPS unit strapped to his forearm to take a fix. It took about a minute for the device to synchronize with three of the constellation of Russian navigation satellites that orbited over the north Pacific. *We're right on.* Shtyrov understood the need to relocate the package from the naval base to the commercial harbor area—the chance of discovery was substantially less. Nevertheless, the reality of the real-world conditions did not sit well with him.

Don't think about it—just do your job.

He took a last look at the surroundings before descending.

Shtyrov joined Chief Dobrynin on the bottom, thirty feet below the surface. Dobrynin's dive light illuminated the work area, its beam angled down. Shtyrov issued a hand signal, directing his assistant to proceed. Using a spade he carried with his dive gear, Dobrynin began excavating a hole. The top half foot of the bottom consisted of muck—silty sediments with the consistency of mush. Below that layer, however, the soil was hardpacked clay. It was slow going with the mini-shovel. Moscow dictated that the unit must be covered by at least fifty centimeters (twenty inches) of firm soil.

Shtyrov checked his watch. They should have departed by now. He reached down to his right calf and removed a dive knife. He signaled to Dobrynin to take a break. With both gloved hands gripping the handle of the knife, Shtyrov jammed the stainless-steel blade into the bottom of the hole.

Ten minutes later, the Spetsnaz operators completed their work and departed.

* * * *

Yuri surfaced to check his bearings in the entrance channel to the Qingdao Naval Base. The ten-story-high harbor surveillance tower was about a hundred yards away. Located on the north side of channel, the observation post marked the landward end of the rock jetty that protected the waterway from waves generated in the northern reaches of Jiaozhou Bay. Yuri hugged the bottom as he crept further into hostile waters. He dialed the DPV back to just two knots. Despite the thermal long johns and jumpsuit he wore under the rubber dry suit, the cold penetrated. He shivered.

As he continued east along the north side of the channel, Yuri noticed the gradual change in ambient light conditions. The gloom eased into a gray tone.

Floodlights—I'm close!

A row of pole lights just beyond the harbor tower illuminated the 1,200-foot-long naval base wharf. Earlier, Yuri had noted the destroyer moored at the west end of the quay.

Yuri had just slowed to one knot when he heard the high-pitched whine of propellers chopping water. The racket commenced without warning.

Patrol boat!

Adrenaline surged into his bloodstream, fear displacing the cold within heartbeats.

Yuri powered down. He sank to the bottom and waited. The din escalated. He looked up but could see nothing through the gloom. The noise peaked and receded.

Whatever produced the noise had moved on, heading west in the navigation channel.

Thank you, Lord!

Relieved, Yuri was about to continue when he noticed his breathing rate. He was gulping gas from the rebreather. *Slow down!* His noisy respirations could give his position away.

Yuri paced his breathing, thankful there was no stream of exhalation bubbles that could reveal his presence. About a minute later, he powered up the DPV. *It should be around the corner ahead.*

* * * *

Shtyrov guided his DPV west in Jiaozhou Bay, cruising just above the bottom at three knots. Dobrynin followed ten feet behind, towed by his own propulsion unit.

The acoustic receiver attached to Shtyrov's rebreather backpack relayed the relative heading of the *P-815*'s homing signal to an LED display strapped to his right forearm. He estimated they had another twenty minutes before reaching the minisub.

* * * *

Yuri rose from the depths at a glacial pace, his head oozing above the water surface.

There you are!

The submarine was about a hundred feet away. The Type 095 nuclear-powered fast-attack submarine occupied the south side of a floating pier that extended seaward from a steel bulkhead. Security floodlights illuminated the exposed hull. Yuri did not observe personnel on the pier or on the sub's casing. Nevertheless, he suspected human eyes and myriad electronic sensors guarded the warship. Releasing a short squirt of air from his buoyancy compensator, he submerged and dropped forty feet to the bottom, where he switched on the DPV. At minimum power, it towed him northwestward at a snail's pace until he passed into the sub's night shadow.

Now directly under the hull about midships, Yuri switched on his dive light using the low illumination setting. He disconnected the tether to the DPV, allowing the propulsion unit to settle to the bottom. On his knees in the mud, Yuri extracted the Remora from the tow bag and used the dive light to illuminate its control panel.

Good, everything's okay.

He pulled open a plastic guard that covered the Remora's activation switch, then used his gloved right index finger to activate the device. The Remora's legs snapped outward from the main cavity. Still holding the huge crab lookalike by the rim of its outer shell covering, Yuri closed the switch guard and set the Remora onto the seabed.

Its ten appendages went to work. Within seconds, it burrowed into the bottom.

Yuri waited another minute to verify the gadget had deployed correctly. Satisfied, he proceeded with the second element of his mission. After removing the infrared flash camera from a thigh pocket of his dry suit, Yuri spent fifteen minutes photographing the underside of the 095 hull taking shots of the ducted propeller assembly, various hull-through valve fittings, sonar arrays, and torpedo tubes.

After completing his spy work, Yuri reattached the DPV's tether to his chest harness and grabbed the unit's handle bar. He switched off his dive light and squeezed the DPV's throttle. Heading toward the main channel at two knots five feet above the bottom, he checked his watch. *Dammit, I'm late.* He goosed the throttle, increasing his speed by fifty percent.

Yuri had travelled about one-third of a mile when it happened. The collision knocked him off course. Before he could react, the DPV plowed into the bottom, dragging Yuri with it.

Something had slammed into his right shoulder. Collecting his bearings, he was relieved to find he had retained the mouthpiece to the rebreather, and he still had gas. His facemask remained in place but had lost its watertight seal. He cleared the flooded mask and switched on his dive light. The diver propulsion vehicle's battery gauge indicated a quarter charge remained. He checked the depth gauge on his left forearm—14.5 meters deep. Yuri next scanned the homing readout unit strapped to his right forearm. The screen was blank.

Govnó!

Yuri used a hand to manipulate the readout display, hoping to reset the unit. No joy. The impact to the rebreather had damaged the sonar receiver attached to the backpack's outer casing, rendering the unit deaf. He was about to restart the DPV when a grayish black hulk blasted by, just inches from his head. It disappeared into the murk within a heartbeat.

What's that? He aimed the dive light's beam at the creature's path. Nothing, not even a bubble trail.

Yuri commenced a three-sixty scan, rotating his body while hovering just above the bottom.

It came back for another pass and this time Yuri blasted it with the light beam. The quarter-ton sea lion broke left, passing just a couple of feet away. *You bastard!*

Knowing what he now faced, Yuri considered his options.

He knew that both Russia and the United States employed marine mammals for anti-diver warfare. Dolphins, seals, and even sea lions guard high-value naval facilities. Trained to use their hunting skills to pummel and sometimes bite subsurface intruders, the militarized creatures are the ultimate underwater guards. *There are not supposed to be any bio-sentries here!*

Yuri and the Spetsnaz operators had checked with the GRU regarding marine mammal activity at all the PLAN fleet anchorages. The latest intelligence reports suggested that China had not yet deployed biological-based weapons. Sea lions also were not common to the waters offshore of China.

This guy must be a rogue—maybe he thinks I'm a rival.

A new revelation flashed. *Damn—maybe he's looking for a mate.*

Yuri pulled up the DPV and steadied himself. He aimed the dive light ahead.

All right, you son of a bitch, make your move. At the edge of the light cone, Yuri caught a glimpse of the enormous bull as he skirted by. Yuri placed the light on the bottom, its beam still directed in the same direction. He retreated to the left five feet and waited.

The sea lion commenced another pass, homing in on the light. Yuri timed it perfectly, driving the DPV full throttle into the sea lion's mid-torso. Startled but not injured, the interloper raced away.

Yuri hoped the inquisitive creature would leave him alone. He checked his watch. *Oh God.*

Yuri powered up the DPV. He had no choice but to retrace his path using reserve course procedures. *I hope they're still there!*

Chapter 48

"Where is he?" Lieutenant Tumanov said.

Spetsnaz operator Shtyrov looked at the watch lashed to the forearm of his dry suit. "He should have returned fifteen minutes ago."

Shtyrov stood beside Tumanov, who remained at the controls of the *P-815*. Shtyrov and Dobrynin had climbed out of the lockin-lockout chamber ten minutes earlier. The minisub hovered at the rendezvous coordinates, ten feet above the bottom.

"Are you still transmitting the signal?" Shtyrov asked.

"Yes, the system is working flawlessly."

"Maybe he was discovered."

"Maybe—but I haven't detected any hostile response. The base remains quiet. Just routine patrol craft activity."

"How long can we wait?"

The *Novosibirsk* waited twelve miles offshore of Qingdao. The *P-815* should have already departed to remain on schedule. If the mini failed to rendezvous within an hour of the scheduled time, the *Novosibirsk* would retreat to deeper waters in the Yellow Sea and wait until the following evening. If the *P-815* failed to make the second hookup, the *Novosibirsk* would end the mission and return to Russia.

"We'll wait ten more minutes," Tumanov said.

* * * *

Yuri remained just above the bottom, heading southwest. Eight percent of the DPV's battery power remained. The tide had turned. The ebb current pushed him eastward. He attempted to compensate but could only guess. Sensing he was off course, Yuri pulled back on the DPV's hand grip and headed topside. Yuri's head emerged from the murk. He faced north. He could see the Jiaozhou Bridge in the distance, floodlights illuminating the 500-feet-high towers. He kicked his fins, pirouetting in place. The city lights of Qingdao glowed to the east.

Yuri raised his right arm about a foot out of the water. As Shtyrov had earlier, Yuri manipulated the GPS unit, allowing it to compute a satellite fix on his position. It was a dangerous maneuver. With the bay waters as flat as a billiards table, radar could possibly detect his exposed form. More likely, however, infrared surveillance cameras might pick up his heat image. Although encased in a dry suit, he remained warmer than the surrounding waters.

It took nearly two minutes before his real-world coordinates were displayed on the GPS unit. A flashing red dot marked his position on a tiny map of Jiaozhou Bay. A red X identified the rendezvous location. He was about half a mile away. Yuri checked the DPV's compass readout and mentally set a new course. He dropped below the surface and gunned the underwater machine.

* * * *

The unmanned patrol craft drifted with the outgoing current, its twin inboard diesels idling. Thirty-three feet in length, the cabinless hull sported a fourteen-foot-high mast packed with sensors that included radar, GPS, and comms. Also attached to the spire was an experimental 3-D laser scanner adapted for security purposes. The rotating scanner head emitted invisible light beams that measured the distance to objects within its path. Adapted to detect low-profile objects projecting above the water surface, the instrument's principal purpose was to detect small craft invisible to radar, such as rubber rafts and rigid-hulled inflatables. The onboard computer controlling the autonomous surface vessel monitored the laser scanner and radar along with a dozen other sensors. The scanner generated up to half a million data points per second. Since the ASV was offshore, the only surface available to generate return reflections from the laser beam was the bay itself.

Near the extreme limit of the scanner's range of half a mile, it detected a disturbance on the surface. The reflected signal did not match images of likely target craft stored in the CPU's memory. Instead, it classified the target as a biologic, likely a porpoise or a seal surfacing for a breath of air. A report of the biologic sighting was transmitted by the ASV's encrypted VHF radio to the security center at the Qingdao naval base.

* * * *

Tumanov remained seated at the *P-815*'s control station. He was alone; Shtyrov had retreated to the galley to join Chief Dobrynin for a hot cup of tea. Co-pilot Nevsky was in the engine room, running a systems check with the engineer. Tumanov stared at the clock on the command console. His self-imposed ten-minute limit had ninety seconds to go.

Dammit! I don't want to leave him. He's a good man.

The minute and half passed.

I'll give him two more minutes but that's it!

Tumanov triggered a master switch on the panel.

Maybe this will help.

Tumanov activated the *P-815*'s main floodlight system, illuminating the waters over the minisub's bow—a procedure that violated security protocols. With just twenty feet of water overhead, the luminous glow might be visible from the air or a nearby ship. Tumanov activated the forward underwater camera. The cockpit screen displayed the mini's submerged bow. Debris in the water column reflected light, creating a snow-like blizzard on a bed of black.

Come on Kirov, where are you?

Yuri swam into view forty seconds later.

Chapter 49

The *Novosibirsk* was underway with the *P-815* once again piggybacking. The submarine headed southward just above the bottom following the fifty-meter contour. Yuri and Shtyrov sat at the mess table in the officer's wardroom with Captain Petrovich. The briefing had started five minutes earlier. Shtyrov provided an accounting of the installation of the recording device.

"The only real problem we had was burying the unit," Shtyrov reported. "There was a layer of soft silt on top. Below was a hard-packed layer—dense material. That took a lot of effort to dig out."

"But you did manage to bury it—correct?" Petrovich asked.

"Yes, sir. It was covered as required. You can't tell that we were there."

"Good. The Chinese routinely scan the harbor bottom of their naval bases looking for foreign plants."

Shtyrov neglected to reveal that the recorder was not installed at the naval base but instead was delivered to the commercial harbor located south of the base. Neither Petrovich nor Kirov was cleared for that information.

Captain Petrovich turned to Yuri. "Okay, your turn."

"Overall, it went well. I was able to deploy the Remora as planned."

"How far into the sub base did you penetrate?"

"All the way. I released the Remora under a Zero-Nine-Five."

That grabbed Petrovich's attention. "No one's done that before. What did you see?"

Yuri reached forward and keyed the laptop sitting on the table. He had already inserted the SIM card from the underwater camera into the computer. He rotated the computer toward Petrovich. "After verifying that the Remora buried itself in the bottom, I took photos of the submerged hull—the camera had an infrared flash."

Both Petrovich and Shtyrov eyed the display.

"It has a ducted prop," Captain Petrovich said. "Looks like what the Americans use."

"Yes, it appeared similar to the newer *Virginia*-class boats."

"Probably a copy," Shtyrov commented.

"I wouldn't be surprised." Petrovich settled back into his chair. "They're very good at reverse engineering."

Yuri advanced to a new photo taken near the stern. "This appears to be a housing for a towed array."

"Reel inside the ballast tank?" Petrovich asked.

"Probably."

Yuri called up another photograph. "Outer doors. Eight tubes total, four on each side."

The three officers spent several minutes examining the photographs. Petrovich summed up, "Nice work, Kirov. Fleet will be pleased. I want to send these home ASAP."

"I'll take them to comms and have them encrypted and transmitted to Vladivostok."

"Good. Let's move on."

Yuri interlocked his fingers. "I made a quick topside observation in the harbor. Besides the Zero-Nine-Five, I spotted a couple of diesel boats moored nearby—Type Zero-Four-Ones."

"Any other nukes?"

"No sir, just the Zero-Nine-Five. But there was a carrier moored to a pier on the opposite side of the harbor from the sub base."

"Must be the *Liaoning*," Shtyrov said.

Petrovich agreed. "Probably—that's what Fleet indicated."

Yuri continued his briefing. "After completing my work in the harbor, I headed back to rendezvous with the mini." He smiled thinly. "That certainly turned out be the most challenging part of the mission."

Captain Petrovich arched an eyebrow; Lieutenant Shtyrov tried to suppress a grin. "I had an encounter with a sea lion—a very big fellow."

"Really," Petrovich said.

Yuri unzipped the top section of his jumpsuit and exposed the right shoulder. He pulled back the sleeve of the T-shirt he wore underneath, revealing an ugly reddish-purple bruise about the size of an orange. "That guy starting playing tag with me. Hit me so hard that he knocked me around like a rag doll."

Dumbfounded, Petrovich said, "Was it a sentry?"

"I don't think so. I was in the bay when it happened, not at the base."

"What was going on?"

Shtyrov jumped in. "I think that critter was in love with Captain-Lieutenant Kirov, sir."

All three laughed.

"I don't know what he wanted. Maybe I was intruding on his territory. Anyway, that sure wasn't a gentle love tap he gave me, more like a challenge."

"That must have been unnerving," Petrovich offered.

"It was. Just imagine a 200-kilo blubber missile coming at you out of the murk." Yuri shuddered. "About the scariest thing I've encountered underwater."

"No doubt."

Yuri described how he evaded the annoying marine mammal and made his way back to the *P-815*.

"Well gentlemen, congratulations on completing your individual tasks. I'm quite pleased with your efforts."

Yuri and Shtyrov signaled their thanks.

"Sir, how long before we arrive at Ningbo?" Yuri asked.

"Thirty-six hours or so. Too shallow here to make a speed run."

"Good. We can use the downtime."

* * * *

As the *Novosibirsk* proceeded southward in international waters offshore of Shandong Province, Commander Yang Yu arrived at the security office in the headquarters building for the North Sea Fleet. His executive officer, Lieutenant Commander Zheng Qin, was waiting in the conference room. He sat in a chair at large oval table. Another officer sat beside the XO.

"Good morning, Captain," Zheng said as he stood.

His companion also pushed her chair away from the table.

"As you were," ordered Yang.

Yang took a seat on the opposite side of the table.

"Tea, captain?" asked Zheng, gesturing to the steaming pot sitting on the nearby counter.

"Please."

After filling a mug and handing it his boss, Zheng returned to his seat and turned to the female sitting to his right. "Captain, this is Lieutenant

Gao Le. She's the security officer for the base. She has something interesting to tell you."

Gao was in her late twenties, petite, with military length black hair. She wore a crisp uniform, subtle makeup, and no jewelry. "Captain, I believe the base may have been targeted by at least one diver earlier this morning."

"What evidence do you have?" Yang asked.

Gao keyed the remote to the slide projector. An aerial image of Jiaozhou Bay filled the screen on a wall next to Yang's side. "Sir, one of the autonomous sentries detected a surface disturbance early this morning." She aimed a pointer at the image; a bright red dot danced on the screen near the entrance to naval base. "The ASV was in this approximate location when its laser scanner detected the disturbance."

Gao advanced to a new PowerPoint slide. "The digital image projecting above the water surface was blurred and nondescript. The ASV interpreted the contact to be a marine mammal."

"So, there was no alarm?"

"That's correct. It transmitted the contact to base but did not register it as a threat. When the unit returned to its mooring, the entire patrol's recorded database was uploaded to our security office. As part of my duties, I review all ASV activity for the previous evening and morning. I noted the subject observation in the bay was classified as a biologic. However, since it was close to the base, I asked our photo recon section to enhance the laser scan image. This is the result."

The image filling the screen startled Captain Yang. "That's a diver!"

"Yes, sir. That's my reading, too."

"What's with the arm projecting up like that?"

"I'm not sure," Gao said. "But it's possible the diver was attempting to either communicate with others or make a GPS fix."

"Did he get inside the harbor?"

"Unknown. None of the bottom sensors detected any threats."

Zheng rejoined the conversation. "Captain, the *Heilong* is the first boat a diver would have encountered after passing through the harbor entrance."

Wang grimaced. "It's the damn Americans again."

Chapter 50

The Ministry of State Security agent drove into the subterranean parking garage in downtown Bellevue, Washington. The driver bypassed the guest parking zone and headed deeper into the basement to the reserved stalls. It was late Thursday afternoon; tenants in the high-rise tower were already leaving the garage.

The Chinese agent drove down the ramp to level two, where he spotted his companion standing in the shadows next to the elevator. The lookout opened the passenger door and climbed inside.

"Is it still there?" asked the driver in Mandarin.

"Yes, one level down. There are open stalls nearby where we can park."

"Good."

The agents descended to the next level, driving past a silver BMW Seven Series that was parked half a dozen stalls from the elevator landing. They parked four stalls away from the vehicle on the opposite aisle, with their Ford Explorer backed into the stall. The passenger removed a smartphone from his jacket and queued up the cell's photo album. He studied half a dozen images of his prey.

The MSS officers had elected to lie low after the aborted assault at Laura Newman's home. The rapid response by local authorities suggested Newman's security system had been upgraded substantially since a previous operation earlier in the year. After leaving the Newman premises, the agents switched to Plan B. They dumped their rented Toyota in a local Park and Ride lot. A deep undercover operative living in Seattle provided quarters and a clean vehicle.

Earlier this morning the senior agent had waited in the office building's lobby by the elevators. Dressed in a suit and carrying a black leather briefcase, he sat in a chair thumbing through the latest edition of the *Wall Street Journal*. After walking out of the garage elevator, Laura Newman stepped past him at 8:55 A.M., her three-inch heels click-clacking on the tile floor. She wore a tweed suit jacket with matching skirt cut an inch above her knees. While Laura waited for an elevator to ride to the twenty-fifth floor, the MSS officer surreptitiously took half a dozen photos of her with his Samsung.

"She's pretty," commented the driver as he also eyed the images on his boss's cell.

"Yes, and rich too."

"I wonder what she did."

"Doesn't matter. We have our orders."

"I know. Still, it seems like a waste."

"Stop thinking about it."

The driver reached into his pocket and removed a pack of cigarettes. He offered a Camel to his partner, who took one. They lit up, both rolling down their car windows.

The MSS operatives were halfway through their smokes when one of the garage elevator doors opened. A tall man wearing a blue blazer jacket and gray trousers stepped out, followed by a female in a tweed ensemble.

"That's her!" The passenger crushed the butt in the ashtray and reached into his coat pocket. He removed the Colt .45 semiautomatic; the suppressor was already attached.

"What about the guy?" the driver asked.

"Collateral damage."

The passenger cracked open the door and started to step out when both targets retreated to the still open elevator.

Surprised, the assassin remained beside the open car door, his pistol at the ready.

"FBI. DROP YOUR WEAPON NOW!"

Startled, the gunman turned to his right, homing in on the female voice. She was two vacant stalls away, crouched down behind the hood of a Chevrolet Suburban. Her nine-millimeter pistol targeted his chest.

The rear door of a van parked on the opposite side of the lane from the Suburban burst open. Four black-clad FBI Hostage Rescue Team agents emerged, each carrying a submachine gun.

The gunman's orders directed that neither he nor his partner could be captured. He ducked down and peered into the open doorway of the Ford. The driver sat rigid in his seat staring at his partner.

The gunman met his partner's eyes. "Sorry, Jin."

An instant later, he fired a single round into the driver's forehead. Without hesitation, the gunman bolted upright and raised his .45 toward the approaching HRT assault team. He was cut down by a hail of gunfire.

* * * *

Michaela Taylor approached the Ford Explorer with both hands still gripping her smoking pistol. One perp lay prostrate on the concrete deck, riddled with nearly twenty rounds. The other man remained in the driver's seat, slumped over the steering wheel.

As the HRT agents circled the hood, each SMG trained on the driver, Taylor advanced to the driver's door. She pulled it open. That's when she spotted the driver's exit wound—a lethal puncture two inches in diameter.

She placed two fingers onto the man's neck, knowing there would be no pulse.

"Clear," she called out.

* * * *

"What's going on?" Laura Newman asked as she arose from her chair.

Cognition's receptionist had just escorted the visitors into Laura's penthouse office unannounced.

"Ms. Newman, my name is Michaela Taylor. I'm with the FBI." She opened a wallet, displaying her credentials. Laura studied the photo ID. Taylor gestured to her side. "This is Agent Todd Rossi." She turned toward the receptionist, who remained in the office threshold. "We need to speak in private."

"It's okay, Jeanette," Laura said. "Please shut the door."

Laura sat down, stunned at the intrusion and suddenly very worried. *It's about Yuri!*

Taylor and Rossi took chairs fronting the desk.

"Ms. Newman, about ten minutes ago there was an incident in this building. Two men were shot in the parking garage. Both expired."

Laura's hand raced to her mouth. "Oh, dear God... Were they my employees?"

"No." Taylor faced Rossi. "Go ahead."

He removed his cell phone and pulled up face shots of the two men, picked up by surveillance cameras the FBI had installed in Laura's building.

"Do you recognize either individual?" Rossi asked.

Laura peered at each image. The men were Asian…Laura's mind instantly went to the Chinese. "I've never seen them before. What were they doing?"

"Both men were armed. They were waiting for someone when we confronted them."

"Waiting for whom?"

"You were their target Ms. Newman," Taylor said.

Laura sat rigid in her chair—astonished. *This can't be happening again!* "Why do you think they were after me?" She clasped her hands to suppress the tremors.

"We've been tracking them," Michaela said. "They were waiting near your vehicle. When our decoy came out of the elevator, they started—"

"Decoy?" interrupted Laura.

"One of our agents dressed in an outfit similar to yours."

They've been following me!

Taylor continued, "These two also made an earlier attempt at your residence. We were able to intervene but they escaped."

Laura's forehead wrinkled. "At my house, what are you—" Laura stopped in mid-sentence. The revelation hit with the impact of an avalanche. The call from the security company. The rush to the safe room. The Sammamish police showing up so quickly.

The FBI has been monitoring my home!

Bewildered, Laura whispered, "What do you want from me?"

Special Agent Taylor removed a tablet from the handbag she carried and activated the screen. She motioned for Laura to take a look.

Laura picked up the device. Yuri's image stared back. It was his official Russian Navy portrait.

"Ms. Newman, where is Captain-Lieutenant Kirov?"

Chapter 51

Laura handed the Surface tablet back to the federal agent. "I'm not going to answer any questions without my attorney present."

Taylor turned the screen so it faced Laura. "Are you aware that this man—the man you have been living with for the past year—is a military intelligence officer with the Russian Federation?"

Laura didn't answer.

"Ms. Newman," joined in Agent Rossi, "were you also aware that Captain-Lieutenant Kirov is an expert in underwater espionage?"

"That's right," Taylor added. "And he just happens to be the general manager of a high-tech underwater technology company that you own. I don't think that's a coincidence."

Laura gripped the armrests of her chair; her fingers turned white from the pressure. Rossi called up a photo on his phone. He turned the screen toward Laura. She gasped at the color image of the corpse—the horrific wound to the skull vividly clear.

Taylor said, "This man and his companion wanted to kill you. And they would have if we had not intervened. Why were they after you?"

Laura turned away from the hideous image. She was on the verge of vomiting.

"Ms. Newman, you need to start cooperating with us right now."

Laura fought the tickle of bile that surged in her throat. "I'm not going to answer any more questions without my attorney present."

"You need to start talking right now."

"Am I under arrest?"

"I can detain you on the basis that you're a material witness regarding the two gunmen in the parking garage."

"I'm going to call my attorney right now." Laura reached for her desk phone and keyed the intercom to her secretary. "Jeanette, call Tim Reveley's office immediately and track him down. Tell him it's an emergency."

Agent Taylor scowled while pursing her lips. "You're making a serious mistake, Ms. Newman. You need to be cooperating with us—not lawyering up."

"There could be more of those gunmen out there," Rossi added.

"That's right. You need us. We can protect you—and your lovely child." Taylor queued up another file on her tablet.

The video showed Maddy crawling on the living room floor toward Amanda as they played a game of chase. Laura lost it.

"You have cameras inside my home! How dare you!"

"It's all legal, Ms. Newman. We have warrants from a federal judge."

Laura turned away, fuming while scared out of her wits. Taylor continued to encourage cooperation but Laura refused to engage. Laura's desk phone rang.

She picked up the handset. "Hello, Tim. I have two FBI agents in my office asking questions…"

Chapter 52

Day 27—Friday

Commander Yang Yu stood atop the sail of the *Heilong*. It was 1:57 P.M. at the Qingdao Naval Base. The officer in charge of the dive team stood on the floating pier below Yang's perch. After spending forty minutes inspecting the submerged hull, the two navy divers climbed back onto the floating dock.

"All clear, Captain," announced the dive officer with an inflated voice.

"Thank you," Yang said. He felt confident that the underwater intruder never made it to the base.

Yang turned to face the chief petty officer in charge of the moorings, who stood on the hull forward of the sail. "Chief, single up the lines and prepare to depart."

"Aye, aye, Captain."

Sailors on the floating pier released the mooring lines from dock cleats. The half dozen line handlers standing on the hull hauled in the lines.

Yang took one last survey of his command and its surroundings. The harbor was clear of vessel traffic. And with still air and slack tide conditions, there was no need for a tug assist.

Yang keyed the microphone he held in his hand. "Maneuvering, minimum power astern."

The quartermaster in the control room repeated the order. Yang spotted a swirl of water at the stern of his ship as the ducted propeller engaged. As the *Heilong* backed out of its slip, the men standing on the floating dock saluted in unison. Yang returned the gesture.

* * * *

The Remora remained on standby while embedded in the bottom sediment. When it detected the telltale sound of the ship's propeller biting into seawater, it backed out of its mud hole and discharged compressed air into its internal bladder. Now neutrally buoyant, the robot activated its jet pump and began to ascend. About a minute and half later, the Remora clamped itself to the underside of *Heilong*'s hull sixty feet forward of the propulsor.

* * * *

Commander Yang remained atop the sail as the submarine headed eastward in Jiaozhou Bay. The radar antenna rotated on its mast ten feet above his head. The deck crew relocated to the interior of the pressure casing and both fore and aft hatches were sealed. Standing next to Yang was his executive officer, who had just ascended the sail's internal ladder.

"Glorious day for our departure, Captain," Lieutenant-Commander Zheng Qin said. "A sure sign of good fortune ahead."

"It is a good day to be at sea for us and the fleet."

The *Liaoning* and a dozen escorts would depart Qingdao later in the evening, also bound for southern waters. Both men stood silently, enjoying the fifteen-knot induced breeze. To the port about 500 yards away was an inbound supertanker, laden with two million barrels of Saudi crude. The ship's product after refining would fuel the Qingdao region's ravenous hydrocarbon appetite for several days before another refill. Three hundred yards ahead was the *Heilong*'s escort. The frigate bristled with fore and aft cannons, torpedo launchers, and assorted missile batteries. Its active sonar pinged the waters, searching for submerged interlopers. Two miles ahead, a PLAN helicopter from the same warship deployed a dozen sonobuoys. The underwater microphones listened for submarines and radioed their findings back to the aircraft for analysis.

Two hours passed. The *Heilong* was well into the Yellow Sea. After receiving an "all clear" encrypted radio broadcast from its escort, Commander Yang and his XO descended into the hull. Yang then issued the dive order.

The Remora remained undetected, firmly attached to the hull. Its acoustic and electronic sensors recorded a treasure trove of digital secrets.

* * * *

Captain Tom Bowman stood beside the sonar watch console in the *Colorado*'s control room, holding a coffee mug. Senior sonar technician Anderson provided an update.

"Captain, it's the same boat we trailed into Qingdao—Master One. Identical submerged acoustic output. Running on a heading of one eight five at fifteen knots. Depth is 115 feet."

"Continue Master One designation. Inform me immediately of any course changes."

"Aye, sir."

The *Colorado*'s commanding officer considered Master One a likely threat. Two days earlier, People's Republic of China's state-run media outlets had launched a barrage of nationwide television and radio propaganda broadcasts condemning the USS *Ronald Reagan* Strike Group's intrusion into the South China Sea. The resulting public outcries demanded action by Beijing, just as the Politburo Standing Committee of the Communist Party had planned.

Captain Bowman returned to his command station near the center of the control room.

Every console and monitoring station was staffed. The tension inside the compartment was electric.

The executive officer stepped away from the plotting table to join the captain. "What do think this guy is up to?" Commander Jenae Mauk asked.

"Based on COMSUBPAC's last report about the *Liaoning* strike force, I'd say Master One is the advance guard. It's probably going to be on the lookout for the likes of us."

"They're behind the eight ball."

"And I intend to keep it that way. We'll remain in its baffles and see what it's really up to."

"Good plan, skipper."

For almost a week, the *Colorado* had loitered fifty to a hundred miles offshore of Qingdao, monitoring the arrival of North Sea Fleet vessels. The high-powered sonar pings this afternoon compelled SSN 788 to investigate.

Although the *Colorado* had a clear acoustic lock on Master One— the *Heilong*—its cutting-edge sensors did not detect the *Novosibirsk* earlier when it arrived offshore of Qingdao. The Russian nuke's sound suppression measures, coupled with Captain Petrovich's skill, evaded the *Colorado*'s sensors.

The *Novosibirsk* was in a similar situation. Its many sensors were blind to the *Colorado*'s presence.

* * * *

Four hundred miles south of the *Heilong* and *Colorado*, the *Novosibirsk* continued on schedule for its next mission. Yuri Kirov had just entered the *P-815*. He was alone. The minisub's crew and the two Spetsnaz divers were in the *Novosibirsk*'s mess, enjoying a meal. Yuri headed aft to the equipment storage locker. It was time to check Lieutenant Tumanov's earlier warning about the exposed dosimeter. Yuri pulled open the locker door and stepped inside. He crouched down due to the pressure hull's curved overhead. The locker was compact, about six feet square. Packed from the deck to the overhead with gear, the storage room contained a collection of spare parts for the mini's power plant, backup electronics for navigation and communication systems, diving equipment, and spy apparatus.

Yuri squatted and reached inside the stacked gear. His hand searched for the cigarette pack-sized device he'd planted earlier beside the fiberglass cases containing the Spetsnaz team's equipment. He extracted the electronic dosimeter and examined the readout.

"Dammit," he muttered.

The LED light was illuminated, signaling exposure.

Tumanov was right—there's radioactive material inside this equipment.

Yuri spent several minutes removing the equipment stacked on top of the two remaining cases containing the special underwater recorders. Both were stored next to the pair of cases housing Yuri's Remoras. He unsnapped the locks on one of the cases, removing the cover. Nestled inside the foam packing was a stainless-steel cylinder about eighteen inches in diameter and two feet long—identical to the unit installed at Qingdao. Yuri extracted the cylinder.

It was heavy, at least fifty pounds. He opened the plastic cover that protected the built-in control panel. A digital keypad sized to accommodate a diver's gloved finger occupied half of the panel space. A classified code was required to activate the recording device, once placed on the bottom. Yuri suspected the code also armed a self-destruct charge—standard on all covert recorders. Should the device be discovered, any attempt to open it without entering the code would detonate a chunk of semtex. Yuri turned the cylinder on its end, examining the hard plastic cover that housed the recording mechanism. He gripped the cover with one hand while holding the cylinder casing with the other. He tried to rotate the plastic cover.

"It won't come off, sir."

Startled, Yuri turned to the side. Shtyrov stood in the passageway beside the storage locker.

The Spetsnaz officer continued, "The boot is fused to the casing to ensure it's watertight and pressure resistant."

"You just about startled the piss out of me, Shtyrov. How long have you been aboard?"

"I just got here. I wanted to check my dive gear for our next mission." Yuri placed the recorder onto the deck and stood.

"What's inside that thing?"

Shtyrov cocked his head. "Sir?"

Yuri handed over the dosimeter. "I placed this next to one of your cases twelve hours ago. It's been exposed. So, I say again, what's inside those recording devices?"

After Lieutenant Shtyrov eyed the LED readout, his stocky frame stiffened. Yuri had caught him in a lie.

Yuri said, "They contain radioactive material. Why?"

"It's part of the power supply, sir."

"I asked you about that earlier. You assured me these units are battery powered."

"I was under orders not to reveal the alternative power source."

"Well, I'm ordering you now. What's going on?"

"It does have a conventional battery system, but there's a backup power system that utilizes a radioactive isotope."

"Why is that needed?"

"I don't know. That information was not provided to me. All I was told was to not reveal the presence of the isotope."

"Why?"

"For transportation purposes."

"Explain."

"As you know, sir, transporting any radioactive materials requires special handling and permits, plus it can scare the crap out of those who handle it or are located near the stuff. By keeping silent, all that hassle goes away."

Yuri glowered.

Shtyrov continued, "I was told the recorders have minimal exposure, no health risks."

Yuri grabbed the dosimeter from Shtyrov and reexamined it. "I don't know about that. I just hope those emissions haven't impacted the

Remoras—or our diving gear." Yuri slipped the dosimeter into a pocket of his jumpsuit and squatted down next to the recorder.

Still addressing Shtyrov, Yuri said, "Help me put this damn thing away and restack the compartment."

"Yes, sir," Shtyrov dropped to knees next to Yuri.

Yuri turned toward his charge. "And Lieutenant, don't ever lie to me again."

* * * *

Four hours after the *Heilong* departed Qingdao, the microcomputer housed inside the Remora's pressure casing executed a preset maneuver. A circular port at the rear end of the robot rotated open. The first of a dozen tennis ball-sized aluminum spheres nested inside the Remora's cargo compartment ejected. A squirt of compressed air from the onboard ballast control tank propelled the ball downward with sufficient thrust to avoid the sub's propeller and rudder assembly.

The sphere descended about thirty feet before its positive buoyancy and drag retarded its downward velocity. It then began a gradual ascent. When the sphere broke the water surface, the Chinese submarine was about half a mile away. Neither the *Heilong* or the trailing *Colorado* detected the ejection and ascent of the sphere, which was now functioning as a buoy. A wire about the diameter of a paper clip emerged from the upper hemisphere. Simultaneously, a tiny counterweight attached to a monofilament line descended from the lower hemisphere. Once deployed, the six-inch antenna broadcast an encrypted signal on a rarely used ultra-high frequency. Neither the *Heilong* nor the *Colorado* detected the radio transmission. Both submarines were too deep. However, Russian military satellites passing over the North Pacific listened for the unique transmission.

Within five minutes of commencing the broadcast, two low-orbit spy birds detected the signal. After collecting data from the satellites, a land-based monitoring station near Vladivostok decrypted the digital information, which allowed calculation of the buoy's earth coordinates. Also processed were compressed data streams of recordings of the *Heilong*'s electronic and acoustic emissions.

The location of the *Heilong* along with its relative course and submerged depth were duly reported to Pacific Fleet Command. The buoy would continue broadcasting on a looped circuit until it exhausted its battery, estimated to range between two and three hours. It would then sink.

Every twenty-four hours, the Remora would repeat same process, allowing the Russian Navy to track and spy on the *Heilong* for at least ten days.

Chapter 53

It was 7:35 A.M. in Sammamish, Washington. Laura Newman walked along the asphalt driveway, cooling down from her forty-minute run. She wore a Seahawks T-shirt, running shorts, and Nikes. The sky remained cloudless, portending another warm summer day.

Laura reached the parking court of her home. Amanda's Honda Civic occupied one of the half dozen guest stalls. Amanda was up; Maddy still slept. Laura looked over her property, hands on her back as she stretched her spine. She wondered where the cameras were located.

They're probably watching me right now.

As she scanned the landscaping and the forest of evergreens that screened the adjacent hillside homes, nothing appeared out of the ordinary. But Laura knew otherwise.

They must still have some cameras inside, too.

She had spent an hour the previous evening searching inside her home, looking for surveillance gear, but found nothing.

How long have they been watching us?

Orbiting the circular planting bed in the center of the parking court, Laura mulled over the timeframe. She had put it together last night while lying in bed. *The surveillance must have started after Yuri left, otherwise they would have arrested him.*

Laura speculated that Yuri was spotted at the Russian Consulate in Houston.

Nick probably knows, but he's an impossible source now.

On several recent occasions Laura was tempted to contact Nicolai Orlov to check on Yuri but refrained. Yuri warned her that the FBI monitored the consulate and it also kept tabs on key personnel. Laura swiped sweat from her brow. The expected "high" from her run had not yet kicked in. She remained anxious.

When FBI Special Agent Michaela Taylor presented the photograph of Yuri, demanding his whereabouts and threatening her arrest, Laura had clammed up. She was pre-warned. Lying to a federal law enforcement official was a felony. Taylor eventually backed off after Laura linked up with her attorney, first by telephone and then Skype. Tim Reveley brokered the deal with Taylor during their impromptu video conference. Laura would submit to a formal interview at the FBI's Seattle Office on Monday.

This afternoon Laura planned to meet with Tim and other attorneys at his Seattle office to strategize for the upcoming FBI interview. *They could have arrested me right in my office but they didn't—why?*

Yesterday afternoon's rude "outing" continued to traumatize Laura. But it was not unexpected.

Thank you again, Lord, for helping me to be prepared.

Reveley had engaged a specialty law firm in Washington, D.C. to assist with Yuri's request for asylum. Two preliminary meetings had been held with key State Department staff. Yuri's name was not disclosed; instead, he was described as an Eastern European high-level foreign intelligence operative seeking refuge in the United States. After conferring with the CIA and FBI, State had expressed interest in proceeding with the asylum process.

Tim Reveley planned to reveal the State Department connection when he and Laura met with the FBI next week. Laura hoped that revelation would tone down agent Taylor's aggressive posture when she met separately for the formal interview. Tim might not be allowed to sit in during that interrogation.

As Laura walked toward the main entry to her home, ready for a shower and a cup of coffee, another matter nagged at her well-being. *What about the Chinese? Are they really after me—again?*

* * * *

Nicolai Orlov had the same questions as Laura Newman. *The Chinese again—that must have been an MSS op!*

Nick sat at his desk in the Houston consulate. He had just completed his daily review of overnight developments in the Western United States, compiled by the night staff. What caught his attention was a link to a news story broadcast the previous evening by a Seattle television station reporting an FBI shootout in Bellevue, Washington.

Nick clicked on the link for a second viewing. The image of a comely blonde holding a microphone in front of the entrance to a parking garage flashed onto to his PC. The reporter recited her spiel:

"Late this afternoon, a shootout took place in this downtown Bellevue parking garage. The FBI reports it tracked two individuals to the garage and prepared to take them into custody for questioning regarding a bank robbery when the men resisted. Gunfire erupted and the two men were killed. None of the FBI agents involved in the confrontation were injured nor were any bystanders.

"Witnesses using the garage at the time of the incident report hearing a barrage of gunfire. The deceased individuals have not been identified but the FBI reported the men were associated with an Asia-based gang suspected of having conducted several bank robberies in the Seattle area.

"There is no bank in this particular building. Its principal tenant is Cognition Consultants, a high-profile IT company. However, a bank is located in the adjacent tower."

Nick turned away from the screen, dumbfounded. *Cognition Consultants—that's Laura's company. That was no bank robbery—they were after Laura.*

The FBI is hiding something!

Nick picked up the handset to his desk phone and dialed the consulate's security officer. A minute later, Captain Oleg Babin walked into Nick's office and took a seat.

"I just went over the daily report," Nick announced. "There was an FBI-involved shooting in the Seattle area yesterday at Laura Newman's company. I think the FBI has been watching her."

"She was shot?"

"No, my gut tells me the FBI was probably trying to protect her." Babin's brow wrinkled, amplifying the shrapnel scar over his right eye. He was unsure where his boss was headed.

Nick spent the next five minutes connecting dots.

Babin assessed the situation and provided his opinion. "Maybe the MSS wanted to interrogate her to find out if she knows where Kirov is?"

"That's possible but unlikely. After what Kirov uncovered, I suspect Beijing is trying to clean up loose ends. Laura Newman is one of them."

"And Captain-Lieutenant Kirov is the other?"

"Yes, plus one other."

"Sir?" Babin said.

"Me."

"But why?"

"Revenge," Nick said. "We collectively torpedoed Beijing's plan to spark a war between Russia and the USA."

Chapter 54

Day 28—Saturday

"We have new orders, gentlemen," Captain Petrovich said, addressing Yuri Kirov and Mikhail Shtyrov. All three sat at the mess table in the officer's wardroom. The *Novosibirsk* continued its southerly track, paralleling China's coast.

Petrovich continued, "Fleet has directed us to bypass the East Sea Fleet and head straight for Hainan Island."

"So Ningbo is no longer part of the mission?" Yuri asked.

"No. It's still on. We'll stop there on our way back, plus Zhanjiang." Petrovich checked his notes. "Fleet reported the *Liaoning* carrier strike force is headed to Yulin. It's behind us, steaming south at twenty knots."

"What's going on, sir?" asked Shtyrov.

"Apparently, the Chinese are massing a taskforce at the Yulin Naval Base on Hainan—prepping for their upcoming South China Sea war game. Fleet wants us to monitor that activity."

"We're still supposed to install recording equipment?" Yuri said.

"Correct, monitor the surface vessels." Petrovich grinned. "And according to Fleet, there will be at least one missile boat moored at Yulin, so you'll get another chance to install one of your bots."

"Interesting," Yuri commented.

"Captain," Shtyrov said, "if the PLAN is assembling a taskforce, won't that make it more difficult for us to install the equipment? With all that floating hardware, their ASW forces will be in full mode."

"That's right, Lieutenant. Fleet indicated that we should expect a robust ASW environment. However, it will not necessarily be directed toward us."

"Americans?" Shtyrov said.

"Yes. The U.S. Navy will have several subs in the area—one of which will likely be a *Virginia* class. Trying to track one of those devil boats will drive the Chinese Navy mad. Our mission will be to stay out of the way of the Americans and let the PLAN flail about as they try to find them. Should be good theatre."

Yuri and Shtyrov chuckled. Petrovich recalled another factor. "Kirov, you'll be interested to know that the Remora you left behind at Qingdao worked."

"It reported in?"

"It did. The boat you targeted is headed south. Fleet speculates that it will screen the taskforce."

"Has it been transmitting data on the boat?"

"It has. I don't have any of the details, only that Fleet is pleased with our work."

"That's great news."

"It is, Kirov. Well done."

"Sir, the boys back in Peter who built the Remora units should get the credit, not me."

"They will, but you deployed it. That counts a lot."

"Thank you."

The three officers spent the next hour planning for the Hainan Island operation and then dispersed.

* * * *

Eight hours later and over 300 nautical miles behind the *Novosibirsk*, the USS *Colorado* continued to stalk the *Heilong*. Captain Bowman stood beside the control room's plotting table. It displayed a digital chart of the Chinese coastline. A red cursor configured as a submarine hull pulsed. Master One—the *Heilong*—was about sixty nautical miles offshore of Ningbo. A similar blue cursor represented the *Colorado*. It trailed the *Heilong* by nearly ten miles.

The *Colorado*'s executive officer walked aft from the pilot's station to join Bowman.

"It's not heading to port, is it?" asked Commander Jenae Mauk.

She had bundled her black hair into a ponytail today.

"No." Bowman tapped the red icon on the glass display with a finger. "Looks like COMSUBPAC may be right about Master One. It's bypassing Ningbo." The port city served as the headquarters for China's East Sea Fleet.

"It could still be heading to Zhanjiang or Hainan Island," Mauk said. "That's where their taskforce is assembling."

"The *Heilong* is their best attack boat. I think it might be tasked with something else." Bowman punched in a couple key strokes on the plotting table's control panel. The screen snapped to a larger scale, which not only displayed the entire coastline of China but also included the South China Sea. Another blue icon, configured as a star, flashed about 500 miles southwest of Manila, in the Philippines.

"You think it's headed for the *Reagan* Strike Group?" Mauk asked.

"I do."

As part of the ongoing dispute between China and its neighbors over control of the South China Sea, the United States routinely moved naval and air assets across the 1.35 million square miles of the international waterway. Stretching from China to Indonesia and Vietnam to the Philippines, the South China Sea was one of the most traveled waterbodies in the world. Over half of all global marine commerce passed through it. The Sea also contained enormous natural resources ranging from subsea oil and gas deposits to vast ocean fisheries.

China, through its policy of incrementalism, was resolute in its ultimate goal to control the South China Sea—lock, stock, and barrel of crude. It blatantly bullied the other nations that bordered the sea, threatening the lesser powers with economic and military retaliation if they dared to challenge China's self-initiated sovereignty. In direct opposition to China's game plan, the United States remained steadfast in its right to transit the international waters and airspace of the South China Sea. Consequently, the U.S. Navy routinely operated throughout the Sea.

To curb China's sea-grab, the *Reagan* Strike Group patrolled the South China Sea. The USS *Ronald Reagan*, CVN 76, was the centerpiece of the Strike Group. The U.S. Navy *Nimitz*-class nuclear powered aircraft carrier with its ninety fixed wing and rotary aircraft embodied the pinnacle of naval power. Surrounded by a dozen other American surface warfare ships and a submarine escort, the *Reagan* Strike Group was a clear demonstration of America's roving sovereignty. And right now, it was in China's backyard thumbing its nose at Beijing.

The *Heilong* was designed and equipped with one principal goal—sink American aircraft carriers. With its deadly ship hunting missiles, it represented a clear and present danger to the *Reagan*. Captain Bowman's orders were unequivocal. Continually track the *Heilong* and if it threatens the *Reagan*, kill it.

Chapter 55

Day 30—Monday

Laura Newman was inside a conference room at the FBI's field office in downtown Seattle. Sitting beside her was attorney Tim Reveley. Dressed in a tailored beige summer suit, Tim was in his early fifties, stood two inches over six feet, and had an agile build. His brunette hair was streaked with gray but remained full and thick. A *magna cum laude* graduate of the University of Washington's School of Law, Tim was a name partner is one of Seattle's larger law firms. Besides representing Cognition Consultants, Tim served as Laura's personal attorney.

"Is it safe to talk in here?" Laura asked.

"It should be while we're alone, but we still need to be cautious."

Laura glanced at her wristwatch. It was 1:04 P.M. "How long do you think this will take?"

"Probably a couple of hours. We'll be lucky to be out of here by three."

"Will I still have to meet with them without you present?"

"That's what they indicated, but that could change."

Laura sulked.

Tim smiled. "When I explain what's been happening, they may reconsider."

"I hope so."

"It's going to be okay, Laura. Just tell what happened."

"They won't believe me."

"Be yourself."

At ten minutes past one o'clock, the door to the conference room opened and FBI Special Agent Michaela Taylor walked inside. She carried a two-inch-thick file folder.

"Good afternoon," she said with a broad smile. She extended her hand to Laura. "Thanks for coming in today."

Taylor and Reveley exchanged salutations.

Taylor took a seat on the opposite side of the table. She placed the folder on the table and opened it. She removed a typed document and studied it.

Taylor looked up, facing Reveley. "I understand you have a statement to make before we proceed with the formal interview."

"Yes. My client is prepared to cooperate fully with your investigation, but there are some underlying facts that I believe are important that the FBI be made aware of first."

Taylor clasped her hands, resting them in front of her. "What facts?"

Reveley scanned the conference room. He noted the ceiling mounted cameras in two corners. A tiny red light on each camera had switched on when Taylor entered the room.

"Is our conversation being video and audio recorded?"

"Yes."

"And are others viewing the live feed of the cameras?"

"That's correct."

"Okay." Tim intertwined his fingers. "First, on behalf of my client, I want to thank the FBI for intervening in the incident that occurred last week. Your efforts undoubtedly saved Ms. Newman from a second kidnapping and likely saved her life."

"What do you mean *second* kidnapping?"

Tim held up a hand. "We'll get to that." He cleared his throat. "My client is aware that the FBI is investigating the status of an individual known as John Kirkwood. Ms. Newman is also aware that Kirkwood is an alias. His real name is Yuri Ivanovich Kirov."

Michaela Taylor chose not respond.

Reveley continued, "Kirov is a captain-lieutenant in the Russian Navy serving as an intelligence officer."

"Where is Kirov?"

"We'll get to that, too. But first you need to know that our law firm in conjunction with an affiliate firm in Washington, D.C., has been in discussion with the State Department concerning asylum for Mr. Kirov."

Taylor glared at Reveley. "We've heard nothing about that."

"Kirov was not yet named. He was simply identified as a high-level intelligence operative from an Eastern European nation."

"That could fit dozens of individuals."

"I will provide evidence that will it narrow down. But first, you need to hear the entire story, which started over a year ago. It will provide the context for your current investigation."

"I'm listening."

Reveley turned toward Laura. "Please tell them what happened—from the very beginning."

Laura faced the FBI interrogator. "About a year and a half ago, Yuri broke into a waterfront house I was staying in at Point Roberts, Washington," she began. "I rented the home to get away from my then-husband…"

Chapter 56

FBI Supervisory Special Agent Ava Diesen sat alone at a conference table on the sixth floor of the Hoover Building. It was half past six o'clock in the evening. She had already called home and informed her husband that would she be late—again. Ava stared at the massive wall-mounted screen at the far end of the video conference center. The digital image of Special Agent Michaela Taylor in the Seattle Field Office peered back. The two federal law enforcement officers connected via a secure link.

"I don't know what to believe," Diesen said. "Her story is so outlandish that it borders on the absurd." Diesen had monitored the interrogation of Laura Newman via the video link.

"I agree, her tale is preposterous—almost."

"What do you mean by that?"

Michaela consulted a notepad before looking back at her boss. "There are several items that we need to consider. First, Captain-Lieutenant Yuri Kirov was and probably still is an officer in the Russian Navy. During the timeframe Newman quoted, DIA already confirmed he was assigned to a nuclear powered submarine based in the Pacific Fleet." She again checked the pad. "It was called the *Neva*."

Diesen remained silent. Taylor continued. "Second fact. During the interview, I had one of our agents call the property management company that Newman said handled the rental of the beach house at Point Roberts. The house in question was and still is in the company's rental pool. Accordingly, we're going to request a court order requiring the company to release its records regarding Newman."

"Okay, so she might have been up there. What else?"

"Newman's attorney claimed they made contact with the State Department about seeking asylum for Kirov. That should be straightforward to verify."

Diesen glanced at her wristwatch. Traffic would still be a nightmare if she left now. "We're working on it from here. I'll probably have something tomorrow on that."

"Great. If we assume for the moment that Kirov was in fact trying to defect, that would bolster her story."

"But he's missing now and she claims she doesn't know where he went after Houston. That may have been part of his strategy all along—time to get out of Dodge."

Taylor sensed she was making little headway with her boss. "Let's say he has returned to Russia and won't be coming back. That still leaves the problem of what to do with Laura Newman."

"Charge her with espionage. She clearly helped the SOB."

Taylor pursed her lips. "Ava, Newman has considerable resources. She will do everything she can to protect herself. If she can back up just part of what she revealed, there's going to be a lot of questions asked about just how secure our naval facilities are in the Northwest and elsewhere. Can you imagine the political fallout from that?"

"Go on."

"At this time, I'm inclined to believe her story."

"So, you accept the nonsense about Kirov's so-called 'spy sub' sinking offshore of where Newman was staying and he washes up on the beach by her house."

"I agree it does sound far-fetched. But if he did take her hostage as she claims, it's possible that he manipulated her into providing assistance. That is a well-known consequence of hostage taking. There is documentation about—"

"Yeah, yeah, I know," interrupted Diesen. "I've heard of the Stockholm Syndrome, too."

Taylor collected her thoughts. "Let's assume that Newman decided to help him—regardless of the reason. If what she reported is true, there must be a record. She claimed that both our Navy and the Canadians were searching for the sub. There would be a record of that activity."

Diesen clasped her hands. "What are you suggesting?"

"Can you contact the Pentagon and check on her story? We could try from here but we have no clout with the DOD."

"I'll take care of it, but don't be surprised if there's nothing."

"I understand." Taylor hesitated. "When you talk to them, please inquire about the other event Newman mentioned—the aborted attack on one of our missile submarines in Puget Sound."

Diesen rolled her eyes. "Come on, Michaela, of all the BS that Newman spewed today, that one really takes the cake. Chinese agents conspiring to sink a Trident missile submarine in Puget Sound to start a war between us and Russia."

"I agree, but we at least need to ask the question of the Navy."

"Okay, I'll ask about it."

Diesen terminated the video conference. She walked back into her office, collected her purse, attaché case, and coat. If she hustled and there were no hiccups on I-66, she might make the last half of her oldest daughter's semifinal soccer game.

Just as she reached her Honda Accord, the revelation hit with the power of a tornado. *The Trident sub base in Puget Sound is one of our most important strategic assets—that's got to be it. What if Kirov's real mission was to spy on it!*

When Ava drove out of the garage, she made up her mind.

I've got to go out there and interview Newman myself.

* * * *

As the sun rose in Hong Kong, Kwan Chi sat at a desk in the office of his Kowloon apartment. He had just checked the draft folder of the Outlook email account he shared with Elena Krestyanova. After downloading the Word document, he typed in the password and opened the encrypted file. Elena's latest report in English text was brief but to the point: *SVR and FSB still searching for Kirov. Believe FBI has him sequestered in a safe house near Washington, D.C. No report yet of what Kirov has revealed. Search continues. Has highest priority with SVR. Will update as information is received. E.*

"Dammit!" Kwan muttered. He had hoped Elena would work a miracle. Kwan composed a new message, also in English: *Received authorization to increase your fee to five hundred thousand USD. Need address ASAP. Pull out all stops. Counting on you. C.*

Chapter 57

The Director of the FBI offered one of the Bureau's jets. Ava Diesen accepted. The Cessna Citation X cruised at 45,000 feet above South Dakota's Badlands National Park. It would touch down at Seattle's Boeing Field at 11:15 A.M. Laura Newman's second interview was set for two o'clock.

It was Ava's first ride aboard an executive jet. The flight was smooth and surprisingly quiet inside the eight-passenger cabin. What impressed Ava most were the seats. The recliners were comfortable with ample room. Each chair came with its own mini workstation that included secure communication links to Headquarters. Accompanying Ava today were two additional passengers—a U.S. Navy Captain and a counterintelligence officer from the CIA.

Her telephone call to a Pentagon contact the previous morning resulted in a firestorm of activity. Within an hour of her inquiry, she received a return call from a senior officer in Naval Intelligence requesting a briefing. Minutes later, she received a similar request from a case officer at the CIA.

All three sat in the forward four-seat section of the cabin. Ava requested a summary from the Naval officer.

Forty-eight-year-old Captain Robert Clark gave his rundown. "The search lasted four days. Both U.S. and Canadian assets were involved. Nothing was found."

A bit stocky for his five-foot eight height, Clark wore a Service Khaki uniform—khaki button-up shirt and trousers.

Ava leaned forward. "Did the search include the waterway where Newman says the Russian sub made its escape?"

Clark pursed his lips while rubbing the back of his salt and pepper hair. "No. We concentrated on the logical route to the ocean."

Ava checked her notepad. "The Strait of Juan de Fuca?"

"Yes."

"So, it's possible what she claimed is true?"

"Maybe." With his brow furrowed, Clark continued. "We just didn't think it was doable—ditto for the Canadians. Those passages are narrow and some are shallow."

"What about the other incursion?" asked CIA officer Steve Osberg.

The oldest of the trio at fifty-six, he had a thick mop of slightly grayed blond hair, Nordic facial features, and the trim five-foot-ten frame of a younger man.

"There we had a positive hit by a P-Three," Clark said. "Definitely a Russian boat."

"P-Three?" Ava asked.

"Aircraft for hunting subs."

"Where did it go?" asked Osberg.

"West, down the Strait of Juan de Fuca."

"Did it reach the ocean?"

Captain Clark grimaced. "We think so but were never able to confirm it."

"Is it possible that was the other submarine Newman mentioned?" Ava said. She paused to consult her notes again. "The one that helped the crippled *Neva*?"

"It's possible, but highly unlikely."

"Why's that? Osberg asked.

"For two Russian submarines to evade detection in our territorial waters is just too unlikely."

Ava decided it was time to move away from the delicate subject matter of Russian spy subs.

She shifted to another hot potato, addressing Osberg. "What about the oil problems in Alaska? Could the PRC be behind those events?"

The CIA officer cupped his hands. "The Russians continue to claim we sabotaged their oil well in the Arctic. That's why they refuse to participate in the oil spill cleanup in Alaska. We remain convinced they countered with the attack on the tanker and the pipeline. There's plenty of evidence pointing straight back to the Kremlin."

"What about the attack on their Sakhalin oil facility?" Captain Clark asked.

"Russians didn't try to pin it us. They claim Chechen rebels took it out."

Ava processed the new information. "So, I gather you don't think much of Newman's accusations that Beijing was behind all of this stuff?"

"We believe Kirov fed her a bunch of BS to motivate her. Beijing and Moscow remain allies—they're tighter than ever, increasing economic ties and conducting joint military operations. If the Kremlin thought the PRC blew up their oil well, they would hit back with a sledgehammer."

"So, who sabotaged the well?"

"Unknown." Osberg gulped from a water bottle. "There's been some talk about eco-terrorism—there's massive opposition to drilling for oil in the Arctic."

"Hmmm," Ava said. She decided to move on. "Steve, what can you tell us about the fellow from Hong Kong, Kwan Chi?"

"He's wealthy. Net worth of several billion. Has a large real estate company with holdings throughout East Asia."

"And North America?"

"Yes," Osberg said. "His company owns office buildings on the West coast from San Diego to Vancouver."

"What about the yacht Newman mentioned, the *Yangzi*?" Ava asked. "Have you been able to examine it?"

"No, not yet. We've asked the Coast Guard to conduct a bottom survey of the wreckage."

Captain Clark rejoined the conversation. "Is that the boat Newman claims blew up?"

"Yes." Ava crossed her legs. "A large yacht purported to be the *Yangzi* caught fire and exploded in international waters about fifty miles offshore of the southern Washington State coastline—just as Newman claims."

"We should have our people involved in that bottom survey."

"That would be welcome. I'll have our Seattle office set it up with Coast Guard." Ava turned to Osberg. "What about Kwan Chi? Have you located him?"

"He's in Hong Kong."

"That puts the kibosh on Newman's claim he was on the yacht when it went down."

Osberg cleared his throat. "Maybe not."

Ava frowned. "What do you mean?"

"Our assets in Hong Kong report he's been convalescing for the past several months. An automobile accident was claimed as the cause. Broke a leg and suffered severe burns to his arms."

"When did the accident occur?" Captain Clark asked.

"Four months ago."

"Interesting," Clark said. "That's close to when the yacht exploded. Maybe he was aboard like she claims and somehow survived."

"Rescue vessels reported finding no survivors," Ava said. "Just a couple of badly burned bodies. How could he have survived?"

CIA officer Osberg responded. "Remember, Newman claimed there were two boats involved, the *Yangzi* and a smaller workboat." He checked his notes. "It was called the *Ella Kay*. Our people located the workboat. It was abandoned at a port facility in Ensenada. We also—"

Ava interrupted. "Are you suggesting the workboat rescued Kwan and took him to Mexico?"

Osberg continued, "We also checked the airport in Ensenada. Four days after the *Yangzi* sank, a Gulfstream registered to one of Kwan's companies landed and then immediately departed."

"Well," Clark muttered, "ten to one he was aboard the workboat. I think Newman is telling the truth."

"That's our conclusion, too," Osberg said.

Ava could only nod.

Osberg removed a file from a folder parked on his workstation table. He extracted a color photograph of Yuri Kirov in his Russian Naval uniform and tossed it onto the table.

"Kwan's activities are important, but the principal reason I'm here is that this GRU officer has been operating in the U.S. and Canada for the past year or so. We want to know what he's really been up to and how he pulled it off. As of right now, Newman is our best avenue for reeling him in."

Ava smiled. "Steve, I think we can all agree on that."

Chapter 58

Laura Newman and attorney Tim Reveley sat on one side of the table in a sterile room at the FBI's Seattle field office. The space was about half the size of the conference room used during Laura's first interview. Special Agents Ava Diesen and Michaela Taylor occupied the opposite side. It was a half past two in the afternoon. The interview started twenty minutes earlier.

Two HD video cameras mounted in the corners of the interrogation room transmitted live images and audio to an adjacent room. U.S. Navy Captain Robert Clark and CIA case officer Steve Osberg observed the proceedings, along with two additional FBI agents. A miniature receiver in Ava's left ear allowed her to hear questions asked by the observers. Taylor was similarly equipped. Both women concealed the devices with their hair.

"Ms. Newman," Ava Diesen said, "before the yacht you were held on travelled from Seattle to Vancouver, did you see the individual known as Kwan Chi?"

"No. The only contact I had at that time was with crew members. I didn't see him until the boat was in Vancouver."

Ava consulted her notes. "What about Elena Krestyanova, the woman working at the Russian trade mission in Vancouver?"

Laura clasped her hands. "She was on the *Yangzi* in Seattle. She came into my cabin a couple of times."

"What for?"

"She negotiated with Yuri for our release."

"You were aware she was an SVR officer?"

"Yes."

"Other than Krestyanova, were the personnel aboard the *Yangzi* of Asian origin?"

"That's correct. Until Yuri and Nick and his men showed up."

"Ah, yes. Let's revisit your relationship with Nicolai Orlov."

The interview continued for another forty minutes when Ava called for a fifteen-minute break.

* * * *

Laura and Tim conferred in a hallway near the restrooms. They spoke in low tones.

"What do you think so far?" asked Laura.

"I think it's going well. They obviously confirmed that you were in contact with the State Department about seeking asylum for John—sorry, Yuri. That really helps."

Laura frowned. "I don't think they believe me about the *Neva*."

"Is there anything that you can think of that might have been left behind to confirm what happened?"

Laura bit her lower lip as she mulled over the question. "We used an ROV—it was left on the bottom."

"ROV?"

"Remotely operated vehicle—an underwater robot. Yuri used it to enter the *Neva* through a torpedo tube."

Tim's eyes ballooned. "Laura, the more I hear about what you went through…incredible."

"The ROV is on the bottom near where the *Neva* was marooned." Laura hesitated as another flashback jelled. "One of the crew, Yuri's friend, died while making a dive. His body is also on the bottom in the same area."

"When you get a chance, you should mention this to Diesen. She's clearly calling the shots. They can order a search of the bottom."

"Okay."

"Can you think of anything else that might have been left behind up there… maybe at the house you rented in Point Roberts?"

"No," Laura said, but the mention of Point Roberts resurrected an old horror. Laura's face rolled into a frown. "They haven't asked anything about Ken—why?"

"They know you were up there to get away from him because of the divorce. There's plenty of documentation that verifies that element of your story."

"But what if they grill me about what happened—you know, what Ken did?"

"Just tell what happened. Remember, it's a crime to lie to federal officers." Reveley placed a hand on Laura's shoulder. "You'll be okay. If things start to get out of hand, I'll intervene."

Laura gave him a weak smile.

Reveley removed his hand. "You're doing a fantastic job."

"Thanks." Laura ran a hand through her hair. "You still want me to show the photo?"

"Absolutely. It will blow them away."

"What about the phones?"

"At this point, I would prefer not to mention them unless they ask the specific question. I'll guide you on how to respond if it comes up."

Laura cast a puzzled look.

"The phones are powerful bargaining chips for you and Yuri. I intend to offer them at the right moment."

"That was Yuri's idea."

"Smart man."

"Yes, he is."

* * * *

While Laura and Tim deliberated, Ava Diesen and Michaela Taylor conferred with Captain Clark and Steve Osberg in the observers' room.

"Parts of her story just don't resonate with me," Clark said. "Conducting a rescue mission as she described is unbelievable. The things she claims Kirov did solo would normally require multiple divers and an armada of surface support vessels."

"Why would she make up something like that?" Ava asked.

"I don't know. Maybe she's trying to cover up something else."

Osberg added his thoughts. "The Russian submarine thing is way out there all right, but her allegations about China's involvement are really over the top."

"I agree," Captain Clark said. "You should pin her down about what she claims happened with the *Kentucky*."

"I will. That's coming up."

* * * *

The break ended and all parties returned to their prior locations. Ava Diesen continued the interview.

"Ms. Newman, I'd like to revisit your statements about what you and Captain-Lieutenant Kirov recovered from the bottom in the—" Ava stopped to view her notes.

Michaela Taylor answered. "In Admiralty Inlet."

"Yes, thank you," Ava said.

Laura clasped her hands to suppress the tremors. "Before we discuss that, I remembered something during the break that might be helpful about the *Neva*."

Ava crossed her arms. "Okay, go ahead."

Laura cleared her throat. "Prior to the rescue of the *Neva*, Yuri used a remotely operated vehicle—an ROV—to survey the damage to the *Neva*."

"This ROV," Ava said. "Please describe it."

"It was a self-propelled underwater robot with a video camera. A cable connected to a boat on the surface where it was controlled."

"Where did this equipment come from?"

Laura cringed at the question. "From Seattle. I arranged for it along with the workboat."

"This was the same workboat you operated from…" Ava glanced at her notes. "The *Hercules*."

"Yes. Anyway, after the collision between the *Neva* and the *Hercules*, the ROV was left on the bottom. It should still be there."

Diesen turned away as a question from Captain Clark broadcast inside her earbud.

She faced Laura. "We need more information on the ROV. What is its size and how long was the tether?"

Laura spread her hands apart. "It was about the size of a standard shopping cart—the basket part of the cart. The cable was the diameter of a pencil. It supplied power to the ROV as well as transmitted data back to the *Hercules*."

Ava listened as Clark made a request and then said, "We need the precise location of where this took place."

"If you can get me a chart, I'll show you the approximate location."

"A nautical chart?"

"Yes, of the Strait of Georgia. You can download it from NOAA's website."

"And Admiralty Inlet, too," added attorney Reveley. He faced Diesen. "Ms. Newman will need that chart also."

Ava turned to Taylor. "Michaela, would you please look into that for me?"

"I'll get right on it." Agent Taylor left the room.

Before Ava Diesen could continue with questions, Laura said, "There's something else to look for on the bottom."

"Go ahead," Ava said, curious

Laura ran a hand though her hair. "One of the *Neva*'s crew, a diver—Yuri's assistant—died. His body is somewhere on the bottom near where the *Neva* was located."

"And how do you know this?"

"I saw him. Yuri used the ROV to recover the body from the torpedo tube. The corpse, still encased in diving gear, was returned to the bottom."

Ava's facial expression remained neutral.

Laura continued, "I know all of this sounds crazy, but it's true. The body was so heavy with gear that it's likely still on the bottom."

Diesen was still questioning Laura about the *Neva* when Michaela Taylor returned. She carried a roll of drawings.

"Sorry it took so long. I had to recruit a tech to print out the charts for me." Taylor unrolled the first map onto the table—NOAA Chart 18421.

The upper half of the thirty-six-inch by forty-eight-inch sheet displayed the southern Strait of Georgia with Point Roberts at the center top.

Laura studied the chart for a few seconds and placed her right index finger southeast of Point Roberts. "The *Neva* sank somewhere in this area."

Ava handed Laura a black felt pen. "Please mark the location with an X and then sign your name and date it."

Laura turned toward Reveley. He nodded his approval. Laura accepted the pen, complied with the request, and returned to her seat.

Agent Diesen pulled the chart toward her side of the table, holding the top half in her hands. She rotated in her chair, allowing the nearest ceiling camera a clear view of the *Neva*'s location. Half a minute later, she returned the chart to the table.

Ava again glanced at her notepad. "Ms. Newman, please continue with your description of the rescue operation."

"As I mentioned, after the ROV located the open hatch inside the *Neva*, Yuri—Captain-Lieutenant Kirov—dove to the bottom and entered—"

"Excuse me," interrupted Michaela Taylor. "How deep again did you say the submarine was?"

"About 720 feet."

"I'm a SCUBA diver. That's crazy deep. How could he make such a dive?"

"He used his military diving gear. Rebreather system with helium."

"Really?"

"Yes, the same gear he used to make his initial escape. That's when he washed up on the beach where I rented the house at Point Roberts."

Michaela eyed her boss, broadcasting her astonishment. She turned toward Laura. "Please continue."

Laura recited her involvement with the *Neva*, moving onto recent events. Chart 18471, Approaches to Admiralty Inlet, covered the conference table.

Laura once again used her finger to mark a location. "It was somewhere in this area, southwest of Point Partridge."

Ava handed over the felt marker pen.

Laura said, "because I'm not as certain as the *Neva*'s location, I'm going to make a circle here."

"This is where Kirov made his dive?"

"That's correct."

Ava picked up the chart, allowing the video camera a clear shot. When she returned the chart to the table, Captain Clark's voice broadcast in her earbud.

Ava listened and then said to Laura, "So, to be clear, this is the location where the weapon was located."

"Yes, Yuri called it a moored mine. It had a watertight casing with the torpedo inside. He said it was designed to be deployed by airplanes and ships because it's too big for submarine torpedo tubes."

"The Mark Twelve?"

"That's right. But Yuri also used the Russian name, which I can't remember. It translated to 'Viper' in English."

"So, it was definitely Russian made?"

"Yes, according to Yuri."

"Hmmm."

Michaela Taylor spoke next. "You said it was buoyant. How was it anchored?"

"There was a concrete block on the bottom. That's where Yuri disconnected the—" Laura stopped talking as the thought jelled. She then turned toward Diesen. "The concrete block—I'm certain that it's still on the bottom. You could send a diver down to verify it."

Ava massaged her forehead. She suffered from jetlag and had slept poorly the previous evening. Her brain was weary from Laura's tale, not knowing what to believe.

"Yes, I suppose we could look for this anchor block after we check out these other areas regarding the submarine, but that's going to take time." Ava looked skeptical. "Quite frankly, Ms. Newman, you have not offered any credible evidence to back up your claims about what Kirov did and how you were involved. I think it is—"

"If I may, Agent Diesen," Tim Reveley said.

"What?"

"We do have hard evidence to offer—right now." Reveley reached down and retrieved his leather briefcase.

He placed the case on the table and opened it. He removed an eight by ten color print and handed it to Ava.

"This is a photograph of the Mark Twelve torpedo mine, aka the Viper. After recovering it from the bottom, Mr. Kirov took the photo while aboard the *Yangzi*. As you can see, Ms. Newman is standing next to the weapon."

Both Ava Diesen and Michaela Taylor stared bug-eyed at the image.

Chapter 59

Day 33—Thursday

Yuri stood next to a widescreen video display in the *Novosibirsk*'s officers' wardroom. Captain Petrovich was on his right, Lieutenant Shtyrov to the left.

"That's impressive," Yuri said. "Must be equivalent to half of the South Sea Fleet."

"More," commented Captain Petrovich.

An aerial color photograph filled the bulkhead-mounted LCD monitor. A Russian recon satellite had captured the image several hours earlier. Pacific Fleet headquarters reformatted the image adding text that identified key elements of the target. Fleet relayed the encrypted image to the *Novosibirsk* using another Russian telecom bird parked over the Pacific. Included with the photo were new orders from headquarters.

The image provided a bird's eye view of a mammoth naval base at the southern tip of China's Hainan Island near the coastal city of Sanya. Located at the PRC's southern limit, Hainan Island bordered the South China Sea and the Gulf of Tonkin. Vietnam was about 200 miles to the west and the Philippines more than 700 miles to the east.

The Yulin Naval Base was one of China's largest and most modern facilities. Created by connecting several offshore islands in Yalong Bay with a series of manmade breakwaters, the resulting seven square miles of sheltered waters provided excellent moorage for an armada of naval craft. For the past two days, the *Novosibirsk* had loitered off Hainan Island's southern coast surveilling the *Liaoning* strike group as it sailed into Yulin.

It joined elements of the South and East Sea fleets already moored at the base, including the PRC's newest aircraft carrier, the *Shandong*.

Warships lined both sides of the twin parallel concrete piers that jutted over half a mile into the breakwater-protected waters of Yalong Bay. The two carriers berthed near the seaward ends of the piers. In several locations, smaller vessels, frigates, and destroyers, rafted together two to three deep next to the piers. Other ships anchored in the bay. In total, thirty-eight surface warships and support vessels occupied the Yulin Naval Base.

"How come the carriers are here instead of at Sanya?" Yuri asked. He referred to Yulin-West, an auxiliary base near Sanya about seven miles west of Yulin. The harbor facility contained an enormous wharf designed to service aircraft carriers.

Captain Petrovich hunched his shoulders. "I don't know. There's nothing about that in our orders."

Lieutenant Shtyrov spoke next. He pointed to the opening in the southern leg of the offshore seawall system. "Captain, the main harbor entrance will no doubt be loaded with sensors. It would not surprise me if they also run nets across, especially at night."

Petrovich altered his stance. "That's exactly what I would do if I were base commander."

"I agree," Yuri said.

He studied the photo, impressed with the layout of Yulin. Surface warfare ships moored at the north end of the base. Nuclear-powered submarines occupied the harbor's eastern shore.

Captain Petrovich gestured near the midpoint of the aerial image. "What about the western opening in the breakwater system? Can you get the mini in there?"

Yuri responded. "It will have similar defenses as the south entrance."

"Well," Petrovich said while eyeing open water near the shoreline, "that leaves the gap from this island to the shore. What about using that approach?"

"It appears shallow in that area, plus it will have sensors."

Shtyrov rejoined the conversation. "Isn't that the area where they have recreational beaches?"

"It is," Petrovich said.

"Then you can expect barriers to keep boaters and swimmers out of the base waters."

Shtyrov touched the screen near the beach and moved his fingers to increase magnification. As the new image materialized, he pointed. "Look, there they are." Several faint parallel lines extending seaward were visible.

The Spetsnaz officer continued, "They're probably float lines, maybe with nets that extend to the bottom. That route will be a real bitch to penetrate." Petrovich looked glum. "You're right."

Dismayed, Yuri pointed to the beach area west of the barriers. "Look at the people, there are hundreds."

The amplified image revealed scores of sunbathers, waders, and swimmers along the shoreline with dozens of paddle boards, jet skis, and sailboats plying the offshore waters.

The Yalong Bay resorts catered to China's thriving middle class. With year-round balmy weather, spectacular sandy beaches, and clean, clear subtropical waters, Hainan's southern shore was China's Hawaii.

Yuri gestured to the nearby military piers. "Very strange place to moor dozens of combat ships and half of your strategic nuclear submarine force—next to waterfront resorts teeming with sunbathing tourists."

"Ballistic missiles and bikini beaches," offered Shtyrov.

The trio laughed.

"So, gentlemen," Petrovich said, "how do we accomplish the mission?"

Indeed, thought Yuri. *How the devil are we going do this and survive?*

Yuri responded. "Captain, we've only got one chance to pull this off. As we did at Qingdao, we'll need to go in together at the same time and then split up. Lieutenant Shtyrov and Chief Dobrynin will head to the main moorage area. I'll make my way to the sub base."

Petrovich's brow arched. "So, you plan to take the mini through the harbor entrance?"

"No. As Shtyrov said, it's too risky to penetrate—that's exactly what the PLAN would expect." Yuri pointed to the rocky island located on the west side of the main entrance to the Yulin base. "We'll lockout from the mini and come ashore in this area. We'll cross over the island and enter the harbor on the opposite side."

"Why not just cross over the breakwater?"

"Too easy. They would be expecting that type of approach. The breakwaters are likely well monitored by cameras and have sensors." Yuri touched the screen on one of the breakwaters, increasing the magnification. The new view displayed a cluster of four-legged interconnected pods. "These breakwaters are composed of precast concrete armor units, not rock." He bent forward for a closer look. "These units look like tetrapods. They're huge and difficult to try climb across."

"So, by using the island that will be easier?" Petrovich asked.

"Less chance of detection." Yuri pointed to the photo. "We'll come out of the water about here on this rock ledge, climb up the slope and then head across the island through the depression area to the inner harbor. We'll use this beach to reenter the water."

"How long is that route?"

Yuri checked the photo scale. "A hundred forty to a hundred fifty meters."

"That's quite a way to lug all of your equipment."

"I know but we'll manage." Yuri faced Shtyrov. "Right, lieutenant?"

"Yes, sir. Three of us should be able to manage the gear."

Yuri again pointed to the photo. "Once we're in the water again, you two head north and I'll go east. We complete our individual assignments and rendezvous back here, where we'll backtrack across the island, and then make our way back to the mini."

"How long will it take?" asked Petrovich.

Yuri reflected on the mission. "We need to allow a minimum of five hours once we depart from the *Novosibirsk*."

"You'll need to be underway before sunrise, which will occur around zero-six-hundred hours. If you have any trouble, I can't wait. Too much risk to *Novosibirsk*."

"I understand, sir. I suggest that we commence the mission at twenty-two-hundred hours tonight. That will give us a couple hours' reserve."

"Okay. Proceed accordingly."

* * * *

As Yuri headed aft to prepare the *P-815* for departure, he remained antsy. *This mission is high risk!*

Orders from Fleet required the Spetsnaz operators to install two recording pods within the main moorage area of the Yulin base to spy on the unusual assembly of surface warships. The underwater sounds collected by the recording devices would provide valuable information on propeller signatures, propulsion systems, and internal hull machinery. *Why risk such an operation now?*

Chinese security would be almost on a wartime level. The Spetsnaz operators would be passing under the hulls of a dozen or more ships in order to place their recorders. Besides evading shipboard and bottom acoustic sensors, Shtyrov and Dobrynin would need to avoid the swarm of autonomous surface vessels that patrolled the harbor waters. As at Qingdao, the ASVs were loaded with anti-sub and anti-swimmer gear. The increased security also threatened Yuri's task. *Why are they insisting it be done now? This is crazy!*

Spying on the assembled PLAN taskforce was only half of the Yulin mission. Yuri's target was about a mile south of the surface fleet moorage along the eastern shore of Yalong Bay. The Yulin submarine base served as the homeport for China's newest and most powerful nuclear submarines. Four modern piers, each more than 700 feet long, extended from the shore into the protected waters of the bay. Four Type 093 fast-attack boats and a newly commissioned Type 095—a sister sub to the *Heilong*—operated from the base. In addition to the hunter-killers, four *Jin*-class Type 094 ballistic missile subs homeported from the base. These behemoths each carried a dozen nuclear armed ICBMs that were capable of reaching anywhere in Russia from patrol zones offshore of China.

Yuri's task did not involve the submarines tied up at the piers. Instead, his destination was about half a mile further south along the shoreline. A *secret sub base inside of a hillside—just incredible!*

When viewed from above, the shoreline aberration was hardly noticeable—a filled platform area about 200 feet long that extended around a hundred feet into the bay from the base of the rocky hillside. At the southern end of the fill was a notched zone about seventy feet wide; it abutted another filled area to the south. The shoreline notch stretched landward to the hillside. It served as the tunnel entrance.

The half-submerged tunnel extended deep into the interior of the hill, opening up into a vast underground cavern designed to protect and service half of China's ballistic submarine fleet. Yuri's assignment was to spy on the underground base.

Like the surface combatants moored to the Yulin Pier, the sub base would be on a similar wartime footing. Penetrating the tunnel to discover the secrets hidden inside the grotto was a formidable undertaking.

To have any hope of completing his mission—and surviving—Yuri could not be detected.

Chapter 60

Day 34—Friday

Yuri was the first to emerge from the water. To his relief, the seas on the west side of the island were calm. About a third of a mile away, ocean swells surged against the sheer rock face of the island's south shore. He removed his dive fins and clipped them to his chest harness. Still clad in his all-black ensemble of dive gear, he scrambled up the rock slope lugging an equipment bag in one hand and carrying his diver propulsion vehicle in the other.

From his perch ten feet above the water, he took stock of the surroundings. Night vision gear would have been helpful, but he could see well enough with reflected light from the quarter moon. The route to the harbor side of the island was just ahead. The dense thigh-high brush would be a nuisance, but the course was just a hundred yards long.

A dull thud rang out. Yuri turned back toward the water. One of his companions had just surfaced and in the process of extracting himself from the water slipped on slime-covered surface. His DPV crashed onto the exposed rock. Dobrynin managed to hang on to the duffle bag he carried. He recovered from the spill and clamored up the rock slope.

"You okay, Chief?" Yuri asked, lending a hand.

"Yeah, slipped on some shit. My DPV's a little banged up."

"Still functional?"

"Yes, I checked it."

"Good."

Yuri looked downslope. He was to about ask about Shtyrov when he spotted the Spetsnaz officer emerge from the sea. No longer buoyant, he struggled with the heavy gear container and his DPV. Dobrynin and Yuri met Shtyrov at the water's edge and helped with the apparatus.

After depositing the equipment onto the ground near the brush line, Yuri addressed Shtyrov. "The launch site is north of here—through the brush."

"That stuff looks nasty."

"We'll manage." Yuri checked the watch strapped to the left wrist of his dry suit. It was set to the local time: 12:23 A.M. "Ready to proceed?"

"Yes, let's go."

It took half an hour for the trio to slog their way up the slope and then descend to the shoreline. The vegetation was challenging. Machetes would have been welcome in several locations. After failing to make progress with their dive knives, they were forced to divert from the planned path, lengthening the journey. Nevertheless, they made it.

The beach on the lee side of the island provided an ideal launch site into Yulin Harbor. The sandy shore descended gently to the water. All three men knelt next to the water's edge. To the north, the warships moored at Yulin were ablaze with shipboard and pier-side lighting.

"Quite a lightshow tonight," Yuri said, his voice a whisper.

Even though the piers were several miles away, he was cautious, knowing that sound travels effortlessly over the water surface.

"Impressive," Shtyrov commented.

"I wonder if the drone patrol boats are out yet," Dobrynin said.

"Count on it," Yuri replied.

Shtyrov cursed. "I hate those things."

Yuri moved on. "Let's make our final equipment checks."

Yuri completed his mental checklist, verifying he was good to go. Dobrynin was next, followed by Shtyrov.

Yuri glanced at the time: 12:58 A.M. "We meet here three hours from now at zero-four-hundred. Since you have farther to go I'll probably be here first." Yuri looked back toward the uplands. He pointed. "I'll conceal myself behind that rock outcrop."

Shtyrov noted the position. "Okay, got it."

"Good luck."

"You too."

Chapter 61

The diver propulsion vehicle towed Yuri just above the bottom at three knots. After half an hour he estimated he was close to the target. Switching off the DPV and adding a squirt of compressed air to his buoyancy compensator, he slowly ascended. When Yuri broke the surface, he faced north. Through his facemask, he could see the nearest dock facility at the Yulin sub base. About a half a mile away, the massive concrete pier glowed in the early-morning darkness, illuminated by dozens of pole-mounted floodlights. Yuri spotted the black silhouette of a low-lying hull adjacent to the pier. *There's a boomer!* The ballistic missile submarine was one of Yuri's landmarks. He pivoted to the right and peered toward the near shore. He was about a hundred yards from the shoreline. The knoll rose from the bay at a steep slope. Like the water, the hillside was dark—barely visible in the frail reflected moonlight. But low to the water, almost in direct line of sight from Yuri's position, he spotted the light.

There it is!

Yuri estimated that the opening in the hillside was at least seventy feet in diameter. About half of the arc was above water. A removable bridge spanning both sides of the tunnel entrance hid the opening from overhead view—a deliberate ploy to thwart spy satellites. Suspended from the overhead rock ceiling, the lights illuminating the tunnel's interior extended deep into the interior of the hill. Fleet intelligence was certain that submarines were moored inside the bored-out cavern but had not yet observed a boat entering or departing the tunnel. It was Yuri's mission to confirm Vladivostok's suspicions.

Yuri was tempted to swim into the tunnel and start exploring. But he couldn't risk it. The Chinese, like the Americans, were obsessed about protecting their submarines—especially those carrying nuclear-tipped ICBMs.

Both Yuri and the navy brass expected that the PLAN saturated the tunnel with safeguards to prevent unauthorized entry—submerged sonar sensors designed to detect a diver or autonomous underwater vehicle, motion and audio detectors in the tunnel's airspace to pick up aerial drones, and armed guards patrolling the shoreline next to the tunnel entrance on the lookout for interlopers. *Time to get to work.*

Yuri released a bubble of air from his BC and sank to the bottom. At fifty feet below the surface, he switched on his light for the first time since starting the dive. Because the bay waters were exceptionally clear, he directed the light beam downward, using his body mass to help shield the resulting glow.

With the DPV parked on the sandy bottom next to his right side, Yuri opened the cargo container he had towed. He removed the probe and placed it on the bottom. The exterior of the unit was similar in appearance to the Remora that Yuri had deployed at the Qingdao—but smaller, about a foot in diameter. It was also reconfigured for a different mission. Nicknamed "Crawlerbot" by Yuri, the robotic apparatus was designed to explore underwater terrain rather than attach itself to the hull of a vessel.

While aboard the *P-815*, Yuri had reprogrammed the basic mission parameters into the Crawlerbot's CPU. Its AI brain would do the rest.

Ready to activate the device, Yuri opened the control panel. A single red LED light adjacent to a mini keypad flashed on and off at one-second intervals. He used his gloved index finger to punch in the four-digit code. The mode light switched to a constant green hue.

All set!

Yuri closed the control panel cover and placed the device on the bottom. Fifteen seconds later, its ten articulated legs extended from the hull. The robot crawled eastward, heading straight for the tunnel entrance.

Good luck, little guy!

Chapter 62

Shtyrov and Dobrynin diverted from the op plan presented to Yuri and Petrovich back aboard the *Novosibirsk*. Included with the revised operation orders transmitted to the *Novosibirsk* by Pacific Fleet headquarters was the codeword OCTOPUS. Both Petrovich and Yuri asked about the code. Shtyrov explained that OCTOPUS required the installation of two recorders instead of just one. His lie was believed.

Instead of swimming to the twin piers berthing the armada of surface warships at the north end of Yalong Bay, the two operators guided their DPVs to the island located just west of the moored fleet. The unnamed island served as the northern anchor of the Yulin Naval Base's protective seawall system. A jetty and concrete pier extended about 2,000 feet south from the island to the base's western navigation entrance.

Shtyrov and Dobrynin scaled the island's rocky slope in the darkness. It was too risky to switch on their lights. Guards patrolling the naval base east of their position across the bay might detect the illumination. The uninhabited island was off-limits to the hordes of tourists residing in the beachfront resorts located west of the island across Yalong Bay. Curious boaters sometimes ignored the warning signs.

It was tough going for the special operators, despite their training. The grade was steeper than expected and the equipment they hauled was hefty. Their destination was about 600 feet away.

Before heading up the hillside, the men hid their dive gear and DPVs in a rocky nook near where they had emerged from the water. They removed the special equipment from cargo containers and strapped the pre-packed backpacks onto their shoulders. After nearly thirty minutes of struggling up the grade and fighting their way through the dense brush, they arrived at the deployment site. Shtyrov looked toward the northeast. Through an opening in the vegetation, he could see the moored warships bathed in the uniform glow of high wattage dock lights.

He gestured with a hand at the distant ships. "This should work fine right here. Direct line of sight to the target."

"Looks good to me, sir," Dobrynin said. "It's well hidden in this area, too."

Paramount to the success of the mission was for the equipment to remain unseen. That's why they traversed through the brush, avoiding game trails and ignoring cleared areas.

"Okay, let's set it up," Shtyrov said.

"Right."

Both men removed their packs and lowered them to the ground. Shtyrov unzipped the canvas cover to his backpack and with Dobrynin's help extracted the black cylinder—referred to as the "package." They set the package on the earth, laying it on its side. Slightly less than two feet diameter and about four feet long, the cylinder weighed ninety pounds. One end of the canister was rounded; the opposite end flat. The exterior casing consisted of a Kevlar epoxy composite. Except for eyebolts protruding from the tube, the package had the appearance of an artillery shell. Dobrynin extracted four one-hundred-twenty foot coils of climbing rope from his pack and handed them to his partner. Shtyrov looped an end of a coil through one of the four eyebolts on the bottom side of the package. He secured the line with a bowline knot. He repeated the same process for the other three bottom eyebolts. Shtyrov next removed four stainless-steel screw anchors, each about three feet long, from his pack. He walked several steps away and dropped to his knees. Employing a metal bar also extracted from his pack, he augured in the first anchor. He next tied the free end of one of the ropes to the anchor. He repeated the same process for the remaining three lines. When completed, the four soil anchors were equally spaced in the corners of an imaginary box about twenty feet square. He tested each anchor, yanking the line as hard as he could.

While Shtyrov worked, Chief Dobrynin took a stainless-steel bottle about a foot in diameter and three feet long from his pack. It contained helium under very high pressure. Attached to the top of the bottle was a rubber hose with high-pressure fittings. Dobrynin removed a deflated fabric bag from the backpack. He unfolded the bag on the ground, careful to avoid puncturing the lightweight black fabric. Surrounding the circular bag, roughly twenty feet in diameter, was a loosely fitted fishnet-like maze of Kevlar strands. The fibers terminated in a steel ring about three inches in diameter located several feet beyond the bottom side of the sack.

Protruding from the same end of the bag was a narrow rubber tube with a plastic valve fitting. Dobrynin connected the valve to the helium flask. Satisfied that the balloon was ready for deployment, Dobrynin turned to his boss. "All set here, sir. Ready for the harness lines?"

"Yes."

Dobrynin handed over two twenty-foot-long lines connected to the balloon harness assembly. Shtyrov secured the ropes to eyebolts protruding from the package's topside, one on each end. Shtyrov inspected the setup from anchors to package to balloon.

"Looks good, Chief. I'm going to arm it now."

"Very good, sir."

Lieutenant Shtyrov knelt next to the package and used a Phillips screwdriver to remove a cover plate from the flat end of the cylinder. Recessed inside were a timer clock and the arming switch. He checked his watch. They were behind schedule. He bent down and set the timer for 5:30 A.M.—half an hour before sunrise. He next flipped a single toggle switch from "SAFE" to "ARMED." A ruby LED light next to the arming switch flashed on.

Inside the package, a timer on the compact lithium ion battery pack was set to charge the coaxial capacitor bank one minute before the scheduled release. Also energized were the firing circuits of the explosive charges in the sequential two-stage coaxial flux compression generators. Each generator consisted of a cylindrical copper armature tube packed with Composition-4 plastic explosive. Surrounding each blast tube was stator winding composed of helical coils of heavy copper wire. Encircling both FCG assemblies were Kevlar jackets. When detonated, the consecutive C-4 blasts would compress the magnetic field generated by the instantaneous discharge of the capacitor bank. Within microseconds, the resulting compressed energy wave would enter the vircator tube. Located at the rounded end of the package, the vircator would transform the compressed magnetic field into ultra-high-powered microwaves. The resulting discharge would produce an energy pulse hundreds of times larger than a typical lightning bolt.

Shtyrov refastened the cover plate of the package and stood up.

"Chief, let's get this thing in the air."

"Okay."

Ten minutes later the package was about a hundred feet overhead, suspended by the helium-filled balloon expanded to just over twenty-two feet in diameter. The two men adjusted the mooring lines to aim the device at its target.

Chapter 63

Yuri tossed his fins and facemask onto the sandy beach next to the diver propulsion vehicle and sat down. Even though the DPV did most of the work towing him to and from the Yulin sub base, he was beat. Mission jitters contributed to his fatigue. He was ahead of schedule by nearly ten minutes, but experience taught him not to let his guard down. "Things" could go downhill in a heartbeat. From his post on the upper level of the beach, Yuri scanned the distant shoreline to the northeast. In the dim moonlight, the submarine moorages remained quiet with no apparent changes in shore lighting or sudden appearance of security vehicles racing along the shoreline; ditto for the tunnel entrance to the underground submarine facility.

Yuri wondered how Shtyrov and Dobrynin were progressing with their assignment. He did not observe any changes along the shoreline or on the twin piers at the north end of the naval base. As far as Yuri knew, the Spetsnaz team was busy installing two acoustic recorders, one under each pier and as close to the aircraft carriers as possible. Yuri removed his gloves and pulled back the hood of his dry suit. He ran his hands through his damp hair. He was heating up. The night air remained in the high eighties Fahrenheit.

Yuri thought about his mission. *I wonder how the bot is doing.*

* * * *

By the time Yuri was halfway back to the beach, the Crawlerbot had reached the entrance to the tunnel. As expected, a retractable barrier blocked the submerged portion of the entrance. The grid pattern of the stainless-steel mesh was about two inches square. It allowed for the ebb and flood of tidal waters but prohibited access to anything larger than the opening area, which included the robot.

The Crawlerbot's AI software computed two penetration scenarios: climb over the mesh or burrow under it. Due to the soft texture of the bottom, it selected the latter as the more expeditious.

Within minutes, the Crawlerbot embedded itself in the bottom. It burrowed under the mesh like a gopher and remerged inside of the tunnel.

The robot crawled down the center of the bore, covering about thirty feet per minute. Shortly after entering the passage, a hostile rock crab using the tunnel as its home challenged the intruder to a duel. The Crawlerbot, more than four times the size of the crab, shoved the challenger aside without deviating from its course. Later, a flounder asleep on the bottom and covered with a thin lens of silt was abruptly awakened when one of the bot's legs clipped a tail fin. The flounder scurried away, leaving a blurred wake. Again, the bot proceeded ahead without interruption.

As the Crawlerbot proceeded further into the subterranean chamber, its acoustic sensors detected faint underwater sounds from myriad machinery sources. With confirmation of a key mission parameter, the bot moved ahead with determined persistence—like a bloodhound on the scent.

* * * *

After an hour, Yuri watched as Lieutenant Shtyrov and CPO Dobrynin emerged from the bay. He met them at the water's edge. "How did it go?" he asked.

"Good, just took a lot longer than planned." Shtyrov pulled back his dive hood. "And you?"

"No problems." Yuri checked his watch—5:03 A.M. "We need to move now."

"Let's go."

Fifteen minutes later, Yuri and the Spetsnaz operators retraced their steps across the island to its western shore. They stood at the edge of the brush line, peering downslope at the rocky beach.

Yuri was about to descend when Dobrynin latched onto one of his arms.

"Patrol boat," he whispered, gesturing with his other hand.

Yuri turned to his right. The boat sped southward about fifty yards away from the breakwater that connected with the north end of the island. The churning white bow wave stood out in the blackness. Navigation lights marked its hull.

"Where'd that come from?" asked Shtyrov.

"Quick, back into the brush," Yuri ordered.

The trio retreated, using the heavy vegetation for concealment. The patrol craft raced by at thirty knots, the deep-throated growl of its twin diesel engines breaking the tranquil pre-dawn silence.

"Dammit," Yuri muttered. "It's one of those autonomous sentries."

Shtyrov said, "That's the first one I've seen here tonight. Maybe it's just a routine patrol."

"Let's hope so." But Yuri had his doubts.

Shtyrov continued, "If it's a perimeter patrol, we're probably okay."

Yuri was about to comment when he noticed the change. The drone throttled back to idle; it was about a quarter of a mile away. Shtyrov uttered a curse. Yuri's eyes remained glued to the faint silhouette of the patrol craft, but it was too far away to make out any details. Nevertheless, he suspected big trouble.

Dobrynin addressed Yuri. "What's it doing, sir?"

"I think it's in ASW mode, probably using its passive sonar."

"The mini?"

Yuri bit his upper lip. "I'm afraid so—we're supposed to rendezvous in that area."

"*Govnó!*"

Chapter 64

Aboard the *P-815*, Lieutenant Tumanov monitored the idling diesels of the autonomous surface vessel. The patrol boat was 720 feet northeast of the minisub. The *P-815* hovered six feet above the bottom; it had been waiting to pick up the dive team for over an hour.

Tumanov's two enlisted crewmen stood nearby as he manned the pilot's console. Nevsky continued to occupy the co-pilot station. The virtual reality headsets both men wore created an artificial three-dimensional image of the water space surrounding the submersible. A flashing red icon at the top right quadrant of the screen revealed the enemy craft.

"Captain, is it looking for us?" asked Nevsky, his voice suppressed.

"I don't know what it's—"

Tumanov was interrupted by a grating clang as a high-powered sonar pulse hammered the hull.

"*Tvoyú mat!*"—son of a bitch—he muttered.

* * * *

"What was that?" asked Shtyrov.

"Active sonar pulse," Yuri said.

All three heard the muted sonar pulse as a slice of its energy telegraphed into the air through the ASV's hull. Mounted to the keel of the patrol craft, the sonar's transmitter was just three feet below the water surface. Seconds later, a floodlight lit up the water surface in front of the drone.

Yuri cursed. "The shore operator remotely switched on a search light."

"It's really hunting the mini," Dobrynin said.

"Yes."

Shtyrov checked his watch and turned to look over his shoulder. "What do we do?"

"Wait and hope Tumanov can shake the thing."

* * * *

Tumanov advanced the throttle to flank while steering the *P-815* toward the southeast. The only chance for escape was to go deep, but they needed time to traverse the shallow nearshore zone before diving.

"Vassi, prepare to launch countermeasures," he ordered.

"Ready, sir."

"Launch number one."

"On the way."

A charge of pressurized seawater ejected a stainless-steel canister from a housing in the minisub's sail. As the *P-815* surged ahead, the neutrally buoyant cylinder remained behind, drifting thirty feet below the surface. About half the size of a standard SCUBA tank, the canister flooded the water column with billions of air bubbles. Within ten seconds, a bubble sphere sixty feet in diameter engulfed the cylinder.

* * * *

"What's that?" Dobrynin said, pointing. Diffracted light from the patrol boat's search beam revealed a deluge of fluorescent bubbles around the drifting robotic craft.

Yuri responded. "Noisemaker from the mini—air bubbles flooding the water to confuse sonar."

"Will it work?" asked Shtyrov.

"I don't know. It's shallow out there. Maybe."

They heard a new sonar pulse from the ASV, followed by another a couple of seconds later.

"The boat is moving now," Dobrynin said.

"Dammit," Yuri muttered. "It's still following the mini."

Shtyrov again checked his wristwatch while looking over his shoulder at the distant Yulin base. Dobrynin observed his boss's action and gestured toward Yuri, who continued to follow the AUV.

Shtyrov faced Yuri. "Sir, we'll need to take cover soon."

Yuri was about to respond when the roar of diesels on full power caught all three by surprise. They turned in unison toward their right. A second patrol craft raced along the seawall, its churning bow wave of white water revealing its location.

"Can they evade two of those things?" Dobrynin asked.

Yuri pursed his lips. "This is just the beginning. More of those damn things are no doubt on the way. They'll swarm the mini."

"What will happen then?"

"The drones carry depth charges. Some may even have homing torpedoes. They will attack and will keep attacking until they kill the mini."

Dobrynin turned away as the reality of Yuri's words sank in.

Shtyrov summed up the tactical situation. "We're screwed."

* * * *

The *P-815* rushed southward at nearly eighteen knots, its power plant pushed well into red zone. Sonar pulses from the pursuing robotic patrol boats were now continuous.

"Launch number four," Tumanov ordered.

"On the way," replied Nevsky.

The air bubbles offered slight protection. The noisy underwater smoke screens diffused the sonar pulses, which helped confuse the AI software used to execute the swarm attack.

The *P-815* crossed the sixty-foot contour. Deep water was just ahead. Once they passed ninety feet Tumanov planned to launch their last countermeasure. The decoy was pre-programmed to execute an evasion program mimicking the minisub. The autonomous decoy would continue south at eighteen knots while Tumanov cut power and piloted the *P-815* westward at four knots.

"We're coming up on deeper water, men," Tumanov said, hope in his voice.

An enormous clang engulfed the hull, shaking the minisub with violence.

"Depth charge attack," Tumanov shouted. "Hang on!"

* * * *

A quarter of a mile away from Yuri and his colleagues, a geyser of seawater mixed with bottom sediment rose thirty feet above the sea surface, followed nearly instantaneously by a muted clap.

"They're attacking the mini with depth charges," Yuri said, his voice strained as he peered into the pre-dawn darkness.

A churning ring of bleached foam marked the detonation point.

"Can they survive?" Chief Dobrynin asked.

"Maybe—if they can avoid a direct hit. The hull is tough. It can a take lot of abuse."

"There's another one," Lieutenant Shtyrov announced, pointing to his left.

A third drone roared across the water, having just come through the southern harbor entrance to the Yulin Naval Base.

Yuri muttered a curse. "This is bad. I've reviewed simulations on these drones. They're going in for a coordinated kill."

"What do we do?" asked Dobrynin.

Yuri was about to respond when Shtyrov said, "I know those boats are autonomous, but they still report back to the base—correct?"

Yuri faced Shtyrov. "Yes, I'm certain base personnel are monitoring everything remotely by encrypted comms. They can override or redirect the attack if they don't like—"

Shtyrov interrupted, "What happens if a drone loses RF contact?"

"With the base controller?"

"Yes."

"I don't know what they do here, but for other locations the drone would automatically revert to default mode if it loses contact with its controller."

"What then?"

"Default mode usually calls for the drone to break off the patrol and return to its base."

Shtyrov checked the watch strapped to the left forearm of the dive suit. "If the mini can hang on for the next minute or so, they've got a chance."

"What are you talking about?"

Another offshore geyser erupted accompanied by a sharp thwack.

"Dammit," Yuri said. "They're getting close!"

* * * *

"Captain, were taking on water in the engine compartment. A seawater intake pipe on the cooling system ruptured."

"Can you band it?" asked Lieutenant Tumanov, addressing the *P-815*'s engineer over the minisub's intercom system.

"I'll get it done—somehow."

"Okay, Chief. I'm sending Sasha back to help."

"I can use him."

Tumanov didn't need to order the crewman. He was already headed aft.

"Skipper, that last one was too damn close," said co-pilot Nevsky.

"I know, but maybe we confused 'em."

The underwater bomb detonated thirty yards away. The resulting shock wave hammered the *P-815*, stressing eardrums and rattling teeth. It also disabled the launch system for the decoy.

With no other options available, Tumanov reversed course and headed northward—back to shallow water. Expecting the target to continue on its speed run to deeper water, the trio of attacking drones probed the depths with active sonar.

Within minutes, however, the AI software guiding the robotic patrol boats would redirect the attack to the *P-815*'s last known position. With three units working together, it wouldn't take long before they discovered the mini lurking in the shallows.

Knowing that the odds of their survival diminished by the minute, Tumanov made the toughest decision of his career. He picked up the intercom mic and keyed the transmit switch.

"This is the captain. Prepare to abandon ship."

Chapter 65

"What are those damn things doing now?" asked Dobrynin, his eyes following the searchlights of the drones.

"Still heading out to sea," Yuri said.

Dobrynin cocked his head. "I don't hear anything. Did they stop dropping depth bombs?"

Shtyrov cut in. "It's going to get real loud in about half a minute, Chief."

Dobrynin glanced at his watch, also strapped to the forearm of his dry suit. "Oh, shit," he muttered.

Puzzled, Yuri turned to face Shtyrov. "What are you talking about?"

The Spetsnaz officer pointed northward, back toward the Yulin Naval Base. "Vlad and I left a surprise package for the PLA Navy."

"Surprise package—what are you—"

A brilliant flash lit up the north shore of the base for just an instant. The hulls of the moored warships—especially the two towering aircraft carriers—cast elongated shadows against the steep hillside that rose from Yalong Bay.

Ten seconds later, the shock wave reached the divers—a sharp thunder slap.

"What have you done?" Yuri demanded, facing Shtyrov.

"Change of orders from Moscow."

"You blew up a damn ship?"

"No, we didn't sink anything. But if it worked right, we took out the entire taskforce."

Yuri gawked at Shtyrov, bewildered and furious.

"We used an e-bomb," the Spetsnaz officer announced.

"EMP?"

"Correct. A focused electromagnetic pulse composed of microwaves—very nasty thing if you happened to have electrical and electronic equipment on the receiving end." Shtyrov pointed with his outstretched hand. "And it looks like it worked as planned."

Yuri looked back at the naval base. "My God," he muttered.

The entire north and east shores of the base were black. Not a single light was visible onshore or aboard any of the dozens of warships moored to the piers or anchored.

* * * *

Tumanov remained at the *P-815*'s pilot's station. His crew stood behind him, huddled around the ladder that provided access to the escape hatch at the top of the sail. Each man wore an escape suit. Designed to protect a crewman ascending from a crippled sub, the suit also provided flotation to prevent drowning and extra thermal protection to ward off the chill of the sea.

Once the minisub broached the surface, Tumanov removed the VR headgear he had used to guide the craft while submerged. He stared at the widescreen display fronting his control console. He had just switched on the forward looking infrared camera. Mounted to the periscope mast, the camera lens swept the sea surface, providing black and white imagery of the surrounding waters.

"Where are they, Captain?" asked Junior Lieutenant Nevsky.

He stood behind Tumanov's seat, eyeing the video display. Expecting to be surrounded by robotic patrol craft, Tumanov worked the joystick controlling the FLIR camera.

"There's one of 'em," Nevsky called out.

"Got it," Tumanov said as he spotted the target on the right side of the screen.

He increased magnification five times. The white splotch near the aft end of the otherwise gray image of the hull stood out prominently. The heat of the engine compartment marked the unmanned patrol boat.

Tumanov checked the bearing of the patrol craft.

Astonished, he called out, "It's heading away from us—back toward the south harbor entrance."

The strobe light at the peak of the patrol drone's radar mast flashed on, along with the standard hull nav lights.

"What's with the lights... and where are the other ones?"

The FLIR camera picked up all three unmanned patrol craft, each one illuminated with marking lights. The three boats proceeded northward in single file, each running at fifteen knots.

* * * *

Yuri continued to reel from the blacked out naval base. From their position on the breakwater island, the entire Hainan Island shoreline to the north and east remained black.

"It was a non-nuclear device?" Yuri asked.

"Of course. Plastic explosives compressed an electrical charge into the pulse."

"There's not a light visible over there. How could that happen?"

"Besides simple power and lighting circuits, that pulse was specifically designed to fry integrated circuits—even hardened ones. Once the computers go down, so does everything else."

The Yulin naval station, like most modern military facilities, relied on computers for virtually every electrically powered and electronically controlled system on the base—from air conditioning controls in the dozens of shoreside buildings to radars and comms aboard every warship in the harbor. The energy released by the Yulin e-bomb generated Terawatt electrical surges in the wiring systems that powered the computers, scorching microchips and erasing hard drives. Yuri reached into a watertight pouch on his dive suit and removed a portable radio. He clicked on the power switch. The display activated.

"This still works."

"The explosive charge that triggered the e-bomb was focused so that at least ninety percent of the pulse was directed toward the target."

Still stunned, Yuri couldn't mask his dismay.

"Look," shouted Dobrynin.

Yuri and Shtyrov turned around. They both spotted the waterborne drone, the strobe on its radio mast flashing. It raced parallel to the island and then disappeared as it turned north into the main harbor entrance.

"There's another one," Dobrynin announced.

Yuri watched the second robotic patrol boat cruise by. Soon after, the third ASV followed in the wake of the others.

Dobrynin commented, "They're heading back in. They must have sunk the mini."

Shtyrov swore.

Yuri stared down at the rocky outcrop they stood on. *Now what?*

The speaker on the radio Yuri held came alive. "Alpha Team, Nomad, radio check."

Despite the washed-out tone of the decrypted transmission, Yuri recognized Tumanov's voice.

"Nomad, this is Alpha. Where are you?"

Chapter 66

"Sir, I apologize for awakening you."

"What is it, Admiral?" asked Chen Shen.

He held a phone to his ear while sitting up in his bed inside the presidential quarters of China's equivalent of the White House—the Zhongnanhai.

"The Yulin base was attacked this morning," Admiral Soo reported.

"Attacked—by whom?"

"Unknown at this time. Some type of electronic warfare, about an hour ago." The chief of staff of the People's Liberation Army-Navy called from his office in the Ministry of Defense.

"Cyber attack?"

"No, physical attack using a directed energy weapon."

President Chen swung his legs over the edge of the mattress. "How much damage?"

"We don't know at this point. Initial reports indicate that the weapon was directed against the moored ships at the base."

Chen's belly flip-flopped as he connected the dots. "The task force—it was massed at Yulin."

"I'm afraid so."

"The carriers—what happened to them?"

"Dead in the water electronically. Nothing works. Teams are assessing the damage. I'll know more soon."

"How could this happen?"

"I don't know yet. But just before the attack, patrol craft guarding the base detected a submarine near the southern entrance to the harbor. We believe the sub was involved but at this time are unsure of what its role was."

Chen cursed as he climbed out of bed. His wife remained asleep, immune to his frequent middle-of-the-night awakenings. "I want a complete briefing by nine o'clock this morning."

"Yes, sir."

Chen returned the telephone handset to its cradle on the bedside table. As he pulled on a silk robe over his pajamas he muttered, "The damn Americans. I know they're behind this!"

* * * *

After collecting the divers offshore of the Yulin base, the *P-815* proceeded southeast for two hours to rendezvous with the *Novosibirsk*. As soon as the *P-815* docked with its host, Captain Petrovich ordered Yuri Kirov and Lieutenant Shtyrov to report to the wardroom. Visibly agitated when the junior officers entered the compartment, Petrovich didn't offer tea. The three men were alone, seated at the mess table. Shtyrov had just provided a briefing on his part of the mission.

"Did you know about this?" Petrovich barked, his fury directed at Yuri.

"No, sir. I'm just as surprised as you are."

Petrovich turned back to face Shtyrov. "Who authorized you to make the attack and why wasn't I told about it in advance?"

"Our operation was planned on a contingency basis before we departed from St. Petersburg. The new orders to proceed to Hainan contained the authorization for us to proceed."

"What authorization?"

"It was the codeword OCTOPUS."

"You said that was your authorization to install multiple recorders."

"A diversion, sir. We were ordered not to reveal any details of OCTOPUS until the mission was complete."

Exasperated, Petrovich rubbed his forehead. He fumed in silence as the tension inside the compartment mounted.

Breaking the ice, Yuri said, "Sir, have you heard anything about the base? Have they deployed any assets?"

"We conducted an ESM sweep twenty minutes ago. Yulin's still dead. No transmissions from anything, shore-based or shipboard." Petrovich remained peeved. "What about you, Kirov? What surprises do you have for me?"

"I deployed the unit as planned."

"Well, after the chaos of this morning, there's no way we're going to able to reinsert you to pick up the damn thing. The PLAN is going to have Yulin locked down for months."

"I agree, sir," Yuri said. "The unit has a default mode like the Remora deployed at Qingdao."

"Will it surface and radio home its data package?"

"Correct." Yuri didn't mention that he had programmed the Crawlerbot to transmit a duplicate data dump via satellite comms to an FTP site Yuri used at Northwest Subsea Dynamics. Only Yuri had the password to access the storage file. It was Yuri's insurance.

"How long before the default mode kicks in?"

"Thirty days from deployment."

Petrovich grimaced. "Assuming it works, which is a huge assumption, if that thing manages to crawl back out of the tunnel into the bay and sits on the bottom waiting to be retrieved, don't be surprised if the Chinese find it before the thirty days are up. They're going to be checking every square meter of the bottom, looking for spy gear."

Yuri did not respond. Exhausted and sleep deprived, he wished the debrief would end so he could crash. But the *Novosibirsk*'s commanding officer was not done.

Petrovich said, "Kirov, how much damage did the mini sustain from the attack?" The *Novosibirsk*'s sonar unit monitored the *P-185*'s entire encounter with the drones.

Caught off guard, Yuri chose his words carefully. "It's a sturdy boat, sir. Lieutenant Tumanov reported they had one seawater intake line that fractured during the depth charge attack. It was banded and held."

"Can it be repaired—with help from our engineering department?"

"It's possible but that will be difficult while it is submerged. Usually, a dry dock is needed to repair seawater intake lines."

"What if we surface? Would that work?"

"Of course." Yuri flashed a questioning gaze. "Do we have another mission, sir?"

"I don't know yet. After we reported picking up the mini, Fleet radioed back ordering us to stand by for a possible follow-up mission."

"Understood, sir."

Yuri turned away, suppressing his frustration. After such a close shave, all he wanted was for the mission to be over. Once he completed his obligation, Admiral Belofsky promised Yuri that his military service commitment would be fulfilled, and he could to return to the United States.

* * * *

In Beijing, the Central Military Commission (CMC) briefing was underway. All members were present including President Chen Shen, who served as Chairman. Vice-Chairman Admiral Soo Xiao stood at the podium next to the theatre-size video screen. Soo had provided a brief overview of the events at the Yulin Naval Base and was now ready to go into details. He advanced the first photograph—a dockside view of the *Shandong*, China's newest aircraft carrier and the pride of the South Sea Fleet. The photo had been recorded an hour earlier by a naval intelligence unit stationed at Yulin. The officer in charge emailed the encrypted images to Beijing from a PLAN administration office in nearby Sanya.

"This is the *Shandong*." Soo gestured to the big screen image of the imposing warship. "From this perspective, you would never know anything was wrong."

Soo advanced to the next slide, which contained a thirty-second-long video clip. "This recording was taken on the bridge after a portable generator from Sanya was brought aboard." The video panned the dozen control consoles centered on the ship's helm. Every screen was either ink black or solid blue. "As you will note, not one of the ship's control systems rebooted."

"What about the other ships in the harbor?" asked one of the seventeen conference participants. The man in a civilian suit sat on the left side of the U-shaped conference table.

Soo responded. "Same as the *Shandong*. Every surface ship in the Black Pearl Taskforce at Yulin suffered the same fate, including the *Liaoning*."

A PLA general equivalent in rank to Soo spoke next. "Admiral, the carriers should never have been based at Yulin. I believe you were duped."

Soo inhaled deeply, expecting the rebuke. "That may be the case. The *Eu Bu* is looking into the possibility as we speak."

Three days earlier, the master computer that controlled the fuel system serving the carrier support wharf at Sanya failed. Because the *Shandong* and *Liaoning* were conventionally powered, they would need to take on fuel oil in order to participate in the Stalking Tiger exercise. Jet fuel for aircraft would also need to be transferred. The PLAN diverted the aircraft carriers to the Yulin Naval Base where the fuel system functioned.

"Were we hacked?" asked the same general.

"Unknown. My technical people are still trying to trace the fault."

"What about our subs?" asked another Army general.

"Those moored in the open bay also lost their electronics. However, the three missile boats moored inside the mountain were shielded and remain operational."

That report brought a collective sigh of relief from all in attendance.

"Sir, was it a cyber-attack that disabled the ship's computers?" The intelligence expert with the PLA Air Force sat on the right side of the table.

"Negative. What happened at Yulin was not a software hack." Soo adjusted his posture while leaning against the lecture stand. "Virtually every control system on the *Shandong* and on the other ships at the base including the *Liaoning* was rendered physically inoperable by a hostile directed high energy pulse."

Soo activated a second video, a clip downloaded from an American military contractor's website. "This video illustrates the attack of a military base by a U.S. Air Force aircraft delivering an EMP device."

Mandarin replaced the original English narration as the video diagrammatically played out the war game attack—approach to the target, release of the weapon, retreat by the aircraft, and then detonation of the e-bomb.

Another civilian bureaucrat spoke next. "Admiral, isn't EMP generated by a nuclear weapon?"

"Nuclear weapons generate EMP as a byproduct of the detonation, but that's not what happened at Yulin. There's no trace of radioactivity associated with the attack." Soo warmed to his topic. "The weapon used at Yulin was triggered by chemical explosives. We have similar devices, as do the Russians and Americans."

Admiral Soo followed up with a brief primer on the mechanics of non-nuclear EMP weapons.

President Chen, occupying the center of the conference table, then asked, "Admiral, how was the device delivered to Yulin?"

"We've ruled out an attack by aircraft. Defensive radars detected no threats."

"What about a low flying cruise missile?"

"Same, sir. The base defenses specifically look for that type of threat. There was none."

"Continue," ordered Chen.

"That leaves only one avenue of attack, Mr. President." Soo advanced to a new slide. "This is an aerial view of Yulin." He used a laser pointer to mark the north end of the base. "Taskforce Black Pearl ships are moored here. Eyewitness accounts from on-duty crew members indicate that the explosion occurred in this area." Soo repositioned the laser pointer to a small island nearest to the warships.

"Admiral, just how did that happen?" asked Chen, his tone peeved.

"The attack came from the sea, most likely by divers from a submarine."

"I thought this base was prepared to deal with that type of activity."

Admiral Soo massaged his temple with a free hand. "Mr. President, we're still trying to sort that out. I can tell you the base did detect the presence of a submarine minutes before the detonation." He redirected the laser pointer to the waters offshore of the southern harbor entrance to the base. "An underwater sensor detected a hostile submerged vessel in this area. Three antisubmarine warfare drone patrol boats were dispatched to investigate. Upon arrival, the lead drone used its sonar to target the intruder. It then directed a coordinated depth charge attack by all three craft."

"They sank the intruder?" Chen asked, encouraged.

"We don't know yet. ASW assets are checking the area as we speak."

"What about the drones—didn't they report back on the attack?"

Soo pursed his lips before responding. "Once Yulin was knocked out by the e-bomb attack, the drones lost communications with the base security center. Without the shore control link, default software for each vessel required it to return to the base."

Chen's face rolled into a scowl. "So, this submarine might have escaped after all."

"It's possible. We'll know more later today."

President Chen squirmed in his chair, his hemorrhoids reacting to the mounting stress. Without regard to the others in attendance, he lit up a cigarette.

After inhaling and releasing a lungful, he once again addressed Admiral Soo. "I know it's early, and I know you don't like to speculate, but I want your best assessment at this time. Are the Americans behind the attack on Yulin?"

"I believe so. Our assets in the U.S. Department of Defense have reported in the past that the Department's research unit called DARPA developed a potent man-portable EMP system. That system was upgraded and may have been deployed against Yulin." Admiral Soo aimed the laser pointer at the aerial image of the base, again marking the island nearest to the piers mooring the Taskforce Black Pearl warships. "Everything points to the Americans detonating the bomb on this island." He lased the area just south of the Yulin base. "They probably used a U.S. Navy SEAL commando team, delivered by submarine. The divers penetrated the harbor and somehow evaded our defenses, which allowed them to install the weapon on the island."

"And the problem with the fuel system on carrier pier?" President Chen asked.

"They may also have been responsible, but it's too early to be sure." Chen took another puff. "Payback for Alaska?"

Admiral Soo narrowed his eyes. "I know we've all been waiting for repercussions, but I'm not sure. I would have expected their response to be much more robust. There was no loss of life associated with the Yulin attack."

"Knocking out half of our fleet is not enough?"

"Violence of action, sir. One EMP blast is minimal."

"Then what do you believe provoked them?"

"They could still be in the dark about what happened in Alaska. My best estimate is they used the e-bomb to shut down Taskforce Black Pearl in order to avoid a confrontation in the South China Sea."

"What about Taiwan?"

"Yes, that too if they somehow figured out our plan."

President Chen crushed the spent cigarette in an ashtray. He dismissed the Commission, requesting that Admiral Soo remain behind.

With the room cleared, Soo joined Chen at the center of the conference table. They sipped tea from porcelain cups, filled from a steaming pot delivered by a presidential aide.

"Admiral, we can't let this go without a response. I have to do something."

"Sir, it's still early. I recommend that we wait a few more days to collect evidence. Forensic teams are scouring the island as we speak."

"What are they looking for?"

"Bomb fragments, trace elements from the explosive—anything that might help identify where the bomb was manufactured."

"Xiao, I can't wait long. There will be leaks about the attack, perhaps even by the Americans to mock us. Our people will be furious when they find out what happened. They'll want answers and I have nothing to offer them." Chen said.

Soo understood Chen's worry. With a downturn in the economy, China's once-burgeoning middle class floundered. Beijing's foremost horror was on the horizon—renewed Tiananmen Square-type protests with legions demanding jobs, free speech, and political reforms.

Admiral Soo returned his cup to the table. "Sir, I may have a way to neutralize what the Americans did at Yulin that will also garner substantial support from the people."

"Tell me more," President Chen said.

Chapter 67

Lieutenant-Commander Zheng Qin knocked on the cabin door of the *Heilong*'s commanding officer.

"Enter."

Zheng opened the door and stepped into the cabin. "You wanted to see to me, Captain."

"Have a seat." Commander Yang Yu gestured to the chair on the opposite side of the table from where he sat.

Although compact, Yang's stateroom was well appointed. His bunk occupied the far corner. A work area next to the table held a computer monitor anchored to a desktop. With the companion keyboard and mouse, Captain Yang had instant digital access to all of the ship's critical systems. Mahogany shelving above the desk contained assorted books and several framed photographs of submarines he previously served aboard. The only personal photo on display was a color portrait of his parents. A doorway near the bed led to Yang's private head, which included a shower.

The *Heilong*'s executive officer sat down. That's when Zheng noticed the navigation chart laid out on the tabletop. "Course change, Captain?"

"Yes, we received new orders." He handed over a printout of the decrypted message received thirty minutes earlier by the *Heilong*'s communications department. While the submarine remained several hundred feet below the surface cruising southwestward at ten knots, a buoy antenna deployed from an aft compartment ascended to just below the water surface for a routine radio check. VHF radio waves broadcast on a loop cycle from South Sea Fleet headquarters at Zhanjiang penetrated five to ten feet into the water column, allowing receipt of the message without the need to raise the radio mast above the sea surface.

Zheng's brow wrinkled as he read. "They don't need us for Taskforce Black Pearl. I don't understand."

"I'm just as surprised."

"Where are these coordinates?" Zheng held up the printout of the sub's new orders, which directed the *Heilong* to depart from the South China Sea and proceed east across the Pacific to a specific set of earth coordinates. Yang rotated the navigation chart of the North Pacific Ocean. He pointed to an X he had penciled in prior to the executive officer's arrival.

Zheng eyed the chart and looked up at the *Heilong*'s commanding officer. "Hawaii?"

"Yes—Pearl Harbor."

* * * *

Aboard the *Colorado*, Commander Thomas Bowman sat at his workstation in the control room reviewing ship maintenance reports. He was listening to his favorite musical score, Richard Rodgers's "Victory at Sea," when an intercom speaker in the overhead blared with a new message.

"Conn, sonar. Master One update."

Bowman switched off his iPod and went to the sonar unit. "What's up, Richey?"

"Sir, Master One has changed course to zero-two-zero and increased speed to twenty-five knots."

"Continue to monitor and report any deviations."

"Aye, aye, Captain."

Bowman addressed the officer of the deck. "Continue following Master One, Mr. Johnson. But remain discreet."

The junior officer acknowledged Bowman's direction and issued new orders to the watch crew.

Bowman walked to the plot table. *Colorado*'s executive officer was already studying the digital map.

"What's the projected course, XO?" Bowman asked.

Jenae Mauk met the CO's eyes. "If Master One continues on this track and speed, it will enter the Luzon Strait in about four hours."

"Hmmm," Bowman said, puzzled. "He's been milling around northern Luzon for the past day. Why the speed run out of the South China Sea now?"

"That is odd. Leaving the area while the *Reagan* is in their backyard."

The USS *Ronald Reagan* Strike Group was headed northward through the South China Sea, bound for its forward-deployed base in

Japan. The fourteen-ship taskforce was a hundred miles off of Luzon Island's western shore.

"I smell a rat." Bowman checked his wristwatch. "We'll continue to shadow Master One for a couple of hours. If he remains on the same heading, we'll call it in to COMSUBPAC."

* * * *

Four hours had passed since the *Heilong* received its new orders. Captain Yang Yu and his executive officer, Zheng Qin, stood at the chart table near the aft end of the *Heilong*'s attack center. Yang propped himself against the waist-high platform. An electronic chart of the North Pacific Ocean filled the table.

"What do you recommend?" Yang asked.

Zheng stabbed the Plexiglas cover over the LCD display with the eraser end of a pencil. "This is our current position in the Luzon Strait. I recommend a course change to one-zero-eight degrees." He reached to the side and entered a command with a keyboard. A red line stretched across the display from the north end of the Philippines to offshore of Oahu's southern shoreline. "That's the shortest route."

"ETA?"

"Ten days at our current speed."

"What about seamounts?"

"None, should be clear the entire route."

"Very well, proceed."

The course change was implemented and the *Heilong* proceeded west toward Hawaii at twenty knots. Several hours later, the Remora secretly anchored to the bottom of submarine's hull woke up. It excreted one of the five remaining tennis ball-sized mini-buoys with a soundless squirt of the seawater. Thrust downward under the hull, the sub passed overhead as the buoy ascended. Once topside, its tiny wire antenna deployed and the encrypted broadcast commenced.

* * * *

Software uploaded to the constellation of Russian military satellites charged with monitoring the Pacific Ocean instructed the spacecraft to listen for a discreet radio transmission. To date, seven separate transmissions had been uploaded and relayed to Moscow.

Red Star Forty-Four, orbiting 265 miles above the Philippines on a polar track, detected the latest broadcast from the Remora's buoy transmitter. Within the hour, a record of the *Heilong*'s travels in the South China Sea over the past twenty-four hours would be transmitted to the Ministry of Defense in Moscow. Of particular interest to the naval analysts reviewing the data would be the *Heilong*'s projected destination.

Chapter 68

Day 35—Saturday

The three men met at a forested compound forty miles north of Moscow. A dozen modern dachas, several support buildings, and a massive guest lodge with conference center were scattered across the 300-acre site. A lake near the center of the facility occupied a third of the compound's area. Reserved for the Kremlin elite, the retreat was surrounded by a ten-foot-high security fence and guarded around the clock by a cadre of Army Special Forces. The facility was on par with America's Camp David.

The Russian leaders occupied the palatial library of the president's residence. Staff were dismissed. The president's wife remained in the couple's Kremlin apartment. The men sat in plush chairs by the window wall, enjoying the view of the lake and the stand of birch trees on the far shore. It was early afternoon.

The President of the Russian Federation raised his shot glass and proposed a toast, "Gentlemen, to the success of Operation Fall Harvest."

The president slammed down the chilled slug of Imperia Vodka. SVR Director Borya Smirnov and FSB General Ivan Golitsin followed his lead.

President Pyotr Lebedev turned to face Golitsin. "The GRU reports the attack was more successful than expected. The men you recruited did well."

"Thank you, sir."

"I'm especially pleased that you were able to take out the carriers, too. That's a real coup!"

"We were lucky with the timing, Mr. President. Our cyber team was able to hack into their system and disable the software controlling the fuel pumps. It will be awhile before they can fix it." Golitsin grinned. "We also left a few digital crumbs pointing back to the Americans."

"Excellent...just outstanding."

SVR director Smirnov addressed Golitsin. "The e-bomb used in the attack on Yulin—should we continue to expect that it will be traced back to the Americans, too?"

"We believe so. It shouldn't take long for China's forensic people to recreate the attack. Based on the damage to their shipboard equipment and land facilities, their scientists will no doubt conclude a directed energy weapon was used. When they discover the detonation point, the gear left behind will implicate the Americans."

The president's spine stiffened. "Just like what those bastards did to us at Sakhalin." He referenced false evidence left behind by Chinese commandos during the sabotage of a colossal oil and gas export facility on a Russian island near Japan.

"Yes, sir," Golitsin said. "The equipment used to inflate the balloon, as well as the ground anchors, were manufactured in the United States. The weapon exploded about thirty meters above the ground. Residue from the explosion will litter the ground and vegetation. When the Chinese check, they will discover that the bomb's electrical components were American-made and C-4 was used for the explosive—also manufactured in the U.S."

Lebedev grunted his satisfaction.

SVR director Smirnov joined in. "We expect the Chinese will fall for the deception. The use of an EMP weapon solves the Americans' immediate problem—revenge for the attacks in Alaska and an efficient way to throttle back the potential for conflict in the South China Sea. They inflict a costly blow to Beijing for its treachery. But since it was a measured response, war is avoided."

"Yes, that fits how the Americans do things—half-assed."

Smirnov raised a hand. "I know. That's why we have the final element of Operation Fall Harvest."

"Are your people implementing the campaign?"

"They are. I gave the order as soon as we had confirmation that the attack succeeded. Our operatives in Beijing, Shanghai, and Hong Kong are busy feeding gossip websites about the attack. The internet is flooded with rumors that the Americans attacked the Yulin base. Beijing is working overtime to shut down the sites but they won't succeed."

"Excellent. What about the final phase?"

Smirnov glanced Golitsin's way. "The general has some new information."

Lebedev faced the FSB director. "Yes?"

"Sir, as you know, we've been tracking one of China's newest attack subs. We now have solid intelligence that within hours of the EMP attack, it was diverted from its patrol in the South China Sea to an apparent new mission. Based on a preliminary analysis, we now believe that submarine is heading toward the American Hawaiian Islands."

"To do what?"

"It doesn't matter. Just the fact that it's heading that way offers us the opportunity to complete the operation in a dramatic fashion."

"I thought the plan was to target U.S. facilities in Japan."

SVR director Smirnov rejoined the conversation. "That option remains, Mr. President. But think of this opportunity."

"Can we move on this quickly?"

"Yes, sir. All we need is your authorization to deploy assets into the area."

"How long will that take?"

Smirnov turned toward General Golitsin. "Ivan, what's the timing?"

"Ten days."

"Very well, proceed—but with this caveat. Once the operation is ready, I must provide the final authorization."

"Yes, sir," both intelligence chiefs replied.

* * * *

Two hours after the meeting at the president's dacha concluded, the *Novosibirsk* received new orders. Commander Petrovich sat at a desk in his cabin working with a laptop computer. He was expecting orders to return to Petropavlovsk, but the new instructions directed him to proceed east to a set of specific coordinates located roughly fifty miles southwest of Oahu Island.

Hawaii—what's going on there? Accompanying Petrovich's orders was an encrypted message for Lieutenant Shtyrov. Petrovich attempted to open the message, but his decryption key would not unlock it.

What the devil?

The latest rebuff from Fleet fueled Petrovich's distrust of his guests. *Damn Spetsnaz!*

Although Captain Petrovich outranked Shtyrov by several grades, the lieutenant and Chief Dobrynin were naval Spetsnaz. As such, they functioned as guests aboard the *Novosibirsk* and carried out their orders independent of the ship's commanding officer. *I'm nothing more than a bus driver!*

Petrovich was exasperated at the turn of events. And then a new thought developed.

Kirov. There was no mention of him in my orders. And who does he really work for anyway?

Petrovich inserted a blank thumb drive into a USB port on his laptop. He copied the encrypted file directed to Shtyrov and removed the drive. He stood and left the cabin.

* * * *

Lieutenant Mikhail Shtyrov and Chief Petty Officer Vladimir Dobrynin were alone aboard the *P-815*. Dobrynin brewed a pot of tea while Shtyrov worked with a laptop computer at the mess table, decoding the message given to him by Captain Petrovich. Dobrynin handed a mug to his boss.

"Thanks, Chief."

Dobrynin took a seat on the opposite side of the table and waited.

About a minute later, Shtyrov looked up from the laptop. "We have a new assignment."

"Zhanjiang?"

"No. We're done with China for now."

Dobrynin squinted.

Shtyrov continued, "We're heading west—to the Hawaiian Islands."

The chief petty officer guessed what was coming next. "Pearl Harbor?"

"Yes, we've been ordered to install one of the specials in the fleet moorage area."

Dobrynin suppressed a gasp. He and Shtyrov, along with others in their elite group, had war-gamed missions directed against the U.S. Navy's Pacific Fleet Headquarters. But this was for real.

"How long until we get there?"

"At our current speed, about ten days."

"Does Petrovich know our mission?"

"No. And our orders direct us not to reveal mission details to anyone aboard the *Novosibirsk,* including the captain."

"This must be linked to what we did in Yulin."

"No doubt."

Dobrynin scratched an ear. "What about Kirov? Can we use him? He knows what he's doing and we might need his help. Pearl Harbor is going to be a bitch to penetrate."

"I know. He's a good man but our orders direct that only you and I are to conduct the mission." Shtyrov crossed his ankles. "Besides, Kirov's GRU. He might be trouble if he knew the details."

"Same for Petrovich."

"Correct. Neither one is prepared for the consequences."

Dobrynin accepted the reality of the circumstances. "What intel did headquarters provide with the orders?"

Shtyrov turned the laptop around so Dobrynin could view the screen. "Very thorough." He clicked through a series of images. "Latest navigation chart of the harbor. Recent satellite aerial photos, locations of bottom sensors."

"Where did those come from?"

Shtyrov zoomed in on the image of the naval base. Over a dozen icons were displayed within the three interior bays—lochs—and along the entrance from the ocean.

"I don't know," Shtyrov said. "If I had to guess, probably someone we paid. You know how Americans are."

"I'd feel better if it were one of our undercovers—more reliable."

"I agree. Still, this helps."

"What else did Fleet provide?"

Shtyrov continued the rundown, seeking input from his subordinate.

They worked well as a team. To everyone aboard the *Novosibirsk*, the two special operators were naval Spetsnaz.

That was true to a point. Both Shtyrov and Dobrynin were originally assigned to naval Spetsnaz units. However, each was subsequently recruited into an ultra-secret organization operated by the FSB, four years earlier for the chief and three for the lieutenant.

Shtyrov and Dobrynin were members of OSNAZ, an abbreviation for *osobovo naznacheniya*—special purpose detachments. OSNAZ originated with the KGB during the Cold War. The principal mission of OSNAZ units was to conduct sabotage and covert action deep inside hostile territory. During the Cold War, OSNAZ was tasked with destroying key military and infrastructure facilities of NATO nations prior to full onset of a war. Within FSB OSNAZ, Shtyrov and Dobrynin were assigned to a *Delfin* or Dolphin combat diver incursion unit, operating from St. Petersburg. On par technically with the U.S. Navy's Naval Special Warfare Development Group (DEVGRU—aka SEAL Team 6), *Delfin* units operated worldwide with absolute stealth and lethality. Although designated military units, OSNAZ

Delfins bypassed the normal Ministry of Defense chain of command. *Delfin* units report to the director of the FSB, who in turn, has a direct line to the president of the Russian Federation.

Chapter 69

Day 36—Sunday

Yuri was inside Captain Petrovich's cabin, seated at the compact table. On the other side, the *Novosibirsk*'s commanding officer vented.

"I don't know what the hell Fleet is up to, but I don't care for it one iota."

"Why Hawaii, sir?"

"I don't know and Shtyrov remains tight lipped. 'Orders,' he claims."

"If I may ask, sir, what were your orders?"

That question scratched a raw nerve. "Transport 'em—like a glorified bus driver." Petrovich massaged his forehead. "And you know what? My orders directed me to follow specific requests from Shtyrov as needed to support his mission." Petrovich sneered. "Can you believe that—a subordinate providing me my operational orders?" He took a gulp from a bottle of water.

"Did Shtyrov confirm his mission is Pearl Harbor?"

"No. Again, citing orders. But the specified coordinates are eighty kilometers offshore of the entrance to the naval base. Where else would they be going?"

"Tumanov taking them in?"

"I assume so. Shtyrov has complete operational control for his mission. I'm directed to provide him with whatever he needs."

"Anything about me in the orders, Captain?"

"Nothing in mine. Has Shtyrov said anything to you?"

"Not a word."

Petrovich clenched his fists. "Kirov, if you get a chance to talk with him and he reveals anything, I'd really appreciate a heads up. I don't care for putting my boat in jeopardy without knowing what's going on."

"I understand, sir. I'll see what I can find—without being pushy about it."

"Thank you."

After leaving the CO's stateroom, Yuri headed aft. He planned to recheck the *P-815*'s cargo compartment. A clue to the Spetsnaz operator's mission might be contained in the special equipment they brought aboard from St. Petersburg.

* * * *

On the opposite side of the Pacific Ocean in the Salish Sea, the underwater survey was underway. It had commenced just after sunset the previous day. The morning sun would rise above the Cascade Mountain range in half an hour. The 140-foot-long workboat plied the still waters of the Strait of Georgia south of Point Roberts, Washington.

Trailing behind the *Titan* was a sidescan sonar towfish. The bullet-tipped cylinder was eight inches in diameter and five feet long. Submerged a hundred feet below the surface, the fish transmitted acoustic energy downward in a fan shape. Sound pulses reflected from the seabed back to the towfish and were transmitted by a fiber optic cable to a receiving unit inside the *Titan*'s main cabin. The receiver converted the reflected energy into digital form and displayed the output on a laptop computer sitting on the mess table. The result was a detailed image of the bottom.

U.S. Navy Captain Robert Clark and CIA officer Steve Osberg sat at the galley table with the Dell laptop. Osberg propped his back in a corner of the booth. He had fallen asleep twenty minutes earlier, his head slumping forward. Captain Clark sat on the opposite side of the table, nursing his fifth cup of coffee for the night. He yawned and stretched his arms. He had the current watch. An electronics technician from the Keyport Naval Undersea Warfare Center near Seattle napped in the crew quarters; he operated the sidescan system. Clark's eyes followed the monotonous bottom plot on the monitor as the *Titan* continued to execute a series of north-south transects—mowing the lawn.

Clark had arranged for the barebones charter of the privately owned workboat. Other than Osberg, the seven-person crew was U.S. Navy including the *Titan*'s acting skipper. All personnel were in civilian clothes.

A U.S. Navy vessel operating in these waters would have raised too many questions.

Clark decided to conduct the survey at night to minimize interaction with the recreational boaters that plied the local waters. The San Juan Islands archipelago was due south. The Canadian Gulf Islands lay westward across the adjacent shipping lanes that separated Washington State from British Columbia. To the north beyond the Point Roberts Peninsula was megacity Vancouver. During daylight hours, hundreds of watercraft sailed in the Strait of Georgia.

Clark eyed the sidescan display, fighting fatigue. It had been a decade since he pulled an all-nighter aboard a ship. He was bored. So far, the sidescan unit had revealed nothing significant. The seabed remained flat with an occasional blip suggesting debris dumped overboard by a passing ship. But that was about to change.

The target was barely noticeable on the left side of the digital plot, about three inches from the solid black line that represented the centerline of the track. It started as a slight smudge indicating a bottom depression. Clark scrutinized the screen in detail.

"What the hell?" he muttered.

The shadow area expanded as the *Titan* continued southward.

"Steve, wake up!"

Osberg looked up, eyes open. "What?"

"We've got something here." He turned the laptop toward the CIA officer.

Osberg scooted across the bench seat to view the screen. "What do you have?"

Captain Clark pointed to the monitor. "That shadow—it's a depression on the bottom, a couple meters deep."

"What's that mean?"

"I've seen these before. Something big grounded out here and left a hole in the bottom."

"How big?"

Clark punched a key on the laptop, freezing the image. He accessed a software tool to measure the length of the target. "The main depression is roughly 120 meters long."

Osberg was now fully awake. "What was the length of the sub?"

"About 110 meters."

"Son of a bitch—Newman was right!"

Chapter 70

Day 38—Tuesday

Supervisory Special Agent Ava Diesen walked into the conference room at the FBI's Seattle Field Office at 8:05 A.M. She greeted the two men already seated at the table. "Good morning, gentlemen."

"Morning," Robert Clark said. He wore civilian garb. CIA counterintelligence officer Steve Osberg smiled.

"You guys must be tired—on that boat all weekend and then Keyport. What time did you get back to Seattle?"

"We arrived at the hotel around ten last night—not too bad," Clark reported.

Ava spent the weekend visiting with her Boeing engineer brother and his family in Woodinville, an affluent suburb east of Seattle. While catching up with her sibling, she kept a close eye on the Yuri Kirov case. She also spent Monday in the Seattle Field Office prepping for the upcoming Newman interview.

"Well, thanks for coming in this morning."

"No problem."

Ava chose a chair across the table from the visitors. After placing a file folder on the tabletop, she said, "As you know, Laura Newman and her attorney are scheduled for a follow-up interview this afternoon. I'd like your help in preparing for it." Ava opened the folder and removed a document marked Secret. She faced Clark. "Captain, I reviewed the summary of the field operations you emailed me. It appears that what was uncovered agrees with Ms. Newman's account of what occurred. Is my understanding correct?"

Clark planted his elbows on the table. "As far-fetched as her story appeared when I first heard it, the evidence we recovered suggests that she's been truthful."

Ava remained skeptical, partly due to her training, but also because of the sheer boldness of Laura Newman's tale.

Captain Clark reached down to remove a document from his briefcase. He passed a color print across the table. "This is a screenshot from one of the sidescan sonar images of the bottom offshore of Point Roberts."

Ava stared at the image. "What am I looking at?"

Clark pointed. "This dark area is a depression in the bottom, about two meters deep. The submarine could have settled into the soft bottom muck at that location after sinking—just as Newman said." Clark passed another photograph. "We found this item a hundred meters away from the depression."

Ava examined the photo—a box-like device with a metal frame and internal cylinders. "What is it?"

"An ROV—remotely operated vehicle."

"The underwater robot she mentioned?"

"Yes."

"Hmmm," Ava muttered. She turned the photo toward Clark and pointed to a thin yellowish cable that trailed away from the ROV. "What is this thing?"

"It's a remnant of the tether that provided electrical power and communications to the ROV." Clark again reached into his briefcase and removed a foot-long length of canary-yellow cable. "Here's a specimen of the tether that was recovered with the ROV."

Ava examined the pencil-diameter specimen. "I need to retain this."

"It's yours."

Ava placed the cable on the table. "Where is the ROV now?"

"It's being examined at Keyport."

"It's evidence. We'll need it back here, too."

"Understand, I'll take care of it."

"Good, anything else?"

"We searched about a thousand meters around the depression, looking for the body of the Russian diver Newman mentioned but didn't find it."

"So, she's lying about that?"

"Not necessarily. Bottom currents are strong. They could easily have transported the corpse out of the search area." Clark hesitated as he extracted another photograph from the folder. "We did find something else during that effort."

He passed the new photo to Ava. She peered at the jumble of metal parts and turned a questioning gaze toward the naval officer.

"I know it's a mess," Clark said. "I didn't know what it was either. But like the ROV, we were able to recover it and it was also sent to Keyport. They examined the debris yesterday but could not identify its source. In that process, however, Cyrillic lettering was discovered on one of the parts."

"I don't remember reading that in your summary."

"They found it after I sent you the report." Clark turned toward Osberg. "When our people couldn't ID the part, I asked the CIA for help. Go ahead, Steve."

"We ran a trace on the number recovered from the debris and received a report back a couple hours ago via secure email." Osberg produced a document and handed it to Ava. "This diagram is from a manual for a Russian rocket torpedo called the *Shkval*. The serial number matches the rocket motor for a heavyweight version of the weapon."

"It's Russian?"

"No question."

"My God," Ava said, astonished. "Is this what caused the sub to sink?"

"The weapon appears to have exploded. If that happened inside the tube, it could have easily sent the boat to the bottom."

"Newman really is telling the truth!"

"That's not all," offered Clark.

"What?" Ava's brow wrinkled.

"While we were on the boat, Steve's people obtained archived radar data from the U.S. Coast Guard's vessel tracking system for Puget Sound along with data mined from AIS."

"What's that?"

"AIS—Automatic Identification System for monitoring marine traffic. Large yachts and commercial vessels are required to carry a transponder that transmits the ship's GPS location."

"Okay."

Osberg took over. "Using the combined data, we were able to reconstruct the route the *Yangzi* took when it departed Seattle with Newman and her child aboard—as she claimed." He paused to unroll an oversized document. "This is a navigation chart of Admiralty Inlet. The red line is the course of the *Yangzi*." He tapped the chart with his index finger. "The superyacht loitered here for almost twenty minutes very early in the morning."

Ava riffled through a folder. She retrieved a document and unfolded it. The poster-size sheet was a copy of the same NOAA chart that Osberg displayed, except that it contained Laura Newman's estimate of where the torpedo mine was placed on the seabed.

Ava placed the chart from her file next to Osberg's. "They're almost the same location."

"Exactly, just as Newman said."

"Then they really tried to sink that *Trident* sub?"

"It appears so," Captain Clark said. "I checked with Kitsap-Bangor and confirmed that the USS *Kentucky* sailed within half a mile of this location, again just as Newman said."

Ava remembered more of Laura's statement. "She said the Chinese used a concrete block to anchor the mine to the bottom."

"That's right. We made a quick side scan sonar pass through that area on our way up to the Strait of Georgia but didn't spot anything. However, with this new information we're going to check it again. I have a team from Bangor on the way this morning. As soon as we finish here, Steve and I are going to hitch a ride on a Coast Guard swift boat and head north to join the survey crew."

"And if you find this concrete block?"

Clark smiled. "The United States Navy will owe Newman and Kirov one hell of a thank you."

Chapter 71

Laura Newman occupied the hot seat again. She and attorney Tim Reveley sat inside the same conference room of the FBI's Seattle Field Office used during her second interview. It was 1:35 P.M. Ava Diesen sat on the opposite side of the table. The FBI Supervisory Special Agent would conduct the interview solo today. Special Agent Michaela Taylor attended to another pressing matter—a new terror threat to the Pacific Northwest.

The preliminaries concluded, Ava commenced the meeting. "Ms. Newman, this is a reminder that you remain under oath."

"I understand."

"Good. I'd like to revisit your earlier statements regarding your abduction and the time you spent aboard the yacht."

"Okay."

Ava glanced at her notes. "You indicated the owner of the *Yangzi* was a Hong Kong businessman by the name of Kwan Chi."

"That's what Yuri told me."

"And how would he know?"

"Nick found out."

"Nick—you mean Nikolai Orlov from the Russian consulate in Houston?"

"Yes, but at the time he was in San Francisco."

"You are aware that Orlov is an intelligence officer for the SVR?"

"Yes. And he's also a friend. He saved my life and Yuri's too."

"But he's still a foreign agent."

"I know." Laura turned away, butterflies taking flight in her belly.

Ava continued. "When you were aboard the *Yangzi*, what interaction did you have with the Russian operative you identified as Elena Krestyanova?"

Laura responded with a puzzled gaze. "She visited me a couple times when I was confined."

"To do what?"

"Negotiate with Yuri for my release."

"Negotiate on behalf of whom?"

Laura grimaced, frustrated. "Kwan Chi… China I guess. Yuri and Nick both said Elena was working for the Chinese government."

"Ms. Krestyanova is the same person you were involved with regarding the *Neva*?"

"Yes."

"You identified her as a Russian intelligence agent during that time?"

"That's right."

"But now you claim she works for the People's Republic of China. Which one is it?"

Laura sensed a trap. "Both. Yuri told me that Elena was 'turned' by the Chinese—I think that's the term he used. Anyway, she was helping Kwan Chi."

"Was she involved with obtaining the torpedo you claimed that Mr. Kirov recovered from the seabed?" Ava handed Laura a copy of the Mark Twelve photo that Reveley had produced in their earlier interview.

"I don't know anything about how they acquired the thing. Neither did Yuri or Nick."

Diesen moved on. "Have you had any recent contact with Ms. Krestyanova?"

"The last time I saw her was when she left the *Yangzi*. Nick sent her ashore for treatment of a gunshot wound."

"Nothing after that?"

"That's right."

"So, you have no knowledge of her current whereabouts."

"Correct."

The interview continued for another forty minutes. Ava Diesen probed. Laura responded. And Tim Reveley observed.

Diesen was about to start another round of questions when a secretary entered the room and handed a note to Ava. She said, "Let's take a ten-minute break. I need to take a quick call."

* * * *

Ava took the call in a vacant office. It was Robert Clark.

"Hang on to your hat, Agent Diesen. We found the concrete anchor block."

"Really!"

"Spotted it on sidescan and just sent an ROV down for positive ID. It's really there."

"Wow."

"We're in the process of recovering the block. Should have it aboard the workboat within an hour."

"Remember, it's evidence."

"We'll get it to you."

"Thanks for letting me know."

"What happens now—with Newman?"

"I'm not sure."

* * * *

Ava Diesen returned to the conference room. She picked up the photograph of the Mark Twelve from the tabletop. The black steel casing housing the Russian torpedo mine looked like a utility pipe. About two and half feet in diameter and over twenty feet long, it occupied deck space in the *Yangzi*'s cargo compartment normally reserved for a thirty-foot tender. Detailed analysis of the photo by FBI technicians verified it was legitimate—no tampering. The fact that the image included Laura added authenticity.

Holding up the photo, Diesen said, "After you and Kirov recovered this device from the seabed, how did you get it aboard the yacht?"

"Yuri and Nick used an internal crane system to pick it up."

"The system used to retrieve boats?"

"Yes. There were other boats in the garage—that's what they called that part of the boat."

"So, when you evacuated from the *Yangzi*, this is how you remembered the Mark Twelve?"

"Yes, it was sitting in the cradle when Nick and I left in the runabout."

"And the other watercraft..." Ava paused to check her notes after placing the photo on the table. "The underwater vehicle your company built—the *Deep Adventurer*—where was it when you left?"

"It was still in the water, tied up next to the boat."

Agent Diesen switched gears. "Ms. Newman, you must realize that your story is quite fantastic."

"But it's true! Everything I told you happened." Laura gripped her hands to suppress the tremors.

Diesen noticed but continued the attack. "The fact that you openly admitted to assisting a foreign agent—a spy—in the recovery of a submarine conducting espionage operations against the United States is—"

"But Yuri told me it was in Canada," interrupted Laura. "Not the U.S. All I wanted to do was save the men who were marooned."

"You could have turned him in."

"He held me hostage."

"You said he released you. What about then?"

"He told me that if our government tried to rescue the crew, they had orders to self-destruct."

"And you believed that?"

"Yes."

Diesen prepared for the final assault. She again picked up the photo of the Mark Twelve. "Other than this photograph, you have provided no solid evidence confirming your story about what happened to the *Yangzi*. I believe you are not being truthful and that you have willingly participated in espionage against the United States."

"No. That's not true!" Laura's eyes teared up. She sank into her chair, defeated.

Tim Reveley came to her defense. "Agent Diesen, we understand the optics of the situation. We encourage you to conduct field investigations both offshore of Point Roberts and in Admiralty Inlet to collect evidence that will validate my client's claims."

Diesen kept her poker face, waiting to see what, if anything, Reveley would offer.

Tim retrieved his briefcase from the floor. He opened the leather case and removed a large Ziploc plastic bag.

Reveley held up the bag. "We do have additional evidence. There are three phones inside. Two cells and one satphone. One of the cells is Elena Krestyanova's. The others belong to Kwan Chi. They were recovered by Mr. Kirov while aboard the *Yangzi*. We believe that forensic analysis of these devices will validate Ms. Newman's testimony regarding her abduction and subsequent actions."

Bingo! Ava thought. She had sensed from early on that Laura Newman had a trump card to play. Now here it was.

Chapter 72

Laura lay stretched out on the deck recliner. It was half past five in the afternoon and still in the mid-eighties. She gazed westward at the dozens of boats rushing across the lake surface in the distance; the drone of one high-powered V-8 drowned out the others. Just a few feet away, Madelyn Grace crawled around her playpen. An oversized deck umbrella shaded both mother and daughter from the sun. Laura wore a sleeveless blouse and pleated shorts. After finishing the interview with the FBI, Laura elected to drive home rather than stopping at the office. Amanda had left half an hour earlier for a dinner date with her boyfriend.

Laura still reeled from the interrogation. Special Agent Ava Diesen was tough to read. When the interview ended, Diesen offered nothing to indicate what would come next. Tim Reveley speculated that it might be a week or more before they heard back from the FBI. It could take that long to run forensic tests on the phones, especially with their encryption software.

The only positive outcome from today's meeting was Diesen's acknowledgement that Laura's home and business would remain under surveillance to circumvent a follow-up attack by MSS operatives. Diesen provided no details, only saying that agents were monitoring both venues. Laura assumed it was a self-serving benefit offered by the FBI. The Chinese threat was possible but Laura suspected that the principal purpose of the federal protection was to trap Yuri.

To supplement whatever the feds were doing, Laura contracted with a private security firm to provide a two-person armed detail at night. The team arrived around ten in the evening and patrolled the grounds until six in the morning. If Yuri were home, Laura wouldn't worry about security, knowing he would protect her and Maddy. But until then she would remain vigilant.

* * * *

Elena Krestyanova stared at the digital image of SVR director Boris Smirnov as she sat in the code room of the trade mission. He wore a business suit with a crimson tie. Elena wore jeans and a sweatshirt.

It was a quarter to midnight in Vancouver; Moscow was ten hours ahead. Smirnov had scheduled the video conference.

"Kwan is clearly worried," Elena said.

"He should be, the son of a bitch."

"He placed another message in the Outlook account yesterday, requesting a progress report on Kirov's whereabouts. As you directed, I responded that the SVR has narrowed it down to one of three locations: Andrews Air Force base, CIA headquarters, or an FBI safe house in Virginia."

"Good, that will give him heartburn."

"He also asked for information about our protocols if we're ever captured. I responded that we're supposed to remain silent, only asking for a representative from our embassy."

"Excellent. We want him to have the illusion of hope that Kirov might not talk." Smirnov remembered another question for his operative. "Tell me about his personal security."

"What do you mean, sir?" Elena said.

"When you last visited him in Hong Kong—his body guards, armored vehicles, personal weapons, those kinds of things."

"At first I didn't notice anything obvious. But later I spotted several guards—very subtle. Whenever he was in public at least two men accompanied him at all times, his driver and another."

"From what you observed, how difficult will it be to get to him?"

Elena digested Smirnov's question. "To take him out—in Hong Kong?"

"Yes."

Elena fought to maintain her composure. "Sir, it's doable. But because of his security, it'll be a bloodbath if it's done in public."

The video call ended five minutes later. Elena stood and walked to her office. *They're going to kill him. And I'm next!*

Chapter 73

Day 39—Wednesday

Nick Orlov sat on a park bench near the consulate. It was the noon hour. He observed no obvious tails; if the FBI had eyes on him, it was from far away. Nick was halfway through a salami and cheese sandwich when his cell chimed. He checked the display. Six-zero-four area code. *Vancouver.*

"Hello," Nick said.

"Hi, Nick."

He recognized the voice straight away. "Elena?"

"Yes, it's me. I'm back in Vancouver."

Nick's heart raced. *What's this about?*

"Welcome back," Nick said. "I received notice the other day that you'd returned." Nick's tone became more personal. "Your shoulder, how are you feeling?"

"Good. It's healing up. Still sore but I'm managing."

She must know it was me—dammit!

"How's it going at the mission?" he asked.

"Same old stuff."

"Traveling?"

"Not much, thankfully. Made one trip west, Hong Kong, and Vladivostok. Probably more coming up. How about you?"

"Just local stuff."

"How do you like Houston?"

"It's certainly not San Francisco but it's okay—too damn hot at times."

Elena asked a couple of follow-up questions about Texas before revealing the purpose of her call.

"Nicky," she said, "I have a little time off coming up and I'd like to take you up on your offer to see the Bay Area." She hesitated. "I really didn't have much of a chance during my last visit. You know—my shoulder."

When stationed at the San Francisco consulate, Nick had invited Elena to visit but nothing ever jelled. *She must want something—but what?* There was only one way to find out.

"Sure," Nick said. "When can you come down?"

"This weekend—if that's not too soon."

"Okay, I'll schedule a trip for a security check of the San Francisco consulate. Send me your flight info and I'll pick you up."

"Fantastic—thank you."

Nick's travels within the United States were restricted to the Houston area by the U.S. State Department. However, he could periodically visit the Bay Area to check on the security of the mothballed consulate. After the call ended, Nick munched on the remains of his lunch while mulling over what had just happened.

She's a traitor!

Maybe not.

Despite Elena's past actions, Nick never had concrete proof that Kwan Chi turned her. He was privy to Elena's original mission—seduce Kwan Chi and turn him into an SVR asset. As part of that effort, Elena outed Yuri and helped facilitate the abduction of Laura and Madelyn Newman.

Moscow must have approved her actions. Otherwise, why would they have returned her to Vancouver? Nick finished the sandwich and used a paper napkin to wipe a trace of mustard from his upper lip.

Maybe I had it all wrong. Could she be innocent?

Walking back to the consulate, Nick smiled at the thought of seeing Elena—especially while revisiting the Bay Area. Despite the trauma that occurred earlier in the year, his longing for Elena bubbled to surface.

Chapter 74

Day 40—Thursday

The USS *Colorado*'s commanding officer sat at his cabin desk. Tom Bowman had just shared a two-page classified message from COMSUBPAC with his XO. Jenae Mauk occupied the visitor's chair next to the desk.

"I think you're right," Mauk said as she returned the decrypted cipher to the captain. "Master One has new marching orders. That has to be tied into what happened at Hainan."

"The Chinese believe we did it."

"No surprise there. It seems like they blame us for everything these days—just like the Russians." Mauk's interest was piqued. "What do you think really happened, Tom?"

Bowman rubbed an ear. "COMSUBPAC confirmed Yulin was subject to an EMP attack. To me, the real question is: Was it from hostile action or self-inflicted?"

"Why would they do it to themselves?"

"They wouldn't do it on purpose. But China has a host of directed energy weapons. If they had an accident or a misfire aboard one of the ships moored at Yulin, that could account for what happened."

"From Master One's actions, it appears Beijing believes they were attacked and is now out for revenge—and Pearl Harbor seems to be the target."

Bowman frowned. "It looks that way. COMSUBPAC is concerned that Master One might try to retaliate with an EMP weapon—tit for tat."

"The boat certainly has the capability with its vertical tubes. It could launch one of its YJ-18 supersonic cruise missiles 300 miles offshore and fly it into the base at wave top level. We'd never see it."

"I know. It's our job to prevent that from happening."

Mauk waited for orders. Bowman didn't hesitate.

"Command has given me broad discretion on how to handle Master One. Once it's close to missile range of Pearl, I intend to neutralize that threat."

* * * *

Nearly fifty miles ahead of the *Colorado*, the *Heilong* cruised eastward in the mid Pacific. The submarine was 660 feet below the surface, running at twenty knots. A few hours earlier, the Chinese warship passed the halfway point of its voyage to the Hawaiian Islands.

Heilong's commanding officer sat in his captain's chair inside the attack center. Yang Yu was oblivious to the threat lurking in the *Heilong*'s wake. None of the submarine's acoustic monitoring systems detected the *Colorado* or any other nearby surface vessels. Yang believed he had this section of the Pacific to himself.

Using the touchscreen feature of the monitor attached to his chair, Yang paged through a collection of color photographs—targets. Stored in the *Heilong*'s mainframe computer were thousands of images of U.S. Navy warships.

He soon found one of the images he was looking for—the *USS Theodore Roosevelt* (CVN-71). The nuclear powered aircraft carrier was nearly 1,100 feet long, carried ninety aircraft, and was crewed by some 5,500 officers and enlisted personnel. South Sea Fleet headquarters provided Commander Yang with the *Roosevelt*'s current location. It was just over a thousand miles ahead of the *Heilong*, also on an eastbound course.

After a six-month deployment in the North Pacific with more than half of that time spent offshore of North Korea, the *Theodore Roosevelt* and its twelve-ship strike group were headed to their homeport in San Diego. However, because the group had spent more than seventy consecutive days at sea, the ships would stop in Pearl Harbor for liberty. The sailors would have five days to enjoy Oahu before completing the voyage home.

In two days, the strike force would sail into Pearl Harbor. As juicy a prize as the *Roosevelt* was, the carrier was not Yang's target. Beijing wanted a measured response to the attack at Yulin. The Central Military Commission selected one of the *Roosevelt*'s escorts as the *Heilong*'s prey—an Arleigh-Burke-class guided missile destroyer. Captain Yang queued up the file of the USS *Halsey* (DDG-97). The ship was 510 feet long and displaced 9,300 tons. Powered by four gas turbines generating 100,000 horsepower, the *Halsey* carried an arsenal of missiles, guns, and torpedoes along with two helicopters.

The *Halsey* had a crew of 260 but the normal complement would be supplemented when the destroyer departed Pearl Harbor. Sixty-seven friends and family members of the crew would embark with the ship for a Tiger Cruise back to San Diego.

The CMC selected the *Halsey* because of its civilian passengers during the trip home. Yang worried, however, that as justified as China was for sinking the warship as retribution for the U.S. attack on Yulin, destroying the *Halsey* with innocents aboard would further enrage the Americans. Despite his reservations, Commander Yang would carry out his orders. *Heilong* would loiter offshore of Pearl Harbor, waiting for the *Halsey* to depart. It would then trail the destroyer. When the ship was halfway home, the *Heilong* would attack with an overwhelming assault of torpedoes and missiles.

* * * *

Captain First Rank Leonid Petrovich lay on his bunk. After nearly twenty-four hours on duty, he had retired to his cabin, handing off control of the *Novosibirsk* to his executive officer. The XO promised not to bother him for the next eight hours—unless a real emergency occurred.

Sleep eluded Petrovich. Instead, he continued to process the latest news. *What is that damn boat up to?*

Several days earlier, *Novosibirsk* received a new ELF bell ringer signal from Kamchatka. He ordered deployment of the VLF buoy antenna. The cipher from Pacific Fleet command was received and decoded. The message notified Petrovich that a Chinese Type 095 nuclear-powered fast attack sub might also be in route to Hawaii. To maintain mission security, Fleet ordered Petrovich to avoid the PLAN sub. The captain was thankful for the warning. The 095 boats were on par with the *Novosibirsk*, which meant he would take great care to avoid the Chinese submarine.

Another issue troubled Petrovich—the Spetsnaz team. Shtyrov and Dobrynin remained aloof, offering no details on their pending assignment. The special operators continued to drill with the *P-815*'s crew, rehearsing the Pearl Harbor mission. Petrovich accepted the cold reality that Fleet had decided not to share mission details with him. What caused him anxiety were his orders to deliver the spies and the *P-815* to the very doorstep of the United States Navy Pacific Fleet headquarters. It was equivalent to an American submarine passing under the Eastern Bosporus Strait Bridge and sailing into Vladivostok's Golden Horn Bay. *This operation is insane. What the devil are those idiots in command thinking?*

* * * *

Nearly 2,500 miles to the west, the apparatus that Yuri left behind at Yulin on Hainan Island woke up. It was 3:12 A.M. local time. After sitting on the bottom listening and recording for a week, the Crawlerbot's AI software algorithms decided it was time to conduct the next phase of its mission. The robot's bladder expanded from a charge of compressed air. Now buoyant, the device ascended, reaching the water surface in fifty seconds. It floated inside the vast subterranean chamber. The water was still. The Crawlerbot's acoustic sensors detected the faint hum from overhead fans used to ventilate the cavern. A recessed panel at the exposed crown of the Crawlerbot's hull rotated open. Inside the cargo compartment, the miniature aerial drone pulsed to life. The Firefly took flight, propelled by twin counter-rotating blades. About the size of a dragonfly, it was virtually silent.

The Firefly rose thirty feet, its bat-like echo-ranging sensors exploring the vast cavern and its contents. The survey took a couple of minutes to complete. Three candidate targets were identified. The drone approached the first candidate. The Firefly's infrared sensors checked for the heat signature of humans. Detecting no guards, it approached the huge black hull of the ballistic missile submarine. Forty-five seconds later, it located the open hatch.

The Firefly hovered five feet over the opening. It switched on its onboard video camera and descended into the interior of the submarine.

Chapter 75

Day 43—Sunday

"Good morning," Nick Orlov said, admiring the sensuous form lying under a blanket on the bed. The beat of pounding surf rushed through the nearby open slider to the deck.

Elena Krestyanova rolled onto her side and looked up. Nick stood beside the bed. Garbed in blue jeans, a T-shirt, and sandals, he held a pair of paper cups stenciled with a familiar logo.

Elena sat up, pulling a sheet over her breasts. She caught a whiff of the intoxicating brew.

"You've been busy."

"Woke up early and went for a walk on the beach. I found a Starbucks just down the road." Nick sat on the side of the mattress and handed the caffè mocha to Elena.

"Umm," she said, savoring the sweet espresso. "This is wonderful. I'm glad you remembered. Thank you."

Nick beamed. "I still love tea but this isn't bad."

"No, it isn't."

Elena had arrived in San Francisco the previous afternoon. Nick picked her up at the airport. Instead of heading north toward downtown, they drove south in Nick's rental—a spiffy VW Beetle convertible. Nick wanted to show Elena his favorite part of California.

The two Russian intelligence officers arrived in Monterey Bay near sunset. Nick randomly selected a beach hotel north of the city, electing not to reserve a room in advance. If the FBI managed to follow the pair despite their combined evasion protocols, the chances that the hotel room might be bugged were sharply reduced. As they finished their coffees, Nick was tempted to shed his clothing and climb back into bed with Elena. Their love-making the previous evening remained fresh on his mind. But that could wait.

"I need a shower," Elena said as she placed her empty cup on a bedside table. She stood, her splendid form on full display. "Where are we going today?"

"You've got to see the aquarium. It's incredible."

"Cool," she said, casting a seductive smile Nick's way. "I'll be ready soon."

While Elena showered, Nick walked onto the balcony and gazed at the bay. It was a cloudless morning. Several hardcore surfers were already riding the swells. He lit up a Winston. Within minutes of meeting Elena the previous afternoon, Nick had noticed the change in her. The new hairstyle was obvious, but her altered demeanor struck him. He'd sensed something was wrong.

Nick couldn't quite pin down the disparity, but he perceived she was troubled. And then there was her shoulder. While in their hurry to shed clothing in anticipation of sex, he had noticed the scar. To repair the shattered collarbone, the surgeon had opened up the left shoulder far beyond the pencil-diameter puncture caused by the nine-millimeter slug.

Nick's feelings for Elena were rekindling, yet he couldn't trust her. Both he and Yuri were certain that Kwan had turned her. Nick himself ordered her returned to Moscow for questioning by the SVR. But then headquarters sent her back to Vancouver as if nothing had happened.

Why?

And now she'd reached out to him. Again, why?

Nick crushed the butt in an ashtray on the deck table. He promised himself that before he dropped Elena off for her return flight to Vancouver, he would find answers to his questions.

* * * *

SVR Director Borya Smirnov sat at an office desk in his country dacha north of Moscow. Although it was late Sunday evening, he was working. The following afternoon he would meet with President Lebedev and FSB General Golitsin to report on the status of Operation Fall Harvest. In anticipation of the briefing, he reviewed the latest communications and intelligence summaries for the mission. He was about to log off his computer when he remembered a minor item. Several days had passed since he had checked on Elena Krestyanova's whereabouts. Smirnov typed the password that provided access to the special file. *What's this?* he wondered as he scanned the tracking data. Expecting Vancouver, he was stunned to see her location. *California! What's she doing there?*

* * * *

The sun kissed the ocean horizon in the cloudless sky. Endless swells expended their energy on the mile-long beach, churning sand and seawater into a turbulent vortex.

Elena and Nick sat hip-to-hip midway up the broad pocket beach. Their shoeless toes probed the white grainy sand, savoring the delicious touch. They both relished the vestiges of the long, wonderful day.

"This truly is a magic place," Elena said. "Thank you for sharing it with me."

"My pleasure." Nick cupped Elena's face with his hands, and kissed her warm, moist lips.

The embrace lasted for half a minute. It would have been so easy to continue to the next phase, but beach walkers strolled nearby, also enjoying the sunset. Nick and Elena were in Carmel-by-the-Sea, a quaint waterfront community bordering the Pacific Ocean in California's Monterey County. After visiting the Monterey Aquarium and lunching at a restaurant in Pebble Beach, they had driven to Carmel. Nick rented a one-bedroom cottage a block from the beach.

"I think I could live here forever," Elena said.

"Me too. It's truly beautiful. Maybe you—we could retire here."

Elena stared westward, silent.

"What's wrong?" Nick said.

Elena remained mute. That's when Nick noticed the tear flowing down her cheek.

Nick placed an arm over her shoulders and pulled her close. "What's the matter?"

"I'll never be able to retire... I don't have much time left."

Nick angled his head to the side, his brow furled. "Are you ill?"

Elena reached up with her right hand. She pulled the collar of her cotton blouse to the side, exposing the clavicle blemish. "The SVR poisoned me."

* * * *

Yuri Kirov waited until the Spetsnaz operators and the *P-815*'s crew departed the minisub. It was the first time in a week that the minisub was not occupied by at least one of the special mission's team members. Just after the *Novosibirsk* started its transpacific run, Shtyrov and Dobrynin moved into the *P-815* and took over.

The team headed to the *Novosibirsk*'s accommodations compartment, ready for a joint meal. They had been rehearsing for days. But rehearsing what? Yuri was determined to find out.

Yuri passed through the *Novosibirsk*'s air lock module, entering the midget. As he expected, the submersible was powered down, except for lighting.

He sat in the pilot's seat and activated the navigation system. He ran into a roadblock after switching on the power. The LCD screen flashed a prompt, requesting a password.

Yuri cursed. He looked over the console and the adjacent co-pilot station, hoping to discover a hidden spot where one of the crew might have penciled the password. No joy. Yuri switched off the console and headed to the cargo compartment. He attempted to examine the Spetsnaz team's equipment but discovered a new padlock on the mini's storage locker. Frustrated, he returned to the galley and brewed a pot of tea.

While sitting at the mess table, he discovered a rolled-up document lying on a shelf near the table. He unfolded the navigation chart.

Someone had hand drawn a series of course lines in red ink starting from offshore in deep water and continuing through the narrow entrance channel into the vast inland harbor. A red X marked the endpoint of the route.

Yuri massaged his forehead as reality set in. *Pearl Harbor—what are they planning to do there?*

* * * *

Nick couldn't sleep. It was a quarter to midnight. He relocated to the cottage's deck just outside the bedroom. Elena remained in the bed, asleep. Nick tilted back the wooden deckchair, his sandals propped up on the nearby table. The soothing beat of distant surf heightened the otherwise still night air. It remained balmy—T-shirt and shorts comfortable. The black overhead sparkled with stars.

Nick lit up and took a deep drag from a Winston. The familiar rush of nicotine helped but his rage persisted.

"Dammit," Nick muttered, appalled at Elena's story.

Several hours earlier while sitting on the beach, Elena let it all out, a deluge that astonished Nick. *What a dreadful childhood!*

Abandoned by her single mother at two years old, Nastasia Vasileva spent the next dozen years trapped in a succession of heartless orphanages on the outskirts of Moscow. Bullied, picked on, and harassed, shy and demure Nastasia endured the institutional torment.

Raped at twelve years old—stinking orphanages!

The forty-four-year-old married attendant visited her bed weekly for half a year, threatening to slit her throat if she told anyone. Only when he was fired for perpetual drunkenness did the abuse cease. Not yet fertile, preteen Nastasia mercifully escaped pregnancy.

Our government should be ashamed of itself.

Nastasia excelled at her schoolwork, but it was her golden mane and blossoming body that attracted the female recruiter from the SVR. Rescued from the child penal colony at fourteen, Nastasia transferred to a special school just blocks away from the Kremlin—an institute of new horrors. The four years of indoctrination were subtle but persistent. When Nastasia and her classmates were ready for university, all but two girls and a boy were deemed acceptable for future service. The graduates moved to their assigned schools with new cover identities, including fictitious, detailed family histories.

Nastasia Vasileva aka Elena Krestyanova accepted her role as a seductress without question. Lacking any family foundation to fall back on for moral clarity, she found it natural to use her sex as a tool of her government. She embraced her work, wishing only to please her superiors—just as the training predicted.

What they did to her was unconscionable. No wonder she broke!

Elena revealed what Nick already suspected. The MSS and Kwan Chi had turned her. She passed on state secrets to fund her exodus—from the SVR, Russia, and Kwan.

That son of a bitch Smirnov—what a prick.

The poison capsule embedded in Elena's collarbone was the final insult. A death bomb with a short fuse.

I've got to help her—but what can I do?

Nick mulled over the notion he'd been developing all evening.

As he inhaled a last lungful from the Winston, the plan jelled.

Chapter 76

"Captain, at Master One's current heading and speed, it will cross the range line in approximately sixty minutes."

Commander Bowman stood beside *Colorado*'s senior sonar technician, who sat at a control room console. "Okay, Richey. Until further notice, I want an update on Master One every five minutes—or sooner if it deviates."

"Aye, sir."

Bowman relocated to the plot table near the center of the compartment. Superimposed onto a digital NOAA chart of the Hawaiian Islands was Master One's track line. A red star marked the *Heilong*'s location. Adjacent to the red star was a blue star. During the past twelve hours, the *Colorado* had closed to within two miles. A green arc also overlaid the electronic plot. The radial arc extended 400 nautical miles from Joint Base Pearl Harbor-Hickam on Oahu Island—a hundred miles farther than the range of Master One's missiles. The red and blue icons closed on the limit line.

Colorado's executive officer joined Bowman. Jenae Mauk stood next to the table, eying the plot.

"He's getting close, Skipper," Mauk said.

"What's your take?"

"This turkey is definitely up to something." Mauk checked the ship's clock on a nearby bulkhead and made a conversion. "The sun is up now. Whatever they have planned, I doubt they'll do it in daylight."

"You're probably right, but we can't take that chance."

"So, we proceed as planned."

"Affirmative.

* * * *

Commander Yang Yu sat in his captain's chair reviewing maintenance reports on his tablet. Although fatigued from the journey across the Pacific, he remained upbeat. His ship and crew were performing well, and he would soon carry out the most important mission of his career. The *Heilong* was approximately 700 kilometers west of Oahu Island. In twenty hours, the submarine would reach the planned holding zone, a patch of the ocean a hundred kilometers southwest of Pearl Harbor. Yang planned to loiter there, waiting for his prey.

The latest radio message from North Sea Fleet headquarters indicated that the USS *Halsey* was due to depart Pearl for San Diego in two days.

Yang surveyed the attack center. All consoles were manned. His XO stood at the forward end of the compartment, monitoring the helm and planes operators. Two minutes earlier, sonar reported no subsurface contacts—just routine surface traffic. Yang finished reading the last report and set the tablet aside. He settled into the plush leather cushion lining the chair back and closed his eyes. Before drifting off Yang pictured Tao, his best friend and lover. He promised himself that they would vacation together during his next leave—maybe in Thailand or Vietnam, somewhere they could relax without condemning eyes.

Yang managed six minutes of bliss when his world turned upside down. The *Heilong*'s hull radiated with an enormous CLANG. Yang woke. Every person in the compartment stared at their captain, each set of eyes broadcasting alarm.

Yang stood, not yet quite certain what had occurred. Another CLANG hammered the submarine's hull. Yang cursed. "The Americans are targeting us!" He turned to face the officer of the watch. "Hard right rudder. All ahead flank. Make your depth 400 meters."

* * * *

"Captain, Master One has increased turns to thirty-plus knots. Heading southeastward and diving."

"Keep the reports coming in, Richey. He's going to try everything in the book and then some to shake us." Commander Bowman stood next to the sonar technician.

"I'll stick on him like superglue, sir."

"Atta boy."

Bowman turned to face *Colorado*'s second in command. "Well, Jenae, we now have his full attention."

"Indeed. How long do we stay on him?"

"We're going to hound him as long as it takes to convince him to return home."

"And if he decides to challenge us?"

"That will be very bad for him."

The *Colorado* closed to within one mile of the *Heilong* before blasting it with a massive ping from its Large Aperture Bow sonar array. Prior to sending the wakeup call, Bowman ordered the *Colorado* to battle stations torpedo. COMSUBPAC's orders were unambiguous. If the *Heilong* did something stupid, Bowman would not hesitate to send it to the bottom.

* * * *

"All stop!" ordered Petrovich.

The *Novosibirsk*'s watch officer repeated the order, and within seconds power to the submarine's propeller shaft was disengaged. Petrovich grabbed an intercom microphone. "Sonar, Captain. Where is that active sonar coming from?"

Everyone in the attack center heard the pulse. Acoustic energy travels approximately four times faster underwater than in the air. The *Novosibirsk* was just over a hundred miles west of the *Colorado*.

Aggravated at the delay in the sonar compartment's response, Petrovich was about to repeat his call when another ping reverberated throughout the attack center.

Petrovich uttered a curse just as the *Novosibirsk*'s senior sonar technician responded. "Captain, sonar. Positive ID on pings. American *Virginia*-class boat, Block Three, LAB sonar array. Range 165 kilometers, bearing zero-one-five degrees relative."

"What's it targeting?"

"Unknown contact, Captain. Rebound signal is weak. I estimate target is close to the emitter—within two kilometers."

Petrovich stepped to the plot table. A digital copy of NOAA Chart 540—Hawaiian Islands—filled the one-meter-square electronic display. The watch officer joined Petrovich.

"Exercise, Captain?" he asked.

"Maybe. But whatever they're up to is far beyond their normal exercise zone." He pointed to a boxed-in area centered on the Kauai Channel between Oahu and Kauai. "This is the designated submarine operating area."

The junior officer noted the 700-kilometer separation between the U.S. Navy's sub operating area and the source of the active sonar emission. "If it's not an exercise, what are they doing?"

"I don't know." Petrovich looked up, meeting his subordinate's eyes. "Order the boat to ultra-quiet. We're going to hover here for a while and see what plays out."

"Understood."

* * * *

Ten hours had passed since the initial encounter and the *Colorado* continued to hound the *Heilong*. After repeated efforts to evade SSN 788, the Chinese submarine ceased high-speed maneuvering and turned to a westerly course—away from Hawaii. The *Colorado* followed two miles behind, periodically harassing the Type 095 boat with active sonar pulses. Three miles to *Colorado*'s starboard, a second American submarine shadowed the *Heilong*. The USS *Olympia* was ready to attack upon orders.

Captain Bowman remained in the *Colorado*'s control room. With Pearl Harbor now over 600 miles in the *Heilong*'s wake, the immediate danger to the homeland from a missile strike was abated. Nevertheless, all six tubes of his vessel contained warshots ready for instant release.

Should the *Heilong* attempt to attack either the *Colorado* or *Olympia*, Bowman was pre-approved to sink it.

Chapter 77

Day 45—Tuesday

The clinic was in an upscale section of Tijuana. The facilities were modern and the staff exceptionally informative and polite. The Mexican coastal city specialized in medical tourism. Nick made the arrangements the day before by phone while in Carmel. They drove to San Diego, staying in a hotel on Coronado Bay that night.

Nick Orlov and Elena Krestyanova had walked across the border two and a half hours earlier. A cab delivered them to the physician's office within ten minutes. At Nick's suggestion, Elena left her cell phone in the hotel room's mini safe along with her travel documents—her official Russian diplomatic papers and four different passports, all but one of her collection of credit cards, and most of her cash. Nick did the same. For reentry into the U.S., Elena and Nick carried their Canadian passports, issued over a year earlier by the SVR. Nick and Elena sat in the reception area of the surgeon's office. It was a few minutes before noon. Elena had already spent an hour-plus in the clinic's medical imaging-radiology unit.

An attractive young woman in green scrubs approached the couple. "Ms. Martin," she said in perfect English, using one of Elena's aliases, "the doctor will see you now."

"I want Nick to come with me."

"Of course."

Dr. Luis Aragón was in his late forties. Five-foot-ten with an athletic build and graying black hair, he was a handsome man. The wall behind his desk displayed a medical degree from the *Facultad de Medicina* of the

Universidad Nacional Autónoma de México. A public research school in Mexico City, UNAM was a world-class university. Adjacent to the diploma were several post-grad accreditations and professional awards.

Aragón spoke English with a mild accent. "The CT scan looks normal, and your clavicle fixation appears to be healing well."

"May we see the scan?" Elena asked.

"Certainly." Dr. Aragón rotated the Dell monitor on his desk.

The hardware used to pin Elena's shattered collarbone together stood out on the black and white image. The splice was solid white. The threads on the screws penetrating the splintered bone were visible.

"What's that?" Nick asked, pointing to a slight protrusion on the top surface of the steel plate.

Aragón studied the image and then typed in a new command on the PC's keyboard. An enlarged view materialized. "That is odd. I assumed it was part of the repair hardware, but the close-up shows that it does not appear to be attached to the plate."

Elena turned away, her fears confirmed.

Nick said, "Could that be what's bothering her—causing the pain?"

Dr. Aragón rubbed his chin. "It's possible. The surrounding tissue might be irritated."

"Can it be removed?" Nick asked.

"Yes, it's a simple procedure. But perhaps I should check with the surgeon who performed the original repair first. I'd like to know what the object is. It's hard for me to believe it was left behind accidently."

Elena faced Nick. "I want it out. I don't care about the risk." She turned back to Aragón. "Can you remove it today?"

"I have a full afternoon of appointments."

Nick understood Elena's urgency. "Doctor, we'll pay double your normal fee if you can do it today."

Aragón called up his calendar on the PC. "I'll schedule it for five o'clock this afternoon."

"Perfect!" Nick said.

Chapter 78

Day 46—Wednesday

Kwan Chi was in his Kowloon apartment. He was sitting on his favorite living room sofa reading the *Hong Kong Economic Times* when the special phone in his office announced the incoming call at 11:10 P.M. Kwan hobbled into the office, annoyed at the shrill tone of the ringer, which he could not mute, and the late hour of the call.

He picked up the handset of the government-issued encrypted telephone. "Kwan here."

"Kwan, there's been an incident that you need to know about. Are you alone so we can speak in private?"

"Yes, sir," Kwan said, recognizing his boss's voice despite the flat, washed out monotone caused by the encryption process.

MSS Deputy Minister of Operations Guo Wing was calling from his Beijing office. "What I'm going to tell you is for your ears only, not to be repeated to anyone else."

"I understand, sir."

"The Navy base on Hainan Island was attacked nine days ago."

"Attacked—what do you mean? I've heard nothing about that on the news."

"And you won't, at least for a while."

"What happened?"

"Over half of the South Sea Fleet was disabled by a directed energy weapon, likely some form of EMP. No fatalities or serious injuries, but widespread damage to electrical systems."

Kwan uttered a curse. "How bad is it?"

"Thirty-eight ships were moored at Yulin, including our two carriers. They're all dead in the water. The pulse fried every computer and power system aboard the ships. The damage even extended to shore-based facilities."

"That's incredible!"

Guo continued, "Only the base was impacted. It's being handled as a local power outage."

Stunned, Kwan rubbed his forehead. "Hainan Island—what about all of those resorts they have down there? Someone is bound to notice something's wrong."

"The Air Force flew in portable power generators and floodlights. The docks and ships are illuminated at night. From the resorts, the base appears to be normal."

"How long will it take to repair the ships?"

"We received the report this evening—I just returned from an emergency CMC briefing. The Navy estimates it will take at least six months, maybe even a year, to replace critical systems. Even then, the electronics and wiring not outright damaged by the attack will remain suspect. The only way to ensure one hundred percent operational security is to remove and replace every computer, electrically operated system, and all power and communications wiring."

"That's awful—almost like starting over."

"Correct. The Navy may end up scrapping half or more of the ships because it might cost less to build new ones."

"Who did this thing?"

"The investigation is underway. It appears the Americans are responsible."

Kwan seethed. "It has to be Kirov. He defected to the United States. He must have told them about the Mark Twelve."

"That's my opinion too," Guo said. "We also know that Kirov's woman has been talking with the FBI."

The reminder jolted Kwan. The MSS unit Guo dispatched to eliminate Laura Newman had failed—twice. "Will the Americans tell the Russians about the Mark Twelve?"

"It's possible, but the fact that Kirov defected will taint anything the Americans offer." Guo's voice deepened. "Fortunately for us, relations between Moscow and Washington remain awful. That gives us time to prepare."

"The Americans are bad enough," Kwan said. "But we can't trust anything about the Russians. They'll cut our throats without hesitation if they figure out what happened."

"I agree. Now's the time to inoculate ourselves as best as we can."

Guo's medical analogy caught Kwan off guard. "What do you mean?"

"All elements of Sea Dragon are being disbanded. The key players involved in hostile operations are being interviewed."

Kwan recognized the codeword "interviewed." To ensure continued silence, security teams would visit all military and intelligence operatives involved in clandestine ops against Russia and the United States during Sea Dragon. Each person would be reminded that any "leaks" would be traced back to the leaker. Not only would that individual be liquidated, but also others in the leaker's immediate and extended families.

Guo continued, "At this time, we believe sufficient confusion remains between the Americans and the Russians regarding our involvement. Should either make a claim against us in the UN or at the Hague, we will deny any involvement and redirect the accusations back to the accusers."

"That sounds like a good plan, but I must reiterate that I do not trust the Russians. If they put it together—"

"I agree," interrupted Guo. "We need to make sure they remain in the dark." The MSS deputy director of operations hesitated. "That's one of the reasons I'm calling you. Are you still in contact with your Russian contact—the female SVR officer you turned?"

"Yes, she's in Vancouver."

"What is she doing for you?"

"Checking to see if the SVR or FSB knows where the Americans might be holding Kirov."

"And?"

"She reported the SVR has it narrowed down to several locations. I'm waiting for a follow-up report from her."

"Could she be playing you?"

"She's motivated by money only. Believe me, sir, if she comes up with actionable intel on Kirov, I will hear from her along with an immediate request for payment."

"I want you to contact her."

"Sir?" Kwan said, impatient for the punchline.

"Tell your agent we have a new assignment for her."

* * * *

Nick Orlov walked into the hotel room. It was a few minutes before ten in the morning in San Diego.

Elena Krestyanova sat on the king-sized bed, her back propped up by pillows stacked against the backboard. The door to the balcony was open. The crystal waters of Coronado Bay sparkled in the background.

"How are you feeling?" Nick asked as he stepped closer.

"Better. The pain's not so bad now."

"Great."

Under Elena's blouse, the dressing over the left collarbone concealed the stitched two-inch-long incision. The pain had kicked in around ten the previous evening, after the local anesthesia that Dr. Aragón administered wore off. It took two doses of the post-op meds provided by Aragón before Elena obtained relief. But Elena didn't mind—she was still alive!

Nick placed a couple of paper bags on a table. He removed a paper cup from one and handed the caffè mocha to Elena.

"Oh, thank you!"

"My pleasure."

Nick removed his caffè latte and opened the lid.

"Were you able to find it?" Elena asked, noting the other bag on the table.

"Yeah. Got it at the local electronics store."

Nick removed the RF testing device from the bag, opened the packing box, and took out the instrument. After inserting the batteries he'd also purchased, he picked up the plastic bag containing the item Dr. Aragón had removed from Elena's clavicle. The cylindrical device was about half the diameter of a pencil and an inch long. Nick held the radio frequency tester next to the metallic tube.

"Son of a bitch," he muttered in Russian.

"What?"

"Just as I thought. It has a micro transmitter inside." Nick held up the plastic bag.

"So, that part of Smirnov's story is true."

"Yeah, it allows 'em to keep track of your whereabouts, but that's it. The stuff about the poison capsule was pure bullshit."

Elena turned away. "Get rid of that thing."

Nick was about to drop the transmitter onto the floor to crush it with the heel of his shoe when Elena's cell phone vibrated on the table. Nick glanced at the cell's display. The incoming text displayed a number with an area code he did not recognize. He handed the phone to Elena.

She opened the text tab and read the message. "It's from Kwan. I need my laptop."

Elena read aloud the decrypted text from Kwan's message in the draft folder of the anonymous Outlook email account they shared.

"That bastard," Nick muttered.

"That he is—and more."

Kwan wanted Elena to lure Nick Orlov to Vancouver for a meeting. The fee he proposed to pay Elena was astonishing. Nick's mind raced.

"We'll accommodate Mr. Kwan," he announced, a wicked smile breaking out. "But not quite the way he's expecting."

Chapter 79

After a cautious approach, the *Novosibirsk* arrived offshore of Oahu in mid-morning. The submarine loitered 800 feet below the surface about twenty-five nautical miles south of the entrance channel to Pearl Harbor. Captain Petrovich ordered a pre-mission briefing in the officer's wardroom. Attending were special operators Shtyrov and Dobrynin and the *P-815*'s commander, Lieutenant Tumanov. Yuri Kirov was also invited to sit in.

Petrovich stood beside the bulkhead-mounted video monitor that displayed an electronic chart of the Hawaiian Islands. "At twenty-one hundred hours local time *Novosibirsk* will proceed north twenty kilometers." Petrovich pointed to a location in the ocean twelve miles south of Pearl Harbor. "The mini will decouple here and proceed to the target."

"Captain," Lieutenant Tumanov said, "it would be beneficial if we could get a little closer before launching."

"I understand, but I have orders. *Novosibirsk* is to remain outside of American territorial limits at all times."

"Even if we have trouble on the way back?" Tumanov asked.

"Affirmative."

P-815's commander masked his disappointment by picking up his mug and drinking the last of his tea.

Petrovich continued. "The mini will head north and enter the outer channel and then proceed..."

Yuri sat beside Tumanov with his hands clasped on top of the conference table. As the briefing continued, he kept an eye on the junior officer. *It shouldn't be much longer.*

Yuri and Tumanov had arrived in the wardroom in advance of the other participants. While Tumanov took a seat, Yuri filled two clean mugs with tea from the kettle on a counter. He also spiked Tumanov's mug. Yuri had concocted the mixture from several items liberated from *P-815*'s first aid locker. The key ingredient was syrup of ipecac, a liquid used to induce vomiting in an effort to remove poisonous material ingested in the stomach. Although outdated and considered ineffective for countering poisons, ipecac remained an efficient substance to make a person puke.

Yuri spotted a bead of perspiration on the lieutenant's brow. Tumanov squirmed in his seat.

Any moment now!

* * * *

Laura Newman made her way down a crowded sidewalk in downtown Bellevue. She had a lunch meeting with an acquaintance from a marketing firm. The restaurant was five minutes away. As she walked, she took the opportunity to call her attorney, Tim Reveley. "Have you heard anything from Diesen?" Laura asked, holding her cell phone to an ear.

"I'm sorry, but no. And nothing from my contact at the Department of Justice."

"This waiting is awful."

"I'll try again with my DOJ contact, but don't be surprised if the FBI continues to stonewall." Tim hesitated. "Remember, Laura, you provided quite a story that will take the feds a while to verify. And who knows what they'll find on those phones?"

"What should I do?"

"Nothing. Just try to relax."

"Okay, thanks."

Laura slipped the phone back into her purse. *Relax—no way!*

With a possible federal criminal indictment looming, Laura's angst remained sky-high. But what really pegged out her worry quotient was Yuri's fate. Weeks had passed since he left. Laura feared she would never see him again.

* * * *

It was late afternoon on the east coast. Ava Diesen sat in a Pentagon conference room. The briefing by analysts from the National Security Agency and the Defense Intelligence Agency had concluded five minutes earlier. The forensic computer experts departed along with senior DOD staff, including several flag officers. Ava and two others had the room to themselves.

"Well, I sure wasn't expecting that outcome," Ava announced, commencing the debrief.

"No kidding," Bob Clark said. The U.S. Navy captain sat across the table from Ava. Clark turned to his right. "I take it you heard about this already."

"Not everything," CIA officer Steve Osberg said. "But enough to connect the dots."

Osberg had arranged for two CIA technical staffers to assist the NSA-DIA forensic team. One was an expert in Mandarin and the other in Russian.

The two cell phones and the satphone Laura Newman and Tim Reveley turned over to the FBI yielded a diamond mine of data. After deciphering the password to Elena Krestyanova's phone, the technicians discovered numerous contacts between Elena and Kwan Chi. Kwan's cell and satphone required more horsepower to decrypt but proved even more valuable.

"What's next with this Kwan Chi character?" Captain Clark asked Diesen.

"If he ever sets foot in the U.S. he will be arrested and charged with espionage."

Osberg commented, "I don't think that will be happening for some time. Our people in Hong Kong indicate he's keeping a low profile."

Captain Clark swiveled in his chair, looking Ava's way. "What about the Laura Newman investigation? We were able to verify a lot of her story about the sub with the fieldwork we conducted…but this phone stuff really seems to vindicate her with Kwan."

Ava pressed her lips. She still could not get over the photograph displayed on the conference room screen half an hour earlier. The image recovered from Elena Krestyanova's phone was texted to Yuri Kirov. The photo was in color; Laura Newman sat on a bed, her legs bare but her torso covered in a pajama top. A strip of duct tape sealed her mouth and plastic cable ties bound her wrists. She cradled her infant daughter in her lap, wrapped in a baby blanket. The front-page headline of the *Seattle Times* was on display next to Madelyn.

Ava crossed her legs. "I agree that Newman's story about being kidnapped by Kwan and his associates has merit. But until we come to a resolution on just what Captain-Lieutenant Kirov has been up to, she will remain under investigation."

Clark turned toward Osberg. "Steve, did your people pick up anything on him?"

"Zero. We have nothing on his whereabouts." The CIA officer recalled another item. "Regardless of what he was doing before, I think the Navy owes Kirov and Ms. Newman big time—remember, you said it yourself."

Clark grinned. "The *Trident* sub—the *Kentucky*."

"Exactly. All of the stuff recovered on the phones confirms her story that the Chinese were trying to sink it in order to start a war between us and Russia."

Clark agreed with Osberg's conclusion but was not yet authorized to confirm it. The data recovered from the phones, the photo of the Mark Twelve torpedo provided by Newman, and the hardware collected from the seabed of Puget Sound and the Strait of Georgia confirmed Laura's allegations. After a briefing at the White House, the president authorized the U.S. Navy to prepare an appropriate response. Turning back the *Heilong* as it closed on Hawaii was just the beginning.

Chapter 80

Yuri's heart raced. He clenched his teeth. His lower spine ached. *Concentrate. You can do this!* Yuri had repeated the mantra to himself half a dozen times. It helped manage the stress.

He was in the *P-815*'s pilot station as the submerged minisub travelled northward at seven knots. The virtual reality headgear made him uneasy. The goggle's computer-generated image of the dredged channel illustrated the route ahead. Superimposed on Yuri's artificial 3-D view of the waterway was the icon of a whirling propeller. The minisub's proximity to the harbor tug required Yuri to constantly adjust the controls.

Wake turbulence from the tractor tug's dual Z-drive thrusters buffeted the *P-815*, causing it to porpoise. If the sail broke the water surface, the submarine might be spotted. Although it was a few minutes after one in the morning, a nearly full moon and residual lighting from both sides of the channel illuminated the waterway.

After detaching from the *Novosibirsk*, the *P-815* stealthily approached the outer buoys marking the entrance channel to Pearl Harbor. The minisub loitered at the entrance, waiting for an inbound vessel. Propeller cavitation and engine noises radiating into the water column from an inbound vessel would mask the *P-815*'s already miniscule acoustic output.

Yuri would have preferred to shadow a conventionally powered craft whose propellers were not as deep as the tractor's. Nonetheless, the tractor tug was the only arriving vessel during the mission's allotted time, so he reluctantly followed it.

Tumanov remained aboard the *Novosibirsk*, confined to the sick bay for twenty-four hours of observation. The *P-815*'s pilot protested, claiming he was fine. But Tumanov was overruled. Captain Petrovich could not take a chance that whatever "bug" afflicted Tumanov might infect the *Novosibirsk*'s crew and/or the minisub's staff.

Yuri regretted making Tumanov ill, but it was the only way he could interject himself into the mission. He feared the two Spetsnaz operators preparing for deployment in an aft compartment were not on an ordinary espionage mission but something truly sinister.

With Tumanov out of commission, Yuri was the natural replacement. Tumanov's co-pilot was too junior to command the vessel. Petrovich ordered Yuri to take over—just as Yuri had planned.

"How close are we to the next sensor?" Yuri said, directing his question to *P-815*'s co-pilot.

"On the starboard about 200 meters away," reported Junior Lieutenant Vassily Nevsky aka "Hollywood".

The handsome twenty-three-year-old occupied a console on the port side of the control station two meters from Yuri. Nevsky had piloted the mini for the first hour but nearly collided with the tugboat, forcing Yuri to take the controls.

"Got it," Yuri said as he advanced the throttle.

The minisub closed on the tugboat until its bow was just five meters away from the tug's stern. The buffeting increased but Yuri had no choice. To help defeat the approaching underwater sensor, Yuri needed to immerse as much of the mini's hull into the tractor tug's wake zone as possible. To protect the naval base from underwater intruders—like the *P-815*—the U.S. Navy had installed a network of acoustic sensors along the Pearl Harbor entrance channel and the interior basins—lochs—that composed the principal moorage areas for the U.S. Pacific Fleet. The hydrophones listened for unauthorized submerged sounds from submersibles and divers.

A civilian contractor working for the U.S. Navy unknowingly supplied the GRU with the complete plan for Pearl Harbor's underwater defense. The California-based company won the low bid for maintenance and testing of the system. Although certified for Top Secret work, the contractor had inferior in-house computer security measures. GRU cyberhackers broke into the company's server and downloaded the plan without triggering a single alarm.

The *P-815* approached a slight bend in the channel. Bishop Point was to the right; Iroquois Point was 2,000 feet ahead on the left.

"Sir, we're abeam of the sensor now."

"Okay."

Dear God, I hope this works. Yuri counted on the tug's underwater racket to shield the mini. Ten minutes passed. The *P-815* in tandem with the harbor tug neared Pearl Harbor's infamous Hospital Point. The main waterway to the U.S. Navy's principal moorage facilities was just ahead on the right.

Yuri could hardly believe what he was doing. Over three quarters of a century earlier, a Japanese midget submarine cruised into Pearl Harbor's battleship row and launched torpedoes against the sitting ducks. Although Japan's sneak air attack devastated the naval base, the minisub also created havoc inside the confined harbor waters.

Nevsky made a new report. "Sir, the barrier to the main channel is approaching."

"I suspect that's where this guy is headed."

Yuri eased off the throttle, allowing the *P-815* to fall behind the tractor tug. The din from the tug receded as it turned eastward into the main channel of the naval base.

Traveling at two knots and just three feet above the bottom, Yuri guided the *P-815* northward into the Ford Island Channel. It was too risky to continue following the tractor tug. A floating barrier extending from Ford Island to the shoreline of the Pearl Harbor Naval Shipyard prevented unauthorized surface craft from entry to the Pacific Fleet's main moorage basin. Although the minisub could easily sail under the barrier, bottom sensors might detect the intrusion. Hugging the bottom, the *P-815* crept northward as Yuri and Junior Lieutenant Nevsky tag teamed. Yuri steered the boat while his co-pilot called out sensor locations and monitored vertical control.

After following the North Channel into the East Loch, Yuri eased back on the throttle and pumped water into the fore and aft ballast tanks. The *P-815* settled onto the mud bottom in mid-channel, around half a mile from the northern end of Ford Island.

Nevsky was about to comment on the unplanned maneuver when he was preempted. "Lieutenant," Yuri said, "I need to check with Shtyrov. You have the conn. Keep monitoring. Any changes, let me know immediately."

"Understood, sir."

Yuri pushed up his goggles. The mini's interior lighting was amber— standard operating procedure for nighttime running conditions.

He climbed out of the pilot's station and headed aft. It was time for a confrontation.

Chapter 81

Yuri Kirov, Lieutenant Shtyrov, and Chief Dobrynin were inside the *P-815*'s accommodation's compartment. Yuri closed the watertight bulkhead door when he entered, ensuring privacy.

The OSNAZ operators used the compartment to assemble equipment and don their diving gear. Both men had already slipped into neoprene dry suits. Two rebreathers lay on one of the bunks, each unit charged with oxygen and the CO_2 absorbent canisters filled. All batteries were charged and electronics calibrated.

"We're close to the departure point," Yuri said. "But before we go any further I want to know what your mission is—everything!"

"With respect, sir, I can't reveal any mission details." Shtyrov stood beside Yuri. Dobrynin sat on the edge of a bunk.

"I know you're not installing recording gear." Yuri gestured to a black cylinder resting on the deck beside Shtyrov's rubber dive boots. "What is that thing?" he demanded.

"Ah, sir, you are out of order. I cannot—"

"Bullshit. What is it for?"

"It's the same type of acoustic recorder we deployed at Qingdao. Once installed, it will record the acoustic signature of every vessel that enters and departs the base."

Yuri was ready for the expected response. "To do that, all you had to do was install it in the main entrance channel. There's no need risking an incursion deep into the harbor like this."

He dropped to his knees next to the cylinder. It was the device he had checked earlier with a dosimeter.

He looked back up Shtyrov. "I want you open it now and show me the backup isotope power system."

"That's impossible. The unit's sealed."

"Well, it's time to unseal it." Yuri grabbed a sheathed dive knife from another bunk stacked with gear and extracted the blade.

He inserted the tip into a recessed joint near the steel canister's midsection and was about to pry the two halves apart when everything went black.

Dobrynin stood above the now prostrate Yuri, a spare two-kilo lead weight from the dive gear locker cupped in his hands. "I had no choice."

"Good job, Chief." Shtyrov knelt next to Yuri. "Let's tie this jackass up and then get going."

"Very good, sir."

Chapter 82

The dive team surfaced, their black-clad heads and shoulders nearly indistinguishable from the dark harbor waters. Their target loomed in the near distance. The USS *Theodore Roosevelt* was ablaze with self-illumination, its 1,092-foot long-hull moored to a massive concrete pier near the mouth of the Halawa Stream. Shtyrov extended his right gloved hand in a thumbs up. Dobrynin nodded his understanding. In unison, the special operators vented air from their buoyancy compensators and sank back into the murk.

After locking out from the *P-815* in Pearl Harbor's East Loch, Shtyrov and Dobrynin had proceeded southeastward just below the surface, towed by individual diver propulsion vehicles. They passed under the east end of the Ford Island Bridge, avoiding the floating barrier that paralleled the north side of the bridge. The security barricade consisted of a floating fence designed to repel surface craft. Suspended from the floating barrier was a recently installed underwater anti-diver net. Extending to the bottom, the plastic mesh fabric contained sensors that could detect efforts to pass through the barrier or to cut the net. Pre-warned about the submerged web, the Russians emerged from the water and walked a dozen steps along the darkened coastline, then reentered the waterway on the south side of the floating barrier. They swam along the shore that housed the Pearl Harbor Visitor Center, passing under the bow of the USS *Bowfin*. Converted into a floating museum, the World War II submarine was one of Pearl Harbor's most visited tourist attractions.

At the southern end of the Visitor Center the divers powered across the mouth of the Halawa Stream to their destination—Naval Station Pearl Harbor's Hotel Pier and the USS *Theodore Roosevelt*.

After venting their BCs, the Russians sank to the harbor bottom just below the *Roosevelt*'s bow. Once the divers swam under the aircraft carrier, Lieutenant Shtyrov switched on his dive light, directing the beam downward. The colossal bulk of the overhead hull created a shadow that suppressed all shipboard and shoreside lighting, creating pitch-dark conditions on the bottom. The supercarrier drew nearly forty feet of water. The tide had just passed the daily low, leaving about five feet of clearance under the keel. The divers followed the keel line, running the DPVs at low power, which rendered the already minimal acoustic signature of the electric drives silent. Uncertain as to what dockside acoustic security measures might be used at Hotel Pier, the divers paced their breathing, taking measured breaths and slowly exhaling into the closed-circuit rebreathers. Shipboard-generated noise from machinery inside the hull radiated into the water, helping mask the divers' incursion. Shtyrov and Dobrynin were prepared to suppress any marine mammal sentries that the U.S. Navy might deploy. Chief Dobrynin carried a hand-held laser. The device emitted an array of irritating light pulses designed to confuse and hopefully scare away any biologics.

After reaching the approximate midpoint of the hull, the divers powered down the DPVs and settled onto the bottom. Lieutenant Shtyrov retrieved the package he had towed. Assisted by Chief Dobrynin, he armed the weapon.

The yield of the nuclear device was eight kilotons—eight thousand tons of TNT. About half the explosive power of the bomb dropped on Hiroshima, it was not a significant weapon in terms of modern nuclear warfare. Nevertheless, it would accomplish the mission. One of the United States' most powerful warships would be vaporized in a heartbeat and the surrounding Pearl Harbor Naval Base rendered impotent for years. The evidence planted by the SVR would point straight back to China—payback for the Yulin Naval Base attack.

With the mission complete, the commandos retreated. But they would not be returning to the *P-815* or the *Novosibirsk*. After retracing their path to near the *Bowfin*, Shtyrov and Dobrynin sank their DPVs and rebreathers. They swam to the nearby shore and climbed up the low bank. Still clad in dry suits, the pair walked in the dark to a waiting vehicle.

An undercover FSB operative waited for the pair in a Ford SUV. She parked the Expedition in an unlit private lot sandwiched between the Pearl Harbor Visitor Center and the east landing of the Ford Island Bridge. She had waited the previous day from 10 P.M. to 6 A.M. She was prepared to come back the next three nights if needed.

Shtyrov keyed the bomb's timer for three hours, which set the detonation time as 6:52 A.M. It was his call; Moscow's orders did not dictate timing.

Waiting until noon would have incinerated legions more as droves of visitors flooded Pearl Harbor's tourist sites. Limiting the carnage to military personnel helped ease Shtyrov's dishonor.

By zero time, both OSNAZ operators would be several hundred miles to the west, resting inside an executive jet. The charter would fly to Seoul, South Korea, and then on to Vladivostok.

Chapter 83

"Untie me, now!" Yuri shouted.

"Shtyrov told us you tried to block their mission." Nevsky squatted beside Yuri's hog-tied frame. Nevsky had just yanked off the duct tape that had sealed Yuri's mouth.

Yuri struggled to right himself. With his hands tied behind his back and his hobbled ankles lashed to his wrists, he remained face down on the deck. "Dammit Nevsky, get these things off me."

Ordered by Shtyrov to keep Yuri tied up until he and Dobrynin returned, Nevsky eventually decided to question Yuri. "What did you do, sir?"

"I confronted 'em. They're not who they say they are."

Nevsky's brow wrinkled.

Yuri continued, "The package they took with them—it's not an underwater recorder."

"What is it?"

"A weapon." Yuri made eye contact with the junior officer. "I suspect it's a nuke."

The junior officer's jaw dropped like the proverbial rock.

"Now untie me. That's a direct order!"

Nevsky worked at the bindings. A minute later, Yuri stood up.

He flexed his hands. "How long ago did they lockout?"

Nevsky checked his wristwatch. "Over an ago. They should have been back by now."

"I don't think they ever planned on returning. They probably have another way out." Yuri reached behind his right ear. The scalp welt was sore to the touch. "Have you heard anything topside?"

"No, sir. Very quiet." Nevsky fidgeted. "Sir, just what do you think they're doing?"

"Earlier, I found a chart they used to plan the mission. Their dive route took them to a quay identified as Hotel Pier. It's where the U.S. Navy moors aircraft carriers."

"The *Roosevelt*! They want to sink it?"

"Obliterate it."

* * * *

Yuri was suited up. He stood next to the open hatchway to the *P-815*'s lockout chamber. Lieutenant Nevsky was at his side.

"All right, Lieutenant, as soon as I'm out, you turn this thing around and backtrack to the ocean as fast as you can. Push it hard—don't worry about sensors. You'll be out of the harbor before they can react. Once you reach the ocean, go deep and really gun it to get back to the *Novosibirsk*." Yuri met Nevsky's eyes. "Vassi, don't worry about what happened earlier with the tug. That was just nerves. You'll do fine now."

"Yes, sir, thank you. I've already programmed in the reciprocal course."

Nevsky understood Yuri's order to leave Pearl Harbor. Detection was a huge concern, but what really motivated him was the prospect of a nuclear detonation.

Yuri adjusted one of the rebreather backpack's shoulder straps. "I'll try to rendezvous with the *Novosibirsk* tonight as we discussed. But if I don't show up in a small boat, don't waste any more time waiting for me. Make sure you tell Captain Petrovich that."

"But how will you get home?"

"I'll figure out another way."

"Understood. Good luck, sir."

"Thank you."

Yuri had no plans to return to Russia. He would either remain in his newly adopted home or die trying.

Chapter 84

Yuri encountered the security barrier on the north side of the Ford Island Bridge near mid-channel. He had intended to swim under the floating fence when he discovered the submerged anti-swimmer net. Recognizing the net's sensor-laden mesh, he diverted to the east, making landfall at the same location where Shtyrov and Dobrynin had exited the water earlier. When Yuri reentered the water, he discovered the OSNAZ commandos' abandoned diving gear scattered on the bottom. The finding confirmed Yuri's suspicion they had another way home.

Spurred by the specter of imminent annihilation, Yuri gunned his DPV and powered southward to Hotel Pier.

Surfacing near the bow of the USS *Theodore Roosevelt*, Yuri spun three-sixty, accessing tactical conditions. It was still dark, but light from the ship revealed its enormous size. He could hear the muted call from a shipboard intercom speaker issuing orders. *Where did they plant the damn thing?*

Yuri was planning his next move when he heard the rumble. He peered westward into the gloom. *Damn!*

The U.S. Navy patrol boat ghosted along the port side of the *Theodore Roosevelt*, its high-powered engines throttled back to minimum. The security vessel was just fifty yards from Yuri when a twenty-million candlepower spotlight flashed on. The beam scanned the harbor waters, working its way toward Yuri.

Yuri vented his buoyancy compensator, and compressed air hissed from the valve. He'd barely submerged when the search beam crossed over his position. All that remained on the surface were residual bubbles from the BC. The searchlight locked onto the froth as the patrol boat advanced.

By the time Yuri sank to the bottom, the security craft was overhead. The rumble of its idling outboard engines polluted the water column with noise. In the darkness he could see a partial silhouette of the thirty-foot-long craft. Refracted light from the searchlight highlighted the hull.

Please God, don't let them find me.

After nearly five minutes, the patrol boat turned and headed westward. *Thank you!*

Grounded in bottom muck, Yuri switched on his dive light. He aimed the beam at the narrow gap under the *Theodore Roosevelt*'s hull. Searching the bottom under the huge ship was going to be a daunting proposition.

This is going to take forever!

Yuri was about to start a grid search when he spotted a slight depression in the muddy bottom ten feet to the south; it appeared to extend southwestward under the hull. He swam to the dent and discovered additional bottom hollows running parallel to the first.

And then it hit.

These are trails.

When Shtyrov and Dobrynin swam under the supercarrier's hull, wake wash from their DPV propellers eroded silts from the top surface layer of the bottom. Yuri throttled up his DPV and followed the furrows.

Chapter 85

When the bottom track lines stopped, Yuri cut power to the DPV. He estimated that he had traveled half the length of the monster hull. He reached up with a gloved hand and touched the *Roosevelt*'s bottom. That's when the revelation hit.

Dammit—I'm probably under one of the reactors!

As Yuri swept the light beam back and forth, probing the surrounding murk, another factor struck. While suspended in the five-foot gap between the barnacle-encrusted steel plates of the overhead hull and the muddy bottom, claustrophobia reared its ugly head. Experienced at diving in enclosed environments, Yuri suppressed his dread. He closed his eyes and slowly inhaled, allowing the oxygen-rich breathing gas to penetrate deep into his lungs.

You can do this. Just focus on the mission.

After several deep inhalations with repeated incantations, the terror passed.

Yuri surveyed his surroundings with the handheld light. The silt-laden bottom had obviously been disturbed by the OSNAZ divers, but there was no sign of the bomb.

Where is it?

Yuri dipped a gloved hand into the soil. It had the consistency of thick pea soup. He extended his arm further into the mud, encountering mild resistance just past elbow length.

Yuri made half a dozen additional random probes but came up empty-handed.

They could have buried it anywhere around here. Now what?

The inspiration came half a minute later when he inadvertently backed into his DPV. The diver propulsion vehicle had sunk about half way into the bottom.

Yes, that could work!

Yuri retrieved the DPV and turned it around, directing its propeller toward the bottom. After inverting his body and bracing his fin-tipped feet against the *Roosevelt's* hull, he switched the unit on. The propeller engaged, and a jet of exhaust water blasted the bottom sediments. Within minutes, the propeller's wash hydraulically dredged a hole two feet deep and nearly ten feet in diameter. Unable to see much because of the ensuing silt cloud, Yuri explored the depression with his hands. It didn't take long.

There you are!

Yuri extracted the eighteen-inch-diameter cylinder from its burial pit, cradling it in his lap as he kneeled on the bottom. Just over two feet in length, the canister's exterior black steel surface was glass-smooth with the exception of a recessed rectangular-shaped section at one end. Yuri pulled open the curved housing that covered the control panel. *Govnó!*

The LED readout ticked off the seconds. The bomb's timer indicated it would detonate in eighty-six minutes.

He searched the panel for an "on-off" switch. No joy.

Now what?

Chapter 86

Yuri surveyed his surroundings. He was on dry land near where he had hauled out earlier. He knelt on the lawn beside the water's edge, using the lush vegetation as cover. *What is this place?* During his earlier visit, he had remained focused on following Shtyrov's and Dobrynin's trails. Although it was still dark, he could see well enough.

What's that?

Yuri took a couple of steps toward the mechanical oddity set among half a dozen towering palm trees. He stared at the antiaircraft gun mount, two sets of twin barrel guns aimed skyward. He took another look around and spotted a ship's propeller in the distance.

This must be a naval museum!

Yuri retreated to the shadows. His DPV and fins, along with the atomic bomb, lay on the lawn next to the shrubs.

He again examined the canister, searching for a way to disarm the weapon. The timer continued the countdown—sixty-three minutes and change. Yuri concluded that once triggered, there was no way to turn back the clock. He cursed Shtyrov and Dobrynin for what they had done—orders or not!

Maybe I can get inside the thing.

Yuri removed his dive knife from its ankle scabbard and probed an edge of the bomb's control panel. He was about to attempt to pry open the housing when common sense intervened.

The damn thing is probably set to blow if tampered with!

Yuri groaned, defeated.

I need to turn myself in. He was on an American naval base. Maybe their specialists could disarm the weapon or take it out to sea and dump it.

But then he thought better of that idea.

Who's going to believe me—a guy in a diving suit claiming to be a Russian naval officer who happens to be carrying a nuclear bomb that's counting down to Armageddon?

After he was written off as a nutcase and locked up in the brig, the bomb would still detonate—either by running down the clock or by U.S. Navy Explosive Ordinance Disposal personnel tinkering with it.

There has to be another way!

Yuri rubbed the side of his head; the swelling from the blow had ballooned. The ache inside his skull worsened.

God, help me—I don't know what to do.

Yuri had no choice but to surrender to the Americans and hope they would believe his story.

As he looked over the grounds of the Pearl Harbor Visitor Center, searching for a way out, he peered northward. Under the concrete span of the nearby Ford Island Bridge, he spotted movement on the water. A boat had had just backed out of a marina slip.

That just might work!

Chapter 87

Yuri oozed from the gloom. His black-hooded head rose above the still waters of Aiea Bay. It remained dark topside but not for long. Through his face mask, he eyed the nearby floating pier. The dock lights along the center walkway revealed he was alone—at least for now. Over a hundred boats were moored at the marina. Some of them might be occupied by liveaboards or transient boaters.

Yuri swam to the edge of the floating pier, where he reached up with both gloved hands and grabbed the edge of the float. He kicked his fin-tipped legs, propelling his bulk upward. After a struggle he managed to haul out onto the top of the foam-filled concrete pontoon. Crouched low on the deck with his fins removed, Yuri parked the facemask on his forehead and took stock of his surroundings. There was no movement on the marina docks, nor did he observe any cabin lights in nearby boats. More of a concern, however, was the security gate on the Ford Island Bridge.

The elevated bridge deck loomed to the south. Owned by the U.S. Navy, the bridge provided restricted access to Pearl Harbor's Ford Island. The gatehouse was about three hundred feet away. Later in the morning, a steady stream of tour buses would flow across the bridge as hundreds of tourists flocked to board the USS *Missouri* memorial. The battleship was permanently moored along the south shore of Ford Island next to the watery grave of the ill-fated USS *Arizona*. Sunk by Japanese aircraft at the onset of World War II, the submerged hulk held the remains of more than 1,100 sailors and Marines.

Yuri unclipped a Dacron line from a D-ring on his chest harness. The rope trailed into the water. He tied the line to a dock cleat, stood, and then took half a dozen steps to his destination, carrying his fins.

The open-deck Boston Whaler Dauntless was twenty-seven feet long with a hardtop canopy and twin 300-horsepower Mercury outboards. He boarded the fiberglass craft, tossing his fins and facemask onto the deck. He stepped to the center-hull cockpit and studied the control console. With his dive knife he pried open a door lock on the starboard side of the console housing. Inside he found a portable toilet—and on the aft bulkhead, a fiberglass cover plate to the instrument panel.

Yuri removed his backpack and buoyancy compensator. Now gear-free, he slipped into the side opening of the boat's head. He removed the cover plate and peered into the electrical guts of the console's instrument panel. Trained in electrical and electronic engineering and schooled in spycraft techniques for bypassing digital security measures, Yuri sidestepped the start key mechanism. In a couple of minutes both outboards ignited, and the instrument console bloomed.

While the Mercs warmed up, Yuri stepped back onto the marina pier and returned to the line he'd tied to the cleat. He tugged on the rope. A few seconds later, he hauled the bomb onto the deck. He checked the timer's LED. Thirty-six minutes remained. *Govnó!*

Yuri synced the stopwatch function of his dive watch with the bomb's timer. He carried the bomb aboard the Whaler, stowing it under the pilot's seat. Life jackets he found in a locker served to cushion the cylinder. Yuri untied the mooring lines and powered the boat away from the dock. As he guided the Dauntless toward Pearl Harbor's North Channel, the sun emerged above Mount Pu'ukawipo'o to the east. In the dim light, he checked the path ahead. No other vessels were active on the waterway.

Yuri eyed the instrument console. Mounted in front of the steering wheel and throttle controls were side-by-side LCD displays. The right screen displayed a continuous profile of real-time water depth; the companion screen contained a digital navigation chart of Pearl Harbor with an icon marking the Whaler's GPS position.

Yuri expected there was a speed limit in the harbor but ignored it. He pushed the throttle control. Within seconds, the runabout's hull stepped up to plane and rushed forward at thirty knots.

Chapter 88

The Boston Whaler raced southward into the Pacific, the drone of the twin Mercs flooding the cockpit. The swells were mild and the wind barely a whisper. Yuri ran the boat at thirty knots—an aggressive open ocean speed. He stood behind the helm; the rush of air sweeping over the console ruffled his hair. He welcomed the artificial breeze. Still suited up, he would have cooked without it.

On the instrument panel the GPS electronic chart showed the Dauntless was about five nautical miles offshore of Oahu. Soundings on the chart showed a depth of 262 fathoms—1,572 feet. *Not deep enough yet!*

Yuri checked his watch. Nine minutes, fifteen seconds and counting. He slammed the throttle to the max. The speedometer peaked at 35 knots. While standing, he braced the small of his back against the helm station seat; his hands white-knuckled the steering wheel.

Two minutes later, Yuri chopped the throttle back to idle. The Whaler backed off plane and settled into the sea. The digital chart indicated the ocean was around 1,800 feet deep. He glanced back toward Oahu, now over six nautical miles away. Honolulu's skyscrapers gleamed in the early morning light. Magnificent Diamond Head towered to the northeast. An All Nippon Airways Boeing 777-300 from Tokyo was on final approach to the Reef Runway at Honolulu's Daniel K. Inouye International Airport.

I hope they made it out okay!

Yuri worried about his submates. The *P-815* was scheduled to rendezvous with the *Novosibirsk* between zero-six-hundred and zero-nine-hundred hours. The linkup coordinates were twelve miles south of the entrance to Pearl Harbor—six miles beyond Yuri's current position.

Time's up. This will have to do!

Yuri hauled the bomb from under the cockpit seat. He struggled to lift the fifty-pound cylinder as the Whaler rolled in the swells. He balanced the eight-kiloton yield nuclear weapon on the runabout's gunnel and shoved it overboard. The canister plopped into the sea and disappeared.

He took another look at his watch: five minutes and fifty-three seconds remained.

Yuri slipped back behind the helm. He engaged the Mercs and turned to the starboard. Within half a minute, the Whaler was headed toward the northeast at full throttle.

Yuri did not know what to expect. He prayed the ocean's ever increasing hydrostatic pressure would crush the bomb casing before it reached the seafloor, rendering the weapon impotent. He feared the flipside. An implosion might result in a pre-detonation.

Chapter 89

Captain Petrovich stood at the base of the airlock as Nevsky descended the ladder from the *P-815*. The minisub had docked with the *Novosibirsk* five minutes earlier.

"Where are the divers?" Petrovich demanded.

"Sir, Lieutenant Shtyrov and Chief Dobrynin didn't return from their mission."

"What happened to them?"

"I don't know. And Captain-Lieutenant Kirov told us to leave without him."

"Where the hell is he?"

"He locked out." Nevsky was clearly uncomfortable. "Apparently, Shtyrov and Dobrynin attacked Kirov before they locked out. I found him tied up."

Petrovich cursed. "Where is Kirov?"

"He went after them. Said something about trying to stop them before the bomb went off."

"What bomb?"

"He said Shtyrov and Dobrynin had a nuke!"

"*Súkas!*"—bastards—yelled Petrovich.

* * * *

Yuri ran the Whaler flat-out, aiming for Honolulu. The boat was two miles away from the drop site. With the twin Mercs screaming, he stood at the helm as the boat blasted across the swells. He braced his lower back against the helm station seat's built-in back support while gripping the steering wheel with both hands. His watch remained strapped to the left forearm of his dry suit. *Thirty-three seconds.*

Yuri reached behind and lowered down the back support. He then scooted up onto the seat, elevating his feet several inches above the fiberglass deck. With his right hand on the helm, he turned to peer over the stern. He again checked his watch. *Seven...six...five...four...three...two...one...zero!*

The nuclear flash radiated through the abyss, transforming the turquoise sea surrounding the runabout to a bleached white pall.

* * * *

"How did Kirov know they had a nuclear weapon?" demanded Petrovich. Nevsky grimaced. "He didn't say, sir. In fact, he provided no details. Only that he ordered us to return to the ocean immediately."

The two officers were in the *Novosibirsk*'s airlock, both still standing next to the ladder. Petrovich was about to ask another question when a colossal underwater pressure wave hammered the submarine.

"*What the hell?*" yelled Petrovich as he and Nevsky were tossed onto the deck.

* * * *

The same pressure wave slammed into the submerged bottom of the Boston Whaler's fiberglass hull with the impact of a freight train.

A slice of the shockwave sped up the supports of the helm station seat, spanking Yuri's backside. The seat's foam padding absorbed most of the impact. By keeping both feet raised above the deck, Yuri prevented injury to his legs.

He backed off the throttles and turned the wheel to the starboard. Watching over the bow, he searched the southern horizon.

Dear God—I hope it was deep enough!

Chapter 90

Nearly 800 miles west of Oahu, the *Colorado*'s sonar sensors detected the detonation. The unique acoustic signature captured the attention of the senior sonar tech. Chief Petty Officer Anderson requested an immediate face to face with the captain.

"What've you got, Richey?" asked Commander Bowman.

"Something big just happened back near Pearl." Anderson keyed up a recording of the detonation on his sonar waterfall display.

Bowman stared at the plot. "What am I looking at?"

"A nuke went off, Captain. Deep down."

"What?"

Anderson pointed to the screen as the recording replayed at quarter speed. "See these pulses here? They're oscillations of an expanding gas bubble as it collapses from water pressure and then reforms. Classic subsea nuke detonation."

"Jesus," muttered Bowman.

"We were trained to ID this type of signature—nuclear depth charges."

"Where did this happen?"

"I've got a preliminary fix. Roughly six nautical miles south of Pearl."

"What kind of surface disturbance?"

"It went off deep, Captain. I'm estimating at least 1,800 feet, maybe more. As I recall, at that depth the pressure really dampens the blast effects."

"Did it break the surface?"

"I don't know. It would depend on the yield."

Bowman massaged his temple, stunned.

"Sir, do we have any exercises going on that might explain this?"

"No, Chief. Something's not right here at all. I've got to call this in."

* * * *

Petrovich raced to the attack center. "Status report," he called out to the watch officer.

"Captain, all compartments report minimal damage. No flooding. Eight casualties, six minor and two with leg fractures."

"How far away was it?"

"Ten kilometers to the north."

"Plot the best course back to base. We need to vacate these waters now."

"Yes, sir."

* * * *

The seas around the Boston Whaler were again tropical blue-green as it wallowed with the swells. Despite the pounding from the underwater shockwave, the sturdy hull remained intact. Still in his dry suit, Yuri stood under the cockpit canopy. A fresh breeze from the north cooled the exposed skin of his face and neck. He waited for the surface blast. But in the distance, all he could see was an undulating mat of foamy seawater erupting over the drop site. It was two minutes past zero. No other boats or aircraft were anywhere near the boiling brew.

Yuri continued to scan the southern horizon. After five minutes, the churning water had dissipated by two-thirds, dispersed by the wind and swells. *Thank you, Lord.*

Yuri turned the Dauntless about and set a return course for Honolulu.

Chapter 91

Yang Yu stared at the digital plot. Zheng Qin was at his side. The *Heilong*'s captain and his second in command stood beside the navigation station in the attack center. A digital chart of the North Pacific Ocean filled the electronic plotting table.

Yang pointed to a pulsing blue star on the e-chart. "Sonar estimates that whatever happened occurred in this area."

Executive officer Zheng said, "It's deep there."

"I know. Sonar's still trying to quantify the source but a preliminary estimate indicated it likely exploded at a depth of around 550 meters."

"What are those dogs up to—firing off one of their nuclear depth charges?" Zheng asked.

"We're too far away for it to be a threat to the boat."

"Intimidation?"

"Perhaps."

"We need to inform Fleet."

"We will but not right now."

"But Fleet needs to—"

"Relax, Zheng In due time. Right now, we need to shake off the Americans. They're still out there."

"Those devils," muttered Zheng. "I bet they stay on our ass all the way back to Qingdao."

Yang ignored his XO's remark. His thoughts centered on the failed mission. *The Americans were waiting!*

We—I—sailed right into their trap. They could have sunk us but chased us away instead.

And the nuke—another not-so-subtle demonstration of their resolve. We're not ready to confront them, not even close.

Chapter 92

Yuri tied up the runabout at the Kewalo Basin Harbor near downtown Honolulu. He gathered his dive gear and walked ashore. At a picnic table in a nearby waterfront park he sought shade under a collection of banyan trees. Although still clad in his dry suit, he fit in with the park users. Clusters of wetsuit-clad surfers rode the offshore breaking waves as legions of waders, swimmers, snorkelers, and paddleboarders explored the nearshore waters.

Yuri sat at the table with the top half of the neoprene dry suit hanging down at his waist. He reached inside the navy-blue jumpsuit he wore under the dive suit and removed a plastic Ziploc bag. Stored inside were his ID documents, some cash, credit cards, and his cell phone.

Yuri switched on the iPhone. He hit a speed dial button and waited. It was 8:07 A.M. in Honolulu. Washington State was three hours ahead.

Yuri smiled when the call connected. "Hi honey, it's me," he said.

Chapter 93

The commander of the U.S. Navy's Pacific fleet stood beside his office desk with the telephone handset glued to his right ear. The secretary of the Department of Defense was on the other end of the encrypted circuit in his Pentagon office.

The four-star admiral stared through his office windows at the waters of Pearl Harbor. "I know this sounds nuts, sir, but he just showed up in a cab at the main gate to the base an hour ago, claiming he had information on the offshore explosion."

"How would he know about that?" asked the secretary.

"He shouldn't know. The media has no clue about what happened. The weapon detonated deep enough offshore that nothing substantial was observed on the surface."

"Who is this guy?"

"The security detail at the gate assumed he was a crackpot, but then he handed over his credentials." The admiral reached down to his desktop and retrieved the leather-bound document. "His name is Yuri Kirov. He's a captain-lieutenant in the Russian Navy—GRU, assigned to submarines."

The secretary muttered a curse and said, "The Russians— they're behind this?"

"I don't know. The base commander has him confined. As soon as I hang up, I'm heading over there to find out what's going on."

"Call me ASAP when you know more. I need to update the president soon."

"Aye, aye, sir."

Chapter 94

Elena and Nick stood in a corner of the American Airlines departure lounge at the San Diego International Airport. It was late afternoon. The flight to Miami was in the final phase of boarding.

"I wish you would reconsider," Elena said.

"I can't... I'm not ready yet." Nick ran a hand across his scalp. His Southwest Airlines flight to Houston would depart in another hour.

"Well, when you're ready, you know how to contact me."

"The Chinese are still out there."

"The plan will work. But if it doesn't, Smirnov will find another way." Elena had hatched the plan from their Coronado Bay hotel room via remote secure comms Nick arranged through the Houston consulate. SVR director Borya Smirnov sanctioned the op.

Nick met Elena's eyes. "You need to be very careful. I don't know what Moscow will do."

"Don't worry. I'll be fine."

But Nick would worry. The SVR and FSB were relentless when tracking down wayward agents, especially those who were privy to the highest level of state secrets. To buy Elena time, they had stopped at a U.S. Post Office before driving to the airport. Elena filled out the transmittal form, using her Vancouver mailing address. Inside the mailing box were her cell phone and the RFID tag surgically removed from her shoulder. Because of the international crossing, it would take several days for the package to make the trip north. During that time, the iPhone would transmit hourly locations.

A loudspeaker broadcast the last boarding call.

"Well, it's time for me to go," Elena said.

"I'll miss you."

Elena stepped into Nick's arms and gave him a deep kiss that electrified him. She broke the embrace. "You rescued me, Nick. I'm forever grateful."

At the gate she handed the agent her first class boarding pass. Just before heading down the jetway, she turned and flashed Nick a sparkling smile.

Nick watched as she disappeared.

Chapter 95

It was evening in Hong Kong. Kwan Chi relaxed in his outdoor hot tub at the peak of the Kowloon high-rise. The Jacuzzi jets massaged his mending body. He was enjoying a splendid California merlot.

As he took in the city's dazzling nightly lightshow, he thought ahead to the operation now in motion.

Soon it will be over.

At Kwan's request, Elena had invited the SVR officer to visit her in Vancouver. Kwan electronically deposited an advance payment of $500,000 US into Elena's anonymous overseas account. The balance of her fee, another half million, would be paid upon completion. It was a payment that would not be made. The MSS hit team was already in place in Vancouver. Both Nick Orlov and Elena Krestyanova were on the target list.

Orlov, that son of bitch! He's just as bad as Kirov.

Kwan would miss Elena, but Guo's orders were unambiguous—cleanup all loose ends.

The timer on the hot tub's jets clicked off. The hiss of the rushing water was replaced by the stillness of the night air.

But not quite that still.

Kwan cocked his head to the side, catching the whisper of another white noise source. He set the wineglass aside and peered toward the harbor, probing the darkness. The aberration materialized with a soft purring sound. He faced the drone, now just ten feet away. Its whirling blades sliced the air with a subdued frenzy.

Kwan stood and shouted a litany of Mandarin curses at the robot while flipping his right middle finger.

The drone inched forward.

Kwan was about to grab the nearby wine bottle to bat the aerial pest when the drone fired.

The nine-millimeter hollow point punched a pencil-diameter hole in Kwan's forehead. He crumpled, sinking to the bottom of the tub. The gore from the exit wound stained the waters a deep crimson.

Chapter 96

Day 50—Sunday

Four federal employees sat around a table inside a conference room at the FBI's Seattle field office. A wall-mounted monitor at the head of the table displayed the image of Yuri Kirov, who sat alone inside an interview room located three doors away down a connecting hallway. The interrogation had started at eight in the morning and continued all day with a couple of bathroom breaks. A clerk brought in sandwiches during the noon hour. It was now 4:35 P.M.

FBI Special Agents Ava Diesen and Michaela Taylor, U.S. Navy Captain Robert Clark, and CIA Officer Steve Osberg had left the interview room five minutes earlier for a quick debrief.

Ava kicked off the discussion, "Well gentlemen, we'd like your thoughts on Captain-Lieutenant Yuri Kirov's tale."

"Just incredible," Captain Clark announced. "Everything he said about the nuke matched what Pacific Fleet has been able to reconstruct. The GPS unit on the runabout he used had the entire trip stored in its memory. Our people at Pearl found the abandoned Russian diving gear on the harbor bottom, and they located the tracks in the mud leading to and from the *Roosevelt.* Everything matches what Kirov said during his original interrogation back at Pearl."

Michaela said, "So you don't believe he was involved in planting the device and then got cold feet?"

Clark clasped his hands. "I suppose that's possible but your own people along with Steve's group traced the charter flight to Vladivostok. That sure looks like a get-out-of-Dodge move to me."

Ava faced Osberg. "Steve, what are your thoughts on the charter?"

"A deliberate ploy. The charter could have made a direct flight to Vladivostok, but that would have left an obvious trail. Filing a flight plan to Seoul wouldn't raise flags. The South Koreans reported that the two passengers on the flight had Russian passports. After refueling, the charter pilots filed a new flight plan to Vladivostok. Total time on the ground in Korea was just over an hour. That jet could have easily made a nonstop flight to Russia from Hawaii." Osberg cleared his throat. "I'm inclined to believe Kirov's story that he discovered the Spetsnaz team's true mission and then took matters in his own hands. Anyway, it sure appears to me he saved the day at Pearl Harbor."

"Okay," Ava said, "I tend to agree that Kirov was truthful regarding the bomb but what about his warning concerning that other naval base in China?" Ava picked up her notepad. "The base in Qingdao. He said the other divers might have left a nuclear weapon there. Why would they do that?"

"That bothered me, too," Clark said. "But if what Kirov suspected is right, Russia was trying to incite a war between us and China. Nuking one of our carriers in Pearl Harbor would call for an immediate response— vaporizing the PLAN naval base at Qingdao, for example."

"So that thing could still be on the bottom?" Osberg said.

"Yes," Clark said. "My guess is that it can be triggered by an acoustic signal. Drop a hydrophone over a bulkhead. Transmit the code. The bomb arms itself and after a pre-set time, BOOM!"

"Well, that hasn't happened," Michaela said.

"Right. The Russian mission failed. Pearl Harbor was not destroyed."

Osberg rejoined the conversation. "Of everything Kirov has told us so far, we need to pass along the Qingdao situation to the DOD and the White House ASAP. They will need to decide what to do, if anything."

"Agreed," Ava announced. "As soon as we finish, I will phone Washington."

"Good," Osberg said.

Ava consulted her notes again. She faced Captain Clark. "Bob, what do you make of his offer to share additional intelligence on Chinese submarines?"

"Intriguing. If the device he described really managed to penetrate the tunnel on Hainan Island and spy on China's missile boats, the intelligence could be invaluable to us."

Ava suppressed a yawn. She was tired and missed her family. "So, guys, what should we do with Kirov?"

"Give him a medal. He's a hero in my book." Captain Clark grinned. "Ditto," Steve said. "Plus grant him asylum. He's earned it." Ava glanced at Agent Taylor, who nodded. Ava agreed with her companions but kept it to herself. She was also aware that the State Department looked favorably on Kirov's asylum request. "Well, those decisions are beyond our pay levels. But for now, if you both agree, Michaela and I can grant his immediate request."

"For sure," Clark said.

"Absolutely," echoed Osberg.

Chapter 97

Yuri stared at the world map taped to a wall in the interrogation room. During the interview, he referred to the map numerous times as he retraced the voyage of the *Novosibirsk*. Worn out and sleep deprived, he could not determine if the American agents believed his story.

More than three days had passed since he had turned himself in at the Pearl Harbor naval base. After hours of questioning by the Navy and FBI in Hawaii, the previous afternoon he was placed aboard a U.S. Air Force C-17 cargo transport jet at Hickam Field and ferried to Joint-Base McCord-Lewis near Tacoma, Washington. A caravan of U.S. Marshals and FBI agents drove Yuri to the FBI field office in downtown Seattle, where he was placed in a holding cell.

Yuri closed his eyes, hoping for a quick catnap before the next round of questioning.

Two minutes later, he roused as the door to the interrogation room opened. Ava Diesen stepped inside. "Mr. Kirov, please follow me. We have another location to meet in."

Yuri stood. He wore a pair of orange coveralls provided by the U.S. Marshal Service—prisoner garb. Yuri followed the FBI agent. She opened the door to the new room and stepped aside, remaining in the hallway.

Yuri crossed the threshold into the visitor lounge. Laura Newman sat on a leather sofa reading a magazine. She looked up.

"Yuri!" she shouted.

Laura rushed to Yuri. They embraced, leaning back only to gaze at each other with hungry eyes.

Ava closed the door.

Laura relaxed her grip. "Are you okay?"

"I'm good, just tired."

"You shaved your beard."

Yuri ran a hand across his chin. "I can grow it again if you like."

"You're fine just the way you are. Besides, you don't need a disguise anymore."

"Oh, yeah. Now that I've been outed, it won't do any good."

Laura beamed. "I have some good news."

"How's that?"

"I know you're going to have more government interviews, but our attorney told me that the State Department intends to grant you asylum. That means you'll be able to stay with me."

Yuri was unable to speak.

Laura hugged him again. "I'm so happy you're home."

Yuri recovered his composure. "I am, too." And then he remembered. "How's Maddy?"

"She's fine. Amanda's watching her now."

Yuri gazed at Laura, his eyes misty. "I'm so blessed to have you in my life. I love you."

"And I love you."

They kissed, a lingering delicious kiss.

Don't miss the next exciting Yuri Kirov thriller

THE VIGILANT SPY

by Jeffrey Layton

Coming soon from Lyrical Underground
An imprint of Kensington Publishing Corp.

Keep reading to enjoy the pulse-pounding first chapter . . .

Chapter 1

The city of nine million woke as first light oozed heavenward from the Yellow Sea. A leaden stratum of low-lying, vapor-rich clouds hovered over the coastal metropolis of Qingdao. Drizzle smeared the windshield as the boat puttered along the one-half-mile-long waterway. Its diesel exhaust lingered over the still waters of the harbor. Along the north flank of the waterway, an immense industrial wharf protruded west into the embayment. Tugboats, workboats, barges, and fishing vessels occupied assorted floating piers that connected to the dogleg-shaped wharf. At the western terminus of the waterway, an offshore breakwater split the channel, providing north and south navigational passageways to and from the adjacent bay.

Elegant, slender buildings jutted skyward twenty to thirty stories along the channel's southern shore. Lights blinked on as hundreds of the tower residents rose to the new day.

Two men stood inside the cabin of the 35-foot-long aluminum-hull workboat as it approached the midpoint of the waterway, known locally as the Middle Harbor. They had patrolled the eastern half of the channel for over an hour, running back and forth, broadcasting the recall signal. The hydrophone dangled three feet below the keel near midships, suspended by a cable secured to a guardrail.

"It should have surfaced by now," said the man standing on the starboard side of the cabin.

In his early thirties with a slim build and a mop of black hair that hung over his ears, he wore coveralls and work boots. A cigarette dangled from his left hand.

"I know. Something's wrong." Like his companion, the pilot was of Central Asian lineage.

He was several years older, half a head shorter, and twenty pounds heavier than his cohort. A ball cap concealed his balding scalp; a navy-blue windbreaker encased his chunky torso. The helmsman spun the steering wheel to port, turning the workboat about. He chopped the throttle to idle, setting the craft adrift.

The observer took another drag and turned to face the pilot. "Ismail, maybe we should boost the signal. The recorder might be buried deeper in the mud than planned."

"Good idea. Go ahead and turn it to max."

Both men were fluent in Mandarin, but when alone they spoke in their native tongue—an offshoot of Turkic.

The observer relocated to the nearby chart table. A laptop sat on the surface. Yusup—a form of Joseph—fingered the keyboard and addressed the pilot. "It's now at maximum strength."

"Okay, I'll make another run."

Ten minutes passed. The boat drifted near the eastern end of the channel.

Ismail, the helmsman, peered at the instrument panel display. "GPS says we're over the coordinates Talgat provided. You see anything?"

"Negative—nothing."

"It should be in this area."

"The recorder must have malfunctioned."

"Maybe."

Yusup crushed the spent butt in an ashtray. "What do you want to do now?" he asked.

Ismail's brow wrinkled as he peered through the windshield. The bow pointed west. The twin wipers were set to cycle at minimum speed. He was about to comment when he noticed a skiff speeding from the bay into the channel's north entrance. Powered by an outboard, it carried five men, all wearing raingear, hardhats, and flotation vests. "We've got visitors."

"Wonder what they're up to."

Using binoculars, both men watched as the skiff tied up to an enormous crane barge moored on the north side of the waterway, about a thousand feet away. The crewmen scurried up a ladder and boarded the barge. Within five minutes, a cloud of blackish soot spewed as a diesel generator powered up.

"What's that rig for?" asked Yusup.

"Some kind of marine construction."

One of the crew boarded a small tugboat tied up to the far side of the crane barge. After starting the engine, the operator engaged the tug's propeller. The tug, still lashed to the barge, began to pull the crane barge away from the pier. Secured to the crane barge on the opposite side was a second steel barge. It was about the same size but with an extra three feet of freeboard.

Yusup squinted. "Now what're they doing?"

"I don't know." Ismail set his binocs aside and advanced the throttle, seeking a closer look.

The tug and double barge combination relocated to the center of the channel near the mouth of the waterway's northern entrance. The huge steel truss boom on the crane barge rotated seaward from the deck. A steel bucket the size of a Ford pickup truck, its jaws wide open, hung over the water suspended by half a dozen steel cables that ran through a huge block at the peak of the crane derrick. Seconds later, the bucket plunged into the water and sank to the bottom. The generator aboard the barge blasted out a fresh plume of exhaust as the crane struggled to lift the payload.

The bucket rose above the water surface, its jaws clamped tight. The crane operator swung the boom across the deck until the bucket hovered over the companion barge. The jaws opened and twenty-four tons of black, gooey stinky bottom muck plopped into the dump barge.

A hundred yards away, Yusup and Ismail observed.

"Shit," muttered Yusup as the revelation registered. "They're dredging the harbor ... could they have dug up the recorder?"

Ismail appeared stunned. "There was nothing about this in the orders."

"That's got to be why we can't find it. What do we now?"

"Let me think."

Ismail searched on his smartphone until he found the article. The port authority proudly advertised the project on its website. The waterway was being dredged to increase water depth for deeper draft vessels—not an unusual activity for such a sprawling enterprise as the Port of Qingdao.

However, what did not follow the norm for China's state-owned port and harbor facility—one of the busiest in the world—was the disposal of the dredged materials from the commercial waterway. Instead of dumping the spoils offshore in deep water or reusing the sediments as fill to create new dry land, the one hundred and fifty thousand cubic yards of bottom muck was allocated for an environmental mitigation project. Mimicking projects sponsored by public ports in the United States and Western Europe, China's Ministry of Environmental Protection funded the Port of Qingdao's "Project Seagrass." Dredged material from the Port's commercial waterway formed the core of a new intertidal island located in nearby Jiaozhou Bay. When filling operations ended with a cap of clean sand, the artificial atoll would cover the area of six soccer fields. Later in the year, the mound was scheduled to be planted with patches of eelgrass—*Zostera marina*—transplanted from donor sites. Over several years, project scientists expected the seagrass to propagate, eventually covering most shallow sections of the knoll. By providing protection for fin fish and shellfish and offering a host of nutrients and microorganisms, the underwater eelgrass forest would offer an oasis for marine life within the otherwise degraded industrial harbor.

After digesting the web article, the two men considered their options.

"There's nothing more we can do," said Yusup as he sucked on another cigarette. "We should just head back to the marina."

"My orders were explicit—recover the recording device at all costs." Ismail remained at the helm, a hand hanging onto the steering wheel.

"Talgat should have known about the dredging project."

"I agree. But still it's my—our problem."

Yusup took a deep drag on the Furongwang. His religion frowned on smoking, but the habit provided good cover for his work.

"So," he said, "what do you want to do?"

Ismail stepped to the navigation table. He pushed the laptop aside to view the nautical chart of Jiaozhou Bay.

"The website said the disposal site is in this area." He pointed with a finger.

"You think we might be able to recover it there?"

"Unlikely. That dredge bucket probably destroyed the recorder. But at least we can make the effort—run a couple of transects with the hydrophone broadcasting the recall signal." Ismail faced his companion. "By checking the dump site, we can make sure that Talgat won't be able to blame us for not completing the mission."

"Good plan. Let's go."

* * * *

After a thirty-minute run across the bay, the workboat slowed to a crawl. Hundreds of rice paddies lined the muddy shore to the north. Southward, a sleek modern bridge dominated the skyline. The world's longest bridge over open water, the Jiaozhou Bay Bridge spanned a distance greater than the width of the English Channel between Dover and Calais. Ismail and Yusup eyed the depth sounder. Built into the instrument panel, the device displayed a profile of the bottom depth.

"This must be the right area," Ismail said. "It's definitely shallower here."

"Only two meters deep, probably exposed at low tides."

"Drop the hydrophone overboard and let's see if we get a response."

"Okay."

The workboat idled, drifting westward with the quarter-knot current. Both men scanned the water around the boat, each hoping the lost recorder would magically pop up to the surface.

"I don't see anything," Yusup announced.

"Neither do I."

"Are we done?"

"Let's make one more run across the site. Then we'll head back."

"All right."

It was a fateful decision. Had the two spies recruited from China's Xinjiang Uyghur Autonomous Region started their return trip after the initial run, they would have survived. But their lifespan was now limited to seconds.

The object the boat crew searched for was buried in bottom sediments about a hundred yards away. The Uyghur dissidents believed they were searching for an acoustic recording device used to spy on the Qingdao Naval Base, located just north of the Port of Qingdao's commercial waterway. It was a lie fed to them by their Russian handler, cover name Talgat. Unknown to Ismail and Yusup, their hydrophone was actually signaling a bomb.

Designed to resist hydrostatic seawater pressure to a depth of over three thousand feet and survive subzero freezing conditions as well as function in temperatures exceeding the boiling point of water, the weapon survived dredging. It lay in wait at the bottom of the bay.

Entombed within the excavated sediment, the audio receiver inside the warhead compartment listened for the command signal. The five feet of mud over the cylindrical steel casing degraded reception significantly. But as the workboat approached, the digital signal from the hydrophone penetrated the muck. Recognizing the acoustic command, the bomb's electrical firing circuit triggered the detonators embedded in the concentric lenses of plastic explosive that surrounded the core. The semtex charges exploded, compressing the tennis ball-sized hollow sphere of uranium-235 to the size of a grape. A microsecond later, the nuclear weapon detonated.

Acknowledgments

Thanks to Cody Hulsey for helping me navigate as an author through the "uncharted waters" of social media. Cody's insights and suggestions are greatly appreciated.

I wish to express my deepest appreciation to Michaela Hamilton, executive editor at Kensington Books, for her critical review of *The Faithful Spy*. Michaela is an extraordinary editor who worked with me to advance the story, just as she did for *The Good Spy* and *The Forever Spy*. Michaela and her talented team at Kensington are a pleasure to work with.

Lastly, I'd like to thank my family, friends, and fans for continuing to encourage me with my writing career.

About the Author

Photo by Michael D. McCarter

Jeffrey Layton launched his Yuri Kirov spy thriller series with *The Good Spy* and continued it with *The Forever Spy*. He is also the author of the acclaimed novels *Vortex One*, *Warhead*, and *Blowout*. Jeff is a professional engineer who specializes in coastal engineering. He uses his knowledge of diving, yachting, offshore engineering, and underwater warfare in the novels he writes. He lives in the Pacific Northwest.

Please visit him at www.jeffreylayton.com.

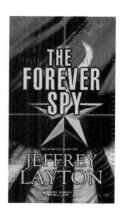 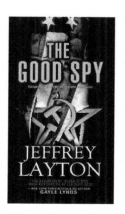

Printed in Great Britain
by Amazon

23602571R00209